REGARDS

REGARDS

THE SELECTED NONFICTION OF
JOHN GREGORY DUNNE

FOREWORD BY CALVIN TRILLIN

THUNDER'S MOUTH PRESS
NEW YORK

REGARDS
The Selected Nonfiction of John Gregory Dunne

Published by
Thunder's Mouth Press
An Imprint of Avalon Publishing Group
245 West 17th Street, 11th Floor
New York, NY 10011

First printing January 2006

ISBN: 1-56025-816-0
ISBN 13: 978-1-56025-816-2

Book design by Pauline Neuwirth, Neuwirth & Associates, Inc.

Printed in the United States
Distributed by Publishers Group West

Contents

FOREWORD

SOMEHOW, I NEVER got around to talking with John Gregory Dunne much about his childhood stutter. We covered a lot of other subjects over the years—he often phoned first thing in the morning to bring me up to speed—but I can't remember asking him whether he thought that the stuttering was a factor in the development of his writing style. After he died, I ran across an answer in the introduction to a collection called *Quintana & Friends*. "I think I became a writer because I stuttered," he wrote. "I had to learn to express myself on paper." His nonfiction pieces were invariably what critics would call closely observed. While reading them, I sometimes wondered whether such intense powers of observation might have owed something to the experiences of a little boy who would have tended to hang back, carefully watching the action, rather than take a chance on the words not coming out as he'd intended. (In *Quintana and Friends*, he recounts having become as a child "precociously observant.") By the time we met—this was about 1962, when we were both writers at *Time* in New York—the stutter was long gone, although I think that he always thought of it as simply being held at bay. His speech, like his writing, was very polished—an anecdote in his telling always sounded like at least a second draft, with the sentences parsed and the paragraphs arranged for dramatic effect—and I always wondered whether that, too, was a hangover from having been a child who had to make certain he could say precisely what he wanted to say before he said it.

However his powers of observation were developed, they turned out to be broad as well as deep. I often found myself surprised at the variety of what drew his gaze. Until I read his piece on Willie Mays, reprinted here, I wouldn't have thought he was paying close attention to baseball. I could not have predicted that his first big project after leaving *Time,* where he had worked mainly in the foreign news section, would turn out to be a book on the California grape strike. Those morning phone calls reflected the catholicity of his interests. He might comment on a piece he'd just seen in the tabloids or in the *Times Literary Supplement.* He might talk about what he'd learned from a bunch of books on World War II he'd been reading. He might give a report on the dinner party he'd attended the night before. Any of this could someday end up in a piece or, somewhat transmogrified, in a novel. John was always on duty.

In one of the essays in this book, he recalls that, in a comic novel I once wrote about working at an unnamed newsmagazine, I'd made him the subject of a claimer, as opposed to a disclaimer. The claimer said, "The character of Andy Wolferman is based on John Gregory Dunne, though it tends to flatter. The other characters are fictional." In the novel, Andy Wolferman was a brilliantly creative gossip who entered the office of the protagonist most mornings with the words "This you will not believe"—the very words, of course, that I used to hear regularly as an entrance line from John Gregory Dunne. Our memories of the conversation we had after the novel's publication vary. As I recall it, Dunne said to me, "Just as a matter of curiosity, why was my character Jewish?"

"That was the 'tends to flatter' part," I said. "You don't want to be lace-curtain Irish all your life, do you?"

"Boarding-school Irish, Calvin," he said. "Boarding-school Irish."

I've clung to my version not simply because that's the way I remember what was said. (Answering a question about using real events in fiction—which might just as well apply to anecdotes— John once said, in a *Paris Review* interview that's included here, "Fact is like clay. You shape it to your own ends.") Making the distinction between boarding-school Irish and lace-curtain Irish is pure Dunne. In all of his writing, he is exquisitely attuned to background and status and class, subjects that a lot of American writers try to avoid. In a piece about making deals in Hollywood, for instance, he introduces his agent like this: "Among Hollywood agents Evarts Ziegler is an anomaly. He went to Princeton, lives in Pasadena (which in Hollywood is considered as recherché as living in Grosse Pointe Farms), and once, I am convinced, hired a very rich young junior agent only because she had gone to Foxcroft." John Gregory Dunne was a writer who always had an interest in where someone had gone to high school—an interest I happen to share.

I don't mean that he was a snob—a product of the boarding-school Irish who liked to lord it over the lace-curtain Irish. He would have corrected me just as quickly if I had placed the Dunnes too high rather than too low on the West Hartford Irish totem pole. Also, he had no illusions about the place of any sort of Irish in a WASP boarding school like Foxcroft. He enjoyed recalling that at the reception his mother gave to introduce her new daughter-in-law to the swells of West Hartford—this was in 1964, after John had married Joan Didion in California—the only two Protestants in attendance were Joan and the society reporter for the Hartford *Courant.*

In fact, you get the impression from Dunne's writing that, despite his boarding-school background and his hobnobbing with movie stars, the sort of Irish-American life he hankered for included regular attendance at Knights of Columbus functions and a couple of uncles in the fire department. He often said that he learned more in his two years as an enlisted man in the Army than he had in four years at Princeton. He loved the cops, and he loved their language. He always called them the cops; I rather doubt that the term "police department" ever passed his lips. He loved the nitty-gritty of American life. In one of the pieces collected here, he writes, "I am drawn to the Santa Monica Courthouse the way some people are drawn to church." He liked to think of himself as a working guy, whose work happened to be at a desk; in one of these essays, he says that what most people don't understand about writing is that it "is manual labor of the mind: a job, like laying pipe."

His interest in the nitty-gritty was part of what made him such a valuable writer on Hollywood. When he began writing about the industry, in *Studio,* it was in the form of a fly-on-the-wall account, enhanced by the penetrating gaze of that particular fly. In his later pieces—and in the book *Monster*—his reporting included his own

Hollywood activities as a screenwriter, even those he characterized as "ignoble." Abstruse film criticism was not his thing. He preferred writing about how the deal was made and why. His response to a pretentious Oscar acceptance speech by a screenwriter, like his response to a lot of film criticism, was to "giggle and hoot." In comparing film-writing to writing for *Time* in the days when *Time* writers were essentially rewrite men (yes, men; when we began at *Time,* there were no female writers), he says in one of these essays, "Why then write for films? Because the money is good. Because doing a screenplay is like doing a combination jigsaw-and-crossword puzzle; it's not writing, but it can be fun. And because the other night, after a screening, we went out to a party with Mike Nichols and Candice Bergen and Warren Beatty and Barbra Streisand. I never did that at *Time.*"

I can confirm that last statement. I would also agree that what we were doing at *Time* in those days was not exactly writing. Still, some of my favorite nonfiction pieces by John, the essays he did in *The New York Review of Books,* were structurally similar to the cover stories he so deftly turned out for *Time.* Now, though, he didn't have to concern himself with *Time's* unforgiving pressure toward compression or with a couple of layers of editors who were themselves rewrite men. Instead of the dispatches that correspondents may have barely had time to write and he may have barely had time to read, he used as raw material his own thoughtful reading of a book or maybe two or three books on the same subject. Years away from a system that had no place for the first-person pronoun, he could enrich the mix with his own experiences and, of course, his own close observations. The resulting product was likely to be both perceptive and entertaining—or, if you looked at writing the way John Gregory Dunne liked to, pipe-laying of the highest order.

—CALVIN TRILLIN
August 2005

GONE HOLLYWOOD

SNEAK

[1969]

✽

THERE WAS NEVER any doubt that the Studio would hold its first preview of *Dr. Dolittle* in Minneapolis. Fox considered the Minnesota capital its lucky city; Robert Wise's production of *The Sound of Music* was first sneaked there and, with the enormous success of that picture, the studio superstitiously kept bringing its major road-show attractions to Minneapolis for their first unveiling before a paid theater audience. With so much money at stake—the budget of *Dr. Dolittle* was close to $18 million—the Studio was unwilling to hold a sneak anywhere around Los Angeles, reasoning that it could get a truer audience reaction in the hinterlands, far from the film-wise and preview-hardened viewers who haunt screenings in and around Hollywood. The plan originally had been to go to Minneapolis on Friday, September 8, and to Tulsa the following evening, but early that week the Tulsa screening was canceled. "If the picture plays, we don't have to go to Tulsa," Richard Fleischer said. "If it doesn't play, why go to Tulsa the next night and get kicked in the ass again? You make some changes, then you go to Tulsa."

Because of the magnitude of *Dr. Dolittle,* the Minneapolis screening attracted twenty-eight Studio personnel from New York and Los Angeles. The major contingent from Los Angeles was booked on Western Airlines Flight 502, leaving at 8:30 A.M. on September 8.

Arthur Jacobs, accompanied by Natalie Trundy, arrived at International Airport nearly an hour before flight time. He was tieless and wearing a dark blazer and he lingered around the escalator coming up from the check-in counters on the ground floor, greeting members of the Fox party as they arrived. His salutation never varied. "I'm not nervous," Jacobs said. "I'm not going to Minneapolis. I'm just here to wave you all goodbye."

"Oh, Arthur," Natalie Trundy said. "Calm down."

"Calm down," Jacobs said. "*Calm down.* You treat me like one of the dogs." He turned to Fleischer. "We've got poodles. She treats me like a poodle."

"You're a very nice-looking poodle, Arthur," Fleischer said.

They milled around the gate, waiting for Flight 502 to be called, Jacobs, Natalie Trundy, Fleischer, Mort Abrahams, Herbert Ross, the choreographer on *Dr. Dolittle,* and Warren Cowan, who was once a partner of Jacobs's in a public-relations firm and whose company, Rogers, Cowan & Brenner, was handling the publicity and promotion for *Dolittle.* At last the flight was called. As Jacobs and Natalie Trundy walked up the ramp, Jacobs turned to Fleischer and said, "I just don't want to go to Minneapolis. Let's go to Vegas instead."

"It would be less of a gamble," Fleischer said.

Jacobs and Natalie Trundy took two seats at the rear of the first-class compartment. Cowan, a short, pudgy man with constantly moving eyes and a voice that sounds somewhat like Daffy Duck's, sat by himself in front of them and spread the New York and Los Angeles papers on his lap. Jacobs could not keep still. "We land at noon," he shouted up the aisle. "At twelve-thirty, we visit the public library. At one o'clock, the museum."

No one laughed except Fleischer, who tried to humor Jacobs. "At one-thirty, the textile factory," Fleischer said.

"And then we have a rest period between eight and eleven this evening," Jacobs said. This was the time scheduled for the screening.

"What I like about you, Arthur, is your calm," Fleischer said.

"Why should I be nervous?" Jacobs said. "It's only eighteen million dollars."

The trip to Minneapolis was uneventful. Most of the Fox people slept, except for Jacobs, who kept prowling the aisle looking for someone to talk to. It had just been announced in the trade press that week that Rex Harrison had bowed out of the musical production of *Goodbye, Mr. Chips* which Gower Champion was scheduled to direct and Jacobs to produce for release by M-G-M. "It was all set," Jacobs said sadly. "Gower and I even went to Paris to see Rex. We drive out to his house in the country and he meets us at the door. 'Marvelous day,' he says. You know the way he talks." Jacobs put on his Rex Harrison voice. " 'Marvelous day. Bloody Mary, anyone, Bloody Mary.' He gets us the Bloody Marys and then he says, 'Now let me tell you why I'm not going to do *Mr. Chips*.' That's the first we heard about it. It was all set. Well, Gower looks at me, picks up his attaché case and says, 'Sorry, I'm going to the airport, I'm going home.' " Jacobs gazed out the window at the clouds. "It was all set," he said. *"All set."*

~

THE FOX PARTY was met at the airport in Minneapolis by Perry Lieber, of the publicity department, who had flown in from Los Angeles the day before to supervise the preview arrangements. Lieber approached the task as if it were—and indeed he seemed to equate it with—the annual pilgrimage of the English royal family from Buckingham Palace to Balmoral. There were none of the ordinary traveler's mundane worries about luggage, accommodations and transportation. Lieber had checked the entire twenty-eight-man Studio contingent into the Radisson Hotel, ordered a fleet of limousines to transport each planeload of Fox people to the hotel, and arranged that all baggage be picked up at the airport and sent immediately to the proper rooms and suites. He gathered baggage tags and dispensed them to waiting functionaries and gave each new arrival an envelope containing his room key and a card listing that person's flight arrangements to New York or Los Angeles the next day, as well as the time that a limousine would pick him up at the hotel for the trip out to the airport.

Jacobs took his envelope and gave it to Natalie Trundy. For a moment, he peered intently at Lieber's tie pin, a musical staff on which the words "The Sound of Music" were written in sharps and flats. "You've got the wrong picture," he said.

"Are you kidding?" Lieber replied boisterously. "This is my

lucky tie pin. You know how *Sound of Music* did and we previewed that here."

Warren Cowan shook his head slowly. "This has got to be the most superstitious movie company in the world," he said.

"If they're so superstitious," Fleischer said, "then why didn't they get Bob Wise to direct this picture?"

Outside the airport, standing beside a limousine, Natalie Trundy pulled out a Kodak Instamatic and began snapping pictures of the Fox party. She was dressed all in white and was wearing pale yellow sunglasses. She aimed her camera at Cowan, but her flashbulb misfired and she asked for one more shot.

"Oh, for God's sake, Natalie," Jacobs said. "Let's get going."

Cowan sat on the jump seat and opened a copy of the *Minneapolis Tribune* to the theater section, where the Studio had placed a teaser advertisement that did not give the name of the picture. The advertisement was headlined "Hollywood Red Carpet Preview."

"They're charging two sixty a ticket," Cowan said. "That's a mistake. You want to get the kids at a preview of a picture like this, and at two sixty a head, it's too steep."

"They should have made it two bucks a couple," Jacobs agreed miserably. At this point, he seemed to see disaster in everything. "To get the Friday night dates."

"It's a mistake," Cowan repeated softly.

As the limousine sped toward downtown Minneapolis, the chauffeur began to issue statistics about the city. "There are fifty-eight lakes and parks within the city limits," he said. No one paid any attention. Jacobs put out one brown cigarettello and lit another.

"Are you going to stand or sit in the theater tonight?" he asked Fleischer.

The director stared out the window at the early autumn foliage. "I'm going to lie down," he said. He patted Jacobs on the knee. "It's only a preview, Arthur," he said.

"Of an eighteen-million-dollar picture," Jacobs said.

~

LUNCH WAS SERVED in the Flame Room of the Radisson. It was after three o'clock and the dining room was deserted, but the kitchen had been kept open for the Fox group. Many had not yet arrived and others were up in their rooms napping. Jacobs had changed into a dark suit and he bounded from table to table.

"Don't forget, we're due at the art museum at three-thirty," he said.

"Arthur's making jokes," Lionel Newman said. The head of the Studio's music department, Newman had arranged the score and conducted it on the sound track. He had arrived in Minneapolis the day before with a Studio sound engineer to help set up the theater for the preview. "Arthur, as a comic, you're a lard-ass."

Jacobs looked chagrined.

"You know what I call this hotel?" Newman said. "Menopause Manor." He smiled at the waitress. "That's okay, honey, I don't mean you. But you got to admit, there's one or two old people staying here. I mean, this hotel talks about the swinging sixties, they don't mean the year, they mean the Geritol set."

Suddenly Jacobs raised his arm and shouted, "The Brinkmans." Standing in the doorway of the Flame Room, with his wife Yvonne, was Leslie Bricusse, the tall, bespectacled young English writer who had written the screenplay, music and lyrics for *Dr. Dolittle.* Jacobs was beside himself. "The Brinkmans are here," he cried to Fleischer. "Brinkmans" was his nickname for the Bricusses. "Did you see them?"

"He could hardly miss, Arthur," Newman said. "You make it seem like the start of World War III."

"Sit over here, Leslie," Jacobs said. He snapped his fingers for the waitress, who was standing right behind him. "We need chairs. Leslie, you want a sandwich, coffee, a drink?"

The Bricusses were pummeled by the Fox people and diffidently gave their order to the waitress. Yvonne Bricusse, a handsome, dark-haired English actress, slipped into a banquette alongside Natalie Trundy, who kissed her on the cheek. She poured herself a cup of coffee.

"What are you wearing to the opening?" Natalie Trundy said.

"New York?" Yvonne Bricusse said.

"Mmmmm," Natalie Trundy said.

"A heavenly thing," Yvonne Bricusse said. "Leslie bought it for

me. Autumn colors, sort of. Burnt orange, with a bow here." She
patted her bosom.

"Divine," Natalie Trundy said. "How about Los Angeles?"

"Nothing yet," Yvonne Bricusse said, sipping her coffee. "I
thought I'd get something made. What do you think of Don Feld?"
Feld is a motion-picture costume designer.

"Heavenly," Natalie Trundy said. She reached over with her fork
and speared a piece of steak off Jacobs's plate. "A lot of feathers,
though."

Yvonne Bricusse brooded for a moment. "Mmmmm," she said.
"I know what you mean. He *does* like feathers." She stirred a spoon
lazily in her coffee cup. "What about you?"

"In the works," Natalie Trundy said. "They're on the drawing
boards, New York, London, Los Angeles, all the openings." She flut-
tered her arms like a ballerina. "I'm going to *float*. I haven't even
talked about colors yet. I want to see how they look on the board."

∾

THAT EVENING, BEFORE the preview, Richard Zanuck hosted a
party for the Fox group at the Minneapolis Press Club on the second floor of the Radisson. Zanuck had just that day returned from
Europe, a combination business and pleasure trip to London and
Paris, then a week vacationing in the South of France with David
and Helen Gurley Brown. He looked tanned and healthy. "I'm
still on Paris time," he said, dipping a cocktail frankfurter into some
mustard. "Stopped off in New York this morning to see a rough cut
of *The Incident,* then back onto a plane out here."

"You can sleep tomorrow," Arthur Jacobs said.

Zanuck shook his head. "I'm going back to Los Angeles at six-
thirty in the morning."

"Why?" Jacobs said.

"I want to go to the Rams game tomorrow night," Zanuck said.

Jacobs looked incredulous. He filtered through the room, stopping
at each little group. "Dick's leaving for L.A. tomorrow at six-thirty.
In the morning. You know why? He wants to go to the Rams game."

At 7:45, Perry Lieber beat on the side of a glass with a fork. He
told the assembled group that the preview started at eight sharp and

that after the picture there would be a supper served in Richard Zanuck's suite on the twelfth floor. The picture was playing just down the street from the hotel at the Mann Theater, one of a chain owned by a Minnesota theater magnate named Ted Mann. Fox had rented the theater for the night, paying off Universal Pictures, one of whose road-show films, *Thoroughly Modern Millie,* was playing there. Three rows of seats had been roped off for the Fox contingent, along with three other seats in the back of the house for Jacobs, Mort Abrahams and Natalie Trundy. Jacobs had specially requested these seats because he is a pacer and wanted to be free to walk around the theater without disturbing anyone. As Jacobs walked into the lobby of the theater, his eye caught a large display for *Camelot,* the Warner Brothers–Seven Arts musical that was to be the Christmas presentation at another Mann house. He stopped in his tracks.

"Oh, my God," he said. He looked at the people spilling into the theater. "Oh, my God, *Camelot.* That's what they'll think they're going to see. Oh, my God."

THE HOUSE LIGHTS went down at 8:13. The audience was composed mainly of young marrieds and the middle-aged. There were almost no children present. Zanuck sat in an aisle seat, with Barbara McLean, the head of the Studio's cutting department, beside him, a pad on her lap, ready to take notes. The overture was played and then a title card flashed on the screen that said, "Equatorial Africa, 1845." The card dissolved into a prologue and Rex Harrison, in frock coat and top hat, rode onto the screen on top of a giraffe. There was no murmur of recognition from the audience. Some of the Studio party began to shift uneasily in their seats. The prologue lasted only a few moments. Harrison, as Dr. Dolittle, the man who could talk to the animals, slipped off the back of the giraffe to treat a crocodile ailing with a toothache. He tied a piece of string to the aching tooth and then tied the other end of the string to the tail of an elephant. At a signal from Dr. Dolittle, the elephant pulled on the cord and the tooth snapped out of the crocodile's mouth. Harrison patted the crocodile on the snout, put its huge molar in his waistcoat pocket, climbed on the back of a passing rhinoceros, and rode through the jungle out of camera range. There was not a whisper out of the audience as the prologue dissolved into the cartoon credits. At the appearance of the title *Dr. Dolittle,* there was a smatter of applause from the Studio contingent, but the clapping was not taken up by those who had paid $2.60 a ticket.

Throughout the first half of the film, the audience was equally unresponsive. Even at the end of the musical numbers, there was only a ripple of approval. At the intermission, David Brown hurried out into the lobby. "I want to hear the comments," he said. The noise in the lobby was muted. Most of the people just sipped soft drinks and talked quietly among themselves. Several of the Fox people blatantly eavesdropped on their conversations. Jacobs stood by one of the doors, his eyes darting wildly. Natalie Trundy leaned against him, her eyes brimming with tears, kneading a Kleenex between her fingers. In the center of the lobby, a circle of Studio executives surrounded Richard Zanuck.

"This is a real dead-ass audience," Zanuck said. "But you've got to remember, this isn't *Sound of Music* or *My Fair Lady.* The audience hasn't been conditioned to the songs for five years like they are with a hit musical."

"This is an original score," Stan Hough said.

Zanuck nodded his head vigorously. "And an original screenplay," he said. The muscles in his jaw popped in and out feverishly. "My God, these people didn't know what they were going to see when they came into the theater. The first thing they see is a guy riding a giraffe."

"It's not like *Sound of Music,*" Hough said.

"Or *My Fair Lady,*" Zanuck said. "Those songs were famous before they even began shooting the picture."

The second half of the picture did not play much better than the first. There was only sporadic laughter and desultory applause for the production numbers. When the house lights finally came on, the only prolonged clapping came from the three rows where the Studio people were sitting. In the lobby, ushers passed out preview cards. Tables had been set up and pencils provided for the members of the audience to fill in their reactions. These cards were more detailed than most preview questionnaires. "PLEASE RATE THE

PICTURE," the cards read. "Excellent. Good. Fair." In another section, the questionnaire asked:

> *How would you rate the performance of the following?*
> *Rex Harrison*
> *Samantha Eggar*
> *Anthony Newley*
> *Richard Attenborough*
>
> *Which scenes did you like the most?*
>
> *Which scenes, if any, did you dislike?*

WE DON'T WANT TO KNOW YOUR NAME, BUT WE WOULD LIKE TO KNOW THE FOLLOWING FACTS ABOUT YOU:

> A. Male—Female
>
> B. Check Age Group You Are In:
> Between 12 and 17
> Between 18 and 30
> Between 31 and 45
> Over 45

THANK YOU VERY MUCH FOR YOUR COURTESY AND COOPERATION.

Jacobs wandered through the lobby. His eyes were bloodshot. Natalie Trundy trailed after him. She had stopped crying, but her eyes were red-rimmed.

"I hear the cards are 75 percent excellent," Jacobs said to no one in particular. He watched a woman chewing on a small yellow pencil as she perused her card. The woman wrote something down, erased it, then wrote something else. Jacobs tried to look over her shoulder, but when she saw him, the woman shielded her comments with her hand.

Ted Ashley, the president of Ashley Famous Artists, Rex Harrison's agents, came up and clapped Jacobs on the back. "Arthur, you've got yourself a picture here," Ashley said. Jacobs waited for him to say something else, but Ashley just slapped him on the back again and went over to talk to Zanuck.

"The audience was kind of quiet," Zanuck said.

Ted Mann, the theater owner, a large blocky man at one of whose theaters *Dr. Dolittle* was going to play when it opened in Minneapolis, elbowed his way to Zanuck's side. "I want you to know, Dick, a year's run," he said. "A year minimum."

"I thought the audience was a little quiet," Zanuck repeated.

"Yes, it was, Dick," Mann said. "But it's the kids who are going to make this picture, and we didn't have many kids here tonight." Mann seemed to search for the proper words. "You've got to realize," he said, "that what we had here tonight was your typically sophisticated Friday night Minneapolis audience."

Zanuck seemed not to hear. "They weren't conditioned to it like *Sound of Music,*" he said.

"That's my point, my point exactly," Mann said. "But they'll be hearing this score for the next four months until the picture opens. By the time December rolls around, they'll know what they're going to see, don't you worry about that, don't you worry at all."

Jacobs looked over at Zanuck. "Over 50 percent excellent," he said.

The theater emptied and the Fox party slowly walked back to the Radisson half a block away. There was little enthusiasm as they rode up the elevator to the party in Zanuck's Villa Suite. The suite was enormous, on two levels, with a large living room and two bedrooms on the balcony above it. A bar had been set up on the balcony and a buffet beside it. The food had not yet arrived. There were only two large bowls of popcorn which were quickly emptied. The room was quiet, with only a slight hum of conversation. Jacobs, Abrahams, Bricusse, Natalie Trundy and Barbara McLean sat around a coffee table totting up the cards, stacking them into piles of "Excellent," "Good" and "Fair." There were 175 cards in all—101 "Excellent," 47 "Good" and 27 "Fair." One viewer had written "Miserable" and another noted that Rex Harrison played Dr. Dolittle "like a male Mary Poppins." Two women objected to a scene with white mice and five to another scene in which Anthony Newley drinks whiskey out of a bottle.

"Those broads are all over forty-five, right?" Jacobs said.

"The 'Fairs' are all over forty-five," Abrahams said.

Ted Mann peered down at the cards. "You've got to realize that this was a typically sophisticated Friday night Minneapolis audience," he repeated.

"What we needed was a lot of kids," Natalie Trundy said. She dabbed at her eyes with a handkerchief and asked someone to bring her a Scotch on the rocks.

It was obvious that the Studio was distressed by the results of the preview. It was not just that the cards were bad—though with $18 million riding on the film, they were considerably less favorable than the Studio might have liked. But what disturbed them even more was the muted reaction of the audience during the screening of the picture.

"I think it's damn silly to come all the way to Minneapolis and then not tell people what they're going to see," Zanuck said. "It's all right to have a sneak in Los Angeles. But you come this goddam far to get away from that inside audience. So tell them what they're going to see. Get the kids out."

Richard Fleischer nursed a drink, stirring it slowly with his finger. "That's right, Dick," he said. "Tell them in the ads." He moved his hand as if he were reading from an advertisement. " '*Dr. Dolittle*— the story of a man who loved animals.' "

"Right," Zanuck said. "They know what they're seeing, they'll break the goddam doors down." He gave his glass to Linda Harrison and asked her to get him another drink. "When we run it next, in San Francisco, maybe, we'll tell them what they're going to see. No goddam teaser ads."

"I'd be mystified," Fleischer said, "if I came into the theater and didn't know what the picture was and the first scene was a guy riding a giraffe."

Jonas Rosenfield, the Studio's vice-president in charge of publicity, who had come from New York for the screening, edged up beside Zanuck. "It's all true," he said. "But we've all got to admit that this was an invaluable preview. We know now how to promote this picture to make it the big success we still know it's going to be."

"This is what previews are for," Owen McLean said.

"Right," Stan Hough said. "This is what we come to Minneapolis for, to find out things like this."

Waiters arrived and laid out a supper of filet mignon on hamburger rolls. Calls were placed to Harrison in France, where he was making another Studio picture, *A Flea in Her Ear,* and to Darryl Zanuck in New York.

When the call to Darryl Zanuck came through, Richard Zanuck and David Brown went into a bedroom and closed the door. The party seemed to settle in. Jacobs still went through the cards, one by one.

"No kids," he said. "Everyone is over thirty."

"It's the kids who'll make this picture a hit," Harry Sokolov said.

In a corner of the room, Owen McLean sat down on a couch beside David Raphel, the Studio's vice-president in charge of foreign sales. "Well, David," McLean said, "what did you think?"

Raphel, a distinguished-looking middle-aged man with a slight foreign accent, wiped a piece of hamburger bun from his lips. "A very useful preview," he said carefully. "This picture will take very special handling to make it the success we all know it's going to be. We mustn't forget the older people. They're the repeaters. The children won't get there unless their grandparents take them. The grandparents, they're the repeaters. Look at *The Sound of Music.*"

"There are people who've seen *Sound of Music* a hundred times," McLean said.

"My point," Raphel said. "My point exactly."

Slowly the party began to break up. It was after one A.M. and a number of Studio people were leaving for Los Angeles at 6:30 the next morning. At the door of Zanuck's suite, Ted Ashley shook hands with Jacobs.

"You've got yourself a picture, Arthur," Ashley said. "It's all up there on the screen."

"It'll work," Jacobs said. "Cut a few things, switch a few things."

"It's going to be great, Arthur," Rosenfield said. He patted Jacobs on the arm. "None of us has any doubts about that."

Zanuck's suite cleared by 1:30 in the morning. At 4 A.M. he called Harry Sokolov and told him to round up Hough, McLean and

David Brown for a meeting in his room. They convened in Zanuck's suite at 4:45 A.M., and for the next hour Zanuck went over the picture reel by reel. Before the meeting broke up, shortly before six, it was tentatively agreed to cut the prologue. A decision was deferred on whether to cut any of the musical numbers. Arthur Jacobs was not present at this meeting.

TINSEL

[1 9 7 4]

THE ONLY TIME I ever met Joseph E. Levine he told me it was snowing in Russia and then left the room. It did not occur to me to mention that it was also snowing outside on Sixth Avenue, because one had the sense that Levine was perhaps the only man in the world not a general to whom snow in Russia was a matter of life or death. I never asked any of his subalterns the significance of the Soviet snow; one became used to cryptic utterance in the Levine organization. "You're hot now," one of his supernumeraries told my wife and me when we checked into Levine's offices to write a screenplay, "but in six months the bloom will be off the rose."

WE WERE SHOOTING. We were behind schedule. We were over budget. Nearly a quarter of a million dollars over budget. The studio was furious. They had held up our final screenplay payment and were threatening to take away our points, or percentage of the profits. We were speaking through lawyers. Studio bookkeepers and accountants combed the books. Talk of injunction was in the air, a showdown meeting arranged.

The studio vice-president wore blue suede Gucci loafers and a white suit with a belt in the back. He was surrounded by his

accountants. He liked to scream. He screamed that we were amateurs. He screamed that only an amateur would rent a house at the
beach for $1,000 a day just to shoot its exterior.

It was a puzzling assertion. In fact the producer had made a good
deal for the house, renting it, for both interiors and exteriors, for an
entire week at only $1,250.

"A thousand dollars a day," the vice-president screamed insis-
tently.

"Who told you that?"

"William."

"Who is William?"

The accountants began to shift uneasily.

"My wife's hairdresser," the vice-president said.

~

WRITING FILMS IS a good deal like writing for *Time* magazine,
except that the pay is better. The film writer is first of all *hired,* and
as an employee, no matter how grandiose his salary, he must tailor
his ideas to those of his employer. He can wheedle, cajole, or even
scream, but if he fails to persuade his employer, he either goes along
or gets out. If he gets out, he is easily replaced. On a recent Barbra
Streisand picture, there was one credited writer, but five others,
including two Academy Award winners, worked on the screenplay.
Now these six people didn't meet at lunch one day and decide to
make a film, you do the plot, you do the humor, you do the flashbacks,
and I'll do the polish. They were all hired, their brains picked by the
producer and the director, and then discarded. In the wisdom of the
Writers Guild, one of these six received a solo credit, but the fingerprints of the other five are smudged all over the finished film.

~

THE FIRST FILM script I wrote, in the summer of 1964, was called
Show Me a Hero, as in Scott Fitzgerald's "Show me a hero and I will
write you a tragedy." It was a measure of the script's worth that neither was it a tragedy nor was the protagonist a hero; she was a heroine. The subject of the yarn—it could not properly be called
anything else—was topical: a woman who had become a national

figure because of her undying love and loyalty to a husband withering away in a Communist prison on a trumped-up charge of espionage. A reporter from a magazine called *Tempo* (I had once worked for *Time* and written for *Life*) is sent to find out what makes this symbol of the good, the true and the beautiful rise above the nation's prevailing moral inertia. (Remember, this was years before the POW wives and Mrs. Commander Lloyd Bucher.) Things are not what they seem. The heroine is a pawn in a right-wing plot. The heroine moreover is living a lie; she never loved her husband. And the husband indeed was a spy, a task he undertook when he discovered that the heroine did not love him. (Not only was he a spy, it turns out, but a setup deliberately blown by his superiors so that a prisoner exchange could be effected with his Communist captors, exchanging him for a famous Red agent who had agreed to double for the CIA behind the Iron Curtain; the famous Red agent, however, had undergone a change of heart and hung himself in his American prison cell rather than turn traitor. This was a subplot.) The young reporter, sickened by these revelations, declares his love *in camera* to the heroine. The heroine reciprocates carnally in a midwinter tryst in either a cottage on Fire Island or a suite at the Radisson Hotel in Minneapolis, a plot point to be worked out later. The military-industrial complex uncovers the illicit romance. The heroine declares herself sick of sham and says she will publicly avow her love for the young reporter. The inhabitant of the Oval Office indicates with all the wisdom of his years that such an avowal of infidelity would be a source of great disillusion to what, in 1964, was not yet known as the Silent Majority. At precisely that moment, the heroine's husband is released from his Communist hell. Love or Duty, which will the heroine choose?

The young reporter says, "I love you, Marjorie," for that is the heroine's name.

And the heroine says, "Oh, Joe," for that is the young reporter's name.

And we fade out before the Great Decision.

∽

MY AGENTS WERE ecstatic when they read the script. A love story by a neophyte writer. What "neophyte" meant in this context was that I had never written a script, which in turn meant that I could be sold for short money and no points, which in turn meant that as the story costs were not top-heavy, a package might be put together with a heavyweight actress/actor/director, which in turn meant that I would be shuffled right off to Buffalo. (I was not as wise in the summer of 1964 as I am in the summer of 1974, but that is what neophyte meant then and that is what neophyte means now.) All the script needed, my agents said, was a few changes and would I come to town to discuss them. Has anyone ever been so young that his heart skipped a beat at the prospect of a script conference with a roomful of William Morris agents? I was, that summer.

There were seven agents crowded in the office, all very short. The meeting was chaired by a henna-haired woman who, after making sure that I was comfortable, assured me that the purpose of the meeting was "constructive criticism."

"Constructive criticism," chorused the other six agents.

"Does anyone have any constructive criticism?" asked the chairperson.

Silence.

"I'm sure someone has some constructive criticism," said the chairperson.

One of the shorter agents raised his hand. "I hope you don't take this amiss," he said to me, "because we all know what we're here for is constructive criticism."

Again the chorus: "Constructive criticism."

"Constructive criticism," I said. Was the heroine too unsympathetic? Was the young reporter too shallow? Or too young?

"Right," said the agent. "Now I'd just like to ask you one thing, uh, and I hope you won't take this personally, it's just constructive criticism, but when you retype the script, I'd like you to make the margins a little wider, if you know what I mean."

I was not sure I did.

"Leave a lot more white space on the page," he added.

There was general nodding around the room. "A good point," the chairperson said.

"White space," I said.

"White space," the agent said.

"That's constructive," the chairperson said.

~

THE BEST TIME to do a picture, if you are a part-time screenwriter, is when you don't need the money. Then you are working because you like either the project or the people (or perhaps both), and your own vanity becomes fused with the vanity fair of the movie business. With luck, the picture might turn out to be pretty good; at worst, you've had a lot of laughs.

~

TECHNIQUE IS EASILY learned. I sat through three consecutive showings of *Seven Days in May* at a second-run drive-in in Long Beach to count the number of sequences that made up a well-crafted movie. (As I remember, there were forty.) But most instructive of all is seeing the bad movies of good directors. Truffaut's *Fahrenheit 451,* Antonioni's *Red Desert,* Peckinpah's *Major Dundee,* Penn's *The Chase*—in each there is a moment or sequence that stands out in such bold relief from the surrounding debris as to make the reasons for its effectiveness clear.

~

SURVEYING THE ARCHITECTURE of even the most mendacious film can be exhilarating. Norman Mailer caught this feeling exactly in *The Deer Park* when the director, Charles Eitel, finds himself absorbed in a meretricious screen story retailed by the producer, Carlyle Munshin: "The professional in Eitel lusted for the new story . . . it was so beautifully false. Professional blood thrived on what was excellently dishonest."

~

KEEP SCENES SHORT. A brothel is a good place for exposition, as is an assembly line or a baton-twirling contest for drum majorettes. In a quieter genre, when two people are talking, have one of them shaving or going to the bathroom or having his ears pierced. A radio dropped in a bathtub is a good way to kill someone and a waffle iron in the face makes a nice visual pattern. Don't forget props: studios call it characterization when an actor is plugged into a menthol inhalator or picks his teeth with a .38 or swabs his ear with a Q-tip.

~

"He used to be a writer," the agent said of his client, the producer. "Now he's a creator.

~

It took my wife and me three years and $2,000 to get our first picture made. It was based on a book called *The Panic in Needle Park* by James Mills and was about two heroin addicts on the streets of New York. We got involved in *Needle Park* because no one was asking us to do any film work. Both my wife and I liked the book and we brought it to my brother, who is a film producer. Between the three of us, we scraped up $1,000 for a year's option against a final purchase price of $17,500 and 5 percent of net profits. It was a year before we finally found time to write a treatment, or dramatic breakdown. By that time, the initial option was up and we had to ante up another $1,000 to hold the book for a second year.

We now had $2,000 of our own money invested in the project and no prospects for laying it off on a studio. Our agents were not sanguine; the story was "too downbeat." They suggested packaging it with Henry Fonda; we suggested that Fonda was perhaps forty years too old for the lead, and countered with Peter Fonda. They said that Peter Fonda was not packageable. Then they suggested writing the whole experience off as a tax loss. Studio after studio turned us down. Then our agents showed the treatment to the Levine organization, and to everyone's surprise, Levine bought it. Months later, we learned why. "Joe never reads anything," one of his executives told us. "You've got to sell him with one line."

We asked what our one line was.

" 'Romeo and Juliet on junk.' "

~

It was from the Levine experience that we learned the importance of guile in writing screenplays. "Romeo and Juliet on junk" was heavy freight, heavier still after we flew to New York and checked into a junkie hotel on the West Side. The roaches in the hotel were the size of gunboats, and neither the sheets nor the towels were changed until we went to Bloomingdale's and bought some of our own. A friend put us in touch with a pusher who dealt marijuana and cocaine to the various movie companies filming in New York. He was a sixteen-year-old high school student with braces on his teeth; his brother was a dealer and his mother an addict and he was the compleat entrepreneur, also dealing heroin from a grocery bike he pedaled around the neighborhood; all his dope was taped to the bottom of the basket on the bicycle.

He introduced us to his customers and for the next several weeks we spent day and night with junkies. We plied them with Hostess Twinkies and they shot up in our room and importuned us for money. Mills's heroine was a lesbian-call-girl-turned-junkie, but during these sessions we found an addict more in keeping with the studio's sensibilities: junkie and hooker Levine would go along with, but lesbian he wasn't into.

It was not exactly the Montagues and the Capulets, but we were stuck with making it seem so. Our solution was to write in a voice-over in which one protagonist or the other would talk about a-heroin-kind-of-love. We never had any intention of recording the voice-over, but it did give Levine's people something they could read to Joe. In one sentence.

～

ANOTHER TRICK. STUDIO executives are notoriously literal-minded, and the easiest way to soothe them when they complain about the mood of a scene is simply to add a stage direction. Thus, if they maintain that:

> BOBBY
> *You dumb bitch*

is too grim, you change the line to:

> BOBBY
> *(Engagingly)*
> *You dumb bitch*

The man in charge of Levine's West Coast office was a former agent who had doffed his agent's black suit for executive suede. (This was during the buckskin-and-fringe period of Hollywood executive life when every studio vice-president looked like Buffalo Bill in tinted glasses.) He had the corner office and the right barber, but he felt a little exposed, in large part because his counterparts in New York were three thousand miles closer than he was to Levine's ear. "Nice guy, smart as a whip," he would say of his Eastern alter ego, "don't trust him." In the middle of a meeting he would often interrupt to ask the names of the more important captains in the better restaurants, and he was an inveterate Gucci-checker and lapel-measurer. Not that he was without self-confidence. "When I go on a set," he liked to say, "things happen."

～

A SCREENWRITER I know was doing a racing picture. "I didn't know you were interested in auto racing," I said.

"I'm not," he said. "Bores me stiff."

"Then how do you handle the racing scenes?"

"With the magic stage direction," he said. " 'SEQUENCE TO BE STAGED BY DIRECTOR.' "

～

FESTIVAL FORTNIGHT IN Cannes. The atmosphere was less film festival than agricultural fair. There were stalls for Scandinavian pornography in the lobby of the Carlton and slide shows explaining the merits of international co-production. The exhibits were run by thick-waisted men who looked like the proprietors of Middle-European Harvester franchises. The conversation was of negative pickup and cross-collateralization, of renting the Yugoslavian army and bribing the Guardia Civil. The lobbies were rich with rumor: Joseph Losey was not speaking to Luchino Visconti. Erich Segal was feuding with Sergio Leone. Buck Henry had seen seven pictures in one day. Jacqueline Susann had met Picasso.

We were staying at the Carlton. It was easy to fall into the pattern. The hall porter brought endless bottles of Château d'Yquem, a studio publicity man handed out crisp, new hundred-franc notes as petty cash, every night there was dinner for six, eight, twelve at La Reserve: it all went on the budget of the picture. We reread *Tender Is the Night*. From the balcony of our suite, we could look down on the Croisette and beyond, past that "bright tan prayer rug of a beach" to Sam Spiegel's yacht bobbing on the Mediterranean. Scott and Zelda, Dick and Nicole Diver, Gerald and Sara Murphy. Abe North. Tommy Barban. Rosemary Hoyt. It would make a great picture; living well *was* the best revenge.

Back in Los Angeles, our agent had already set the ball rolling. *Tender Is the Night* was available; Fox held the remake rights and no additional payments had to be made to the Fitzgerald estate. We would, as the agents say, "take a meeting."

The vice-president in charge of production met us in his office. He had not, he said, read the "basic material," but the story department had pulled out a synopsis made in 1945. He showed us the synopsis: five pages, single-spaced. A few lines caught my eye: "On their way to Paris, Dick and Nicole and Abe and Rosemary visit the trenches of a World War I battlefield. Later, waiting for a train, an orchestra breaks into 'Yes, We Have No Bananas.' "

I handed the synopsis back to the vice-president in charge of production.

"I would gather," he said carefully, "that what interests you about this property is the glamour and glitter of the Edwardian age."

We never wrote the picture.

～

FILM FESTIVAL WARDROBE: faded Levis, tie-dyed T-shirt, torn bush coat, paint-spattered tennis sneakers, and a velvet dinner jacket.

～

THERE ARE WRITERS in Hollywood with the reputation of being a "good meeting," as in "Irving is a fantastic meeting." A good meeting thinks fast on his feet, can argue forcibly that the sun rises in the east, and even more forcibly that it rises in the west if that is the way the studio sees it. He is an interpreter of silences and a reader of eyebrow movement, a master of options, strategic withdrawals, and tactical advances. And he has a fund of good gossip to bridge that awkward moment when he deposits the blame for one of his bad ideas on someone else's doorstep.

～

I AM A terrible meeting. During the conferences on *Tender Is the Night,* the vice-president in charge of production asked how we planned to deal with the ending. We would not take Dick Diver to upstate New York as Fitzgerald did, my wife said. Instead we would end the picture with the penultimate scene in the novel: Dick blessing the Riviera beach with the papal cross as he prepared to leave France.

This was not exactly what the vice-president in charge of production had in mind. Couldn't "the two young people"—he could never remember the Divers' name from the synopsis, so always referred to them as "the two young people"—get back together?

It would seem, I said, to defeat the point of the book.

"That might be so," he said. "But your audience today would like to see these two young people get back together. Your audience today likes your up ending."

I made an attempt to be a good meeting. "But Ali MacGraw," I found myself saying, "died at the end of *Love Story.*"

Nicole Diver, meet Jenny Cavalleri.

～

THE PRODUCER HAD a mechanical joint roller because he could never get the hang of building his own. He poured the grass evenly, fiddled with the roller, and presto! a joint that looked like a Camel. He took a man-sized hit. "The day I got busted for dope," he said, "was the day I left the Republican Party and the Catholic Church."

～

THE STORY CONFERENCE is to screenwriting what crab grass is to the lawn. It encourages the most spurious sense of collaboration: if it allows the producer to feel "creative," it makes the writer ever more aware that he is an employee. Everyone involved feels impelled to pump significance into the most banal bloodletter; rarely this side of academe does one hear more about "illusion versus reality" than one does in a story conference, usually in a story conference about a western. Every sentence tends to begin with "What if . . ." as in "What if the young doctor blows up the boat?"

"As an existential act?"

"Right."

"The illusion-versus-reality type thing?"

"Right on."

"But his wife's in the boat."

"What if he only thought she was?"

"There's your illusion versus reality again."

∽

IN AN EFFORT to cut the losses, we have generally tried to hold story conferences at home. We live fifty miles up the coast from town, and the very length of the ride along the Pacific can turn what began as a meeting into an adventure. And always there is lunch, the same story-conference lunch: a cold leek soup, antipasto, baguettes of French bread, fruit, Brie, and white wine. The lunch is programmed to reinforce the notion that the turf is ours, and that it would be bad form for a guest to push aberrant ideas; we are no longer employees, but host and hostess. Sometimes it works.

∽

THE PRODUCER WAS showing me around his lavishly appointed office. His shelves were stocked with pre-Columbian artifacts and there were two Picasso etchings on the walls. "Here's a Miró," he said, adding helpfully "M-I-R-O."

∽

ONCE YOU ACCEPT the idea that says because you get paid $200,000 to write a script and the director gets $500,000 to direct it, he's $300,000 smarter than you are, then Hollywood becomes a very amusing place to work.

∽

"YOU'RE A MEL," a producer told a screenwriter friend of mine. The statement perplexed my friend, whose name was not Mel.

"Screenwriters are all named Mel," the producer explained. "Mel Frank. Mel Shavelson. Mel Panama . . ."

"*Norman* Panama," my friend interrupted.

"He's still a Mel," the producer said. "Producers are named Marty. In this town, the Martys hire the Mels."

THE SCREENWRITER WAS bearish on the box-office prospects of his new film. I mentioned the director's considerable following on college campuses, but the writer was unimpressed. "Straight to cult," he said of the new picture. "It'll be a hit at Bloomingdale's."

AT LEAST TWICE a year I am asked to prepare an obituary on the death of Hollywood. I am always a veritable Old Testament of parables that no one outside of Hollywood seems to understand, all of them attesting to the health of the industry. There is my Marty Erlichman parable. Marty Erlichman is Barbra Streisand's manager. At the opening of a blockbuster hit I had a hand in writing for his client, Erlichman kept staring at me, as if trying to place the face. Suddenly he snapped his fingers and said, "You must be someone's manager." The point being that when times are flush, the manager's ultimate accolade is to think that someone who looks interesting must also be a manager, like himself.

Then there is my Phil Feldman parable. Phil Feldman is the president of a film company from whom I tried to promote a free trip to New York. I had written a picture for his company, the picture was a hit and I figured why not, I'm entitled. Two, three, five weeks went by and he never answered my "Dear Mr. Feldman" letter. So I decided to write him another:

Dear Phil,

I was immensely warmed and cheered by your letter. It really made us both chuckle.

I mentioned the proposal to our agents and they said it was definitely an option worth considering.

Mazel.

John

Two days later I got a call from Feldman's office. The boss was on a rampage. He could not find the file copy of the letter he had never written me and now he had forgotten which proposal he had never made which I was allegedly discussing with my agents. If it were a new proposal, he did not want me to take it to Paramount. I explained that it was a joke, that he had never written a letter (that being the point of the exercise), but that I knew there were three words that would always make a movie executive's palms twitch: "proposal," "agents" and "option."

When I offered these parables to the last editor who had asked me to write of Hollywood's death rattle, he could not see the lesson, remaining convinced that the industry was in a terminal coma. Or perhaps he just had trouble imagining Old Testament prophets named Marty and Phil.

~

I HAVE COME to dread Academy Award time each spring. The Oscars are always good for an annual smirk in the press, from Andrew Sarris in the *Village Voice,* say, or Vincent Canby in the *New York Times.* The choices are "moribund," the ceremony "tacky." As a matter of fact, the smirkers have never understood either the Academy or its awards. (I have no ax to grind; although eligible, I have by choice not joined the Academy of Motion Picture Arts & Sciences, as I would by choice not join any critics' circle or society or organized sucker list of whatever name.) The Academy is essentially a trade union of some 3,000 members, a mixture of below-the-line sound men and lighting men, special-effects men and PR people, film editors and set dressers, as well as above-the-line actors and directors, producers and writers. The awards are the awards of any union in any company town, a vote for jobs, and hits provide jobs, flops don't. If the New York film critics, most of whom work for union-organized publications, opened their membership to several thousand typesetters from the Typographical Union and projectionists from IATSE and secretaries from the Newspaper Guild, I suspect that the Academy's choices would seem a lot less moribund.

~

A STUDIO EXECUTIVE came to a writer friend of mine and said he had an idea for a film. "We're all very excited about it," the executive said. "The sky's the limit on development money."

"What's the idea?" the writer said.

"Relationships," the executive said. He beamed and pulled on his pipe.

The writer stared at him for a long time, waiting for him to add something else. "You mean men and women?" he said finally.

"That'd be part of it."

~

MY WIFE AND I were once taken to lunch by a producer with a hot idea: "World War II."

"What do you want to do with it?"

"You're the writers."

~

FOR THE RECORD, we have also been asked to do "an extension of *The Graduate*" and "*Rebel Without a Cause*" in the west Valley, with a girl in the James Dean part."

~

IT WAS A deal in search of a story: Paul Newman and Robert Redford as New York police officers David Durk and Frank Serpico. Durk and Serpico, the two cops who had blown the whistle on corruption in the New York Police Department and forced the creation of the Knapp Commission. David Durk, the button-down gray-flannel-suit cop, graduate of Amherst College, former student of Alfred Kazin's. Frank Serpico, the undercover cop, who swung with chicks, wore a beard and a ring in his ear. Paul Newman as Durk. Robert

Redford as Serpico, Butch and Sundance in the Big Apple, over a million beans between them, plus a percentage of the gross. Only they did not have a script.

The writer and the director of *Butch Cassidy and the Sundance Kid* had jointly turned down the project before we were approached, and when we listened to the tapes and read the two magazine articles on which the screenplay would be based, we knew why: there was no story. Especially no story when both Newman and Redford had script approval, as did the director: the writer on a project in which two superstars plus a director have script approval stands a good chance of getting ground into little pieces. We declined.

But in Hollywood when you turn down a go project with two superstars, it is generally assumed that you only want more money. The ante was sweetened; again we declined. And sweetened again: our agent intimated that he could get us $100,000 for a first draft, and that he would ". . . work out the down side later." (I might add here that it is a good rule of thumb to cut an agent's intimation by 50 percent.) The head of the studio called at 7:30 A.M. and said he was glad we were coming aboard. I waffled. Again the ante went up. There was so much money involved that my palms began to sweat. And still we did not want to do the script.

It was the appearance of Sam Peckinpah in the package that made us change from "no" to "maybe." We had first met him in the bad years when he could not get work because of a distinctly un-Hollywood penchant for telling people exactly what he thought of them, their ancestors, their wives and children. We had often talked of doing a picture together, but nothing ever came of it. Now there were stars, money, and a studio; the only thing there wasn't, in fact, was a story.

Peckinpah had never met Paul Newman, and so a dinner was arranged at Newman's house in Malibu. We had not seen Sam in over a year, and he was as unmellow as ever. He said that he did not much like Redford and that if he had directed *Butch Cassidy* it would have been a better picture. Newman, who had some distinct reservations about the violence in Peckinpah films, never lost his aplomb. He had just finished directing *Sometimes a Great Notion,* from which the original director had been fired, and he said that he had ". . . cut it from a disaster into a failure." It was the kind of remark that Peck-inpah, the director, could appreciate. Newman and Peckinpah—they were two professionals feeling each other out, and they seemed to like each other.

We talked about red wine. We talked about studio accounting. In fact we talked about everything except Durk and Serpico, which was the point of the exercise. It was only after we left, standing with Sam out in front of Newman's house, that the subject even came up.

"Sam," I said, "what the hell is this picture all about?"

"Write me a Western," Peckinpah said.

"Jesus, Sam, it's about two cops in New York City."

A small smile. "Every story is a Western."

We must have looked bewildered. As if lecturing to two rather slow small children, Sam said, "You put the hare in front of the hound and let the hound chase the hare."

"Oh."

"Simple."

We never wrote the picture.

～

THE WOMAN IN our script had a twelve-year-old child. "If you're not married to that kid," Ali MacGraw's agent whispered at a party, "I can get Ali to read the script."

～

WE HAVE, IN the course of a dozen or so films, stayed in suites at the St. Francis Hotel in San Francisco, the Ambassador East in Chicago, the Regency in New York, the Connaught in London, the Carlton in Cannes, the Eden in Rome, L'Hotel in Paris, and the Tequendama in Bogotá. I say this only to suggest one attraction about working in films that goes largely unmentioned: the attrac-tion of borrowed luxury. Contracts specify an expense allowance of $1,000 a week and there is always a chauffeured limousine to help the traveler navigate a strange city. In every way, the minor fix is in. Hand an expired passport to a production manager and within hours he will return it, renewed. Land in a foreign capital and a pub-lic relations man will glide you through customs, dispensing francs or lire or pesos or pound notes. ("If you have any dope, best tell me now so I can clear things," a PR man advised me at Heathrow; I received the same counsel from his opposite number at Orly.) The ripoff is endemic; studio bookkeeping is so byzantine that none of the profit participants ever really expect to see their points and as a result are not inspired to economy up front. It is this tendency toward largesse that makes a movie company on location so easy to spot. They laugh a little too long in hotel restaurants and talk a little too loud and drink a little too much; they always stick together and are the object of an attention they pretend to ignore. They are like exiles spending the currency of a government which, unbeknownst to the locals, collapsed yesterday.

~

WE WERE ASKED to write a picture for Barbra Streisand. Unfortunately we did not think much of the book we had been asked to adapt; we had, in fact, turned it down twice before Streisand was involved. But such was the lure of Streisand that we were almost able to convince ourselves that she could make even this story work. The director encouraged this delusion; he had not liked the book either, but with the Streisand magic, he said, perhaps we could pull it off.

With some trepidation, we entered into negotiation. But so seductive is the mythology of deal making that our reservations for the moment evaporated. It is all an elaborate entertainment. There are no surprises in a deal; both sides are aware beforehand of the broad strokes in the final settlement, yet the charade of haggling goes on. The sums involved often resemble the national debt of an emerging nation, frequently causing the negotiators to absent themselves from reality. "I know janitors who make $75,000," our agent once said, as he advised us to turn down a deal.

We were kept abreast of the negotiation by telephone. After an initial thrust and parry, our screenplay fee was set at $100,000. On signing, we would receive $15,000 and, on delivery of the first draft, another $35,000. For two sets of revisions, we would get another $25,000, and on the first day of principal photography, if no other writers had been called in, the final $25,000. The delivery date on the first draft was twelve weeks after a negotiated start date. At any point after the first draft we could be fired, but even if we were replaced and our script dismissed as unusable, we would receive the minimum first-draft payment of $50,000.

The fee was easy; now the real bargaining began. Our agent asked for points, which in a Streisand picture could be considerable. But unless they are also partners in the production, writers of an adaptation rarely get points, mainly because producers are unwilling to give a piece up front to a writer they might ultimately want to fire. Thus our request for points was turned down flat. Our agent then informed the producers: no piece, no script.

The game was now the deal, not the screenplay. Instead of points, the producers offered a deferment out of profits. The first offer was for $25,000, and, when that was turned down, they raised the deferment to $50,000. Our agent accepted and then began to work out when and how the deferment would be paid. After much haggling, it was agreed that the deferment would be in two equal payments, the first at 2.2 times the actual negative cost of the picture (at which point the film would be past break-even and into initial profits), the second at 3.5 times negative. Payment would be pari passu (or pro-rated) with others holding a deferment position. So finally, after three weeks of negotiation, what had been established was that if we wrote the picture and if there were no other writers and if the picture was made and if it went into profits, we would make $150,000.

We balked. Not over the deal, but over the book. Even the possibility of $150,000 did not make us like it any better. More meetings, more bargaining. So much time had been expended on the negotiations that the producers were reluctant to audition other writers, even in the face of our desire to bow out of the project. Finally we suggested a compromise: instead of taking a lump-sum first payment, which would tie us into the picture for months, we would give the producers three weeks during which we would try to work out a viable narrative from the book. At the end of the three weeks, we would either go ahead under the original terms or call it a day. As guarantee of our good faith, our agent stipulated that we would work for $2,500 a week, or half our weekly rate. (Actually we did not have a weekly rate, but now he could claim we did, and he had a deal memo to prove it.)

And so we went to work. On the fifth day, we told our agent to get us out of the deal.

"How badly do you want out?" he said.

"They don't have to pay us."

We never wrote the picture.

~

SCENE 235 TOOK place in a cafeteria. The time was night. KATE was having a cup of coffee with her lover, HUGH, a kind of young Eric Hoffer with patch pockets. They run into Kate's former lover, WARREN, a black academic who describes himself as "less a Tom than a Thomist." Warren and Hugh, who have never met, immediately take to each other. Their rapport makes Kate so nervous that she leaves the restaurant.

The actress objected to the scene. "So she's balled both guys. What's there to be nervous about?"

"She just is," my wife said.

"Do you get nervous when you're in the same room with two guys you've slept with?" the actress asked.

"Yes," my wife said.

The director, the producer, and I assiduously began examining our fingernails.

"Well, I didn't know the picture was about *your* hangups," the actress said.

~

SHIRLEY MacLAINE CAME to lunch to discuss *January and February,* as did Julie Andrews; we flew to Tucson to discuss it with Joanne Woodward and to San Francisco for meetings with Natalie Wood. For each of these ladies we rewrote the picture, by the by, adding some filigreeing from Vanessa Redgrave and Faye Dunaway. Which is how a picture about a social worker in Detroit and Cleveland evolved effortlessly into a script about a college professor's wife in Pomona whose life comes to a crisis at the Ojai Music Festival.

Then we quit the picture.

GONE HOLLYWOOD

[1976]

I ONCE HEARD a screenwriter accepting an Academy Award say, rather sententiously, "In the beginning was the Word." Actually the line is not accurate. Actually, in Hollywood, that line would go through a step outline, treatment, three drafts, polish, additional dialogue and an arbitration by the Writers Guild. Actually the line would come out, "In the beginning were the Writers."

In the beginning, my wife and I were the writers on our last picture and remained so through three drafts, an arbitration, a threatened breach-of-contract suit and a sizable legal (read "cash") settlement for agreeing not to file that suit, which we never had any intentions of doing in the first place. As closely as I can figure, we were followed on the picture, officially and unofficially, by fourteen writers. The film is called *A Star Is Born* and stars Barbara Streisand and Kris Kristofferson, and I can pinpoint the exact moment when it was conceived. It was at one o'clock in the afternoon on the first day of July 1973, when I turned to my wife, while passing the Aloha Tower in downtown Honolulu on our way to the airport, and said sixteen words I would often later regret: "James Taylor and Carly Simon in a rock-and-roll version of *A Star Is Born*."

It was a project that had everything. (A project is a property with one "element," although not a "bankable" element. A bankable element is a star or a director, and once there is a bankable element, a project becomes a "go-project." A writer is a nonbankable element but is nonetheless essential, as the screenplay is the bait to land the fish, or the bankable element.) With two previous Oscar-nominated versions, *A Star Is Born* had "title identification" and a story so well known that its last line, "Hello, everyone, this is Mrs. Norman Maine," had passed into the repertoire of every gay cabaret act in the land. Furthermore, the prospects for a hit sound-track album were so great, according to the Warner Bros. music people, that anything the picture brought in would be gravy. And if the music people were higher on Carly Simon, whose career was soaring, than they were on James Taylor, whose career then was not, they at least gave us a line we could incorporate into the screenplay: "Don't worry about James, if you don't use him, we can always find something for him to do, maybe a house in Malibu." In fact, the project had only one drawback, about which we kept a discreet silence: we had never seen *A Star Is Born* in any of its prior incarnations. Nor had we any intention of seeing *A Star Is Born,* or of reading the scripts, treatments, synopses or memorandums pertaining to any previous version. We were only interested in a movie about the rock-and-roll business, but the only way we could get a studio to underwrite the screenplay was to dress it up in what they perceived as an old but very well-cut suit of clothes. As long as there was a superficial resemblance to that classic story we had never seen, we would not be in breach of contract.

That there was an element of hustle in all of this is a given. Hustle is a basic ingredient of a screenwriter's life. Writing for the screen is not done in a vacuum but more or less at the whim of agents, stars, directors, producers, studio executives and the wives, husbands, lovers, mistresses and assorted rough trade of all the above. "The screenplay is written by a salaried writer under the supervision of a producer," Raymond Chandler once wrote, "by an employee without power or decision over the uses of his craft, without ownership of it, and however extravagantly paid, almost without honor for it." It is useful to remember here that most producers used to be agents and theirs is a world that has only one frame of critical reference: "piece of shit." The highest praise this world can bestow on a screenplay is, "It's not your run-of-the-mill piece of shit," which usually means that McQueen is reading it, at which point it either becomes a go-project or reverts back to just another piece of shit.

This basically excremental view of screenwriting sets the tone for the studios' financial dealings with writers. The business-affairs lawyers who make a studio's deals have all the ethics and charm of Meyer Lansky or Abbadabba Berman, the man who fixed the numbers racket and who was usually described as the Mob's "strange genius." It thus behooves a writer to have a banker's familiarity with such niceties of deal making as cutoffs and conversions and change-of-elements ("the worst clause in this business," my agent says) and pari passu and the most-favored-nation clause and gross players and cross-collateralization and definition and first position and point reduction and abatement and rolling break. ("You can chase a rolling break around the world and never see it," was another piece of wisdom imparted by my agent, making it sound like the perfect wave.) These are all points designed to deprive the writer legally of what his contract otherwise stipulates he is getting. The general view is that screenwriters are overpaid, but at least half of what they ask for they will see only under conditions so arcane as to relegate full payment to cloud-cuckooland.

Part of what a writer gets paid for is not to remind a "pay-or-play" star or director (pay-or-play means the element gets paid whether the go-project goes or not) that he was the only one there when the pages were blank. The moment when the star and the director begin to talk about "my film" and "my concept," the writer is on his way out the door. He becomes an embarrassment to these conceptualizers; his presence casts a pall over "their" film. A number of pay-or-play elements have their own security-blanket rewriters, who come in without credit to restitch the last sequence on *The Missouri Breaks* or pull together *The Marathon Man,* punch up *The Bad News Bears* or hold Robert Redford's hand on *All the President's Men.* This is how movies are written. It is a business, and for every writer who doesn't like it, there are a thousand ready to take his place.

If in Hollywood the screenwriter is viewed as an overpaid purveyor of ordure, in other precincts he is labeled as Gone Hollywood. I have never been quite clear what Going Hollywood meant exactly, except that as a unique selling proposition it's a lot sexier than Going University of Iowa Writers' Workshop. There is something wonderfully Calvinistic about the concept, especially as it is most firmly held by those most insane to Go—the dreary cineasts who spend every waking hour in a darkened theater, emerging only to write about The Film in a language said to be English. They bewail the fact that Hollywood is a business run by businessmen for a profit (an *aperçu* akin to discovering that the Pacific is an ocean), yet for all their *ars gratia artis*–prop, every mail brings their scripts and treatments to some despised mogul's desk. The ecology of Hollywood eludes them. It never seems to occur to these film buffs that the wretched De Laurentiis *Mandingo* pays for the De Laurentiis Altman, that the Irwin Allen disaster epic underwrites the small Paul Mazursky film.

No one, however, makes us write movies. We do it because we like the action, even playing against a heavy deck, and because writing screenplays, especially before the pay-or-play money becomes oppressive, is a lot of fun. The possibilities are infinite; it is only the probabilities that are finite. We started *A Star Is Born* by going on the road with rock groups, three weeks of one-night stands in the armpit auditoria and cities of the land. The trip was a blur. In Chicago a groupie talked about mainlining adrenaline. "It only makes you scared," she said, "for twenty minutes." In a dressing room in Cleveland, one of the Led Zeppelin had penciled on the wall, "Call KL 5-2033 for good head." I called KL 5-2033 (no other identification given) and KL 5-2033 asked my room number at the Hollenden House, any friend of the Zeppelin was a friend of hers. In a motel in Johnstown, Pennsylvania, I spent the better part of an afternoon listening to Uriah Heep's bass player debate the pros and cons of a fretless neck on a Gibson; I was in Buffalo before I learned that a Gibson was a guitar. From Buffalo, the itinerary to Allentown, Pennsylvania, involved two Allegheny flights and a three-hour layover in Pittsburgh. The producer didn't like any of the above elements, so we are perhaps the only people in the world ever to take a Cadillac limousine from Buffalo to Allentown, total cost $435, with a chauffeur who looked as if he had been the wheelman on most of the important Mafia hits in upstate New York. He wore a black chauffeur suit with red piping, red, white and blue high-heel clogs, and stuck in his waistband was the kind of .357 magnum cannon that Clint Eastwood used in *Dirty Harry.*

The first draft of *A Star Is Born* included in one way or another all these people, and it took six months to write. It took one more draft and another six months to make us thoroughly sick of the project. I recall the second six months only as an endless argument, carried on over commissary lunches and studio meetings, usually about who the pay-or-play elements should be. I could never understand why our opinions were so desperately sought, since we had only to voice them to have them ignored. Our first choice to direct was Warren Beatty, whom the studio did not see as a director, our second Mike Nichols, whom the studio did not see as a director on this picture, and after that we kept our mouths shut. Our agents sent the script to Peter Bogdanovich, for which transgression we fired them; his opinion of the script matched ours of his pictures. A director finally came aboard, but as he was going through a messy divorce and as he was trying to put his mother into a tax-shelter condominium in Florida and as he was interviewing UCLA housekeepers who didn't wear brassieres and as he had a number of other projects in various stages of development, his time was fragmented. When the studio would not make him pay-or-play, he left. *A Star Is Born* was becoming a career, and we asked our lawyer to get us out.

Enter Barbra Streisand. We had met her several years before at a dinner party given by her agent, Sue Mengers. When we were introduced, she had said, "Hello," and then without pausing for breath, "What do you think of fidelity in marriage?" The question apparently had a point, for some months later we were asked to write a picture for her on marital infidelity. We didn't, but here she was again, with the muscle to move out the original producer and replace him with her lover, Jon Peters. Venality forced us to reconsider our intention to quit; with Barbra Streisand involved, we knew we weren't going to get poor.

Our relationship with Streisand and Peters was extremely cordial. We drank a lot of wine and blew a few cools and our daughter played with Barbra's son. I wasn't crazy about their playing in the cage with the pet lion cub, but I figured what the hell, this was Hollywood. We also saw *A Star Is Born* for the first time. But Barbra was working on another picture and when it was finished she wanted to take a long vacation. We were also hearing talk about "my film" and "my concept." Barbra and Jon saw the picture as being about their own somewhat turbulent love affair, which didn't leave much room for existential ironies. She also thought the man had the better part, which was true. As her company was now financing the picture, it began to look like a long summer. Two weeks after Barbra Streisand came in, we again asked our lawyer for an out.

Enter Catch-22. We couldn't just quit, because we then would have been in breach of contract and lost our "points," or percentage of the profits, and we regarded those points as our combat pay, our veterans' benefits. Nor could we be fired, because then we would have left with our points intact, and the business people would have none of that. They wanted us to give some of our points back, which we refused to do until it was stipulated that we could leave without being in breach. It took eight weeks to negotiate this point, eight weeks during which we wrote a third draft, although we were not in contact, on advice of our lawyer, with anyone actually involved in the making of the film. Finally, almost fifteen months to the day after I uttered those sixteen words while passing the Aloha Tower in downtown Honolulu, a settlement was signed and we were out of *A Star Is Born*.

This story has a postscript. A year, ten writers and another legal action after we left *A Star Is Born*, the president of Warner Bros, asked our agent if we would consider returning to repair the damage. The price discussed for four weeks was the same as our original fee for fifteen months. For two heady days we paid off our mortgage, priced a Mercedes and laid away our daughter's tuition to Radcliffe. Then we said no. We never knew how firm the offer was, but in any case *A Star Is Born* was a part of our life that was over and going back would have served no purpose. Now, a year after that, we are back in the movie business again, this time with an original story. The other day I told it to a producer friend. "That," he said, "is not a piece of shit."

pages out into the audience, a symbolic act meant either (I am not sure which) as a statement against the auteur theory or as a *tableau vivant* of the loneliness of the writer's life.

The second eulogist was the ex-husband of a movie star. The deceased, he said, had been kind and gentle and truthful, although no boy scout, and he had also been a lonely man. To illustrate the degree of loneliness, he told the following story: "If I hadn't seen him for a long time, the phone would ring and a voice would say, 'What's up? Is your sauna unoccupied?' And he would drive into town and we would go into the sauna and afterwards we would talk for an hour or two. Only after he left would I stop and think, 'He drove all the way in from Malibu to use my sauna in West Hollywood.' And I know there are a lot of saunas he could have used in Malibu that were a lot closer than mine in West Hollywood."

~

IT WAS DIFFICULT not to reflect on this funeral while reading *The Craft of Screenwriting*, a collection of John Brady's long interviews with six screenwriters—the late Paddy Chayevsky, William Goldman, Ernest Lehman, Paul Schrader, Neil Simon, and Robert Towne. "In the beginning," screenwriters are fond of saying, "is the Word." Screenwriters in fact are given to such rhetorical flourishes. "The holy chore of screenwriting," one called his trade recently in a letter quoted in the *Los Angeles Times*, while another, musing about a screenplay of his that he felt had been brutalized by other thumbs, complained: "If it had been properly dramatized, we could have achieved catharsis in the grand tragic sense, the Aristotelian sense, and the audience would have wept at the finale."[1]

Mr. Brady slips easily into this fancy diction himself, never more so than in his capsule descriptions of his interviewees: Chayevsky, a "pugnacious, poetic wordsmith"; Goldman, whom "Scott Fitzgerald, Nathanael West and his other literary forebears could only have envied and admired"; Lehman, "a transitional giant"; Towne, who "pursues his own art as the forger of strikingly original screenplays." (I suspect the word "forger" might make Towne a tad uneasy.) Although his *curriculum vitae* gives no indication that he has ever worked on a picture,[2] Mr. Brady has a theory: auteurism is on the wane, the director is in retreat, "the screenwriter . . . is more pow-erful than ever before." No longer are writers "schmucks with Underwoods," as Jack Warner called them, the protagonists of a hundred bad Hollywood novels, abused and ill-considered, over-paid, oversexed underachievers, victims of credit-stealing and pedes-trian directors, their work gangbanged, their spirits broken. "The road from doormat to . . . dominance on a project," Brady says, "has been long and winding." The millennium has arrived, the Word is supreme, "the era of the screenwriter as superstar is at hand."

This of course is tendentious malarkey, malarkey that Brady can't even get his interviewees to swallow. "The niggers of the industry," Robert Towne (*Chinatown, Shampoo*) calls screenwriters. A screenwriter is a "bastardized thing," says Paul Schrader (*Taxi Driver, American Gigolo*), "half a filmmaker." In the longest and most interesting interview in the book, William Goldman (*Butch Cassidy and the Sundance Kid, All the President's Men*) variously calls screen-writing a "craft," "carpentry," and "shitwork." For Ernest Lehman (*North by Northwest, The Sweet Smell of Success*), with nearly thirty years of screen credits, it is *plus ça change.* . . . "I don't think things have changed as much as they appear to have changed," Lehman says. "Marginal improvements at best, mostly in the area of financial rewards." In other words the schmucks with Underwoods are now schmucks with word processors.

Despite four generally fascinating interviews (the exceptions are those with Chayevsky and Simon, Simon being more interested in the theater and Chayevsky in maintaining his ego), Brady seems to com-prehend neither the realities of screenwriting nor the terms his inter-viewees accept. "Movies are like wars," Towne says in response to a request for a "short course in screenwriting." "The guy who becomes an expert is the guy who doesn't get killed." The military metaphor runs through all the conversations. These are men who recognize that screenwriters are mercenaries interchangeable even on each other's pictures. Alvin Sargent (*Julia, Ordinary People*) rewrote with-out credit Goldman's screenplay of *All the President's Men* and Towne rewrote Schrader's script of *The Yakuza* and (also without credit) the ending of Goldman's *Marathon Man*. "I think it's shit," Goldman says of that new ending, although not unsympathetically:

"Let me say again, though, that they [Towne and director John Schlesinger] didn't make it that way because they thought they were doing it wrong. Everybody's under the gun. The pressures of making a movie are tremendous. The writer gets a certain chance at tranquility because there's nothing till the screenplay is in. But when you are on the floor the pressures are murderous. . . . So when they came up with that ending, nobody sat around and said, 'How can we ruin the ending of this thing?' "

～

IT WOULD BE useful at this point to describe what a screenplay is, the restrictions under which it is written and most importantly how it is made into a picture. A screenplay is 120 typewritten pages designed to be a motion picture, 120 pages because the rule of thumb is that one screenplay page accounts for one minute of film time. These 120 pages are broken down into scenes and locations and dialogue and narrative. Because it is so skeletal, so fragmented, a form in which words are secondary to potential images, a screenplay is difficult to read; the better a script reads, the better it is to be suspicious of the script. It is also essential to remember that a screenplay exists in a vacuum; it has no life of its own. As such, there is really no such thing as a good screenplay; there are only good pictures. An unmade screenplay is consigned to limbo, which means, reduced to the simplest terms, that the screenplay that is made is a good screenplay.

From the moment he or she is signed, the screenwriter is subject to limitations that make the holy chore something less than sanctified. The first is the inflexible length; it calls for a predetermination, a schematic approach that fiction, for example, does not demand. Screenplays are charted as much as they are written—how many scenes, how many pages per scene, how long each scene will play. Time is money. Fifteen extra pages mean fifteen minutes of film time. Since cut and finished film is shot at the rate of approximately two minutes a day, that means seven and a half days at a minimum of $60,000 a day, which does not include the "overages" paid to star actors nor take into consideration scenes that call for extras, chases, exteriors (which are subject to the vagaries of the sun not to mention, if a scene is shot on a city street, the necessity for crowd control), and special effects, all of which are more expensive than a simple two-scene, or two actors talking. The mathematics are staggering: for these fifteen pages $1 million and up. Which is not to say that a cagey screenwriter will not turn in a 135-page first draft. "That lets everybody be creative when they get it," William Goldman says. "That means that the producer will be able to say, 'Well, we must cut fifteen pages out of this.'"

The limitation inherent in letting "everybody be creative" is an absolute of screenwriting. There is first the producer and then the financing organization and then the director and finally the stars, and each element has suggestions, suggestions that have the effect of law unless the screenwriter is very articulate and quick on his feet. Schrader calls the four distinct versions of his *Hardcore* script the Milius, the McElwaine, the Beatty, and the Scott after his producer; the studio executive who bought it; and two stars, Warren Beatty, who wanted to do *Hardcore* but insisted that a daughter who became a porno actress in the script be changed into a wife who became a porno actress, and then backed out of the picture after this change was made, and George C. Scott, who finally did do the script—with the daughter Schrader originally intended.

If a writer produces and/or directs his own script, he circumvents several levels of suggestions, but there is still the studio, which puts up the money, and the star, and if a star wants a daughter rewritten into a wife, the studio will back him up. Beatty and Woody Allen have come closest to circumventing all suggestions. In Beatty's John Reed picture, *Reds*, he stars, produces, directs, and takes a writing credit. The last phrase is used advisedly; Beatty does not write as much as he supervises, in the manner of an architect, teams of writers who in effect work under the pseudonym Warren Beatty. "A Warren Beatty Film" is a far more accurate credit than "Screenplay by Warren Beatty."

Suggestions are especially prevalent on an adaptation of a novel. Invariably a novel has to be replotted to fit into screenplay form. Scenes must be rearranged in order to create a narrative, characters combined or eliminated, parenthetical statements and modifying or subordinate clauses turned into scenes, a wife transposed into a mother, a funeral into a wedding (because it is easier to introduce characters and get rid of exposition at a wedding than at a funeral, where the audience might be distracted wondering who died). This offers an endless forum of suggestions. The suggestions are not necessarily bad—they are sometimes quite good—but they do tend to take the screenwriter away from that beginning where there was the Word. "You can almost say there are two entirely different versions of any screenplay," Goldman notes. "There's the stuff written before a movie is a go project and there is what's written when the movie is actually going to be shot. And sometimes they have very little to do with each other."

The experienced screenwriter is aware of all these restrictions, of all the choices that will be forfeited down the line, and tries to accommodate them within what Scott Fitzgerald called the "private grammar" of pictures. The rules are different. "You always attack a movie scene as *late* as you possibly can," Goldman says.

> "You always come into a scene at the *last* possible moment. . . . You truncate . . . as much as you can. . . . Get on, get on. The camera is relentless. Makes you keep running."

Rarely does a dialogue scene run more than five pages; five pages equal five minutes, a long time to watch two people talk. Before the technique became a television cliché, exposition was often played against some kind of violence or conflict; Chayevsky used an off-screen narrator for exposition because he thought it saved him twenty minutes of film time. Exposition, however, is usually the first thing to go in the cutting room; a picture moves so fast and is so apparently realistic that the rigor of plot is not always necessary. Towne prefers soft openings. "A splashy beginning to hook an audience," he says, results "with an almost mathematical certainty" in a sag twenty minutes later. "It's been my experience that an audience will forgive you almost anything at the *beginning* of a picture," he says, "but almost nothing at the end." Dialogue is usually functional. The novelist Brian Moore told me that after working out a scene with Alfred Hitchcock on *Torn Curtain*, Hitchcock would say, "In the old days, Brian, I'd bring in a man now and have him dialogue this in."

Structure "is the single most important thing contributed by the screenwriter," says Goldman. "It's a terrible thing for a writer to admit, but in terms of screenwriting dialogue really doesn't matter as much as in plays and books—because you have the camera."

And with the camera comes the director, to screenwriters the most pernicious reality of picture-making. "The weak link in almost every film," Gore Vidal told *Rolling Stone* last year. The encomiums roll in from Brady's interviewees. "Pricks," says Towne. "Jealous, petty and frustrated," says Goldman. Ernest Lehman recalls his experiences with Mike Nichols on *Who's Afraid of Virginia Woolf?* with almost palpable pain: "There were a lot of creative conflicts between Mike and me. A lot of give-and-take. He gave and I took."

WHAT OF COURSE sets screenwriters' teeth on edge is the auteur theory, the idea that if film is an art, the director is the artist. I confess that I am less unsympathetic to the auteur theory than most screenwriters. I suspect that what upsets screenwriters is not so much the theory as the word. Auteur. The tony frenchiness of it plays right into the pretensions and pretentiousness of many directors. Since a number of directors perceive their inability to understand words as the mark of the artist, their embrace of the word "auteur" drives screenwriters mad. (I personally find "filmmaker" far more odious, available as it is to every squalid hustler/promoter/producer/executive, many of whom have taken to calling themselves "complete filmmakers," even in one case a "compleat filmmaker.") The captain of the ship theory would be far less provocative; the senior partner theory, the CEO theory.

However grudgingly, screenwriters accept that a director must be in charge when a picture is shooting. "Just another foreman," Stirling Silliphant (*In the Heat of the Night*) says in Brady's introduction. Directing, Silliphant continues, is "an unforgiving routine of administration and traffic control." This is self-serving, and fails to acknowledge that the writer must, by the nature of the medium, cede to the director certain essential writer's functions—pace, mood, style, point-of-view, rhythm, texture. While it is true, as Goldman says, that there are seven major elements on any picture—

writer, director, producer, cameraman, production designer, actors, and editor—the director hires most of them, and more importantly can fire them if they do not give him what he wants. With the cameraman and the designer, the director controls the look and texture of the picture, with the cutter the pace and the rhythm and the point-of-view. Imagine a novelist giving up those functions.

A good director—and unfortunately a bad one as well—directs the writer as much as he directs the actors on the set. "On the continuity and story line" of *The Third Man*, Graham Greene wrote in his autobiography *Ways of Escape*, "Carol Reed and I worked closely together when I came back with him to Vienna to write the screenplay, covering miles of carpet each day, acting scenes at each other." Brian Moore and Ernest Lehman each spent months in a room with Hitchcock, working out the scenarios of *Torn Curtain* and *North by Northwest*; Hitchcock always maintained that for him the picture was finished when he was finished with the writer. ("All of Hitchcock's successes were primarily writers' films," Stanley Kauffmann contends breezily in *Living Images*. Not true. Hitchcock was always the writer of a Hitchcock picture; the credited writers dialogued it in.) My wife and I once spent fourteen weeks in an office in New York with Otto Preminger, five hours a day broken in the middle by lunch at La Côte Basque. Preminger cherished distractions. Managers would stop by and interrupt script conferences to introduce him to Miss Universe contestants they had signed to personal service contracts. I met Miss Philippines and Miss Ceylon; Miss Peru was scheduled for Thursday afternoon.

～

THE MORE POLITIC director always pays lip service to the script. "The script is everything." "It all begins with the script." "There is no movie without the script." This has become a litany in the Writers Guild Newsletter. Notice, however, the word "script"; never "scriptwriter." When a director, Alan Pakula, for example, says the script is everything, he means *his* version of the script, the script he must shoot, and will not shoot if it does not meet his specifications. A director once said a script I wrote was a one-span bridge and needed to be a two-span bridge; he meant that the climax came too early and that the screenplay needed another climactic moment closer to the end. He was right. We worked together for six days in a London hotel room fashioning that second span and all the attendant body work. I wrote every word, but to say that the director's mark was not all over that script would be ridiculous. On the other hand, a less articulate director dunned me so persistently for a "relationship" that I finally said with some asperity that the leading lady was being paid several million dollars to act that relationship and if she could not act it she should be fired; instead I was.

Towne and Schrader, both of whom have directed, say that having a script rewritten is a director's prerogative. "Everything is and should be rewritten," Towne says. "Movies are not done under laboratory conditions. . . . You are always miscalculating in a movie, partially because of the disparity between what you see on the set and what you see on the screen. No matter how skilled you are in anticipating what the image is going to look like finally, you still can be fooled. So you have to rewrite, and be rewritten—not because the original is necessarily badly *written*, but because, ultimately, if it doesn't *work* for a film, it's bad." This is an admission that most screenwriters, the majority who do not direct, are not willing to make. In a script, everything seems possible; every scene plays, every line sparkles, every actor is perfect for his part. The reality, as Schrader says, is that "every idea goes through a series of diminutions. From the moment an idea is conceived, every step of the process diminishes it. By the time the movie is released, it is a tattered shadow of what you imagined it to be. . . . When you are writing, it is all in the mind."

Where it always works, where the screenwriter is a whole and not half a filmmaker. Sometimes, when a writer of distinction works with a director of distinction, even that half can be quite satisfying. Graham Greene and Carol Reed were the most successful of collaborators in *The Fallen Idol* and *The Third Man*; their skills and outlook and interests not only coincided but were complementary. Raymond Chandler and Billy Wilder detested each other, but out of that friction came *Double Indemnity*. It should be noted, however, that these collaborations produced melodramas, a form particularly suited to motion pictures. It should also be noted that a "writer of distinction" has always found that distinction in work other than screenwriting.

～

IN THE EVERYDAY world, professional screenwriters are fated to be chronic malcontents whose value is measured in dollars. "People are going to respect a writer they pay $250,000 to for a script a lot more than a writer they pay $50,000," Schrader says. How true. It is a Hessian ethic, and perhaps the ultimate Hessian is Goldman. His interview is laced with the sour wisdom of the veteran campaigner whose credits are like wound stripes. Rarely has a screenwriter understood so well that there is more to a script than words. In *All the President's Men*, Goldman was faced with the fact that Robert Redford was not only going to play Bob Woodward, he was also the producer, a parlay that would scare off actors of a comparable stature.

"The [Carl] Bernstein part had to not just be *good*," Goldman says, "it had to be . . . as bulletproof as one could make it . . . *appealing* enough to nail Dustin or Al Pacino." In *A Bridge Too Far*, the problem was that none of the historical figures to be played by the dozen stars had died in the mad dash to capture a bridgehead at Arnhem. "You can't have a war film in which everybody lives," Goldman says. "I mean, I can't have James Gavin dying. He's alive up in Boston, right? Since we had to be authentic, one of the craft problems, in addition to making a dozen star parts, was inventing memorable small characters that I could in fact kill off so that the audience would be moved. The problem is finding air space amid all the material for a three-scene role of someone who can die."

It is this battle-scarred pragmatism that has helped push Goldman's price to a million dollars for an adaptation. He is the definition of, to use Mr. Brady's wretched phrase, "the screenwriter as superstar," a superstar who says: "I don't even have very much respect for someone who is just a screenwriter in terms of writing." Mr. Brady plunges on, undeterred. What, according to Brady, are the fruits of superstardom? "Acceptance, applause and acclaim . . . more original screenplays, more money and more mention in the movie press."

More mention in the movie press.

In the beginning is the Word indeed.

POSTSCRIPT TO HESSIANS

I BEGAN THIS piece with a funeral. More or less the same funeral turned up a few years later to another point, and with different cast and set decoration, in my novel *The Red White and Blue.* In the later incarnation, I recycled the screenwriter's sixteen-year-old girl friend, his confession that his pubic hair was turning gray, and the eulogist's story of the screenwriter coming in from the beach to use his sauna (the eulogist himself I completely changed). When this piece appeared in *The New York Review of Books,* the screenwriter's last wife asked a mutual friend if I was going to use the scene in a novel. In truth I had never met the screenwriter and had only gone to the funeral out of curiosity, to see who would attend the last rites of an important Hollywood writer. I sat with two friends, one the international bounder I mentioned earlier to whom the deceased had confided about his graying (and who became, in the novel's funeral scene, the model for my dead screenwriter), and the other Gore Vidal, who at one point during the service leaned over and whispered to me, "Are you working?" Again in truth I had no intention of using the scene in a book, and indeed the novel I was working on at the time would not have accommodated it.

Obviously, however, the funeral had made an impression. Early on in *The Red White and Blue,* I needed a set piece that would culminate in the narrator's learning that his brother and his ex-wife had been murdered. As the narrator of the novel was at that point in his life a screenwriter, I thought the set piece should be laid in Hollywood, a gilded venue in sharp and necessary contrast to the fact of the assassinations. I toyed with a number of settings, but kept coming back to the funeral because of the opportunity it presented both for exposition and for laying out the social architecture against which much of the book would be played. So no, I had not planned to use the scene in a novel, but of course yes, it was always there waiting to be retrieved. And the answer to Gore Vidal's question should have been "Always."

NOTES

[1.] James Poe on his screenplay of *They Shoot Horses, Don't They?* quoted in *The Hollywood Screenwriter,* edited by Richard Corliss (Avon, 1972), p. 191.

[2.] There has long been a mini-controversy between hoi-polloi critics who say "movies" and ivory-tower critics who say "film." "Would you call a book a 'readie?'" "an adherent of "film" once asked, as if this were a telling thrust. No, but I wouldn't call a book a sabago stock, sixty-pound weight, either. People in the business almost invariably say "picture," except when talking to critics, when they lapse into "film." (Many below-the-line people—the crew—simply say "show.")

DEALING

[1 9 8 3]

THIS IS A Hollywood story. It begins in Switzerland. It has stopovers in London and New York. It ends in Burbank and in Brentwood Park. Most of it takes place over the telephone. It is about money and it is about power and it is about pride and it is about vanity. It is about a deal. And it is with a deal, a succession of deals, that a motion picture gets off the ground.

In the fall of 1982, George Roy Hill, the movie director (*The Sting,* for which he won an Academy Award, and *Butch Cassidy and the Sundance Kid,* among others), traveled to Switzerland to meet the English novelist David Cornwell, who is better known under his nom de plume, John le Carré. The reason for George Hill's trip to Switzerland was David Cornwell's recently completed novel, *The Little Drummer Girl.* George Hill had read the new novel in manuscript form, and his enthusiasm was so high that he wanted to make a motion picture from the book. As it happens, the attorney for both George Hill and David Cornwell is Morton L. Leavy, counsel for a Park Avenue entertainment law firm. Morton Leavy was in London on business, and from London he arranged for his two clients to meet.

The meeting in Switzerland was a success. (In spite of Morton Leavy's best efforts, George Hill and David Cornwell had never previously met.) Cornwell agreed that Hill was the director he wanted for *The Little Drummer Girl,* and so Morton Leavy opened negotiations with Warner Bros. to buy the book. Warners was the choice because George Hill's Pan Arts Corporation has a financing and distribution deal with that studio, a deal of course negotiated by Morton Leavy. The package of George Hill and *The Little Drummer Girl* was so appealing to Warners that Morton Leavy was able to conclude a deal quickly. Warners would buy the book and assign it to Pan Arts; and George Hill, with Warners' money, would produce and direct the film.

It was at this point that I received a telephone call from my motion picture agent, Evarts Ziegler of the Ziegler, Diskant Agency in Los Angeles. Among Hollywood agents Evarts Ziegler is an anomaly. He went to Princeton, lives in Pasadena (which in Hollywood is considered as recherché as living in Grosse Pointe Farms), and once, I am convinced, hired a very rich young junior agent only because she had gone to Foxcroft. ("You'll like her," he had told me in the Ivy League drawl he still affects, "she went to Foxcroft," the implication being that he and I, both Princetonians, were perhaps the only two people in Hollywood who had ever heard of Foxcroft.) On the grapevine, Evarts Ziegler had picked up word of the Cornwell-Hill negotiation with Warners, and because the project would need a screenwriter he wondered if we—my wife, Joan Didion, and I—would like to read *The Little Drummer Girl.* He had already talked to George Hill's office and said there was interest at Pan Arts in having us write the screenplay of the book. As *interest* is one of those Hollywood words as slippery as quicksilver—I knew that Evarts Ziegler was interested in our writing the screenplay, but I was less sure how interested George Hill was—I told Evarts Ziegler that I would get back to him. I saw no point in interrupting the novel I had just begun, and the novel Joan was halfway through, to read *The Little Drummer Girl* if there was no real chance of our being asked to do the screenplay.

And so I called Morton Leavy in New York. Again as it happens, Morton Leavy is my attorney as well as George Hill's and David Cornwell's. It is not all that unusual a situation. There are only a handful of good entertainment/literary lawyers, and they are constantly balancing the conflicting concerns of clients who work with each other, who wish to work with each other, who detest each other, sue each other, marry and divorce each other. Morton Leavy is short, round, and benign; he looks, as I have often told him in the fifteen years he has been our attorney, like a Jewish Dr. Dolittle. He is so scrupulous that my wife and I once felt free to leave the country when he agreed to referee a negotiation she was having with her publisher and one I was having with my publisher. The twin negotiations—each for a new novel—needed a referee because my publisher was married to my wife's publisher, a situation further complicated by the competitive strains between my literary agent and my wife's literary agent, each of whom wished to negotiate a better deal than the other. I might add here that Morton Leavy was most aware of these strains as he is also the attorney for both my literary agent and my wife's literary agent. We told him to keep the peace between the two of them, that we did not wish to be played off against each other, but that we also wanted the best deals possible.

Morton Leavy's success as a referee was such that the only real difference between my contract and my wife's contract was that she would receive fifty more free copies of her book when it was published than I would when mine was. Both my publisher and my wife's publisher called Morton Leavy a son of a bitch, which he took as praise for a job well done. I tell you this in such detail only to indicate that I knew Morton Leavy would scrupulously guard the interests of both David Cornwell and George Hill when I asked him if there was more than an outside chance of our writing the screenplay of *The Little Drummer Girl.*

No, Morton Leavy said, the chances were slight. As the leading character in the novel was an English actress and as much of the narrative action took place in seedy third-rate English repertory theaters, David Cornwell, who could make such demands per his contract, was insisting on an English screenwriter familiar with the theater and provincial repertory companies. It was to settle on an English writer that George Hill had flown to Europe to meet with David Cornwell. I thanked Morton Leavy, then called Evarts Ziegler back and said that we would pass up the opportunity to read *The Little Drummer Girl.*

Several months passed. Then, early in December 1982, there was a message on my answering service from Pat Kelley, the president of George Hill's Pan Arts Corporation. I suspected the call might have something to do with *The Little Drummer Girl,* for no other reason than that it had been nine years since last I had talked to Pat Kelley, and that time over another picture with which we were both associated, *A Star Is Born.* Pat Kelley was then president of First Artists Corporation, the company making that movie, and he had okayed the settlement Morton Leavy had negotiated to get us out of *A Star Is Born* when Barbra Streisand and her consort, Jon Peters, wanted us fired off the screenplay. They also wanted three of our contractual net-profit points returned, which transformed the firing into a settlement and made it a very sticky proposition. That settlement negotiation was a triumph for Morton Leavy and a windfall for us, as ultimately we earned more by being fired and losing those three points than we would have made if we had remained on the picture under the terms of our original contract. To our surprise, First Artists had approved all of Morton Leavy's proposals, including a stipulation that we share in the music and record royalties, a clause not previously included in our contract. It turned out that Pat Kelley was leaving First Artists, and I have often wondered if his approval of our settlement was perhaps his way of saying goodbye to the strong and demanding egos of Jon Peters and Barbra Streisand.

Before returning the call from Pat Kelley, I telephoned Morton Leavy in New York and asked him if *The Little Drummer Girl* might have something to do with the message. Yes, he said. George Hill and David Cornwell had agreed on an English writer acceptable to both, but he was not available until the end of February. As George Hill wanted to start shooting *The Little Drummer Girl* in late summer, the English writer had been ruled out. George needed someone who could begin work immediately. Hence the call.

With this information in hand, I called Pat Kelley back. We exchanged pleasantries for a few moments as if I did not know why he was calling and as if he did not know I knew why he was calling. Then we got down to business. Had we heard that George was going to do *The Little Drummer Girl?* I mumbled that I had heard rumors to that effect. Had I read the book? No. Would I like to read it? Yes. Were we available? To that question I have the standard answer: one could always make oneself available if the project and the personalities were of interest, and the combination of a George Roy Hill production and a John le Carré novel was absolutely intriguing, and the conflict in the Middle East that was the subject of this book was something that touched all our lives every day . . . et cetera and so forth. Pat Kelley had been around long enough to know exactly what that bullshit meant: a definite and enthusiastic *maybe.* He said he would messenger over two copies of the bound galleys of *The Little Drummer Girl* that afternoon. He also said that George was at the Mayo Clinic for his annual checkup and would be in Los Angeles late in the week beginning December 6. If Joan and I liked the book, he said, perhaps we could all meet. It was a conversation of subjunctives with no commitments on either side.

It took us five days to read *The Little Drummer Girl.* Reading a book for adaptation into a screenplay is different from reading for pleasure. It is a relentless, carnivorous read in which the book is reduced to its barest bones; it is from these bones that a screenplay is constructed. One reads slowly, spitting out the fat and the gristle and the extraneous joints. At the end of this five-day read, I was not sure I liked *The Little Drummer Girl* (it is all but impossible to "like" any book read in this fashion), but I was sure there was a movie in it, and I was equally sure that Joan and I knew how to write the screenplay. When George Hill arrived in Los Angeles the end of that week, he called and we agreed to meet at our house in Brentwood over the weekend of December 11 and 12.

Time was now important. One of the attractions of working on the screenplay of *The Little Drummer Girl* for both my wife and me was that we both had a block of time open from mid-December through the end of January 1983, with no conflicting commitments. We were already scheduled to leave on Saturday, December 18, for Barbados, where we were spending Christmas at the house of friends, and where we could work through the holidays. This meant we had to see if we were in sync with George Hill (and he with us) and work out a deal before we flew to Barbados. Joan and I agreed that if a deal could not be worked out by the end of business hours December 17 we would pass on the project. We saw no point in

wasting endless infuriating weeks in that Hollywood form of pro-
tracted combat: the negotiation.

George Hill arrived at our house promptly at one o'clock on Saturday, December 11. We had known him casually since he made *The
Sting,* which was produced by Michael and Julia Phillips, who were
friends and neighbors of ours some years before when we had lived
in the farthest reaches of Malibu. George comes from a rich Catholic
family in Minnesota, graduated from Yale, and also has a degree
from Trinity College, Dublin. He served in the marines in World
War II and in Korea, and at sixty he still looks like the marine officer he once was—slender, cold eyes, close-cropped hair. Early in his
career, he was a stage actor both in Ireland and with Margaret
Webster's Shakespeare Repertory Company; I cannot imagine much
warmth coming across the footlights. His profit participation in
Butch Cassidy and *The Sting* has made him millions, but he is famous
in the movie business for never picking up a check. His dress can
best be described as nondescript, or perhaps janitorial. A producer
who once worked on a project with him told me that George would
brag that he bought his clothes at an army surplus store in Santa
Monica, where he could get khaki pants for under ten dollars; in our
brief contacts I never had any reason to doubt this.

Before he came that Saturday, I called two writers who had written pictures for him to find out what George was like to work with.
It was as if they were quoting from the same text. Both said he had
the best story sense of any director with whom they had ever been associated, both said he was absolutely tenacious about not giving up
any point he had settled on but that he would yield if an argument
was persuasive enough, both said he thought he was a good writer but
was not, both said he could occasionally be a terrible pain in the ass,
and both said unequivocally that they would work with him again.
I had also taken the trouble to look up all the writer credits on his
pictures. Unlike many directors, he does not use multiple writers on
a screenplay. One writer works on a script from beginning to end,
which meant that George had enormous confidence in his ability to
get exactly what he wanted from a screenwriter.

There was almost no preliminary feeling each other out. We settled right into work. What was the book about? What was the line

of the movie? What could be eliminated? What was necessary? We continued over an antipasto lunch in the kitchen; Joan and I each had a beer, George had cheap French white wine. By the end of that first day, we were blocking out a possible opening of the picture on a bulletin board. On Sunday the procedure was repeated. Joan had made chili so hot that it made our scalps sweat. More beer, another bottle of $3.49 Château Thieuley. By late Sunday afternoon we had tentatively blocked out the first forty-five minutes or so of *The Little Drummer Girl* on three-by-five index cards. I do not by any means suggest that this would have been the narrative line of the picture. It only meant that we did seem to be in sync with each other.

George talked about scheduling. He said he would like to begin shooting in late August. We said we would like to work in Barbados over Christmas. He asked if it would be possible for us to work with him for a few days in New York on our way home from Barbados. We said this would be no problem. He asked if we could have a first draft by the end of February. We were thinking the end of January, but we did not tell him that. He said the money people would talk the first thing Monday morning. We kept the index cards when he left. Writers can have meetings with prospective employers, but under Writers Guild rules nothing can be written without remuneration. It looked as if we were going to write the screenplay of *The Little Drummer Girl.* We alerted Evarts Ziegler at his home in Pasadena and Morton Leavy in New York.

But of course we did not write the screenplay of *The Little Drummer Girl.* Money was the ostensible reason the deal fell apart, but the negotiation actually foundered on the twin rocks of Hollywood deal-making—hubris and ego—in equal measure ours and George Hill's. The reason that negotiations take so long in Hollywood—it is common for contracts not to be signed until long after a picture is in release—is that the negotiation establishes the channel of power, the chain of command. Making an individual back down over money in the negotiation process is one quick and clear way to establish that power, to show who is boss. The production company can do this because it has one unassailable advantage: Everyone wants to make a movie. The line is long, the chosen are few, and the chosen learn to suck wind—or someone else is chosen.

It is a situation in which the only leverage my wife and I have ever had is that we do not particularly care if we ever write another movie. We have a professional life quite independent of motion pictures, and we are not dependent on screenplays for our living. We like writing them, even insofar as the collaboration inherent in moviemaking is antithetical to the very reason one becomes a writer in the first place, but we do not like to suck wind. This attitude encourages intractability, and we were thus set on a collision course with George Hill. A rich former marine who never reaches for a tab and who buys his khaki pants at an army surplus store is the definition of intractable.

That Monday morning, however, everyone was sanguine. Evarts Ziegler said that he would ask for $500,000 guaranteed for us: the picture had to cost over $20 million; George Hill and David Cornwell must be getting $2.5 million between them, so $500,000 for us was not out of line; we had to establish a position. That is how agents think and that is how agents talk. I told Evarts Ziegler he was crazy. We wanted this deal to work; there were only five days to make it work before we left for Barbados; there was no time to waste fishing for a guaranteed five hundred grand. We wanted only what we had received on the last deal he had negotiated on our behalf, a remake of an old classic at another studio: a guaranteed $300,000 for a first draft and one set of changes, against a final fee of $450,000 if there was no shared credit, and a profit participation.

The numbers were staggering, but then so were those accruing to George Hill and David Cornwell, not to mention the millions that any major star would receive for starring in *The Little Drummer Girl*. It deserves to be mentioned here that one purpose of these huge fees is to establish respect; in the constitution of Hollywood, a million-dollar director has half a million dollars more respect than a $500,000 director. This is why the Eleventh Commandment of a motion picture negotiation is Thou shalt not take less than thy last deal. Everyone knows what everyone else makes (this information is passed around like popcorn at a movie), and the person who violates this Eleventh Commandment is seen not as a model of restraint and moderation but as a plain goddamn fool.

The negotiation was between Evarts Ziegler and a business-affairs lawyer at Warners, but the lawyer was only a conduit for

George Hill. After some initial sparring between Evarts Ziegler and Pat Kelley, the Warners lawyer countered with George Hill's offer: a guaranteed $250,000 for a first draft and a set of changes ("a set of changes" is essentially doodling or fixing that can be accomplished in a short specified period, never more than ten working days; a "draft" is a complete rewrite with a whole schedule of remuneration). This guarantee was against a total fee of $450,000 if we received solo credit, with a back-end profit participation to be worked out later. (In a picture as expensive as *The Little Drummer Girl* promised to be, with at least one and probably more elements having a gross participation, the chance of any net profits was practically nil.) Thus at the end of that first day of negotiating, the actual difference between what we wanted and what was offered was the $50,000 in the first-draft guarantee, in Hollywood terms a piddling sum, which is an indication of how far removed the picture business is from the real world. An agreement seemed imminent.

But there was no movement. Monday dissolved into Tuesday into Wednesday. Although that $50,000 would have been made up the next step down the line (that is, in the second draft), George Hill refused to budge, as did we. It was that rarest of negotiations, one in which neither party would give an inch. In retrospect, I am sure the money was irrelevant. George Hill conducts a negotiation as if it were a captain's mast or a summary court-martial. That it was Warners' money and not his that would ultimately be paid was beside the point; price is set by the commanding officer, not by the marketplace or the Eleventh Commandment. I find it an admirable trait, perhaps because I had the means to say bugger off. As the Friday deadline approached, this mutual display of ego and hubris finally caused the negotiation to fall apart.

I sent the two sets of galleys back to Pan Arts with a note saying that as money seemed to be tight, bound galleys were too expensive to keep. Evarts Ziegler could not believe the deal had fallen apart over $50,000, nor could Morton Leavy. "Listen, I will deny ever saying this if you quote me," a Warners executive whispered to me at dinner some weeks later, "but I would never blow a deal for fifty grand." George Hill would, and so would I. It is something perhaps only another pain in the ass would understand.

There is no moral to this story, no lessons to be drawn. It is only the story of a deal, an encapsulated version of every deal. Deals fall apart; the center holds; mere anarchy is not then loosed upon the motion picture industry. Other deals are made. George Hill moved quickly to sign a new writer, Loring Mandel, who is yet another Morton Leavy client. The day after the deal collapsed, we received by messenger a case of wine of such grandeur—six bottles of Château Haut-Brion 1976 and six of Château Lafite Rothschild 1979—that I called the wine merchant to ask its cost. The 1976 Haut-Brion was $80 a bottle; the 1979 Lafite Rothschild, $60 a bottle; the case was $840, less a 10 percent case discount, which brought the price to $756. The card accompanying the wine said only one word: "George." I immediately sent a note to him at his apartment in New York, also with only one word: "Thanks."

The studio insists that the $756 will not be buried in the budget of *The Little Drummer Girl,* which would be a first in the history of the motion picture business. It is safe to assume, however, that if any of our conversations with George Hill over that weekend in December turn up in the screenplay, the $756 will be a bargain. We then would have worked those two days for approximately one-twentieth of what we would have been paid per day under the deal George had offered. The sad thing is that neither my wife nor I will ever be able to drink a single drop of the Haut-Brion or the Lafite Rothschild. We both have migraines, and red wine is a migraine trigger.

HOLLYWOOD:
OPENING MOVES

[1996]

❧

IN THE SPRING of 1988, my wife, Joan Didion, and I were approached about writing a screenplay based on a book by Alanna Nash called *Golden Girl*, a biography of the late network correspondent and anchorwoman Jessica Savitch. In the spring of 1996, the motion picture made from our screenplay, now called *Up Close & Personal*, with Robert Redford and Michelle Pfeiffer, and no longer about Jessica Savitch, was released. What follows, drawn from a longer account, is about some of the opening moves in selling a screenplay in Hollywood, years before the first day of principal photography—the day when the actors finally appear before the camera.

TWO CENTS A PAGE

I FIRST MET John Foreman in my sophomore year at Princeton, at a cocktail party my brother gave in New York. John was from Pocatello, Idaho, had taught English literature at Stephens College in Missouri after service in the Navy in World War II, then had abandoned academe to become a show-business press agent. He was shepherding a client at the party that day, a neophyte film actress promoting a

Gary Cooper western in which she appeared. The picture was *High Noon* and the actress was Grace Kelly.

It was almost twenty years before I saw John again, when he hired my wife and me to rewrite a screenplay for Joanne Woodward. During the intervening two decades, John had metamorphosed, first into an enormously successful motion picture agent, one of the founders of Creative Management Associates, or CMA, the power packaging agency of the Sixties and Seventies, and then into an equally successful film producer—of *Butch Cassidy and The Sundance Kid, Sometimes a Great Notion*, and *The Life and Times of Judge Roy Bean*, among other pictures. His partner in the Newman-Foreman Production Company was Paul Newman, whose agent he had once been.

The screenplay for Joanne Woodward did not work out. It had been an original script by Joyce Carol Oates called *The Verbal Structure of a Woman's Life*, and was about a blue-collar interracial love affair in Detroit and Cleveland. Ms. Oates departed the project after her contractual rewrites, and, after a draft or two by my wife and me, so did Ms. Woodward. Always the optimist, John had us rewrite the picture for a series of actresses, including Vanessa Redgrave, Faye Dunaway, Natalie Wood, Julie Andrews, and Shirley MacLaine, none of whom "committed" to the picture, but each of whom wanted to see an additional draft, with her own input. We did so many drafts that I protested to John that we were working for two cents a page. Detroit and Cleveland gave way to Hartford and New Haven, then San Francisco and Sacramento, and finally, by some alchemy I still do not totally understand, the blue-collar interracial love story, by this time retitled *January, February*, was situated at the Ojai Music Festival. There it blessedly died.

John was a welcome companion at the better by-invitation-only Hollywood funerals, where he could be counted on to have the last scurrilously hilarious gossip about the recently departed. We talked regularly, and it was he who, in 1973, put together our notion of a rock-and-roll version of *A Star Is Born*, which he developed with us and from which he was then unceremoniously elbowed aside as producer, with only token payment, by Barbra Streisand and her then-consort, Jon Peters.

Several times we gave him titles we found intriguing—a railroad western called *Hundredth Meridian*, an oil field thriller called *North Slope*—and John did the production deals with the studios and arranged meetings with actors and directors and set up location scouts, even though we had little more than the title and the notion that we would address the screenplay when we had finished whatever book one or the other of us happened to be then writing. *North Slope*, for example, consisted in its entirety of a production deal and some photographs of oil wells on Alaska's North Slope in an annual report of a now-defunct oil drilling concern in which we owned a few shares. No money ever changed hands, but we knew that it could if we were ever up against it, that a deal was in place, and then there would be offices and travel allowances and a production number against which expenses could be allocated and a guaranteed pay-or-play fee for a first draft, set of changes, and polish.

THE 1988 WRITERS' STRIKE

HOLLYWOOD FUNCTIONS LARGELY on the kind of personal relationship we had with John Foreman. Picture executives on a roll invariably tell interviewers that the secret of their success is an ability to maintain "good relationships" with the talent; "I don't just work with these guys," this executive mantra goes, "they're my friends." In such an insular and inbred community, a labor strike, or more precisely, an "above the line" labor strike ("above the line" meaning "talent," or actors, directors, and writers; the technical people are "below the line") tears apart the fictions that keep the industry going, putting into play envy and other ugly truths better left unstated. Writers in fact are the only above-the-line players who regularly go on strike; I have walked picket lines in three of the four labor stoppages since 1969, when I became a member of the Writers Guild of America, or WGA, the closed-shop union to which all screenwriters must belong, missing the fourth only when I moved away from Los Angeles.

From the earliest days of the motion picture industry (always in Hollywood referred to as "the Industry"), the screenwriter has been regarded at best as an anomalous necessity, at worst as a curse to be borne. In 1922, Cecil B. DeMille offered a $1,000 prize to anyone who, in three hundred words or less, could come up with "an idea that would send a thrill through the world." "It may be a freight brakeman or a millionaire," Mr. DeMille wrote in the *Los Angeles Times*, "a starving beggar or a society queen." It could even be "a grocery clerk somewhere who has a terrific and forceful idea boiling in his soul." The brakeman, the millionaire, the beggar, the society queen, and the grocery clerk need not bother about putting the idea into scenario form. "We have our own trained scenario writers," DeMille wrote, "who can work out the technical details of plot better than anyone else." It was as if the screenwriter lacked the kind of soul in which an idea might boil and ultimately send a thrill through the world, but could contribute what Mr. DeMille dismissed as a technical detail—the plot.

∼

BEATING UP ON screenwriters is a Hollywood blood sport; everyone in the business thinks he or she can write, if only time could be found. That writers find the time is evidence of their inferior position in the food chain. In the Industry, they are regarded as chronic malcontents, overpaid and undertalented, the Hollywood version of Hessians, measuring their worth in dollars, since ownership of their words belongs to those who hire and fire them. "Schmucks with Underwoods," Jack Warner, the most pernicious of the brothers Warner, called screenwriters, and the impression persists, especially among the freeloading hacks on the show business beat, except that today writers are seen as schmucks with laptops. "They've accepted the idea of being third-class citizens, the industry's pain in the ass." Frank Pierson, an Academy Award–winning screenwriter (for *Dog Day Afternoon*) and the WGA negotiator (and later Guild president) told my wife when she was researching a piece about the 1988 strike. "Our position is that maybe someday we could forget the old joke about the Polish starlet, you know, she thought she could get ahead by fucking the writer."

The screenwriter's problem is that he is neither a writer, in the sense that a script is not meant to be read but seen and its quality only then judged, nor is he a filmmaker, in the sense that he is not in control of the finished product, granting to the director, as the medium dictates, such writer's concerns as style, mood, pace, rhythm, texture, and point of view, much of which is manufactured in the cutting room, where the director is sovereign. Early script drafts, before a director is involved, invariably contain too much exposition and explanation; this is for the benefit of the studio executives, who are seldom fluent in the grammar of film, and have a hard time visualizing the picture that will be made from a script. The writer's presence on the set, furthermore, is generally discouraged as a threat to the director's vision. Although ritual obeisance is paid to the script, rarely is it paid to the individual scriptwriter. Prevailing Industry wisdom is that the more writers there are on a script, the better that script will be. On our version of *A Star Is Born*, eight of the thirteen writers who actually worked on the script filed for credit; in the WGA's credit arbitration, Joan and I received first credit and Frank Pierson, the last writer on the screenplay, other than Barbra Streisand and Jon Peters, second position.

Perhaps no one has a more pungent explanation for what he calls "the historic hatred Hollywood has always had for screenwriters" than Robert Towne, the author of *Shampoo* and *Chinatown* (for which he won an Oscar), and one of the best film writers of the last thirty years. "Until the screenwriter does his job, nobody else has a job," Towne wrote in an essay for the quarterly *Scenario*. "In other words, he is the asshole who keeps everyone else from going to work." That he or she is regarded as such, and more importantly is aware of it, is one of the major reasons that writers strike so regularly, whatever the ostensible creative, monetary, and benefit issues between labor and management. However cost-ineffective a writers' strike may in the end prove to be, it is an option that inflicts a certain amount of payback inconvenience, a satisfying if ultimately self-destructive revolt of the assholes.

~

THE 1988 STRIKE lasted five months. Since more screenplays are assigned than are actually written, and more written than can possibly be produced, the studios decided to seize the opportunity offered by the strike to write off, under the legal doctrine of *force majeure* (an unexpected and disruptive event such as a labor dispute that may operate to excuse a party from a contract), hundreds of projects in development, and avoid the necessity of paying for them once the strike was settled. Any strike offers a certain house-cleaning benefit to the studios, allowing them to get rid of a lot of dead wood and drop projects they don't really want to make. In our case, contracts were cancelled on *North Slope*, on a western about the California water wars called *Water*, and on an adaptation of my novel *Dutch Shea, Jr*. These had all been kept alive in case we needed an infusion of cash, and since we had just moved from Los Angeles to New York, and since the move was more costly than we had antic-ipated, we had been counting on one of them coming through.

Now we had to find a picture from scratch. We had a further financial incentive for doing so quickly: I had undergone a cardiac procedure called angioplasty in the fall of 1987, and it was imper-ative that we remain covered by the Writers Guild health plan, which requires a continuum of television or motion picture work to remain in effect.

Only one of our pre-strike projects was still breathing, and that one on life support. It was a script we had written for Lorimar Pic-tures called *Playland*. Lorimar had taken over an old deal we had with MGM to write an updated musical version of *Mildred Pierce*, and asked us if instead we were willing to do a screenplay about the gangster Bugsy Siegel. We were initially as unexcited about Bugsy Siegel as Lorimar was about *Mildred Pierce* as a musical. There was, however, something naggingly persistent about the Siegel idea; we went back to Lorimar and suggested that instead of a straight-up Bugsy Siegel story we do an original script about a generic Jewish gangster who comes to Hollywood and falls in love with Shirley Temple. Not the real Shirley Temple, of course, but a major child star, seventeen years old, trying to cross over into grown-up parts, a child-woman with the vocabulary of a longshoreman and the morals of a mink. Lorimar gave us the go-ahead, and an enthusias-tic response when we delivered a first draft of *Playland* shortly before the strike began.

Behind the scenes, however, the big business of Hollywood intervened: Lorimar was bought by Warner Bros. For *Playland* and the other Lorimar feature projects in the deal, this transaction was the kiss of death. Although we owed another draft, we knew it was unlikely that Warner's would proceed. Their executives were frightened enough of getting burned by projects they themselves had greenlighted without having to take the fall for projects picked up from another studio. "We inherited all these little orphans from Lorimar," a Warner's vice-president named Lucy Fisher said by way of setting the tone for our one *Playland* meeting. Of course the meeting generated a set of notes. In Hollywood, a meeting without notes is a meeting that never took place. Since senior studio executives consider it beneath their dignity to jot down or even remember the thoughts they advance at script meetings, notes arc always transcribed by ambitious assistants, called "Creative Executives," or CEs, who often add their own spin to the mix. Jargon is the currency of a CE's notes. A screenplay must have a "creative arc" ending in "resolution," or a "controlling idea" leading to "the inevitable climax"; major characters inevitably lack "motivation," and sometimes "basic motivation."

Warner's notes were signed by an entity identified only by the title CREATIVE, and they began, "We feel this project has a lot of potential," the translation of which means file and forget. That Warren Beatty was also said to be developing a Bugsy Siegel project left us feeling even more orphaned, but *Playland* did not fall entirely between the cracks; the unproduced screenplay jumpstarted a dormant novel of mine that was finally published six years later under the same title.

In early August 1988, the strike was finally settled, on terms the Guild membership had turned down in June. It was at this juncture that we heard once again from John Foreman.

THE PACKAGE

HARD TIMES HAD visited John, as they do most people in Hollywood, particularly as they get older and there is no nest egg from a huge hit laid away; the well-earned retirement benefits enjoyed by senior executives in corporate America, with a pension and medical insurance and a golden parachute, are not usually available. After he was bumped from *A Star Is Born*, John had produced two very good pictures directed by John Huston, *The Man Who Would Be King* and *Prizzi's Honor*, but both had taken years before they were made, and because Huston was an insurance risk—chronic emphysema and advancing age being the reasons—budgets and fees were slashed to the bone. John had always been like a junkyard dog with a picture, never letting go of it, even when it would have been to his advantage to do so. To him the important thing was getting the picture on, no matter what humiliations and belt-tightening financial incursions were dealt him by the money people. Now he had a project and he had a partner, a casually dressed good-old-boy Beverly Hills lawyer named E. Gregory Hookstratten, who is always called "the Hook."

The Hook's affable demeanor did little to mask a reputation as a fiercely combative agent for professional athletes (O.J. Simpson and Marcus Allen being two) and especially for television newscasters, both local and network, with NBC's Tom Brokaw and Bryant Gumbel the jewels of his client list. In Jessica Savitch's troubled later years, the Hook became her agent, and for a brief interlude they had a romance. Through this association, he controlled the film rights to Alanna Nash's biography of Savitch, *Golden Girl*, which was then in galleys. The Hook was used to dealing with the treacherous egos and plays of the sports and television news worlds, and was smart enough to know that he would not be at ease with the equally treacherous but differently nuanced egos and plays of the picture business. To guide him through this minefield, he called John Foreman, who had once been his neighbor in Beverly Hills, and John called us in New York.

What John wanted was to "attach" writers to *Golden Girl*, so that when he went to lay the package off on a studio, with himself and the Hook as its producers, he could say that Joan and I were what in Hollywood is called an "element," although it was our considered opinion that a writer's value as an element was at best questionable, and certainly not "bankable," i.e., sufficient to attract a studio's investment in a film. John mentioned bankable actresses and directors, the usual A-list suspects, all of whom, he assured us, without actually offering any proof, would kill to become involved in this picture. This was normal pre-pitch stroking and was understood as such, since he knew and we knew that no first-string actress or director would ever make a commitment without seeing a script.

~

HAD IT NOT been for the strike and the dumping of our other film projects, it is unlikely that we would have even opened the *Golden Girl* galleys. The main attraction of this embryonic project was that it was the only picture we had been offered since the strike ended. If a studio could be interested in the package, the money would ease the burden of carrying two apartments in New York, one of which we were trying to sell in a plummeting real estate market, and get us back on the WGA health plan. In the meantime, we had pressing non-movie commitments. I had to go to Germany and Ireland to research a long-overdue book, and Joan was under assignment to cover both the Democratic National Convention in Atlanta and the Republican convention in New Orleans. We had promised to visit friends in Italy late in the summer, and we told John that we would read the galleys while we were gone.

Although John pressed us to commit on the basis of his enthusiasm alone, we refused. We needed something more, and saw no point in being attached for months to a project that had little possibility of attracting studio financing. If we liked the book, and if he could set it up before something more viable came our way, we would become involved. We told John, however, that we would not attend any session to pitch *Golden Girl* to a prospective buyer; we are not among those writers known in Hollywood as "good meetings," those with the gift of schmoozing an idea so successfully— as if getting that idea down on paper was only a matter of some incidental typing—that studio executives pressed development funds on them.

As it happened, we liked *Golden Girl*, and when we returned home we told John that he could use our names to try to set it up.

A BUYER'S MARKET

IT WAS A buyer's market. Once profligate in developing scripts, only a fraction of which ever went into production (it was not unusual for writers to make several hundred thousand dollars a year for years on end without ever seeing a picture go before the cameras), the studios, having humbled the writers in the strike and thinned their inventory of expensive development projects, were in a feisty, fee-cutting mood. Speculative scripts, many written during the strike (the only kind of screen work WGA members could do, as it was without recompense), were the rage. The beauty of a spec script was that it was finished, could be read and discarded at a sitting if found wanting, or put into production quickly if desirable. The bidding wars on the hotter spec scripts, mainly action thrillers like *The Last Boy Scout, Radio Flyer*, and *Ultimatum*, sent prices through the roof; a million dollars became the floor bid when an auction was held.

Toward the development project, however, the project adapted from a book or a play or a magazine article, and then converted into a screenplay, the studios in this post-strike era brought an accountant's green eyeshade. WGA rules mandate that writers receive a significant portion of their fee upon signing, in other words before a word is written, and the balance of their first-draft payment upon delivery to the studio. The inexorability of these payments is what makes studios sullen, and they try to control the content of the script by endless meetings, often with as many as a dozen people present, all of them offering their ideas about what the script should be. To attend one of these meetings is to understand the cold truth of the saying that a camel is a horse made by a committee.

Neither John Foreman nor we were under any illusions that *Golden Girl* would be easy to sell. There had been a time in the late Sixties and early Seventies, the period of *Darling* and *Easy Rider* and *Midnight Cowboy*, when the life of Jessica Savitch would have been an eminently feasible subject for a film, with a possibility of a tidy profit if the picture was produced under strict budgetary constraints. Her story was a perfect cautionary gloss on the perils of the counter-culture: a small town girl with more ambition than brains, an overactive libido, a sexual ambivalence, a tenuous hold on the truth, a taste for controlled substances, a longtime abusive Svengali relationship, a certain mental instability, a glamour job, and then in 1983 a final reckoning, at age thirty-five, that seemed ordained by the Fates—death by drowning with her last lover in three feet of Delaware Canal mud after a freak automobile accident. This was not a tale, however cautionary, much valued in the climate of the late Eighties, when "high concept"—a picture that could be described in a single line, such as *Flashdance* (blue-collar woman steelworker in the Rust Belt becomes a ballerina) or *Top Gun* (cowboy Navy jet jockeys train and love at Mach 2), pushed along by a hit music track—was in vogue. Studio after studio passed on *Golden Girl*. Then, shortly after Thanksgiving 1988, John called from Los Angeles to say that he had received a nibble from an unlikely source—The Walt Disney Company.

THE MONSTER

ONCE KNOWN MAINLY for its animated features and the cartoon shorts of Mickey Mouse and Donald Duck, WDPc (as Walt Disney Pictures is referred to in its contracts), with Michael Eisner as its CEO and Jeffrey Katzenberg as its head of motion picture production, had become a Hollywood powerhouse. After a string of tightly budgeted commercial hits, Disney in 1988 was on a roll, and believed it had found a formula, sure-fire as long as that formula—family entertainment that did not too rigorously tax the imagination—was controlled by its own executives. The bottom line was the final arbiter and the audience that mattered was the company's stockholders, with whom WDPc enjoyed an extraordinarily profitable fiduciary rapport. To the studio's studied indifference, the brand-name actors and filmmakers used to getting top dollar and their own way tended to take their wares elsewhere.

Toward those members of the creative community not coveted by other studios, WDPc's attitude was to take no prisoners. Late one evening, at a back table in Le Dôme, a Sunset Strip restaurant much favored by the Industry, a producer friend of ours and his screenwriter, a best-selling novelist we also know, argued vigorously against the changes Disney was demanding in a picture already in production. The president of the Disney division overseeing the picture, who was paying for dinner, suddenly demanded silence.

He was, he said, forced by the writer's intransigence to take the monster out of its cage.

In the silence that ensued, the division president reached under the table, pretended to grab a small predatory prehistoric animal from its lair, and then as if he was clutching the creature by the neck in his fist, exhibited his empty, claw-like hand to the people around the table. He asked the screenwriter if he saw the monster, and the writer, not knowing what else to do, nodded yes.

I'm going to put it back in its cage now, the executive said, drawing each word out, and I never want you to force me to bring it out again. Then he mimed putting the monster back into its cage under the table. When he was done, the executive asked the writer, Do you know what the monster is?

The writer shook his head.

The executive said, "It's *our money*."

In time, after an extended run of box office failures, the executive himself met the monster, and was fired the way studio presidents are fired: he was allowed to work out his contract as a Disney independent producer.

MEET & GREET

THE REPUTATION FOR being difficult to deal with was one Disney at that time actively encouraged. With Katzenberg its point man, the studio had taken a consistently hard line during the strike, and a collegial spirit toward the people it had under contract was seen as such a lesser virtue that some who worked there called it Mouschwitz or Duckau, after its two most famous cartoon characters. Though we had been adamant about not attending pitch meetings, John Foreman called to ask if, since Katzenberg was going to be in New York on December 9th, we would agree just this once to meet with him.

I was reluctant. I did not think *Golden Girl* the sort of picture Disney would ever make and thought a meeting with Katzenberg a waste of time. Joan was practical: she said my cardiac distress, however optimistic the prognosis, was still an unknown factor; we needed the health insurance and this was the only project in sight. Together we pared *Golden Girl* down to a one-sentence pitch: the story of an ugly duckling with nothing much going for her who reinvents herself at great effort and greater cost into a golden girl.

On the appointed day, Joan went to see Katzenberg by herself. It is well to remember that Hollywood is largely a boy's club. The presence of a woman at a studio meeting tends to make male executives uneasy. Whenever Joan and I are at a script conference, the questions are invariably directed at me; for years Joan was tolerated only as an "honorary guy," or perhaps an "associate guy," whose primary function was to take notes. This mindset is prevalent even to this day. "Is John there?" an executive's assistant will say over the telephone when calling for his master. "This is Joan." "Tell John to call when he gets home."

We have always maintained contractually that as screenwriters (our only professional collaboration) one of us equals both, and her going solo to meet Katzenberg would establish that premise with Disney. There was also the thought that my continued lack of enthusiasm for the meeting might prove contagious. Hobbled by a household accident that had taken most of the skin off her right shin from knee to ankle (a heavy tabletop had fallen on her leg while she was checking a storage closet before a Thanksgiving party we were giving), and unable to get a cab, Joan walked fourteen blocks through the snow to Disney's Park Avenue offices.

The purpose of such a meet-and-greet is to allow the executive to size up the supplicant. Katzenberg had not read *Golden Girl*, but he was aware of the less savory details of Jessica Savitch's life. He liked the ugly duckling idea; it was the kind of narrative he wanted, and he was also responsive to the television background against which it would be played. He did have reservations, and here I quote Joan's notes of that first meeting: "Wants to know what is going to happen in this picture that will make the audience walk out feeling uplifted, good about something and good about themselves." With subjunctives and qualifiers in place, Katzenberg indicated that Disney could make an offer if somewhere in Savitch's messy life we could find an angle that would fit within the studio's story parameters. With this as our Christmas holiday project, it was agreed that we would meet again in Los Angeles after the New Year with the full Disney creative team.

THE SUITS

TO SEE WHAT kind of deal Disney might be contemplating, we called our agents at International Creative Management, Jeffrey Berg and Patty Detroit. With one timeout, Jeff Berg has been our motion picture agent since his graduation, with an honors degree in English, from the University of California at Berkeley in 1969, and we, as marginal screenwriters, were given him as clients. Like so many in Hollywood, he comes from a show-business background. His father, Dick Berg, was a top television writer and producer; our first screen credit was on a TV show Dick Berg produced—wheels within wheels. Jeff Berg was now the president of ICM, a descendant of CMA, the agency John Foreman had helped start—more wheels within wheels. Early in his career, we had fired him and the agency when his superiors tried to include us in a package in which we did not wish to be included, but in time we returned because we found no one with whom we were more comfortable, although ever since we have told him the second time is easy.

Berg and Detroit spelled out the new realities: our first draft fee would be nearly 60 percent less than it had been before the strike; we would have to write more drafts to get a smaller total fee, the biggest chunk of which would be loaded onto the back end, payable only if, after shooting ended, it was adjudicated that we were due either a solo or shared credit. "Net points," or a share of net profits, would be negligible, with a ceiling on the amount we could even hypothetically receive; the payoff on net points has become such a rarity, as a result of the Industry's elastic accounting practices, that they are dismissed as "brownie points." The offer was take it or leave it. We took, and agreed in principle to a deal that also called for a nominal producers' development fee, what is called "walking around money," for John Foreman and Ed Hookstratten.

Late in January 1989, Foreman, Hookstratten, Joan, and I went to WDPc's Burbank headquarters to meet with Katzenberg, David Hoberman, the president of Touchstone Pictures, the division to which the project was assigned, and a full studio support team of vice-presidents and creative executives—the "suits," so called because they all came to work uniformed in jacket and tie. In the seven weeks since Joan's New York meeting with Katzenberg, she and I had expanded on the idea of Savitch as an ugly-duckling-turned-golden-girl. In the notes we prepared for the Burbank meeting, we wrote that Savitch was

> moving in the very fast, very bigtime, very demanding, very seduc-
> tive world of network news which she fails to understand is a
> MEN'S CLUB, in which, when she gets close to achieving her goal,
> she is closed out. She is closed out in the traditional way: it is said
> that she is unstable, that she sleeps around, that she uses drugs,
> drink, sex, whatever, in her "relentless" drive to succeed; that she is
> in short, "too ambitious." The double bind.

It was the most positive spin we could put on the life of a news-caster whom David Brinkley had once publicly labeled "the dumb-est woman I ever met."

The subordinate suits waited for Katzenberg to open the questioning. Did she have to die in the end? he wanted to know. It was a question we had anticipated. If the character was not called Jessica Savitch, we answered carefully, then it was not necessary that she die. Disney, with its family reputation, was also uncomfortable with Savitch's addiction to cocaine. The transformation had begun, and the caveats started to add up, if only inferentially. Savitch had once had an affair with the CBS newscaster Ed Bradley, and we surmised that the interracial nature of that relationship might be another source of discomfort for Disney's core audience. Her abortions could also pose a problem, as could her two marriages, especially the second, to a gay gynecologist who, less than a year after they married, hanged himself from a crossbeam in the basement of her Philadelphia home. And it was clear that an uplifting story that would make an audience feel good about itself was not going to encompass any allusion either to Savitch's suicide attempts or to the lesbian episodes in her life.

Then there was Ron Kershaw, the antisocial, alcoholic news director who through most of Savitch's professional career (and through both of her marriages) was her lover, mentor, and tormentor. Something of a genius broadcast gypsy, Kershaw skipped from city to city and channel to channel, successfully reconfiguring news departments and finding new Galatea reporters and anchors on whom he could work his magic. "She only existed electronically," Kershaw told Alanna Nash about Savitch, and it was he, according to *Golden Girl*, who taught her the smile that became her on-the-air trademark. "You've got to show teeth," he told Savitch. "Teeth is vulnerability in primates, whether you're a chimp or Dan Rather." Kershaw was also an aggressor who, when he was not feeding Savitch cocaine, regularly beat her black and blue.

If Savitch was not Disney's ideal heroine, Kershaw (who has since died of cancer) left something to be desired as a romantic hero. Still, Disney was willing to go to a first draft before offering any specific suggestions, which would then, of course, have the force of law. When we left Burbank that day, this is what we knew: that as long as Disney was footing the bills, Jessica Savitch would cease to be a factor in the Jessica Savitch screenplay. To persist in writing her story under Disney's rules would be like writing a biography of Charles Lindbergh without mentioning the kidnapping and murder of his son, the trial and execution of Bruno Hauptmann for those crimes, and Lindbergh's flirtation with fascism and America First. What we did not know was that it would take six more years, four more contracts, two other writers, and twenty-seven drafts of our own before the picture that resulted from this meeting reached its first day of principal photography.

AN AMERICAN
EDUCATION

QUEBEC ZERO

[1967]

❧

IT IS EIGHTY-SIX miles from Malmstrom Air Force Base to Quebec Zero, and in the winter, with ice glazing the roads and snow drifting over the Montana range country and the Rockies hidden under a coverlet of clouds, the easiest way to get there is by helicopter. It was cold and crowded in the chopper. There were two other crews besides the three men I was with, one bound for Romeo Zero, the other for Tango Zero, and what struck me about them first was how young they were. Some were boys barely into their twenties, the oldest a year or two younger than I am. Age is not something I brood over, but theirs was a responsibility I did not wish to have on my own shoulders, for entombed out there in steel and concrete capsules sixty feet beneath the rolling prairie, they would, if they were ever called upon to do so, blow the world to pieces.

I had arrived at Malmstrom the day before, driven past the enormous sign at the gate that said PEACE . . . IS OUR PROFESSION. Malmstrom is the headquarters of the Strategic Air Command's 341st Strategic Missile Wing, and for hundreds of square miles around the base, an area the size of several New England states, the wheatland is planted with the wing's own special crop, two hundred nuclear Minuteman I and II missiles, each sheathed in its own individual silo and rooted deep beneath the surface of the plain.

Twenty-four hours a day the missiles are on alert, electronically trained on targets thousands of miles distant. The purpose of my visit was to spend a twenty-four-hour tour of duty with one of the crews that control each ten Minutemen, to see what it was like, how it worked on the mind, to have World War III only an arm's length away.

The command capsule I was assigned to was designated Quebec Zero ("Quebec" being the letter "Q" in the military phonetic alphabet), its missiles Quebec eleven through twenty. The crew commander was a short, smiling thirty-three-year-old Texan, Captain James W. Wilson; his alternate, Captain Laster B. Meads, twenty-nine, was a large, slow-talking North Carolinian. The third crew member was First Lieutenant Charles L. Thysell, a twenty-four-year-old Minnesotan who, in his spare time, under the auspices of the Air Force, was studying for a master's degree. We were briefed early in the morning with the nineteen other crews in the wing going on alert that day. Watches were synchronized, weather information given, and after I was asked to leave the room, there was an EWO check. I asked one of the officers what EWO meant. "Emergency war orders," he said.

The helicopter got lost on our way to Quebec Zero. There are no markings on the endless range, nothing but plowed-under wheat fields and an occasional herd of Black Angus cattle huddled against the cold. We circled low over the blast doors of a missile silo to get our bearings. It was innocuous-looking, almost flush with the ground, easy to miss from the air. I tried to visualize the doors opening and the missile lumbering off into space toward its target. Later I asked Wilson if he knew where the missile was headed. "As far as I'm concerned it's just sitting on target," he said. "I don't need to know what that target is, and I don't care." There seemed to be a clear psychological advantage in thinking that at the end of the Minuteman's long arc lay only an abstraction known as "the target."

It was nearly an hour before we got to Quebec Zero. Though it is surrounded by fertile Montana wheat fields, there is not a blade of grass within the fenced-in area. If grass does begin to grow, Wilson explained, it is killed immediately, thus precluding the danger that a grass fire could flash down into the capsule. The one building within the enclosure is painted a bilious military green and contains a kitchen, a dining area, a lounge with television set and nine bedrooms for the capsule crew and other personnel. Wilson and Thysell were to pull the first shift. Each strapped on a snubnosed .38 and then they took the elevator down into the capsule. Because of the exchange of classified orders and information, I was not allowed to witness the changeover of old and new crews, and so I went into the dining room to get lunch. Not until the second cup of coffee did it occur to me that one of the reasons that crew members carried sidearms was to use on each other in the event that either went berserk below.

Shortly after noon I went down into the command capsule. It sits to the left of the elevator behind a huge six-and-a-half-ton blast door. The room is approximately fifty feet long by thirty feet wide, divided down the middle by a bank of computers and electronic encoding and encrypting devices. At right angles to each other, some fifteen feet apart, are the two consoles where the commander and his deputy sit. On the deputy's console is a bank of green, amber, red and white lights which constantly tell the status of each of the ten missiles commanded by the capsule. Every few seconds the missiles are electronically interrogated. A slight beeping noise and a blinking light on the deputy's panel signal a change in status or a minor malfunction. When this happens, the deputy dials the missile electronically. Seconds later an electronic printer spits out a series of numbers detailing the fault. Except for major maintenance, faults are corrected automatically. The missiles seem to have an independent existence, keyed only to a series of cryptic legends printed on the deputy's console: INHIBIT, HOLD, NO-GO, SECURITY FAULT, WARHEAD ALARM, STATUS CHANGE. And then, from the top, the cold, logical progression: STRATEGIC ALERT, ENABLED, LAUNCH COMMAND, LAUNCH IN PROGRESS, MISSILE AWAY.

It is MISSILE AWAY that is the first and last reason for Quebec Zero. The means to carry out this command are located in a small red safe, roughly eight inches square, above the deputy's console. The safe is secured by two ordinary combination locks, which change as the crews change. Each crew member brings his own lock on duty, adjusted to his own secret combination. When he goes down into the capsule, he fastens that lock to the strongbox. The fact that each crew member knows the combination of only his own lock is a fail-safe to prevent any one man from breaking into the strongbox, for inside are the keys with which the missiles are armed and launched.

For my benefit, Wilson and Thysell outlined the steps following a presidential strike order, relayed through SAC. The entire procedure takes less than three minutes. First the crew members decode and authenticate the order, using classified documents. Then they go through a launch checklist. When this is completed, they unlock the safe. Inside are the keys and additional coded documents to further validate the go-code message. "If these check out," Wilson said matter-of-factly, "then I'm going to war." Each man inserts a key in his console. The keys must be turned simultaneously, and since the consoles are so far apart, it is physically impossible for one man to turn both at once. The turning of the keys activates the missiles and is known as "one launch vote." Before the missiles can be fired, however, this same procedure must be repeated by another capsule in the squadron, Romeo Zero, say, or Tango Zero. Only with the receipt of this "second launch vote" are the missiles actually blasted from their silos. "So you see, nothing can go wrong," Wilson said. "Four guys in two different capsules have to go nuts at the same time. I've heard the odds against that are something like one in eight million."

Somehow I did not find the odds appealing, nor did it seem entirely plausible that only an insane man would want to turn the keys. Perhaps what surprised me most was the discovery that the fail-safe was actually less elaborate than I had imagined: that four men, whatever their mental state, could launch a flight of nuclear missiles without any outside orders. I asked if the President could rescind a launch order after the missiles were airborne, if there was a mechanism that could destroy them before they reached their target. Wilson shook his head. "Once they're gone, they're gone," he said. "Goodbye."

I did not know whether to be chilled or reassured that awe had vanished, that life in the capsule could settle into a routine. Perhaps ennui was the most effective safeguard against mental hazard. The minutes ticked away. Every four hours one of the crew went topside to get some sleep. Lights blinked, gauges quivered, the console beeped, the speaker warbled. "Oil Burner 4 low level route closed to all SAC aircraft. . . . Change frequency to 06320 Echo 1." A fault light flashed, and the printer spewed forth numbers: "306, 320, 322, 336." The effect was dehumanizing. I count myself a stable person, but as the hours wore on, I could not take my eyes off the red strongbox. I had an insane urge to break into the safe, take a key and turn it in the keyhole. I wanted to see what would happen.

The night seemed endless. I went topside and slept a troubled sleep. When I went back down into the capsule at 4 A.M., the conversation turned prosaic. There among the computers and switches we talked about barbecued chicken and French toast with boysenberry sauce. I watched the clock. And then it was time to go. The new crew had arrived. I went outside with Wilson and watched him burn the secret codes and messages in a small incinerator. We waited in the thin, cold sunlight for the helicopter, stamping our feet on the hard, brown turf. I had a plane to catch, and I did not shower or shave before I got on it. I wanted to go home.

INDUCTION DAY

[1968]

WEDNESDAY IS INDUCTION day in Oakland. It was shortly before six o'clock on this particular Wednesday in March when I passed the toll station on the Bay Bridge from San Francisco and headed for the induction center. On the seat beside me was a leaflet from the Peace and Freedom Party saying that Richard Kunst, a twenty-four-year-old graduate student in Chinese language and literature at Berkeley, was going to refuse induction that morning. He had decided to become a "non-cooperator with the Selective Service System," the leaflet said, "in order to resist American militarism in Vietnam and the system of conscription which is its mainstay." The leaflet called for a support demonstration "to encourage other inductees arriving at the Induction Center to join in saying 'NO' to the system which oppresses them."

Oakland is not one of the more inspiring cities in America—"There is no 'there' there when you get there," Gertrude Stein once said—and the induction center is in one of its less inspiring sections. It occupies four floors in a drably anonymous nine-story building that is surrounded by cheap hotels, a bowling-supply store, sheet-music shops, and $3 income-tax advisers. The center handles inductees and enlistees from all over northern California and western Nevada. The building was still locked by the time I parked my car, but the first inductees had already begun to arrive. They milled in small groups on the sidewalk, strangers all, yawning, not talking to one another. Most carried airlines bags and some slumped on the sidewalk, their backs leaning against the building, and stared vacantly into space. I remember the day I was inducted. At the time it seemed the most desolate day of my life.

Diagonally across the street, by the garage the police use as their command post for possible induction disturbances, four prowl cars were parked by the curb. One of them glided across the street as the first demonstrator arrived. She was a middle-aged woman in a cloth coat and she began passing out pamphlets that asked: "Why are we fighting in Vietnam? Because big corporations in the United States have billions of dollars invested abroad which would be lost if these revolutions succeed. Anti-Communism means risking your life to protect the property of the rich at the expense of the poor." The police car followed slowly behind the woman. She reached into her bag and drew out an enormous fruitcake wrapped in tinfoil. She offered some to the policeman. He seemed nonplused. "Too many calories, I'm afraid," he said.

The inductees watched the scene in silence. The woman named the son of a prominent national figure and asked why he had not been drafted. "Because he's a fairy, lady," one of the inductees said. The group around him began to laugh, and with wrists limp, they minced and simpered along the sidewalk. "Oh, to be a queen for today," one of them said. Most of the young men just watched phlegmatically. Some stuffed leaflets into their pockets. A youth crossed the street carrying a large placard that said, "What are you dying in Vietnam for?" An inductee sidled up to him. "For you, jerk," he said.

At precisely half past six, as the doors to the induction center opened, the installation commander walked around the corner. The draftees parted to let him past. His name was Clyde A. Cortez, he was an Army lieutenant colonel, and on his uniform jacket were stepped row after row of decorations, campaign ribbons, combat stars and clusters. I asked Colonel Cortez if I could go inside to see how the Army handled a refusal to report for induction. He brooded for a moment. "Why not?" he said finally. Just inside the front door was taped a sign forbidding the carrying of placards of any description and the distribution of seditious pamphlets and leaflets. "If they got any, we give them a receipt for it and they can pick it up when they leave," Colonel Cortez said. He was a stocky, swarthy Latin and he spoke in a slow military drawl. "It's their private property, you know."

I asked if he anticipated any trouble. "No, just another Wednesday," he said. He pointed across the street. "This Oakland police force, they're good people, a real bunch of professionals." He looked at my notebook. "You people are always writing about these demonstrators," he said reproachfully. "If you want to write about something, you should write about these Salvation Army ladies come down here every Wednesday. They're real fine people. They give these boys shaving kits, you know, toothpaste and razor blades. Nothing but name brands."

One of Colonel Cortez's officers explained to me that each draft resister is informed that under the Universal Military Training and Service Act he is subject to five years in prison and a $10,000 fine if he refuses induction. If he still refuses, he is asked to sign a statement that says, "I refuse to be inducted into the armed forces of the United States." I asked what would happen if an inductee would not sign. "I guess you'd have to say he was uncooperative," Colonel Cortez said. "But we don't arrest people or anything like that. We just forward his papers to the appropriate authorities."

Shortly before seven Richard Kunst entered the induction center. He was a handsome young man with a trim blond beard. He had his wife and a friend with him. Kunst's wife was a quiet, attractive young woman with a ban-the-bomb emblem pinned to her coat. It was several moments before anyone took any notice of Kunst. He finally spoke to a sergeant, who waved his thumb over his shoulder and mumbled, "Oh, yeah, you want to talk to the lieutenant." The sergeant yawned, the lieutenant seemed embarrassed. The officer informed Kunst of the penalties and asked him to wait until an FBI agent arrived at the station to witness his refusal to report. Kunst cleared his throat. "I think my wife is as valid a witness as an FBI man," he said. The lieutenant shrugged. A few steps away Colonel

Cortez made a show of not paying attention and examined his hat-band. The friend and Kunst's wife signed as witnesses, but then Kunst himself refused to sign the papers. "No, I don't think I will," he said. Less than three minutes had passed. Kunst looked around. Colonel Cortez was still examining his hatband. With his friend and his wife, Kunst walked out of the center.

"That was a quickie," Colonel Cortez said. "Some of these kids go around and around for fifteen, twenty minutes."

A demonstration was forming outside, and Colonel Cortez asked if I wanted to watch from his second-floor office. The Venetian blinds were drawn tight. Colonel Cortez loosened his jacket and peeked out through the blinds. Down on the sidewalk there were about fifty demonstrators marching slowly in a circle in front of the induction center. Kunst and his wife circled hand in hand. One of the marchers was carrying a sign that said, PAX AMERICA NOT POX AMERICA. Colonel Cortez sipped a cup of coffee and eased back into his chair. "In the old days," he said, "people used to rally *for* the military." He got up and peeked through the blinds again. "This bunch must have made a bad connection. There's no TV down there. They like to be interviewed, these kids." He chuckled softly. "Some-one must have messed up."

He was back in his chair again. "You ever spend any time in the military?" he asked. I told him I had spent fifteen months in the Army in Germany. "I was there at the end of the war," he said. "Living in a castle. I was guarding Göding's wife before he, uh, did himself in there. I used to talk to Emmy a lot." He mused on this awhile and then we went down the hall to get another cup of coffee. A group of enlisted men was watching the marchers out the window. There was a brief cheer below as one of the demonstrators burned his induction papers. "I got a friend in the FBI," Colonel Cortez said, "and he tells me these kids will burn anything—library cards, envelopes, pieces of paper, anything. Why, there was one kid he told me about, he burned his so-called draft card five times."

We went back into his office. Colonel Cortez went to the blinds again. The marchers had begun to sing peace songs. "I sure wish we had a tape recorder," Colonel Cortez said. "It gets mighty quiet around here in the afternoon. We had that singing on tape, we could have ourselves a little serenade after lunch."

It was all over by 7:45. As suddenly as they came, the marchers had dispersed. "Just another Wednesday," Colonel Cortez said. "A lot of these kids, they got an eight-o'clock class at UC. You saw them, the ones with the book bags. They don't like to miss that class." He nodded his head as if he understood. "They do some marching, get it out of their system, then make that eight-o'clock class."

We shook hands. "Don't forget those Salvation Army ladies," Colonel Cortez said.

MEMENTO DELANO

[1971]

It was a long time before I returned to Delano. I passed it a number of times on my way to Sacramento, where I have family, but I never had the urge to stop. It was not a place of old friends and warm memories. It was a place where I had been and a place I was glad to leave. There was something sad and brooding about it, an endless, unfinished chapter straddling Highway 99. I remembered the last time I had been there. It was four years ago, in March 1967, and I stopped only by accident. I was driving from Sacramento to Los Angeles, that interminable drive, like driving four hundred miles on a pool table, comforted only by the car radio and the valley deejays' version of hard rock—a little Burt Bacharach, a touch of the Fifth Dimension. There was no traffic, the speedometer needle kept inching up. I had no intention of stopping in Delano, but just outside the city limits, I noticed that I needed gas. As I cruised onto the freeway off-ramp, I noticed the blinking red light of the Highway Patrol.

The officer was very young, twenty-two at the outside, with one of those OCS haircuts, all skin on the sides, a part and two inches on the top. He was wearing smoked sunglasses and a lot of Mennen's Skin Bracer. He was very courteous.

"You were going eighty-five in a seventy zone," the patrolman said.

There was no argument. I sat in the front seat of his patrol car and gave him my driver's license. He asked my occupation. I told him. He put his pen down.

"You know about this grape strike here? That's a good story."

I told him I was in the process of writing it. For what magazine, he wanted to know. He was interested now. He had inserted the carbon paper, but still had not made a mark on the ticket. I told him the name of the magazine.

"Is that a liberal magazine or a conservative magazine?"

"They let you think pretty much what you want."

It seemed to satisfy him. He carefully put his pen back into his shirt pocket and closed the flap over it.

"You ever met this Cesar Chavez?"

"Yes."

He was closing his summons book. "He a Communist?"

"No."

The youth was silent for a moment. Then he unbuttoned his shirt flap and took out his pen. He reopened his summons book. "You were doing eighty-five in a seventy zone," he said.

～

IN A SENSE, after four years, this brief encounter with the California Highway Patrol remains my most vivid impression of Delano. When asked "What was it like?" or "What does it all mean?" it is with difficulty that I can recall anything else. There are other things I remember, of course, but they are all equally tangential to what was happening. In no sense could they be used to make a point, to show a moral. I remember a cool night in the foothills of the Sierra when a panicky young farm worker was casually seduced by a California golden girl. I remember the boy still desperately picking on his guitar even as he was being led off to the bedroom and I remember that the next morning when the girl knocked on my door to wake me up she wasn't wearing any clothes. I remember a grower named Jack Pandol, whom I liked personally better than anyone I met in Delano, telling me that he really had very little in common with his brother-in-law, who was also a farmer, and when I asked why, he said simply, "He's in alfalfa. I'm in grapes."

I did not sense then, as I do now, the gulf between all I heard and read about the issues—the "story"—and what strikes me now increasingly as the "real," those moments that have no function in the "story," but which seem in retrospect more interesting, more imaginatively to the point, more evocative of how we live and what we feel. Jack Pandol's story about his alfalfa-growing brother-in-law was real and said more about what it was like to be a grower than all the cant I heard and all the account books I read that hot summer. There was in it the sense of being alone, of embattlement, the feeling that if he didn't have much in common with his brother-in-law, he was going to have even less in common with Chavez. And the California golden girl's seduction of the young farm worker was real. It is clear to me now that no amount of good faith on her part could bridge the chasm of social and sexual custom between them. She worked hard and loyally for Chavez, but in the end I think she had even less communion with the *campesinos* than Pandol.

I think I became further estranged from the events in Delano by the promiscuity of the attention lavished on Chavez. The insatiable appetites of instant communication have necessitated a whole new set of media ground rules, predicated not only on the recording of fact but also on the projection of glamour and image and promise. The result of this cultural nymphomania is that we have become a nation of ten-minute celebrities. People, issues and causes hit the charts like rock groups, and with approximately as much staying power. For all the wrong reasons, Chavez had all the right credentials—mysticism, nonviolence, the nobility of the soil. But distastefully implicit in instant apotheosis is the notion of causes lost; saints generally fail and when they do not, the constant scrutiny of public attention causes a certain moral devaluation. Enthusiasm for a cause is generally in inverse proportion to actual involvement. One could fete grape workers, as the rich and beautiful once did on a Long Island estate, without thinking about, if indeed one even knew about, the Suffolk County potato workers only a few miles away living in conditions equally as wretched as any pickers in the Great Central Valley of California.

And so I followed the strike from afar. Desultorily I kept a file, neatly packaging the headlines in a series of folders. *Note & file:* Chavez boycotts table grapes nationally; *cross-reference:* Lindsay administration halts purchase of grapes by New York city institutions; *cross-reference:* Pentagon increases grape purchases to help growers. *Note & file:* Chavez embarks on a penitential fast; *cross-reference:* Robert Kennedy and Cesar Chavez—who stands to gain the most? *Note & file:* 1969—large crop, depressed prices, boycott; *cross-reference:* strike speeds automation. *Note & file:* 1970—short crop, recession, boycott. *Note & file:* July 29, 1970—Delano growers capitulate, sign three-year contract with Chavez. "We are happy peace has come to this valley," says a growers' spokesman. "It has been a mutual victory."

"Mutual victory"—the phrase had the hollow sound of rhetoric and too often the territory behind rhetoric is mined with equivocation. I wondered who, if anyone, really was victorious in Delano, wondered if victory was tinctured with ambiguity. And so for the first time in four years I returned to Delano, goaded there by the instinctive feeling that there are no solutions, only at best amelioration, and never ultimate answers, final truths.

~

I've never talked to Cesar Chavez. But you know, I've been around longer than he has and I think I know these people better than he does. Maybe he'd learn something if he talked to me.
— FORMER U.S. SENATOR GEORGE MURPHY
(R., CAL.), MAY 1969

IT WAS ROBERT KENNEDY who legitimized Chavez. Prior to 1966, when the U.S. Senate Subcommittee on Migratory Labor held hearings in the valley, no Democrat would touch the Chavez movement. It had always been necessary to attract a few Southern votes in order for prolabor legislation to pass in the Congress, and Southern agrarians would not toss a bone toward labor unless farm workers were excluded from all provisions of any proposed bill. Robert Kennedy was no stranger either to expedience or to good politics and, along with most of organized labor, saw little to be gained by an identification with Chavez. But he was persuaded to attend the hearings in March 1966 by one of his aides, Peter Edelman, acting in concert with a handful of union officials alive to the drama in Delano. Even while flying to California, Kennedy was reluctant to get involved, demanding of his staff, "Why am I going?" He finally showed up at the hearings a day late. The effect was electric, a perfect meeting of complementary mystiques. Kennedy—ruthless, arrogant, a predator in the corridors of power. And Chavez—nonviolent, Christian, mystical, not without a moral imperative of his own.

For the next two years, it was almost impossible to think of Chavez except in conjunction with Robert Kennedy. The Kennedys sponged up ideas, and implicit in Chavez was the inexorable strength of an idea whose time had come. Kennedy's real concern for the farm workers helped soften his image as a self-serving keeper of his brother's flame and in turn plugged Chavez into the power outlets of Washington and New York. For the first time Chavez became fashionable, a national figure registering on the nation's moral thermometer. Robert Kennedy and Cesar Chavez—the names seemed wired into the same circuitry, the one a spokesman, the other a symbol for the constituency of the dispossessed.

Whatever the readings on fame's Geiger counter, it was a bad time in Delano. The strike, in 1968, was mired in quicksand. An attempt to organize the grape ranches of the Coachella Valley had failed miserably. The threat of violence was in the air. A newspaper in India reported a $10,000 bounty on Chavez's head. However unsubstantiated the rumor, bounty spelled contract, and contract spelled hit. Bodyguards dogged Chavez's footsteps and a German shepherd watchdog patrolled his door. And then Robert Kennedy was killed the same day that Chavez had dispatched platoons into the barrios of East Los Angeles to round up votes for his benefactor in the California Democratic primary. Chavez showed up at Kennedy's funeral at St. Patrick's Cathedral in New York characteristically late, dressed in a sweater. He marched to an empty pew and stood throughout the ceremony, to the mounting annoyance of a group of U.S. Senators whose view he was blocking.

The strike had begun to lose its momentum the year before. Perelli-Minetti was the last Delano grower to sign with Chavez, and even that was by default. The grower had originally settled with the Teamsters, an agreement bitterly assailed by Chavez as a sweetheart contract, and it was only after the two unions had arbitrated their jurisdictions that UFWOC inherited the Perelli-Minetti workers. Chavez's next target was the Guimarra Vineyards, the largest table-grape growers in America, themselves controlling 10 percent of the annual crop. His strategy was a San Joaquin Valley version of the domino theory: knock over Guimarra and the other growers had to fall in line. But the Guimarras were a rough bunch of boys, a network of Sicilian fathers and brothers and sons and sons-in-law not especially known for their enlightened views about the labor movement. Even their lawyer was one of their own, John Guimarra, Jr., then not thirty, a Stanford Law School graduate who gave up an Orange County law practice to come home as the family's counsel and spokesman.

The strike against Guimarra proved one thing—there wasn't a picket line in the world that could force a grower to agree to a contract. It was next to impossible to certify a strike. Workers who were pulled out were readily replaced by scabs and green-carders—foreign nationals (in this case Mexicans) with U.S. work permits, or green cards. The pickers were usually out of town working at another farm before the applicable state agencies even arrived to verify their departure. Though green-carders were legally enjoined against working in a strike situation, they were free to work if no strike had been certified. And in the conflicting claims as to the number of workers who actually walked out at a struck farm, I am inclined for one reason to lean more toward the grower's figure than the union's: it simply defied all logic for a picker to go out on strike. However grandiose (by grower standards) a picker's hourly wage, his annual income was barely at subsistence level, if indeed that high. Given that picking is one of the most miserable jobs known to man, it is usually—for whatever social or cultural reasons—the best a picker can hold. So no matter how much he favored the union, he would have had to be a sainted fanatic to go on strike and further heighten both his own and his family's level of misery.

Against Guimarra, Chavez needed another edge and he fell back on the boycott he had used so successfully against Schenley and Di Giorgio. Both these concerns were public corporations, however, susceptible to stockholder pressure, and both had a line of consumer products that could be successfully boycotted. Table grapes were another thing altogether. There was no label identification; a bunch of grapes was a bunch of grapes. The problem did not seem to deter Chavez. He seems to regard a boycott almost as a religious experience. "It's like quicksand," he says. "It's irreversible. Once it gets going, it creates a life of its own. It reaches a point where nothing can stop it. It's like trying to fight the wind."

At first the Guimarras were equal to the blow. When UFWOC prevailed on stores to stop buying the Guimarra label, the firm began borrowing labels from other growers and using them in place of its own. Even a rebuke from the Food and Drug Administration charging that label switching was contrary to federal regulations did not deter the grower. By the end of 1967, Guimarra was using, by union count, 105 different labels. In retaliation, UFWOC early in 1968 extended its boycott beyond Guimarra to include every California grower of table grapes.

As the growers dug in, there was within the union a certain impatience, a certain fraying of the precepts of nonviolence. The imperceptible erosion of the growers' position was not particularly heady to union militants steeped in the literature of the headlines, the combat communiqués from the core cities. There was a new truculence in the air; packing crates were burned, tires slashed, scabs roughed up. Chavez was not unaware of the nascent violence. Late in February 1968, he quietly began a penitential fast to redirect the movement back onto its nonviolent course. Only on the sixth day of the fast did he alert aides to what he was doing. No one had to be apprised of its exploitative potential. The circus aspect of the next seventeen days (the fast lasted twenty-three days) dismayed a number of Chavez's staunchest supporters who, while not doubting his intentions, nevertheless deplored the manner in which union aides pandered to the media that flocked to Delano. If not actively choreographing the fast, UFWOC officials did little to discourage the faithful who seemed to equate it with the Second Coming. Tents were pitched for farm workers maintaining a vigil for Chavez, and old women crawled on their knees from the highway to the quarters where he was lodged for the duration of the fast.

Whatever its indulgences, the fast was like a hypodermic full of pure adrenaline pumped into the union. It seemed to find new resolve, new strength. But the fast had also endangered Chavez's always perilous health. One of his legs is shorter than the other, one side of his pelvis smaller. Six months after his fast, his energies depleted, Chavez was hospitalized. His condition was diagnosed as a degenerating spinal disc. For months he remained virtually an invalid, resisting treatment. Then early in 1969, Senator Edward Kennedy, at his own expense, sent Dr. Janet Travell, the back specialist who had treated John Kennedy, to Delano to look at Chavez. Dr. Travell concluded that Chavez's problem was not spinal but the result of muscular breakdown in his back. Her treatment (among other things, she prescribed a rocking chair) gradually freed Chavez from his bed. Without pain for the first time in nearly a dozen years, he could turn his full attention to a strike that by mid-1969 seemed endless.

~

IN JOHN GUIMARRA, JR., the growers had their most impressive spokesman. In contrast to the primitives of the elder generation, his normality seemed practically epicene. Not for him any vulgar Red-baiting; even the ritualistic evocation of outside agitation was toned down. The 1968 election gave the growers a friendly administration in Washington and an almost immediate by-product was a substantial jump in the Pentagon's purchase of table grapes. Pentagon spokesmen indignantly denied that the increased purchases were meant to undercut the boycott, claiming instead that military *chefs de cuisine* had merely whipped up a number of new grape delicacies. The growers even developed a degree of media sophistication of their own. The California Table Grape Growers Association hired J. Walter Thompson, the nation's largest advertising agency, to come up with a campaign extolling table grapes (it seemed impossible for a while to pick up a service magazine without the eyes feasting on some alchemy of grapes and sour cream and brown sugar) and also engaged Whitaker & Baxter, a public-relations firm specializing in political causes (it handled the American Medical Association's effort against Medicare), to produce material countering the boycott. The gist of this campaign was that Chavez was being kept alive not so much by fuzzy-minded urban liberals boycotting grapes as by the greed of the AFL-CIO. Organized labor, according to this argument, had developed with age a severe case of varicose veins. While union membership continues to increase, the percentage of the population it represents decreases; there are fewer blue-collar workers, while white-collar workers are difficult to organize. Therefore the attraction of the nation's two million farm workers. UFWOC's dues are $3.50 a month, $7,000,000 a month if all two million workers are organized, $84,000,000 a year in the coffers of the AFL-CIO.

The beauty of such an argument is that innuendo does the work. But beyond the rhetoric, the growers were hurting. In New York, the world's largest market for table grapes, the boycott had cut the number of railroad boxcars unloaded in 1968 by a third; in Baltimore by nearly half. Many supermarket chains simply refused to carry California table grapes. In some instances, their motives were not altogether humanitarian. Union locals hinted broadly that, unless grapes came out of the stores, butchers and retail clerks would not cross UFWOC picket lines. Not long after the NLRB put a stop to such intimidation, fires were discovered in at least three New York A&Ps, cause in each instance unknown, although it was the considered opinion of the city's chief fire marshal that the boycott might have been a contributing factor. If a message was intended, it was received loud and clear. Across the country, grapes disappeared from the shelves.

The success of the boycott was enhanced by the uncertain state of the economy. Agriculture is a carnivorous business. Farmers feed on the misfortunes of their own; a disastrous frost in Arizona profits the growers of the same crop in the San Joaquin Valley. Crops are subject to roller-coaster fluctuations. The large harvest in 1969 depressed grape prices; the short crop in 1970 was more susceptible to strike and boycott. What the Nixon economists called a "seasonal adjustment" was a full-fledged recession and it was bleeding growers as it bled the rest of the country. The grape business was plagued by bankruptcies. Money was short, interest was high. Farmers were paying 9 and 10 percent for bank loans to start their crop; the shakier the grower's finances, the higher the interest he had to pay.

His predicament, however, was not designed to elicit much sympathy. Though growers might claim that they were getting stuck with someone else's check, the bill for a hundred years of often malevolent paternalism was now being called in. If that bill seemed inflated by a surcharge of moral indignation, one had only to remember how long past due it was. The growers had finally run afoul of the times. Halfway around the world, the nation was involved in a hated, pernicious war. It was a house divided, doubting itself, forced to examine charges that it was racist both at home and abroad. It was difficult to conjure up a charismatic grower; the words just did not adhere. A man with thousands of acres worth millions of dollars simply did not have the emotional appeal of a faceless crowd of brown-skinned men, women and children eking out a fetid existence, crammed into substandard housing, isolated by language and custom from a community that scorned them. Never mind that the grower was mortgaged to the eyeballs, strangling on 9 and 10 percent interest payments. In the summer of 1970, high interest rates did not sing like food stamps.

The first break came from a handful of growers in the Coachella Valley. They signed with UFWOC and boxes of their grapes, adorned with the union's black-eagle emblem, were exempted from the boycott. After the May harvest, the union growers found their grapes bringing 25¢ to $1 more per box than those of the boycotted farmers. The lesson was not lost on the Delano growers. Late one night in July, John Guimarra, Jr., made his move. From a pay telephone at a dance he was attending in Bakersfield, he called Jerome Cohen, UFWOC's lawyer, in Delano. He told Cohen that he was flying out of Bakersfield at nine the next morning on a mission that could have "drastic consequences" for the grape industry; he asked if he could meet with Chavez before he made this "major move." (He did not mention what this major move was, and when I asked him six months later, he still refused. "It's water under the bridge," Guimarra said.) Cohen got hold of Chavez, who had been making a speech that night in San Rafael. Tired though he was, Chavez agreed to an immediate meeting. At 2 A.M., the parties met at the

Stardust Motel in Delano and negotiated for the next six hours. Early Sunday morning they had reached tentative agreement. That same day Guimarra presented the agreement to the other Delano growers. I asked him how they had reacted. "Well, we had already stuck our foot in the water and I guess they thought it wouldn't hurt to see where negotiations led," Guimarra recalled. "But I wouldn't say any of the growers jumped up and down and said, 'Gee, hand me a contract.'"

Three days later, the twenty-six Delano growers signed a contract with UFWOC. The agreement called for $1.80 an hour, plus 20¢ per box incentive pay the first year, escalating to $2.10 an hour the third. Outwardly there was a sense of collective relief that after five years hostilities had ended. But there were still some residual hard feelings. Most centered on the stipulation that Chavez would supply every worker from a union hiring hall. Privately there was not a grower in Delano who thought UFWOC could deliver a full crew in time for the harvest. (The question was academic that first summer, as the harvest was already underway when the contract was signed and growers had full crews in the fields.) If UFWOC has not supplied enough workers by the start of the harvest, the contract allows growers to hire pickers on their own. But farmers fear that if they are forced to wait that long, their crops might start to rot. I asked John Guimarra, Jr., what action he would take in this eventuality.

"I'll burn your book," he replied without hesitation.*

∾

THAT WAS THE end of the grape strike. The lettuce strike in Salinas had already begun. Even as the conflict in Delano was winding down, Chavez had informed the lettuce growers in the Salinas Valley that he wished to organize their field workers. With almost indecent haste, the Salinas growers responded by soliciting the Teamsters, and twenty-four hours before the Delano contract was

---

* The book referred to is *Delano: The Story of the California Grape Strike*, which was published in 1967. This piece appeared as an afterword in a new edition of that book, published in 1971.

signed, they announced an agreement allowing the Teamsters to represent their field hands. Whatever the Teamsters were, what they were not was a union run by a radical Mexican mystic, and to the growers this was a most seductive enticement.

Since Chavez and the Teamsters had agreed three years before not to poach on each other's territory, the Salinas announcement was tantamount to a declaration of war. Late in August, Chavez struck the Salinas ranches. On the first day of the strike, between five and seven thousand workers walked off the job. The mood at UFWOC was euphoric. Never before had Chavez been able to pull workers out of the fields in any substantial numbers. The effect on the growers was immediate. Railroad carloads of lettuce shipped out of Salinas slipped from a normal 250 a day to as low as thirty-five. In some areas the wholesale price of lettuce soared from $1.75 a crate to $6; in Los Angeles supermarkets the retail price rose 10¢ a head in a single day. Grower losses mounted to $500,000 a day. The numbers were enough to convince a few of the larger Salinas growers to sign with UFWOC. "The Teamsters had our contract," said a spokesman for Inter-Harvest, a subsidiary of United Fruit, "but UFWOC had our workers."

The majority of Salinas growers did not see it that way. In vain they tried to get an injunction against the strike, claiming they were the victims of a jurisdictional dispute between UFWOC and the Teamsters; a judge in Santa Maria ruled against the injunction on the grounds that there was insufficient evidence that the Teamsters actually had the support of the field workers. The Teamsters seemed to be schizophrenic about the whole thing. On the one hand, Teamster antipathy toward Chavez and his "smelly hippies" had long been documented; on the other, the Teamsters could count. The Teamster solution was to renege on its contracts with the growers and turn them over to UFWOC. The growers would have none of it; a marriage of convenience was still a marriage. It was an unprecedented situation—management holding to the sanctity of contracts for workers the union no longer wanted to represent. Not quite sure what to do, the Teamsters bent a few UFWOC skulls to keep in practice and talked a lot about law and order. Nor did the uncompromising majesty of the law make it seem any less droll. Less than three weeks after the Santa Maria decision, a judge in Salinas, ruling on virtually the same evidence, issued a permanent injunction against all UFWOC strike activity in the Salinas area.

Chavez's response was immediate. Hardly were his picket lines withdrawn than he ordered a nationwide boycott of all non-UFWOC lettuce in California and Arizona. Almost predictably hewing to the script of Delano, the first two growers to yield, Freshpict and Pic 'N Pac, were both subsidiaries of large consumer corporations (Purex and S. S. Pierce) concerned that a boycott might spread to their more visible packaged products on supermarket shelves. The other Salinas growers had no such concerns and, except for one defection, stood firm. In Salinas's least dreary restaurant, Caesar Salad was renamed Salinas Valley Salad (it was an affront to the palate under any name). Ironically, Chavez's most prominent foe in Salinas, Bud Antle, Inc., was not really a particular UFWOC target. In a situation almost unique in California, Bud Antle's lettuce workers had been under union contract since 1961. Not that Bud Antle's intentions in allowing the organization of their field workers were entirely altruistic. Nine years before, the Teamsters had lent the financially straitened company $1,000,000 and the quid pro quo was a union contract for, among others, the lettuce workers. Though he frequently alluded to the Teamster loan, Chavez had no real wish to challenge the contract. But in an across-the-board boycott, things get broken; it was the classic case of the omelet and the egg.

The boycott against Bud Antle landed Chavez in jail for the first time in his organizing career. Under court injunction to end the boycott against the firm, Chavez refused. Three weeks before Christmas 1970, a Salinas judge ordered him into jail until he did so. However legally impeccable the court order, the jailing of Chavez backfired emotionally against the growers. In plain terms, the lettuce boycott had been up to this point a flop. Five grinding years of strike and boycott against the grape growers had simply run down the batteries of Chavez's supporters. His incarceration, however, was an instant recharge. A vigil was set up outside the Salinas county jail. The star names pilgrimaged to Salinas, led by the widows Coretta King and Ethel Kennedy, whose very presence was a stark reminder of those insane few months in 1968 when martyrdom seemed the only resolution to the nation's problems. On Christmas Eve, Chavez was released from jail pending a hearing on his case by a higher tribunal. But his jailing had given the boycott so much momentum that the Teamsters announced a boycott of their own, a boycott against the loading or unloading of any UFWOC-picked crops, at least until UFWOC called off its campaign against Bud Antle. The permutations seemed limitless. It was as if the lessons of Delano were written on the wind.

～

FACTS:

There are five million Mexican Americans in the United States. They are the nation's second largest minority. Almost 90 percent live in the five southwestern states of Arizona, California, Colorado, New Mexico and Texas. They comprise 15 percent of the population of Texas, 10 percent of the population of California and 28 percent of the population of New Mexico. More than one-third live in "official" poverty on incomes of less than $3,000 a year. Their birth rate is twice the national average, and the mortality rate for infants less than a year old is twice that of Anglos. Their median age is eleven years less than that of the Anglo; 42 percent of the Mexican-American population is under the age of fifteen. They average approximately eight years of schooling, four years fewer than the Anglos. Half of all Mexican Americans who enter high school drop out before finishing. The Mexican-American unemployment rate is twice that of Anglos, and almost 80 percent work at unskilled or semiskilled jobs.

～

THE HARVEST FROM the grape strike is like a short crop in a good year. Because of Chavez and Chavez alone, it is now possible to predict that all farm labor will be organized in the foreseeable future. Perhaps not by UFWOC. Old habits die hard, and for growers a farm union is hard enough to swallow without Chavez as a chaser. Most would cheerfully sign their workers over to something like the International Ladies Garment Workers Union if they thought it was the only way to thwart him. Even grower associations are now calling for farm labor to come under the umbrella of the National Labor Relations Board, and the sound of their platitudes is heard in the land: "It is time that farm workers be allowed to join the 1970s. Too long have they been cut off from the mainstream of the American labor movement." (Applause.) Six years ago this might have been enough to buy off a strike. Not now. Success has made Chavez very sophisticated and he is in no hurry to embrace the NLRB. As amended by the Taft-Hartley and Landrum-Griffin acts, the NLRB now prohibits the two major weapons in Chavez's arsenal—secondary boycotts and organizational strikes. He is very much aware that since the passage of these two amendments no large group of unskilled labor has been organized. Until adjustments can be made, inclusion under the NLRB is a lollipop Chavez would just as soon forswear.

And yet beyond UFWOC's demonstrable success, beyond its cool reading of the times, there is little room for euphoria. The nagging thought persists that the strike in Delano was irrelevant except as an abstraction. Victory there was like administering sedatives to a terminal cancer patient, a mercy, a kindness, death-easing rather than life-saving, a victory finally important less for its fulfilled intentions than for what, unintended, it presaged. Higher wages, a fund of new members, greater independence from management—these traditional benchmarks of labor achievement do not really apply to Delano. In the narrowest sense, a union of farm workers can only lighten its members' burden of misery. The figures are simply too relentless. Nearly 700,000 workers earned wages in California's fields and vineyards in 1967 (the most recent year for which comprehensive statistics are available), and while they earned $1.78 an hour on the farm, their average annual income for *all* work, both farm and nonfarm, was only $1,709. And though the 700,000 included foremen, crew leaders, supervisors and other year-round employees, only 31,000 earned as much as $5,000 that year in farm work.

There is simply too little future in farm work. While farms grow bigger and productivity increases, the number of farm workers steadily declines. Four percent of California's growers own nearly 70 percent of the farm land; eight percent hire over 70 percent of the farm labor. Over the last twenty-five years, the number of farms in California has been cut by more than half. Cities roll past the suburbs into the country, swallowing up small farms that historically soaked up the glut in the labor market, farms far more valuable to the grower as subdivisions than they ever were as acreage. Two years ago, less than two percent of the wine grapes in Fresno County were harvested by machine; the estimate for 1971 is more than 30 percent. In three years the Fresno County Economic Opportunities Commission predicts that 65 percent of the wine and raisin grapes in the San Joaquin Valley will be picked mechanically. Even table grapes could be picked automatically were consumers willing to buy them in boxes, like strawberries, instead of insisting on the esthetic appeal of bunches. It is estimated that mechanical pickers will cost Fresno County farm workers nearly $2 million in wages during 1971 and that by 1973 some 4,500 heads of families will be displaced by machines.

Growers recite these figures as if they were graven on stone. There is little doubt that Chavez has speeded up the wheels of automation, but the implication is that no one ever dreamed of it until he came along; indeed that, were it not for Chavez, no machine ever developed, no matter how economical, could ever separate a grower from his beloved workers. Engagingly enough, the growers really believe it.

~

THE CURIOUS THING about Cesar Chavez is that he is as little understood by those who would canonize him as by those who would condemn him. To the saint-makers, Chavez seemed the perfect candidate. His crusade was devoid of the ambiguities of urban conflict. With the farm workers there were no nagging worries about the mugging down the block, the rape across the street, the car boosted in front of the house. It was a cause populated by simple Mexican peasants with noble agrarian ideas, not by surly unemployables with low IQs and Molotov cocktails.

All that is missing in this fancy is any apprehension of where the real importance of Cesar Chavez lies. The saintly virtues he had aplenty; it is doubtful that the media would have been attracted to him were it not for those virtues, and without the attention of the media the strike could not have survived. But Chavez also had the virtues of the labor leader, less applauded publicly perhaps, but no less admirable in the rough going—a will of iron, a certain deviousness, an ability to hang tough in the clinches. Together these twin disciplines kept what often seemed a hopeless struggle alive for six years, six years that kindled an idea that made the idealized nuances of Delano pale by comparison.

For the ultimate impact of Delano will be felt not so much on the farm as in the city. In the vineyards, Chavez fertilized an ethnic and cultural pride ungerminated for generations, but it was in the barrio that this new sense of racial identity flourished as if in a hothouse. Once four-fifths of the Mexican-American population lived in the rural outback, but as the farm worker became a technological as well as a social victim, his young deserted the hoe for the car wash. Today that same four-fifths float through the urban barrio like travelers without passports, politically impoverished, spiritually disenfranchised. State and municipal governments have so carefully charted the electoral maps that it is impossible for a Mexican American to get elected without Anglo sufferance. California's only Mexican-American congressman depends on Anglo suburbs for more than half his support and in the state legislature the gerrymandering is even more effective; there was in 1971 only one Mexican assemblyman and no state senator. It was a system that placed high premium on the Tio Taco, or Uncle Tom.

But since Delano there is an impatience in the barrio with the old formulas and old deals and old alliances, a dissatisfaction with a diet of crumbs, a mood—more than surly, if not yet militant—undermining and finally beginning to crack the ghetto's historic inertia. Drive down Whittier Boulevard in East Los Angeles, a slum in the Southern California manner, street after street of tiny bungalows and parched lawns and old cars, a grid of monotony. The signs are unnoticed at first, catching the eye only after the second or third sighting, whitewashed on fences and abandoned storefronts, the paint splattered and uneven, signs painted on the run in the dark of night, *"Es mejor morir de pie que vivir de rodillas"*—"Better to die standing than live on your knees." The words are those of

Emiliano Zapata, but the spirit that wrote them there was fired by Cesar Chavez.

It is with the young that the new mood is most prevalent. On the streets they sell orange posters that say nothing more than *"La Raza."* At Lincoln High School in East Los Angeles, students walked out on strike as a protest against overcrowding and neglect, a strike that challenged the passivity of their elders as much as it did the apathy of the Anglo community. Go to any protest meeting in East Los Angeles and the doors are guarded by an indigenous force of young vigilantes called the Brown Berets. ("We needed a gimmick, we needed a name," one of their leaders told a reporter from *Time.* "We thought of calling ourselves the Young Citizens for Community Action, but that didn't sound right. We tried Young Chicanos, but that didn't work either. We thought of wearing big sombreros, but we figured people would just laugh at us. So we hit on the beret and someone said, 'Why not the Brown Berets?' And it clicked with all of us.")

The pride that Chavez helped awaken took on a different tone in the barrio than in the vineyards. The farm workers' movement was essentially nonviolent, an effort based on keeping and exhibiting the moral advantage. But in East Los Angeles today the tendency is to pick up life's lessons less from Gandhi than from the blacks. Traditionally, brown and black have been hostile, each grappling for that single spot on the bottom rung of the social ladder. To the Mexican American the Anglo world held out the bangle of assimilation, a bribe to the few that kept the many docile. Denied to blacks, assimilation for years robbed the Chicano community of a nucleus of leadership. Today the forfeiture of this newly acquired cultural awareness seems to the young Chicano a prohibitive price to pay. The new courses in social bribery are taught by the blacks.

What the barrio is learning from the blacks is the political sex appeal of violence. Three times in the past year, East Los Angeles has erupted. The body count is still low, less than the fingers on one hand, hardly enough to merit a headline outside Los Angeles County. The official riposte is a call for more law and order. The charges of police brutality clash with the accusations of outside agitation. But beyond the rhetoric there is new attention focused on the ghetto. The vocabulary of the dispossessed is threat and riot, the Esperanto of a crisis-reacting society, italicizing the poverty and discrimination and social deprivation in a way that no funded study or government commission ever could.

Like Malcolm X and Martin Luther King, Jr., Cesar Chavez stands astride history less for what he accomplished than for what he is. Like them, he has forged "in the smithy of his soul," in Joyce's phrase, the "uncreated conscience" of a people. He is the manifestation of *la raza,* less the saint his admirers make him out to be than a moral obsessive, drilling into the decay of a system that has become a mortuary of hopes. We are a nation with a notoriously short attention span, needing saints but building them into a planned obsolescence. The man who survives this curse of instant apotheosis becomes, like Cesar Chavez, acutely uncomfortable to have around, a visionary ever demanding our enlistment as he tries to force the stronghold of forgotten possibilities. He demands only that we be better. It is a simple demand, and a terrifying one.

～

THERE IS SOMETHING exquisite about rural California in January. It is the month of the rains, a clear, cold, almost refrigerated rain, invigorating as an amphetamine. The hills are so green they seem carpeted in Astroturf. Peacocks preen by the side of the road. The wail of a train whistle, almost unheard since childhood, pierces the valley. In Delano there was a semblance of peace. On Main Street the bumper stickers that once said "Boycott Grapes" or "Buy California Grapes" were faded and peeling, like scar tissue from a fight everyone said they wished to forget. Out past the Voice of America transmitters on the Garces Highway, hard by the municipal dump, UFWOC has a new headquarters complex called Forty Acres. There is a gas station and an office and miscellaneous dilapidated buildings. What struck me most was how quiet it was. Underneath that vast empty sky at Forty Acres, even the lettuce strike was discussed with as little fervor as the weather. It was as if after five years of continuous combat everyone had come down with an attack of rhetorical laryngitis. Downtown there is talk of diversification, of attracting industry to Delano, of an industrial park. I was told about the labor pool—20 percent unemployment in the winter—and how a one-crop town needs to get into other things. The Chamber of Commerce and the city council have established the Delano Economic Expansion Project (DEEP) to lure industry into the area, and hired the former manager of the Hanford (California) Chamber of Commerce to head it up. "One thing Cesar Chavez did for us," he says. "In Hanford I spent a whole lot of time trying to get people to know where Hanford is. In Delano I haven't had to do that." There was one other thing I noticed in Delano. I didn't know if it was a DEEP project or not. The sign on the outskirts of town used to say, "Hungry? Tired? Car Trouble? Need Gas? Stop in Delano." There is a new sign now out on Highway 99. It says, "DELANO. WELCOME ANY-TIME."

ON THE KENNEDYS

[1 9 8 2]

THERE ARE NO new facts about the Kennedys, only new attitudes, a literature that, like the automobile industry, puts new
bodies on old chassis. First there were those huge, polluting gas guz-
zlers, the Sorensen and the Schlesinger, like Chrysler and Ford, now
discredited and nearly bankrupt: useful only insofar as their parts
can be cannibalized for nuts and bolts, their gushy excesses, like tail-
fins, always good for sport. Conspiracy is a small but durable seller,
retooled every year or so. And these days revisionism is the hottest
item off the assembly line, each model sleek and economical, with
a racy name, "Destroyer," say, or "Marauder."

In *The Kennedy Imprisonment*, Garry Wills flashes his Marauder
across the high plains of Camelot like a night rider—burn the
barn, destroy the crops, take no prisoners, scorch the myth as if it
were the earth itself. The myth of the Kennedys—and the hold—
was always the hold of the renegade rich, out there on the frontier
beyond accountability. There are no legends about the Duponts; the
legends are about Howard Hughes. Nor do the Rockefellers quicken
the pulse the way the Kennedys did, and do. The Rockefellers only
have money and a foundation and a museum and a bank and suits
with vests. Nelson Rockefeller supervised Diego Rivera at the

beginning of his working life and at the end was supervising expensive reproductions; ironic but not the stuff of legend.

～

THE KENNEDYS SHARED only one attitude with the traditional American rich: they assumed that the possessors of great wealth constituted a real if unacknowledged—this is a republic, after all—nobility. With the aid of the "cool media" and a gut understanding of the power that media could wield, they pushed this proposition one step further: the Kennedys were not merely noble, they were regal, and by shrewd manipulation of the media, the divine right of their sovereignty was acknowledged. They knighted what Wills calls "honorary Kennedys," and we remember the names and MOSs of these troops as we remember second cousins and family retainers—Red Fay and Kenny O'Donnell and Larry O'Brien and Dave Powers and Joe Gargan and Paul Markham, the gutter Irish NCOs who told the jokes and kept the grunts in step and did the dirty work and cleaned up afterward. The officers' mess was positively Dickensian in the breadth of its arriviste and aristocratic pretensions—the Bundys and the Rostows and McNamara and Dillon and Rusk and poor Adlai Stevenson and poor Chester Bowles. Even the gazeteers of this brigade carried colors. Joseph Alsop was William Howard Russell and Theodore H. White brevetted himself Sir Thomas Malory; Arthur Schlesinger prowled around the perimeter of the encampment like Mr. Samgrass in *Brideshead Revisited*.

Then Dallas, then the kitchen of the Ambassador Hotel in Los Angeles. The myth was lit into an eternal flame and honorary Kennedys were anointed its keepers. The thousand days of John Kennedy became Camelot, the eighty-five days of Robert Kennedy's last campaign the end of promise. Those early hagiographies, born of grief and saturated with blood, had all the elements of pop mythology. Charisma became commitment and the Kennedys' renewal each election season with a different set of values, a new set of priorities, was turned into a virtue—the pragmatic virtue of flexibility, the flexible virtue of pragmatism. There were no failures in Camelot, no warts spotted by the valet biographers.

Garry Wills buys none of it. His John Kennedy looks like the Elephant Man—a liar, a cheat, a philanderer, a war lover who waged war less successfully abroad than against the very government he was elected to lead. In Wills's view, John Kennedy was the first Green Beret—a force Kennedy commissioned—and the enemy he sought to destabilize, to terminate with extreme prejudice, was his own bureaucracy. Command was fun, power exhilarating, throw caution to the wind. Vietnam was one of the hangovers produced by this heady wine.

It was a style of leadership to which John Kennedy came naturally. He was his father's son, and that was but the first cell of the many prisons in which Wills finds the Kennedys incarcerated. Joseph P. Kennedy was a randy raider, Harvard-educated but always a parvenu on-the-make mick to classmates who booed him, this emissary from Franklin Roosevelt, at their twenty-fifth reunion. He was not so much a businessman as a predator of other men's businesses. Always traveling fast, traveling light, he struck and moved on and struck again. The running of his various enterprises was not for him or his sons; that was the chore of flunkies and sons-in-law. Joseph Kennedy had "no ideology but achievement," and he created "a kind of space platform out of his own career, one from which the children could fly out to their own achievements and come back for refueling."

The raider collected women as he collected companies. Rose Kennedy visited his bed often enough to produce nine children and suffered gracefully when her husband invited Gloria Swanson, for years the official mistress, and other more casual conquests to Hyannis Port, and Swanson even on a liner to Europe with him and Rose. Rose Kennedy offered up, as the Catholic women of her generation were taught to do, every mortification and every humiliation as an opportunity for a plenary indulgence, markers against her time in purgatory. Her husband made passes at the daughters of his friends and at the friends of his daughters and used Arthur Krock, the conservative and seemingly punctilious resident oracle of *The New York Times*, as an ex-officio pimp who stashed discarded Kennedy girl friends in the various newsrooms of Washington.

"What are you, our staff procurer?" a Washington newspaper editor asked Krock in 1941, and it took Krock nearly thirty years to
realize that was indeed his role, both literally and figuratively, with
his putative friends, Joseph Kennedy & Sons.

⮑

FOR MOST AMERICAN Irish Catholics, the only real sins are sins of
the flesh, but to Joseph Kennedy that notion was parochial school nun
stuff, part of the baggage of Catholic guilt and ethnicity he jetti-
soned early. The Kennedys, as seen by Wills, were only "semi-Irish"
and superficially Catholic. They were citizens of the world of
celebrity and touched down in Palm Beach and Hyannis Port and
logged in safari time on the zebra stripes of El Morocco. Not for them
harp Boston politicians "with outlandish nicknames like Knocko
and Onions." Massachusetts was where they were registered to vote
and Mass where they were photographed with Cardinal Cushing.

The Kennedys were mid-Atlantic people before the term was
invented, "semi-English," as Wills calls them. Father and (especially) children were absolutely moony over the virtues of the English aristocracy in that way that only rich Americans can get. John
Kennedy went to England to study under Harold Laski and said that
David Ormsby-Gore was the brightest man he'd ever met, a statement that makes him sound like Sebastian Flyte's teddy bear. The
very model of the politician he aspired to be was Queen Victoria's
Whig prime minister, Lord Melbourne—languid, horny, a man of
state sustained by family and contemptuous of outsiders—and he
was equally taken by John Buchan's idea of "adventurer-aristocrats,
who could save the people by guiding them, sometimes without
their knowledge." Democracy in spite of the people, in other words.
Wills pinpoints the carcinoma inherent in this hubris:

> The world of aristocratic rakes like Melbourne has an underside, the
> dark area where T.E. Lawrence moves, and Richard Hannay, and
> James Bond, all the Green Berets and gentlemen spies of the CIA.
> Presiding over this potentially dangerous world is the honor of the
> aristocrats, their code of national service.

It is John Kennedy's honor, from those earliest days in England, that Wills finds suspect. If he was a prisoner of family, he was also a prisoner of image, one maximum-security slammer leading inevitably to another. "The whole point of being a Kennedy, in the father's scheme of things, was to look good." To make John Kennedy look good, his father saw to it that *Why England Slept* was published. John Kennedy's tutor thought it "much too long, wordy, repetitious," its "fundamental premise never analysed," but what did he know, he had never met a payroll. Joseph Kennedy asked the family ponce, Arthur Krock, to rewrite and retitle the book, himself supplied a hodgepodge of charts and statistics that never actually quite made any point, and got Henry Luce to attach a foreword. No stranger to this game himself, Luce saw that a book by the son of Franklin Roosevelt's ambassador to the Court of St. James offered a perfect opportunity both to push Wendell Willkie and to take a swat at Roosevelt. Only Harold Laski seemed to see through the whole charade. "In a good university, half a hundred seniors do books like this as part of their normal work in their final year," he wrote Joseph Kennedy. "I don't honestly think any publisher would have looked at that book of Jack's if he had not been your son, and if you had not been ambassador."

Perhaps because of his time in the movie business, Joseph Kennedy seemed to share the Jack Warner view that writers were "schmucks with Underwoods," and that there would always be schmucks—if not Harold Laski—available to make his boys look good. It was not enough that John Kennedy exhibited rare physical courage when PT-109 went down and he saved the life of one of his crew members. First John Hersey and then Robert Donovan buffed courage into heroism, both writers begging the essential question: how does a glorified speedboat get run over in the dark by a heavier, slower and more ponderous enemy destroyer? John Kennedy's version was that the 109 was "attempting a torpedo attack," but the Navy's medal and citations board would not swallow that and rewrote the citation for his Navy and Marine Corps Medal, changing the "attack" into a simple "collision," adding that he had "contributed to the saving of several lives." Cliff

Robertson played the part in the movie; John Kennedy's personal choice, Warren Beatty, turned it down.

~

NEXT TO ARTHUR KROCK, no writer ever made a Kennedy look better than the young Senator Kennedy's amanuensis and aide-de-camp, Theodore Sorensen. He had a way with words and (especially in *Kennedy*) a highly selective memory. Every Kennedy was a hero to this exemplary servant; he was Hudson to their Bellamys and he kept his trap shut. Joseph Kennedy thought books made the man—"You would be surprised how a book that really makes the grade with high-class people stands you in good stead for years to come," the ambassador once said—and he was not choosy about who wrote them as long as a son could claim authorship.

Thus *Profiles in Courage* was fabricated; "John F. Kennedy" was the nom de plume used by Sorensen and Georgetown historian Jules Davids, who "put [the book] together much like a major speech." This was well within the rules of political deceit and did not exceed them until Arthur Krock, turning one last trick for his favorite John, began to lobby for a Pulitzer Prize for the book and its alleged author, the senator from Massachusetts and seeker after the presidency. The Pulitzer judges chose Alpheus Mason's *Harlan Fiske Stone: Pillar of the Law* for the prize, but were overruled by the board, which—denying improper influence—awarded *Profiles in Courage* the laurel, one member of the Pulitzer board making the engaging claim that the board was swayed by his twelve-year-old grandson's enjoyment of the book, which presumably the lad liked better than *Harlan Fiske Stone*. "The incremental touches of glamour were always sought," Wills writes about this prisoner of image. "The unflattering notes were censored. The collision became an attack. . . . Reality was all a matter of rearranging appearances for the electorate."

In the Wills version, the lust for image meant a sentence in still another prison, that of charisma. John Kennedy, author/hero, the first president born in the twentieth century, had the junior line officer's contempt for the general staff, in particular for that ultimate staff officer, general of the Army Dwight David Eisenhower. Both as military man and as president, Eisenhower was the quintessential bureaucratic manager, a delegator of responsibilities, an advocate of caution who thought of crises in terms of—and on a scale with—the Normandy landings. His career was predicated on channels and chains of command, which gave him an intuitive grasp of bureaucracy and an inchoate respect for its procedures. It is a respect shared—hindsight, perhaps—by Wills, who finds bureaucracy the best governor against the imperial presidency.

The Kennedy concept of leadership was that of a commando leader (or a PT boat skipper, for that matter)—lightning strikes against the forces of darkness, be those forces poverty, Big Steel, Fidel Castro, or a bunch of obstreperous slopes in the jungles of Indochina. It was this very impetuosity that the cumbersome bureaucracy tended to thwart, and John Kennedy put that bureaucracy on his administration's hit list: outflank the bureaucrats, seal them off from the schemes of his government, operate with mobile tactical squads recruited by and answerable only to the oval office.* Here was charisma in action, charisma in the true, rather than the vulgar, sense of the word. "Insofar as the charismatic leader asserts an entirely personal authority," Wills says, "he *delegitimates* the traditional and legal authorities." The Green Berets, the Peace Corps, military advisers to Vietnam—there seemed no understanding in Camelot that these romantic Chindits, operating outside regular channels of command, would only create new bureaucracies of their own, outlaw tumors which by their very dependence on the host body must ultimately metastasize and adhere to the older bureaucracy.

∼

KENNEDY CHARISMA WAS the cult of personality carried, in a democracy, to the exosphere: the president as a strong leader in the Buchan tradition, "willing to administer timely jolts to the people as a form of therapy." The timely jolt was often a timely goose. There was a high butch about that Kennedy administration, an obsession with metaphorical genitalia. Balls, ballsy, ballsiness, nuts—these were the calibrations of worth, and often of wit. "A Stevenson

---

* One of the lesser legacies of Camelot is the upper-casing of "Oval Office." Sorensen blamed the Nixon crowd for this, but Wills points out that Theodore White began capitalizing the office in *The Making of the President, 1960.*

with balls," Joseph Alsop called John Kennedy, and the *mot* was fon-
dled all the way into the oval office. In turn, John Kennedy dismissed
the allegedly timid as "holding their nuts" or "grabbing their balls."

The problem with such ballsiness was a constant need to thrust.
Crisis was a way to milk the gland, sixteen crises by Theodore
Sorensen's gleeful count, in the administration's first eight months
alone. It is this appetite for crisis, particularly the taste for foreign
adventurism, that draws Wills's most withering scrutiny. There was
of course the Bay of Pigs, a legacy from the Eisenhower administration, the hagiographers have advised us, as if only an ingrate
would turn down such an inheritance. "The truth is," Wills writes,

> that Kennedy went ahead with the Cuban action, not to complete
> what he inherited from Eisenhower, but to mark his difference
> from Eisenhower. . . . He would be bold where he accused Eisen-
> hower of timidity. . . .
>
> Kennedy was a prisoner of his own taste for crisis, for being in the
> midst of the action. . . . The growing size of the invasion army—
> 1,400 men—made the administration hostage to its own agents.
> Their visibility made them an "asset" that had to be used immedi-
> ately or moved in a way that would waste the asset. . . . Once again,
> acquiring a "capability" chained one to its use, so that decision
> became a kind of resignation to the inevitable. . . . Thus do options
> bind, making "freedom of maneuver" a straitjacket for the mind.

Wills believes, contrary to the conventional wisdom of the
hagiographers, that the failure of the Bay of Pigs invasion taught
John Kennedy nothing. Rather, John and Robert Kennedy were
confirmed in their perception of Fidel Castro as a dagger at the
throat. Getting rid of him seemed the administration's highest
priority. Secret select committees drew up plans and tables of
organization—Operation Mongoose and Task Force W and Special
Group Augmented and Special Group CI (for counter-
insurgency)—and with a nod and a wink from the highest echelons
of government the Mob was contacted about whacking Castro out.
(John Kennedy, Lyndon Johnson claimed, was running "a damn

Murder Incorporated in the Caribbean.") Castro knew what was going on and the missiles he imported from Russia were no more offensive, in the Wills version, than the secret war Washington was waging against him. The very fact of this secret war, Wills contends, punctures any pretense that John Kennedy acted with "restraint" during the Cuban missile crisis; instead the necessity of camouflaging his sordid and shadowy "guerrilla strategy" chained him to a policy of high-risk confrontation and bluster.

As with Cuba, so with Vietnam, war on an ad hoc, CI basis, "There was no reluctance to be 'drawn into' Vietnam," Wills writes. "We welcomed it as a laboratory to test our troops. . . . There was no dove position in Kennedy's administration that stood for withdrawal. The doves were for winning the war by gentler methods." Crisis, always crisis, crisis courted, crisis incited: crisis was finally the syphilis of Camelot, and it has infected, in Wills's telling, every subsequent president. "Over and over in our recent history Presidents have claimed they had to act tough in order to *disarm* those demanding that they act tough. The only way to become a peacemaker is first to disarm the warmakers by making a little successful war."

~

WILLS'S CASE AGAINST the Kennedys is supple and elegant, an extended essay rather than history, and therefore not overburdened by any cargo of facts that might shift and rock the tidy line of argument. He is often bracingly meanspirited, about Eugene McCarthy ("an interesting study in the pride of people trained to embrace humility"), who once stiffed him with a check at Elaine's (dinner for two, plus brandy)—an impolitic thing to do to a writer—and about the more onanistic of the toady courtiers, about Theodore White, who seemed to find sanctifying grace in the Kennedy presence, about Arthur Schlesinger, presented as a tame chaplain ever ready to offer absolution to his mentors from the confessional of history. In the proliferation of honorary Kennedys, layer upon layer around each brother, Wills shrewdly finds a bloated and largely ineffective bureaucracy of sycophants, liabilities where once they were a source of strength, "too many of them now and too few real

Kennedys." It was this bureaucracy that sprang into action after Chappaquiddick, crisis managers who managed the solution that scarred the protagonist.

Wills's John Kennedy is a horror, more Picture than Dorian Gray, a president who "did not so much elevate the office as cripple those who held it after him. . . . Inheriting a delegitimated set of procedures, they were compelled to go outside the procedures too—further delegitimating the office they held." About Robert Kennedy, Wills is ambivalent; in him Wills sees what might have been had he not been his brother's brother, yet had he been the first of the line, would Robert Kennedy ever have been anything more than the nasty piece of work who cozied up to Senator Joseph McCarthy? Toward Edward Kennedy, Wills is patronizing, seeing in him a boozily effective senator condemned to be last keeper of the flame, his life "a permanent floating Irish wake," sorting out friends "according to which brother they accompanied to meet his killer."

The problem with revisionism, however, is that it is too often the mirror image of hagiography, a faith with an orthodoxy of its own. For all its many virtues, *The Kennedy Imprisonment* is ultimately unsatisfying, brought down less by its attitude toward the Kennedys than by the Jesuitical rigidity of its premise, its narrative. Narrative is arbitrary and tendentious, useful to the historian only insofar as it throws people and events into an original perspective or relief. The notion of the Kennedys as prisoners—prisoners of legend, prisoners of sex, of family, of image, of charisma, of power— is a romantic idea, a novelist's conceit that Norman Mailer first tried out in *An American Dream*. Mailer had it all and he had it first—the Cardinal and the girls and the Mob and the flunkies and the pet columnists and the spooks and the wartime heroics; his Stephen Rojak was a true prisoner of celebrity.

⌣

IT IS NOT just that this landscape has already been strip-mined. Part of the fascination with the Kennedys has always been prurient, and Wills is not exempt. The Kennedy administration was sexy, and its sexiness as much as its policies was discussed by the huge army of the knowing. The girls of the thousand days fueled the fantasies of the knowing: Angie Dickinson, Marilyn Monroe, Judith Campbell Exner, who was on loan from Momo Giancana. Wills has a seminarian's interest in the Kennedy's sexual imperialism. For all his excursions into Montaigne and Chesterton, for all the allusions to Carlyle and Bagehot, it is Mrs. Exner's biography that seems to excite him, and the endless erections and the girls crossed off a list like things to do.

Wills uses Mrs. Exner (who noted that John Kennedy, because of his back, could only perform in the missionary position, with his partner the missionary) and Burton Hersh (whose book Wills never troubles to identify by title) and Mr. and Mrs. Clay Blair the way Mailer used Maurice Zolotow in *Marilyn*—as producers of factoids he can alchemize into meditations. Thus Robert Kennedy could not halt J. Edgar Hoover's crusade against Martin Luther King because Hoover might release information the FBI director had gathered about a John Kennedy bedmate, early in World War II, with Nazi connections. Thus Robert Kennedy could not run forcefully, in 1968, against Lyndon Johnson because Hoover and Johnson because Hoover and Johnson knew all about Mrs. Exner and that "damn Murder Incorporated in the Caribbean" and might use it.

Tumescence as the arbiter of national policy is the plot machinery of trash novels. The imposition of this colorful and vulgar narrative finally makes Wills a prisoner of his own premise, and his book as airless and claustrophobic as the slammers to which he has sentenced the Kennedys. There is no Kennedy success offered, not even an extenuating circumstance—not the test ban treaty, and certainly not Soviet expansionism in Berlin and Eastern Europe. John Kennedy, who did not write *Profiles in Courage*, is compared, to his disadvantage, to Janet Cooke, who made up her Pulitzer Prize–winning *Washington Post* feature. There was some dark purpose in inviting Pablo Casals to the White House; the so-called Kennedy cultural revolution only signified a need to exact an "abject profession of servility" from the Kennedy courtiers.

There is a whiff of the Inquisition here, a high whine from the pulpit of revisionism, a sermon on every stone, a lesson on every pin. Wills does not accept mitigating evidence and the only defense he allows is the collective sin of the Kennedy forebears. There is no point in arguing that charisma was not invented by John Kennedy, or political deception, no point in claiming that politicians have always acted out of an inflated self-importance and nations out of an unenlightened self-interest, often with beneficial results. This is a kangaroo court and the verdict was in the judge's pocket before the charges on the indictment were read. The end result is that *The Kennedy Imprisonment* becomes just another oddity in the automobile graveyard of Kennedyana, another model, like the Sorensen and the Schlesinger, future historians can scavenge for parts.

An American
Education

❧

I.

Q. *So my first question is, have you at any time been a member of the Communist Party?*

A. *I would like to answer that by saying that I am not a member of the Communist Party. However, as to the second part of your question I will stand on the fifth amendment and refuse to answer this question because I feel it could incriminate me.*

Q. *Well, actually I asked you only one question, whether you had ever been a member. You state you are not a member now?*

A. *Yes.*

Q. *When did you withdraw from the Communist Party?*

A. *I would have to decline, sir, on the same ground.*

Testimony before the House Committee on Un-American Activities,
Los Angeles, California, September 19, 1951

THE RICHARD AND Hinda Rosenthal Foundation Award is given every year by the American Academy and Institute of Arts and

Letters to one painter and to one "American work of fiction published during the preceding twelve months which, though not a
commercial success, is a considerable literary achievement." Over
the years, this prize has been awarded to novels by, among others,
Bernard Malamud, John Updike, Thomas Pynchon, Joyce Carol
Oates, and Diane Johnson.

The book chosen this year was *Famous All Over Town*, an ebulliently
funny first novel by Danny Santiago about an indomitable young Chicano growing up in the East Los Angeles barrio. The citation for the
Rosenthal Award, presented by John Kenneth Galbraith at the Academy and Institute's annual ceremonial last May 16th, read:

> *Famous All Over Town* adds luster to the enlarging literary genre of
> immigrant experience, of social, cultural and psychological
> threshold-crossing. . . . The durable young narrator spins across a
> multi-colored scene of crime, racial violence and extremes of dislo-
> cation, seeking and perhaps finding his own space. The exuberant
> mixes with the nerve-wracking; and throughout sly slippages of lan-
> guage enact a comedy on the theme of communication.

Danny Santiago did not show up at the ceremony to pick up the
$5,000 check that came with his Rosenthal Award. His absence was
in keeping with a long-established pattern of reclusiveness. There is
no photograph of Danny Santiago on the dust jacket of *Famous All
Over Town*. His agent and publisher have never laid eyes on him. Neither have they ever spoken to him on the telephone. Danny Santiago
claims to have no telephone. His address is a post office box in Pacific
Grove, California, a modest settlement on the Monterey peninsula.
All communication with Danny Santiago goes through this Pacific
Grove post office box. Danny Santiago refuses to be interviewed and
therefore did no publicity on behalf of *Famous All Over Town*. It is as
if Danny Santiago did not exist, and in a way he does not.

~

AS IT HAPPENS, I have known the author of *Famous All Over Town*
for the past eighteen years. He was my landlord when my wife and
I lived in Hollywood. Danny Santiago, strictly speaking, is not his

name. He is not a Chicano. Nor is he young. He is seventy-three years old. He is an Anglo. He is a graduate of Andover and Yale. He was the only member of the Yale class of 1933 to major in classical Greek. He is a prize-winning playwright. He is the co-author of the book of a hit musical comedy that played 654 performances on Broadway.

He was a screenwriter. He worked with Charlie Chaplin on *The Great Dictator*. He was a member of the Communist party. He worked as a volunteer social worker in East Los Angeles. He was one of 152 people named, on September 19, 1951, by a single witness before the House Committee on Un-American Activities, which was investigating Communist infiltration of the movie industry. He was subpoenaed to appear before the Committee. He declined under oath to say whether he had ever been a member of the Party, which he had, in fact, officially left three years earlier. He was blacklisted. He wrote monster pictures under an assumed name. He continued, along with his wife, to do volunteer work in East Los Angeles through the 1950s and into the Sixties. In 1968, he showed me some stories he had written about the neighborhood where he had been a social worker for so many years. As a result, I became a reluctant co-conspirator in his establishing the identity of Danny Santiago. His name is Daniel James. "Danny Santiago," of course, is Dan James translated into Spanish.

2.

Q. *Will you state your full name, Mr. James?*

A. *Daniel Lewis James.*

Q. *When and where were you born?*

A. *In Kansas City, Missouri, January 14, 1911.*

Testimony before the House Committee on Un-American Activities, Los Angeles, California, September 19, 1951

DAN JAMES'S GRANDFATHER was the first cousin of Frank and Jesse James. This grandfather went to Brown. His grandmother was in the first graduating class at Vassar. His father graduated from Yale. The Jameses of Kansas City were Midwestern gentry, importers and purveyors of fine china—Spode and Haviland—which they sold throughout the Midwest and the border states. The business—T.M. James & Sons—flourished. Daniel James's maternal grandfather purchased the home of a robber baron in Kansas City who had gone broke. I have seen a photograph of this house, which has long since been razed. It was a house of which Soames Forsyte might have approved, the house of a man of property, huge, in the convention of the day, dominated by a tower and punctuated by turrets and gables and cupolas and verandas, and it was in this house that Daniel James was born in 1911, his parents' only child.

D. L. JAMES, HIS father, was himself a Galsworthy creation, a businessman-aesthete in the manner of young Jolyon Forsyte, who painted. When he was not selling china, D. L. James was a playwright, his plays occasionally produced in stock and little theaters and foreign and amateur productions, at work at the time of his death in 1944 on a five-act play on his kinsman, Jesse James, about whom his feelings were ambivalent; he could not decide, according to his son, whether Jesse was more sinned against than sinning. "My father met anybody interesting who came to Kansas City," Daniel James says. "There was a little luncheon group of all the intellectuals in Kansas City, which numbered between nine and thirteen, I think."[1] Walter Hampden, the actor, was a friend of D. L. James, as were Karl Menninger and Thomas Hart Benton. Sinclair Lewis came to call.

It was only natural that from 1914 on D. L. James would spend his summers, with his wife and young son, in Carmel, California. A kind of *manqué* literary life could exist there for him as it did among the Kansas City intellectuals because in neither venue would it be put to the test of reality. There is a visual splendor about Carmel that is almost dreamlike, a soft-focus mirage of dunes and crashing white water and guano-washed rock islets and sheer cliffs falling into the surf and forests and meadows and clinging mists and wind-bent stands of cypress; the place tends to create a pervading, even comforting sense that no artistic accomplishment could ever match the landscape. Carmel was "an outpost of bohemia," Kevin Starr wrote in *Americans and the California Dream, 1850–1915*, a place of "artists, near artists and would-be artists." There was something moony about their attempt to merge art and nature. The California novelist Mary Austin (author of *The Ford*) wore long robes, rode a white horse, and worked in a tree house. It was the perfect spot to contemplate Jesse James as the fog rolled in and the years rolled by.

In 1918, D. L. James commissioned the project which was to be his monument. He had bought some property on a promontory near Point Lobos, a few miles from Carmel, and invited an acquaintance, the great California architect Charles Sumner Greene, to take a look at the site. Charles Greene was fifty, a partner with his brother Henry Mather Greene in the firm of Greene & Greene. The Greene brothers were craftsmen, virtuosos in wood and glass. For a quarter of a century in southern California, particularly in Pasadena, they had elevated the prairie house of Louis Sullivan into a mystical idea, the bungalow as a pre-Raphaelite vision. Stone was not their usual medium, but Charles Greene was so challenged by D. L. James's wind-buffeted point that two days later, unsolicited, he submitted a set of rough preliminary sketches for a stone house of such intricate design that it would be almost impossible to tell where cliff ended and house began. D. L. James immediately engaged him to begin work.

CONSTRUCTION TOOK FIVE years. Charles Greene was always on the site, supervising the quarrying, the cutting, and the laying of the stone, all of it indigenous to Carmel. The house is U-shaped, as if fitted to the contours of the point; its granite walls are two to three feet thick and the stones are set irregularly into the facade with broken faces exposed. The effect is medieval.

Although the house has only one story, it has several levels adhering to the topography of the cliff. The ceilings in the living room and library are sixteen feet high and every one of the house's seven rooms has an arched window opening onto the ocean a hundred feet or so below. Charles Greene revised his plans constantly, tearing out walls and replacing them if he were dissatisfied with the masonry or the workmanship. Costs escalated. In 1922, D. L. James finally called a halt before Charles Greene could complete an office on a lower elevation or put his own stamp on the interiors, as was his plan. The final cost, astonishingly, even allowing for the dollar's soundness in that period, was less than $90,000.

The house is called Seaward and it has been the home of Daniel James and his wife Lilith since his mother's final illness in 1968. It is a work of art, with all the baggage that phrase might carry. "This house was the answer to my father's dream of immortality, which he did not achieve in his writing," Daniel James says. The legacy would prove as well to be an enduring financial and psychological burden for the son. "Who am I to have this?" he asks rhetorically. "In my bad moments I've often felt all those tons of rock walls balancing on the back of my neck." Whatever he accomplished, he would always measure that accomplishment against the house.

3.

DAN JAMES IS six feet six inches tall. He was cross-eyed until he was fourteen, a condition that nourished a tendency toward introspection. He missed a year at Yale because of tuberculosis. He majored in Greek "because it was a different thing to do." He was informed more by Carmel than he was by either Yale or the mercantile Midwest. He knew Lincoln Steffens and Ella Winter and was exposed to what Kevin Starr has called Carmel's "loquacious socialism" and "posturing reformism." He was "progressive" as a matter of course, but it was not until his last year at Yale, after his sojourn in a Connecticut TB sanitorium, that he became politically active. He joined the John Reed Club and walked in a hunger march to Hartford.

He graduated into the Depression, but at least into a job, as a china salesman for T. M. James & Sons. His territory was Oklahoma and southern Missouri. The dust bowl was not the best place those days for a drummer of fine china. Dan James remembers once flourishing stops where stores had been boarded up and the towns had ceased to exist. "I was giving away things from my sample case," he recalls. "People who used to order Haviland were asking for a cup and saucer they could sell for ten cents."

~

THAT A YOUNG man of genteel Midwestern background, his only real experience in the marketplace a family sinecure peddling Limoges in the path of a national disaster, could wind up the 1930s a member of the Communist party and working for Charlie Chaplin was a not atypical story of that time. Carmel was the stage where Dan James blocked out the major scene changes in his life, the place to which he would always return after his forays into the job market. From Carmel he went to work briefly in the Oklahoma oil fields, a job secured for him by a relative who owned an oil drilling company. At first the Yale man as a swamper—a colorful name for a truck driver's assistant, loader, gofer, and handyman—was sent to fetch circle stretchers and left-handed monkey wrenches, but in time he learned that "this is what it felt like to make a living." Loading and unloading truckloads of pipe, the Yale man began to dream that one day he might "organize the workers." After a few months, however, he returned to Kansas City—"my own man"—to marry for the first time. In the face of this "explosion of domesticity" and a bout with hepatitis that doctors thought might signal a recurrence of his tuberculosis, the allure of the working-class life began to recede.

He retreated to Carmel, and at his father's instigation he began to write for the first time. The two Jameses, father and son, collaborated on a play about the 1934 West Coast longshoremen's strike. "It was your typical strike play," Dan James remembers. "There was the strike. There was the Irish family of dock-workers. And of course there was the little kid who gets shot." When the play was finished, he and his wife went to New York sure that one of the burgeoning new left-wing theater groups would produce it. His exposure to the reality principle was swift. He recalls the reaction of one producer's reader: "After reading the play, she said, 'You're a nice young man. But I think very possibly you should do something else besides writing.' I resented it slightly."

For a while, James and his wife stayed on in New York. He wrote more unproduced plays and worked as an extra in John Howard Lawson's *Marching Song*, a strike drama he considered far inferior to his own. The experience on stage in *Marching Song* had one postscript unforeseen at the time. A few years later, Lawson (always known as "Jack") became a major functionary and dialectician of the Communist party in Hollywood—the "Grand High Poo-Bah," in the words of one informer before the House Committee on Un-American Activities[2]—and it was he who would vouch for Dan James and his progressivism when he joined the Party.

New York palled, and in time James returned to Carmel. He busied himself in local theatricals and inchoate political activism. His marriage foundered. Then one day in 1938, Charlie Chaplin came to call at his father's house by the sea. "My father was the kind of man Chaplin would be brought to see if he was visiting in Carmel," Dan James says. Chaplin was just beginning work on *The Great Dictator*. Not long after this first meeting, Dan James wrote Chaplin in Hollywood and asked him for a job. He was hired for $80 a week.

Last June, in Carmel, I asked him why Chaplin would hire an assistant with no experience making movies. "He wanted to meet John Steinbeck, who I knew," Dan James said. "Not that he couldn't have met Steinbeck on his own. And he had a history of hiring tall, well-bred assistants who knew what fork to use."

4.

Q. *What has been your record of employment?*

A. . . . *I began writing in 1935, or 1936. The first years were extremely difficult, learning my craft and so forth. In 1938, I came here to Hollywood, was employed in an independent studio as a sort of junior writer-assistant to a producer. After that I wrote a play called* Winter Soldiers, *which was produced in New York City in the fall of 1942. This was then sold to Edward Small. I did a screenplay on it, but . . . the screenplay was shelved. I then engaged with my wife in working on her original story of what turned out to be a musical comedy*, Bloomer Girl. *Since that period, my fortunes have been rather bad. I have written a novel, which was not published, a couple of plays, numerous short stories, and so forth.*

Dan James, testifying before the House Committee on Un-American Activities, Los Angeles, California, September 19, 1951

CHARLIE CHAPLIN WAS the first of what Dan James calls his surrogate fathers. To be in Chaplin's employ was in fact to be included in a kind of family conspiracy. "I'm sure that Chaplin felt the Nazis could capture me and pull out my fingernails," Dan James says, "and I would never turn against him." During the writing and shooting of *The Great Dictator*, James was Chaplin's shadow, taking notes on everything he said and did—scraps of dialogue, bits of business, pieces of pantomime. He would type up these notes, often adding dialogue and suggestions of his own, and Chaplin would pull them apart the next day and start over. Writing the screenplay of *The Great Dictator* was a matter of "going forward one inch and going back three." Chaplin's half-brother Syd was usually on hand. "Syd was very ingenious with gags," James recalls. "He was terrified the picture was going to get too heavy. 'You're a comedian,' Syd would say. 'Let's do some funny stuff here. Let's do something funny.' "

James's other surrogate father was the Communist party. He had joined in 1938, his membership vetted and seconded by John Howard Lawson. Other than premature antifascism, no epiphany led him into the Party. It was more a romantic adventure, a leap that he remembers today, forty-six years later, with detachment and I suspect a certain rue. "I was now supporting myself," he says ironically, "and it was time to join my comrades in the working class.' "

He was a member of the working class who lunched nearly every day with his employer. In a restaurant a few blocks from Chaplin's studio in Hollywood, James and the great dictator would argue about politics. "Chaplin called himself an anarchist," James said. "He assumed I was a member of the Party, but he never asked. He wondered how I could justify the Nazi-Soviet Pact." In fact, James had no trouble with the Party line: the pact bought time for the Soviet Union to arm itself and created in Poland a buffer zone between Germany and Russia. It was an argument Chaplin hooted as specious and deluded.

James and his employer also talked about women. Chaplin always had girl trouble, and when he had a problem with one girl, his usual solution was to add another to his stable. In Carmel, he had become interested in the companion of one of James's closest friends, interested enough to offer the friend a job on *The Great Dictator* so that the girl might be more available. Her name was Dorothy Comingore and she was later cast by Orson Welles as the second Mrs. Charles Foster Kane in *Citizen Kane*. Subsequently she married a screenwriter named Richard Collins, another close friend of Dan James and also a Communist. In one of those coincidences in which the period abounds, Richard Collins, in 1951, purged himself before the House Committee on Un-American Activities and in private session not only named Dan James as a Party member but also suggested that he might be a cooperative witness. Dan James and Richard Collins never spoke again.

～

THOSE EARLY YEARS in Hollywood were the most productive of Dan James's life. In 1940, he was married again, to Lilith Stanward, a divorced ballerina with a small daughter he later adopted. The Party dominated their social and professional lives. For Hollywood's Communists, social activity was predicated on the raising of money—benefits and balls and fund-raisers for the Party, for the antifascist fronts, for the Anti-Nazi League, for British and Russian War Relief. Dan James remembers old czarist and White Russian émigrés meeting uneasily with Hollywood Reds at the Russian War Relief benefits, making common cause because of the danger of Mother Russia.

The Party meetings seemed endless. Days were spent, James recalls, on a pamphlet titled, "What Means This Strike in Steel?" At another meeting, there was a Talmudic argument about whether it was worse for Louis B. Mayer, as a Jew, to own race horses than it would be for a gentile boss to do so. For screenwriters, the meetings were directed toward identifying the class struggle in the pictures they wrote. Melodrama was the approved form, James says, because the bad boss and the crooked sheriff basic to the melodramatic plot were the classic characters of agitprop.

It was a B-picture mentality and by and large the Party attracted B-picture writers. "The Hollywood writer was a highly paid domestic," Murray Kempton noted with cruel accuracy in his 1955 book, *Part of Our Time*. "He was that most unfortunate of craftsmen, the man of talent who once hoped to be a genius and is treated like a lackey."

> In 1941, Leo C. Rosten polled a group of Hollywood professionals on their attitude toward the medium. He found that 133 out of 165 scriptwriters thought the movies were terrible. No other group registered so total a revulsion to the boss's product and no other group turned up so many persons susceptible to the Communist pull.

Years later, Dan James remarked to me that writers with first-rate credentials outside Hollywood—John O'Hara, Scott Fitzgerald, Robert E. Sherwood—rarely joined the Party, however left-wing their politics. Tax returns confirmed the stigma of the second-rate. "Of the seventeen scriptwriters listed by Leo Rosten as Hollywood's highest paid in 1938," Kempton reported in *Part of Our Time*, "only one has since been identified as a Communist."

Germany's invasion of Russia in 1941 eliminated the embarrassment of the Nazi-Soviet Pact for Hollywood's Communists—Stalin became Uncle Joe overnight—and six months later Pearl Harbor elevated most of the Party's anti-fascist fund-raising to the level of patriotic duty. Because of his tuberculosis, Dan James was 4-F, but in any case the Party's position was that its writer members could serve the cause of the proletariat more effectively at the typewriter than at the front. James's contribution to this effort was a play called *Winter Soldiers*, which in 1942 won the Sidney Howard Memorial Award, a $1,500 prize given by The Playwrights Company "to the young American playwright showing the most promise." *Winter Soldiers* was too expensive for The Playwrights Company to mount on Broadway—it had eleven scenes and forty-two speaking parts—but James used his prize money to help finance a production at New York's New School for Social Research, with a cast of unpaid professional actors.

Winter Soldiers is a curious relic, a celebration of the "little people" and a love song to the Soviet Union so melodious that I was
surprised, when I read it again recently, that it could have been produced, even in 1942 when the *Wehrmacht* was at the gates of both
Moscow and Stalingrad; *Song of Russia* is gritty by comparison.
The play roams over Yugoslavia, Austria, Czechoslovakia, Poland,
and Russia—five countries Dan James had never visited—and tells
the story of a united anti-Nazi underground movement, its members hiding in caves and huts all over central Europe, who with dar-
ing and courage and dynamite and picks and old rifles stop the
German troop train carrying the regiment assigned to lead the
assault on Moscow.

The German officers are bad. Told that a timetable is "impossible," a general shouts, "In the German language, that Jewish word
no longer exists." On a Russian collective farm, Comrade Katya,
before going out to fight the Nazis, remembers her reward for finishing the harvest two weeks early: "They sent me to Moscow. I saw
Comrade Stalin."

An artifact of its time, *Winter Soldiers* makes Dan James grimace
today. "Creaky," he says. "Seedy." The play had the good fortune to be
reviewed the same day the headlines in *The New York Times* read: RUS-
SIANS BREAK NAZI DON DEFENSE LINE. SOVIETS LIST GAINS.
100,000 NAZIS ARE SAID TO HAVE BEEN KILLED IN LAST TEN
DAYS. Lewis Nichols, the *Times*'s reviewer, called *Winter Soldiers*
"exciting and moving . . . a perfect portrait of that other column which
also carries on the war for freedom." Other reviewers praised the play
as well and Burns Mantle selected it for *Best Plays of 1942–1943*.

~

WINTER SOLDIERS PLAYED only twenty-five performances, but for
the first time James felt himself a functioning professional writer.
Back home in Los Angeles, he was hired to write a screenplay of
Winter Soldiers, a project that never got off the ground. At the same
time, however, Lilith James had come up with a play idea of her
own, the product of a Party-endorsed workshop on women's rights.
Her idea was to highlight the emancipation of women through her
heroine's campaign to exchange the hoop skirt for bloomers. She and

Dan collaborated on the play and brought it to Harold Arlen and E.Y. Harburg, who thought it would make a perfect libretto for a musical. Thus *Bloomer Girl* was born. The Jameses worked on several drafts of the book and then were joined by two more experienced librettists, who made more room for song and dance by planing away the dialectic. On October 5, 1944, *Bloomer Girl* opened in New York and was an instant hit.

It should have been the best of times, but it was the worst, the beginning of an unproductive period for Dan James that would last twenty-five years. He went to work on a play for Paul Robeson, adapted from a novel by Howard Fast, but the play was, in his word, "terrible." For a few months, he and Lilith, who was pregnant, returned to Kansas City, "to my bourgeois roots." The trip was research for a novel of manners, *The Hockadays*, about the upper middle class and its pleasures. *The Hockadays* did not find a publisher.

At the same time, his enthusiasm for the Communist party had begun to wane with the end of the war. "We all saw a rosy future after the war," he wrote me recently.

> A very brave and progressive new world. It seems very stupid now, but if you'd been there you'd have felt it. We even believed with fascism dead, the Soviet Union would relax its internal repression (which previously when we admitted it, we blamed on the need to prepare for war). Again history took a turn. The San Francisco conference to create the United Nations proved no better than Wilson's old League of Nations in 1919. We tried to blame it all on the US of course, but we began to be very doubtful as we saw the Iron Curtain go down in Eastern Europe. And the wartime coalition of which we were a tiny part collapsed and we found ourselves isolated. . . . Our credibility in the labor movement was destroyed because of our war-time no-strike stand. Liberals and progressives were happy to give us the cold shoulder. And in Hollywood the whole movement collapsed under the weight of the poor Ten who went to Washington as heroes and came back as enemies of the people. . . . Anyway it's when I started moving away from the Party, and of course the debacle of the Wallace campaign in '48 sealed the coffin. When I left, don't get the idea that it was a purely intellectual decision. There was plenty of fear in

there, really chilling fear and with some reason in view of what happened later. And shame because of that fear. . . .

Three years after they left the Party Dan and Lilith James were called to testify in front of the House Committee on Un-American Activities. In the interim, naming names had become a cottage industry in Hollywood. The Jameses' friend Richard Collins named them in closed session. In open session, Martin Berkeley took the trouble to spell out Dan's name: "Also in our group were Dan James, J-A-M-E-S. . . ." Again in open session, Leo Townsend, who was perhaps the Jameses' closest friend in the Party, reduced hair-splitting to a fine, even comic, art:

Q. *Were you acquainted with a person by the name of Dan James?*

A. *I know Dan James.*

Q. *Did you of your own knowledge know that he was a member of the Communist Party?*

A. *I had heard that he had left the Communist Party. I don't know whether you would consider that knowledge of membership.*

Q. *Well, did you hear that from him or from some outside source?*

A. *I heard it from him.*

Q. *Well, I think that is direct testimony. Now, what were the circumstances under which you heard it from him?*

A. *Simply that I had told him that I had been out since 1948 and that he told he had also left the Party.*

Dan and Lilith James were subpoenaed by the Committee in the summer of 1951. Dan was playing tennis on the court in the back yard of his house on Franklin Avenue in Hollywood with a producer from whom he was trying to hustle a screenplay assignment. "It was not the most propitious moment," he recalls. I asked the Jameses not long ago why they had been summoned while so many others who were named had not been called. "They thought we would snitch," Lilith James said. "They knew we had left the Party and assumed we would cooperate." Had it ever crossed their minds? Never. Their position was that while they would say they were not members of the Party, they would decline to answer if they ever had been. "I expect no applause either from this Committee, nor from the *People's World* nor from the *Daily Worker*," Dan James stated under oath. "This is a lonely, lonely position, and I assure you that when I am saying that I am not a Communist, I am meaning it."

With his sense of the theatrical, Dan James carried in his pocket, from his father's library in Carmel, a first edition of *Candide*, which he hoped to introduce into testimony with the admonition that Voltaire had published it under a pseudonym—M. Le Docteur Ralph—and if the Committee worked its will, American writers as well would have to disguise their identities. The Committee would have none of this playlet and cut him off before he could begin.

～

ON THE EVIDENCE of a photograph in the *Los Angeles Times* the next day, Lilith James wore a hat when she testified. She has always been an intensely private woman and the witness table was for her neither a platform nor a podium. She said she was not a Communist and then simply declined to answer further questions. Asked if she had been a member of the Party "on Sunday of this past week," and then on Monday or Tuesday or in 1944, she replied only, "I decline." When it became obvious she would not cooperate, Congressman Clyde Doyle of California tried to wheedle and coax with appeals to her motherhood. "Are there some little Jameses?" he asked, and then, "You've got some young children growing up. Why don't you help us in the field of communistic influences in Hollywood?"

"I feel it is quite possible to be opposed to communism," Lilith James said, "and its principles and its alliance to the Soviet Union and to be in support of our government, our government's policy in Korea, which I certainly am, and still feel it is not an American rule to have to name names of people when it will influence their lives and their families and their children. This is not my reason for declining. I decline on the grounds of the Fifth Amendment. But this is my position."

A moment later she was excused. The Jameses remember the day of their testimony as the same day the Hollywood Freeway opened.

5.

IN THE FALL OF 1966, almost fifteen years to the day after Dan and Lilith James testified before the Committee, my wife and I and our infant daughter moved into their house on Franklin Avenue in Hollywood. The rent was cheap, the place vast, on the lines of an abandoned fraternity house. The neighborhood had known better days. Bette Davis had lived on one corner, Preston Sturges on the other; the Canadian consulate was a block away, the Japanese consulate at the time of Pearl Harbor across the street. Now the pimps and junkies were beginning to take over Hollywood Boulevard, a block south. There was a whorehouse in a brand new high-rise down the street, Synanon owned one house in the neighborhood, a Dr. Feelgood was dispensing amphetamines like gumdrops in another, and the former Japanese consulate, boarded up, was a crash pad for a therapy group.

We saw a good deal of the Jameses. They also owned the tiny bungalow next door and when it was not rented they would move down from Carmel. We intuited political trouble almost immediately. In our basement, there were cartons upon cartons of the *New Masses* and Dan James, although he was only fifty-five, was a writer who did not seem to write anymore. We made the inductive leap. Our questioning was indirect, their answers oblique. The implicit reserve was finally breached one day when Dan showed us a piece in *New Masses*, written in 1946 by Albert Maltz, later one of the Hollywood Ten. "I have come to believe that the accepted understanding of art as a weapon is not a useful guide but a strait jacket," Maltz had written. "I have felt this in my own work and in the work of others. In order to write at all, it has become necessary for me to repudiate it and abandon it."

Unexceptional as Maltz's statement seemed, James said it had caused a furor in its day. Party leaders arrived from New York to re-educate Maltz. There were a number of meetings, kangaroo courts, as it were, to persuade him to recant. One of the sessions had taken place in what was now our living room. "On that couch," James said, "Albert Maltz made his famous recantation." I could not imagine the scene or why Maltz had submitted to such an inquisition. "Whatever happened to 'fuck off'?" I asked. "You don't understand," James replied. "That was the pull of the Party."

~

POLITICS NO LONGER appeared to exert any pull on him at all. On May Day, 1967, I took James with me to Watts to hear the leader of a Maoist splinter group speak. I had met the Maoist when I was working on a piece and found him interesting in the way fanatics often are. He was wearing camouflage fatigues and a fatigue hat crowned with a red star. None of the blacks playing in the park where he spoke paid him the slightest heed. He talked about the "ruling class" and the "workers" and how the day was nigh when the workers would "arise." James soon wanted to leave. We drove back to Hollywood in silence. He seemed sunk in depression. "I made that same speech thirty years ago," he finally explained. "Some things never change."

In time, the Jameses filled in the blanks in the preceding fifteen years. The blacklist precluded what movie work was available. When *Bloomer Girl* appeared on television in the early Fifties, it appeared without the Jameses' credit. Using a family name, Daniel Hyatt, Dan worked on the scripts of two monster pictures, *The Giant Behemoth* and *Gorgo*, each of which ended with either Gorgo or the giant behemoth trampling, eating, and generally dismantling London. They rarely saw old Party friends. "The people we knew best were either stool pigeons or had fled to Europe," Dan James recalls. There was also another reason: money was never the problem with the Jameses that it was with so many others on the blacklist, a situation they found embarrassing. "We didn't have to go out and sell insurance like others did," Lilith James remembers. "There was a little family money. The *Bloomer Girl* money kept coming in. We owned our house. We had no mortgage."

The people the Jameses did see were increasingly on the Hispanic east side of Los Angeles. In 1948 they spent a weekend visiting an interracial camp in Glendale; this led to an invitation to re-create the traditional Mexican Christmas *posadas* on Lamar Street in Lincoln Heights. "The action, of course," Dan wrote in a letter not long ago, "is that Mary and Joseph (played by eight-year-old kids) with the Christ child in arms go from door to door looking for a night's shelter. They're turned away from several on one absurd excuse or another till finally the last door is opened and in they go, with all their candle-bearing followers. We wrote various little dialog scenes for the doorways and taught the kids the *posadas* songs. It grew into a big neighborhood event. We blocked off the street (without a police permit) and from a telephone pole ended the evening with several *piñatas*. We got quite famous."

~

THUS WAS PLANTED the seed for *Famous All Over Town*. The experience satisfied what Dan James describes now as "a need for flight. . . . As many of the comrades took off for Europe and elsewhere, we moved into East L.A. and started making a new life for ourselves there." For the next fifteen years, the Jameses' activities were concentrated on three square blocks in Lincoln Heights, a neighborhood of tiny bungalows with Gothic trim, no larger than a Mexican village and equally confined, bounded on two sides by the tracks and marshaling yards of the Southern Pacific Railroad, on a third by the dry concrete trough called the Los Angeles River. With only the street names changed, it was the place that James would re-create thirty years later as Danny Santiago. The Jameses formed and worked with various teenage clubs, "their names," Dan recalls, "a product of total democracy." There were the Hepkitties and the Bluebirds and the Lamar Tigers. In a letter he wrote me, he remembers

> football, basketball, baseball with eastside playground teams (we usually lost). Beach picnics, trips to snow, various interracial camps in San Bernardino mtns. After a year when the boys started inspecting the girls we started the Starlifters, coed (if you can call it ed). Mostly dancing and volleyball in Methodist church basement. . . . Next Los Compadres Club, whose nucleus were members of the old Hepkitties now married with children. Around 12 couples. Made

an old two car garage into a clubhouse with beer bar. Bowling, dancing in clubhouse and elsewhere, overnight camping trips. Emphasis on keeping the boys and girls together, which was revolutionary in that tradition. Once ALMOST voted a black couple into the club. The Compadres then with 7 other groups, mostly oldtime neighborhood gang veterans, to form the Lincoln Heights Scholarship Federation, which held a largely successful dance at the Hollywood Palladium and gave out a dozen small scholarships with the proceeds. . . .

But this was only part of it. This is how we met the kids. Their families came through *compadrazco*, though our friendships began in our earlier years on Lamar when we sought permission for their daughters to join the club, go on camping trips, etc. Over the years we baptized seven babies and acted as *compadres de matrimonio* to 3 couples, which gave us a special relation with some 20 families, to be asked to all celebrations from birth to death. . . . Our closest *compadre* was Lalo Rios and it was his family and his wife Connie's that we knew best. We baptized Lalo's Ruben and five years later shared 24 hour watches as Ruben died of leukemia. We baptized their third son Tomas and in '74 we buried Lalo who we thought would one day bury us, another agonizing vigil. And now we stay with his widow when we're in L.A. . . .

In recent years it's been mostly funerals and there's only one father left of the old original Hepkitties. We've lost track of most of our club members, except the ones united to us by *compadrazco*, but at the funerals they turn up once in a while. So you can say over the past 35 years we've known four generations of Mexicanos in their best and worst of times. We even brushed elbows with the end of their great-great-grandfathers. . . .

6.

EARLY IN 1968, Dan James asked me to read some stories he had written about East Los Angeles. The stories were the early chapters of *Famous All Over Town* and were drawn of course from his experiences on the east side. I thought they were very good—tough, funny, unsentimental, and undogmatic—but I was not enthusiastic about his wish to send them out under the name "Danny Santiago." I had nothing against pseudonyms—I had once used the name "Algernon Hogg" because the magazine I worked for discouraged staff writers from contributing to other publications—but the idea of an Anglo presenting himself as a Chicano I found troubling. I had spent a period myself in East Los Angeles working on a book about Cesar Chavez and my instinct was that this particular kind of literary deception could, if discovered (and presupposing the stories were successful), have unpleasant extraliterary ramifications.

James, however, was adamant. He felt that for nearly twenty years he had been unable to write under his own name both because of the blacklist and because he had lost confidence in his own ability. "I wish I could tell you how I feel about Danny Santiago," he wrote from Carmel, where he and Lilith had gone back to live permanently.

> He's so much freer than I am myself. He seems to know how he feels about everything and none of the ifs, ands and buts that I'm plagued with. I don't plan to make a great cops and robbers bit out of him, but now at any rate I can't let him go. Maybe he'll prove a straitjacket later on. We'll see. In any event, unless you feel too guilty about this mild little deception of mine, I'd like you to send on the stories to Brandt. . . .

～

CARL BRANDT WAS then my agent, and on March 25, 1968, I sent him the stories, with an obfuscating covering letter that never once mentioned either the author's real or putative name (I assumed the title page and the return address would do the trick). In time, the stories began to appear, in *Redbook* and *Playboy*; in 1971, "The Somebody" was chosen for Martha Foley's annual collection, *Best American Short Stories*. ("The Somebody," in different form, became the final chapter of *Famous All Over Town*.) We corresponded fitfully with the Jameses, all too often about the rent, which they needed and we had trouble paying. "PS. Did somebody forget January rent?" Dan wrote on January 8, 1969. In December: "The mystery is partially solved. Your note arrived today with check #1333 dated November 20."

In January 1971, we moved from Franklin Avenue to the beach, where we had bought a house. Occasionally we would spend a weekend with the Jameses in Carmel or drive down to see them if we were in San Francisco. At times we would send them friends who wanted to see the house. The one they appreciated most was a Cuban diplomat from the United Nations traveling on the West Coast for the first time. The Cuban's companion was a young Spanish woman who worked for Spain's trade mission in New York. When the couple arrived in Carmel, the Jameses invited them to spend the night. The next day Dan James called to report that the woman's father was an old Falangist who had fought with Franco's Blue Division alongside the *Wehrmacht* on the Russian front. It would have been about the same time he was working on *Winter Soldiers*. "Imagine it," he said. "An old Stalinist, a Cuban communist and the daughter of a Blue Division veteran getting drunk and arguing politics in Carmel."

～

DANNY SANTIAGO CONTINUED to work.[3] At the suggestion of Carl Brandt (who still did not know his client's true identity), James began shaping his published and unpublished stories into a novel. After a number of rejections, the completed manuscript was finally accepted by Simon and Schuster. Editing was accomplished by mail, via the postal drop in Pacific Grove. James's letters to his agent and his publisher were in a perfectly mimetic Danny Santiago persona—slangy, contentious, touchy, defensive. *¿Quién es mas macho?* The Eastern gringos gave the benefit of the doubt to the eccentric and erratic young Chicano novelist.

Famous All Over Town was published in March 1983, to no fanfare. The world described was that three-block area of Lincoln Heights where Dan and Lilith James had been granted *compadrazco*. The novel's narrator, Chato Medina, is a fourteen-year-old street-smart kid with an IQ of 135, resisting assimilation by a voracious

Anglo culture he sees as dominated by the Southern Pacific Railroad, which wants to buy up and pave over his block in the interest of better freight management. He is equally divorced from the rural Mexico of his grandparents, a Valhalla he deprecates as a place where "they milk each other's goats."

Chato lives by his considerable wits on that brink where the comic adventure can easily flip into casual violence. With quick tongue and sharp eye, he is ever the observer of his family—his spirited sister Lena (christened Tranquilina, but never tranquil), his placid, preoccupied baby-machine mother, and especially his blustery, ham-handed father: "My father is very loud in stores speaking Spanish, but in English you can barely hear him."

The Medinas exist in a secondhand way: "Day-olds from the bakery, dented tomato cans, sunburned shirts from store windows, never two chairs alike and lucky if one shoe matched the other." They buy their clothes from the "As-Is" bin at the Goodwill, "fishing through boxes raw off the trucks before anything was washed or fumigated." But Chato is never a victim of his circumstances. He is a victor, a vivid historian of his own life: "There's my cousin Cuca and my cousin Kika and Lalo and Lola and Rosario the boy and Rosario the girl and my Uncle Benedicto that the priest put a curse on him for what he done in the bell tower."

Given my rooting interest, I found *Famous All Over Town* a lunatic success, a Chicano *Bildungsroman* by a septuagenarian ex-Stalinist aristocrat from Kansas City. There is no trace of the didacticism of *Winter Soldiers*, no hint of the author's history, either of his communism or his apostasy. This is not social realism, not a proletarian novel; James's Southern Pacific is not Frank Norris's octopus. *Famous All Over Town* takes the form of a classic novel of initiation, and Chato Medina could be read as a Hispanic Holden Caufield. His weapons against the world are brains and humor, his language an eloquent and scrambled mixture of Spanish and English.

The Anglo characters—a Jewish teacher, a homosexual doctor with an unrequited yen for Chato—are the book's weakest, flat and obvious, and when I asked James if this were intentional, another layer of sophisticated deception to disguise his identity further, he only laughed. The novel received generally excellent notices, from Anglo and Chicano reviewers alike, and then last May the Rosenthal Award. A day or so later, I was coincidentally asked by the editors of *The New York Review of Books* if I would like to use the book as a springboard for a piece we had long contemplated on East Los Angeles. I said there were complications, and then sent their letter to Carmel along with a note of my own asking Dan James if "Danny would like to come in from the cold."

7.

WHEN I VISITED the Jameses in Carmel in June, Lilith James was clearly uncomfortable at any public acknowledgment of their Party membership. It was not out of any sense of regret at once having been a member. She was entirely comfortable with her actions and her past, but she did not wish her children—now both grown women—to live with any possible burden of these actions. Her attitude, moreover, had not changed in the thirty-three years since her appearance before the Committee: it was nobody's business then and it was nobody's business now. She finally agreed because "Danny Santiago" had long made her uneasy and she knew that if Dan went public he could not go public selectively.

We talked that weekend, and over the telephone the next few weeks, on and on, as if we were Party members discussing what means this strike in steel. I reread the books on the blacklist. If the Jameses were mentioned at all, they were mentioned only in passing. They were not brand-name screenwriters or celebrity informers, nor did they have the theater or literary constituencies of Lillian Hellman or Dashiell Hammett. After talking to the Jameses so often over the years, I found most of these books, especially those written by people never personally involved, irrelevant and even spurious, often vulgar in language, so flushed with second-hand outrage that they lack any real sense of the period, its social nuances or its particular ironies.

I read the testimony of Dan and Lilith James and the testimony of their accusers. The passage of time has made them benign about those who informed on them. In the mid-1960s, they had been in touch with Leo Townsend but, in Dan James's words, "it wasn't fun anymore." I was struck by one irony in the testimony of Richard Collins. A prodigious namer of other names besides the Jameses, Collins also made the most persuasive case of any witness I have read against the idea of Party minions poisoning the minds of moviegoers:

> Since the basic policy isn't in the hands of the writer or the director but in the hands of the owners of the studio, who are not at all interested in this propaganda, the chances of any real presentation of Communist material or what is termed Communist material in terms of the Communist Party or foreign policy are, I think, extremely unlikely.

Dan James remembered Richard Collins's testimony as "thoughtful" and wondered if he were still alive.

What struck me that weekend in Carmel was how deeply ingrained the character of Danny Santiago was on Dan James. As one has difficulty telling where the rocks end and his house begins, so it is with Dan and Danny. Danny was the only persona in which Dan could write, even in his letters to my wife and me, who have shared his secret for sixteen years. I asked if he had considered the possibility of being accused of manufacturing a hoax. He shrugged and said the book itself was the only answer. If the book were good, it was good under whatever identity the author chose to use, the way the books of B. Traven were good. Nor would he consider that *Famous All Over Town* was a tour de force. "I spent thirty-five years working on this book," he said, "twenty years learning what it was all about, the last fifteen writing it. You don't spend thirty-five years on a tour de force."

When we returned to Los Angeles, my wife and I drove down to Lamar Street in Lincoln Heights. The entire three blocks had been flattened to make a parking lot for the piggy-back trailers that ride the Southern Pacific flatcars. In the book, when the Southern Pacific succeeds in condemning the neighborhood, Chato Medina writes his name in Crayola on every flat surface in the area. It is the gesture that makes him "famous all over town." I had no Crayola in the car. If I had, I would have written four words on the sidewalk of Lamar Street: "Dan and Lilith James."

NOTES

[1] From an interview with Daniel James and his wife, Lilith, June 2 and 3, 1984, conducted and taped by myself and my wife, Joan Didion. Many of Dan James's quotes in this piece come from that interview.

[2] Martin Berkeley, quoted in *The New York Times*, September 20, 1951.

[3] So as not to run afoul of the Internal Revenue Service, James had set up a Danny Santiago bank account, using his own Social Security number.

To Live and Die in L.A.

[1991]

❧

I.

THERE WAS A display of Bar-B-Q equipment in the window of the 24-hour Boys Market. Three blocks over, on South Orchard Avenue, a Sparkletts truck slowly made its way down the street and parked in front of a new Chrysler Cordoba with a bumper sticker that said, "This ain't the Mayflower, but your daughter came across in it." Down at the corner, a Mexican gardener, sweating profusely under the pale flat July sun, loaded his power lawn mower on the small flatbed attached to his pickup. The lawns on South Orchard were all closely trimmed and the small neat bungalows hedged with fuchsia and hydrangea and marigolds and petunias. It was a quiet neighborhood, a neighborhood of pride and fresh paint, a neighborhood that did not threaten. It was the neighborhood where, on the third day of January 1979, officers Edward M. Hopson, Badge No. 13541, and Lloyd W. O'Callaghan, Jr., Badge No. 21216, Los Angeles Police Department, unloaded twelve shots at Eula Mae Love, who resided at 11926 South Orchard.

Eight shots hit Eula Love—a penetrating wound of the right foot, a perforating wound of the left lower leg, a perforating wound of the left thigh, a perforating wound through the left upper arm, a penetrating wound of the right thigh, a second perforating wound of the left thigh, and a third perforating wound of the same left thigh. These seven wounds were described in Autopsy Report No. 79-00133, filed by the Los Angeles County Medical Examiner, as "not immediately life-threatening." The eighth gunshot wound, according to Report No. 79-00133, was "a penetrating wound of the chest . . . [whose] track passes through the skin, fat and muscle of the left anterior chest wall, enters the left thoracic cavity through the second intercostal space, perforates the upper lobe of the lung, enters the mediastinum and perforates the body of T5, exits the right pleural cavity through the sixth intercostal space adjacent to the spinal column and ends in the muscle of the right posterior chest wall. . . . OPINION: This gunshot wound is immediately life-threatening."

I read the autopsy report in a document entitled "Report on Fatal Shooting of Mrs. Eula Mae Love—Special Investigations Division Case No. 100-2070," which the Los Angeles County District Attorney's Office sent unsolicited to the news media. In the report, the D.A.'s office collated and interpreted the testimony of fifty-two witnesses, laid out the applicable law, and, on the basis of the evidence, reached the conclusion that "Officer O'Callaghan and Officer Hopson did not commit a criminal act when they shot Mrs. Love." There was no conclusion, however, as to the tactical judgment exercised by the two officers. "The tragic shooting of Eula Love has had a profound effect on Los Angeles," the covering letter from District Attorney John K. Van de Kamp read. "The entire community needs to be sensitized again to the value of reverence and respect for life."

This bureaucratic piety paled before the fact of Eula Mae Love on the autopsy table: "This is the well-developed, obese, unembalmed body of a 64-inch, 175-pound, 39-year-old Negro female. There is bleeding from both nostrils and pink froth in the mouth. The breasts are large and pendulous. The abdomen is convex. The extremities are unremarkable except for the effect of the gunshot wounds. No surgical scars or tattoos are noted on the body. There are no deformities. Examination of the limbs and antecubital fossae does not reveal any evidence of needle tracks."

Alive, Eula Mae Love was a widow of six months. Her late husband was a professional cook with an annual income of $15,000. When he died, she was left with his monthly Social Security checks totaling $680, a mortgage of $192.18 a month, and three daughters, the two youngest of whom lived with her in the house on South Orchard. Eula Love's gas bill was six months and $69 overdue, her water bill $80 delinquent. The Department of Water & Power wanted to shut off her lights and water that January 3, but did not have the manpower available. Not so the Southern California Gas Company. A serviceman for the gas company arrived at 11926 South Orchard and told Eula Mae Love that she would either have to pay an installment of $22.09 on her gas bill or have her service disconnected. In the words of Report No. 100-2070, "She became irrational and verbally abusive." When the serviceman went to the gas meter, Eula Love hit him with a shovel, causing, as the report continues, "an abrasion, laceration and marked swelling just below the elbow."

After the gas man retreated, Eula Love walked to the Boys Market, a three-minute trip from her house, and purchased one money order for $22.09 (the minimum amount necessary to keep her gas connected) and a second for $192.18 (the amount of her house payment); in her purse, according to the coroner's report, there was an additional $155.16 in cash and a Social Security check for $440.40 making a total of $809.83. Meanwhile, the gas man made an assault complaint against Eula Love to the Los Angeles Police Department. Two other gas company employees, in separate vehicles, were dispatched to South Orchard to attempt collection from Eula Love or to cut off her service. The gas company, as Report No. 100-2070 indicates, also requested from the LAPD "officer assistance to insure that there would be no further violence." At the corner of South Orchard and 120th Street, Eula Love confronted one of the servicemen, who remained in his truck, and when he said he was only there to read a book, she once more became abusive. She went into her house and emerged with a boning knife and began hacking at a tree. Moments later, officers Hopson and O'Callaghan pulled up, summoned by a message on their police radio: "415— business dispute. Meet the gas man at 11926 South Orchard,

Code 2." In the LAPD signal manual, Code 2 means urgent but not requiring red light and siren. Hopson and O'Callaghan exited their black and white, guns drawn.

Consider the situation confronting Hopson and O'Callaghan. They did not know that William Love had died of sickle cell anemia six months before. They did not know that Eula Mae Love had a $22.09 money order for the gas company in her purse. They saw only an enraged woman holding an eleven-inch blade, five and a half inches of handle. Eula Love screamed at the two officers. She said they had homosexual eating habits. She said they fornicated with their mothers. She told them to use their weapons. She told them to kiss her ass. Suddenly O'Callaghan knocked the knife from Eula Love's grasp with his nightstick. She retrieved it before he could kick it away. In the next two and a half to four seconds, the two officers—one eight feet from Eula Love, the other twelve feet away—squeezed off twelve shots.

It is the shame of most of us who write that only riot or death brings us to South Central Los Angeles: riot or death or the ritual night ride, in the interests of research, with the officers of the 77th Division, or that biennial ceremony in which the white hand takes the black pulse. We bring out-of-town relatives to the Watts Towers, pay the obligatory obeisance to the artisanship of Simon Rodia, and head for the Harbor Freeway before the sun sinks. It is my personal shame that the "whiteness" of Eula Love's house-proud neighborhood made her death seem so much more pertinent; this, after all, was a neighborhood where annuals were planted and cultivated, where hibachis and charcoal briquets were sold at the Boys, where mountain-pure bottled water was delivered to the kitchen bubbler. The corollary was even more shameful: Would the death of Eula Love have been easier to swallow had she been shot in a development east of the Harbor Freeway, where welfare and food stamps were the coin of the realm and the wail of Code 1 was the local rhythm and blues?

I became obsessed with Eula Love. I bought an eleven-inch boning knife and practiced throwing it in my back yard, holding it both by the blade, as the LAPD claimed Eula Love had, and by the handle, as three witnesses claimed she had. I replayed an incident of twelve years before when my wife, with cause, once tried to kill me. She stood on the landing in our house in Hollywood with a pair of scissors in her hand, threatening to throw them at me, promising to throw them at me. I stayed out of range. I knew she had a bad arm. I knew she threw like a girl. And I knew the scissors had no balance. I talked. Quietly. Reasonably. And out of range. The moment passed. The fury died. We are still married, I like to think happily.

I kept wondering why Hopson and O'Callaghan could not defuse the situation. I kept wondering why they perceived Eula Love, even with a kitchen knife in her hand, as an immediate threat. This was a short, fat, hysterical woman, an "obese . . . 64-inch, 175-pound . . . Negro female. . . . The breasts are large and pendulous. The abdomen is convex." But the LAPD would admit no error. In this respect, policemen are like doctors and lawyers and writers. When under attack, draw your wagons into a circle. There was no mistake in judgment, there was no violation of departmental firearm policy—although one deputy chief on the three-officer shooting board issued a sharp dissent. This momentary embarrassment did not deflect the department from its conclusion about the events on South Orchard: This was a good shoot. "She decided to solve her problem with a knife," said Chief Daryl Gates. "That's why it happened." Chief Gates seemed to see Eula Love as not unlike the James Coburn character in *The Magnificent Seven,* who could draw his blade and snap it into a gunslinger before said gunslinger could clear his six-shooter.

In fact Daryl Gates had been a public relations disaster in the sixteen months he had then been police chief, a profile in incompetence, and I suspect it was this public apprehension that accounted for the continuing fascination with Eula Love. One week after succeeding Ed Davis as chief, and in need of a bold stroke to emerge from the shadow of that loose cannon, Gates held a press conference and produced Peter Mark Jones as the Hillside Strangler. Jones was fingered by one George Shamshak, a small-time Boston hood and snitch, who was acutely uncomfortable at the prospect of doing time in a Massachusetts slammer in the company of a number of cons his squealing had helped put inside. By fingering Jones, a casual acquaintance, Shamshak hoped that California authorities would grant him a favor and let him do his time in a more congenial West Coast joint. The hitch was that Jones was clean. At a second press conference Gates was forced to announce that his case had sprung a leak; at a third, he announced that Jones had been released from custody and issued him a public apology. He maintained that Shamshak, however, remained a "prime suspect"; a few weeks later, Shamshak was cleared of Strangler involvement.

Public apology has been a feature of Gates's tenure. In a city of over a million Chicanos, he said that Mexicans had not risen in the LAPD because they were lazy; bingo—an apology to the Chicano community. Small wonder Gates fastened on Eula Love; on his terms, the incident at 11926 South Orchard was a successful operation, a chance to recoup after the joke he had made of himself and his department in the Shamshak/Jones circus. There was no one to be released on a writ of habeas corpus, no apologies for false arrest. Eula Love provided an opportunity to take the offensive. In a speech to the County Bar Association covered on local TV, Gates attacked the press for "wringing every single drop, every tear" from the Love case. His voice oozing sarcasm, he referred to Eula Love as "the poor widow trying to keep her house and home together." The "poor widow" did not owe $22, he said; "it was $64 or a $67 gas bill and it had been delinquent for six months," and what was more she had better than $700 in her purse. The implication was that Eula Love was a deadbeat and his department was not about to take a ration of guff from any deadbeat.

Gates on television that night was a man with moral athlete's foot. And he was not through. When Mayor Tom Bradley suggested that officers Hopson and O'Callaghan might have taken more time to calm Eula Love down, Gates was back at the barricades. "I don't agree with the mayor's statement that they could have tried to talk her out of it," he said. "They did that, they did that." Yes, they did. According to the D.A.'s report, Hopson and O'Callaghan arrived on the scene at 4:15 P.M.; according to Fire Department records, an ambulance was summoned at 4:21. Six minutes, including the lag time between the shooting and the call for the ambulance. Six whole minutes. Three hundred sixty seconds.

I have driven a number of times now past Eula Love's house on South Orchard. I park in the street where Hopson and O'Callaghan parked and I eat peaches and Bing cherries bought at the Boys and I keep wondering about the two officers and those six minutes. I wonder what their hurry was. Did they have a date? Was that Wednesday their bowling night? "I think they had every right and opportunity and justification to do what they did," Daryl Gates has said. His own words suggest why some people call cops pigs.

2.

MY FATHER'S WAS the first dead body I ever saw. He died suddenly, of a ruptured aorta, three days after my fourteenth birthday. I kissed him goodbye in the morning, a healthy vigorous man of fifty-one, and when I came home from school that afternoon the oxygen tanks on the back porch were like a psychic barricade, Stygian signposts. I was not a stranger to the cryptograms of death. My father was a surgeon, and when he talked about his practice his words were often encoded in body English—a slight shrug, a raised eyebrow, an almost imperceptible shake of the head: the cannibal cells had taken the high ground. His wake was held in the house, and for four days I was a figure of some importance. Adults— Thomas Moylan and Terence McNulty, May Toomey, the Clarkin sisters—would grasp my hand and avoid my eyes and mumble that wonderful Irish benediction, "I'm sorry for your trouble." But late in the evening, when the mourners were gone and the drinks put away and when the only lights in the living room were the candles flickering around the casket, I would sneak downstairs in my pajamas and stare at my father's face. I tried to will him to breathe. I tried to coax movement into fingers bound with rosary beads. I listened for a heartbeat, as years later I would bend over my infant daughter's crib and listen for her heartbeat. I wonder still if I told him that last morning that I loved him. I do remember that the Brooklyn Dodgers, with Vic Lombardi pitching, beat the Pittsburgh Pirates that day.

What provoked these vivid memories of my father's death were two visits I made recently to the Los Angeles County Morgue. My guides were two homicide detectives with thirty-four years' experience between them in the department. Whenever I meet a cop, I am struck by a certain element of performance in his persona, a sense that the handcuffs hanging from the back of his heavy leather belt are the ultimate social equalizer. There is a willingness to push, a tendency to show off. In their office at Robbery-Homicide, one of the cops was wearing a dark brown tie with a pattern of beige diamonds. He pulled the tie and the polyester expanded and each diamond formed the words "Fuck You." The cop smiled. "It's my courtroom tie."

The two officers pulled out files of murders and murderers past:

"Dear Sir: With reference to the above subject, who was executed at Walla Walla on July 15, 1949 . . ."

"Dear Sir: I would greatly appreciate it if you would question Ray Dempsey Gardner who, I understand, is to be executed in Utah State Penitentiary for a similar crime."

"Dear Sir: This man is a professional hitchhiker and murderer."

A professional hitchhiker and murderer. On the road since the age of fourteen. With six known bodies left beside the highways and byways of his professional hitchhiking. Here was a true foot soldier in the armies of the night. I looked at forensic photographs as the two detectives scrutinized my face for signs of queasiness. I stared at a Polaroid photograph of a two-year-old—"30 months old, 30 inches tall, 30 pounds"—whose nipples had been pulled off with a pair of pliers. The two cops talked about the child in the photograph as if they were mechanics talking about a classic Corvette with a broken camshaft. I fell into their rhythm until it was time to go to the morgue.

The morgue on a Monday morning after a weekend during which a Santa Ana was blowing resembles an airline crash site after a jet has gone in. There had been ten murders in Los Angeles County during the preceding twenty-four hours. Bodies were undressed and weighed on a large industrial scale in an anteroom. Bodies lined both sides of the corridor outside the autopsy room. Murder victims, accident victims, suicides, ODs. Bodies that had simply died. Old people, young people, babies. Male, female, black, white, yellow, brown. Peaceful, contorted, resigned, smashed, battered, bruised. Wistful. Each body was marked with a toe tag listing the victim's name (John or Jane Doe if the name was unknown), cause of death, date, and an identification number signifying the body's ranking in the year's count to date; the numbers that Monday morning in the fall had passed 12,000.

It was a festival of death. On the walls were autopsy photographs of particular or bizarre interest. I backed up into a dead arm, moved forward and was hit by a gurney carrying yet another body. This one was a murder victim, thrown over a cliff not a hundred yards from a house in which I had once lived. The bullet in his back had not passed entirely out through his chest; when the younger of the two detectives asked me to feel the shell protruding from the victim's sternum, I passed. I wished I had taken the cigar the detective had offered outside. It was not that the smell was bad; it was just constant. I looked into one room and saw a man being embalmed. The fluid was pumping into his body through his groin. In another room, an attendant was having a snack; his thermos bottle was perched on the desiccated chest of the aged female body on the table. In yet another room, I saw a body being prepared for viewing by next of kin; it was strapped on a table and the table was lifted and the face photographed by a closed-circuit television camera and the picture beamed to the next of kin in a room somewhere else in the complex. There were no keening relatives in the morgue. It was a place of business, and there was raucous laughter, even a Polish joke in the corridor. Q: What do 1776, 1812, and 1914 have in common? A: They are adjoining rooms in the Warsaw Hilton. I heard myself laugh uproariously and then instinctively I checked the toe tag of the body beside me to see if he was Polish, as if he possibly could have taken offense.

The autopsy room was not like the television show *Quincy*. There were seven autopsy tables and on each there was a body in some stage of dismemberment; on a side table there was an infant whose skin had been cut at the base of the skull and peeled up over its face. It was the first time I realized that the facial features are indeed a mask. There was dried blood on the floor and there was dried blood on the telephone and there were jars full of organs and chemical beakers filled with body fluids. And there was noise, noise that time and distance have made me remember as having an almost factory intensity: the noise of the electric saw that cuts through the skull and of the chisel used to crack the spine and of the instrument like pruning shears used to cut the rib cage. I looked at the exposed viscera and brains and bits of bone and cartilage and I wondered how all the pieces would fit back into a body that would wear a suit and a tie in its casket and perhaps have rosary beads coiled through its fingers.

The cold room, where the bodies are kept prior to their postmortems, is the eeriest place in the morgue. It seemed immense the first time I saw it, a room shaped like a croquet wicket, with tier after tier after tier of bodies, up one leg of the wicket, across the arm and down the other leg. On each tier were five plastic stretchers and each stretcher was Tiffany blue and on each was a body, sometimes two, head to toe. What strikes me now, weeks later, is how the room seemed to shrink between visits; I think the reason is that the mind is simply not equipped at first to assimilate hundreds of bodies in such a cramped surrounding; giving it size somehow made it seem more reasonable until the brain could adjust, to realize that this was not television or the movies where each body in a morgue has its own wall crypt.

The temperature in the cold room was approximately 30 degrees, cold enough to keep the smell of formaldehyde and decay bearable. Most of the bodies were wrapped in white butcher paper (another vivid departure from television), and when my detective hosts ripped the paper to show me a particularly choice corpse, the sound of the tearing seemed to reverberate off the walls. One tier of blue stretchers seemed to hold only babies in what appeared to be paper bags; I was not prepared to examine them too closely. Another aisle, the sound of more paper tearing, this time to expose a bearded biker with a Harley-Davidson tattoo on his right arm and on his left a tattoo of a death's head with Mercury wings. In the exact center of his chest, there was a perfect circular hole the size of a Ping-Pong ball. The biker was a suicide; his old lady had split and he had blown himself away. With a twelve-gauge, one detective insisted, and the other said no, and the first reached into the dead biker's open wound, searched for a moment and then, triumphantly, produced a piece of wadding from the hole in the dead man's chest. "I told you it was a twelve-gauge," he said. As we left the cold room, the first detective showed me a novelty card that read "Eat a toad for breakfast and that will be as bad as you will feel all day."

There is no dignity in death: This was the litany my detective friends kept repeating in the corridors and in the decomp room and in the autopsy room and in the cold room. And of course they were right. There is no dignity when death is merely a professional by-product, when those hundreds of bodies are like so many ball bearings in a gear factory. I think that is why I thought so much about my father after I left the morgue. I tried to dredge up every memory of him that I could, good and bad. I remember once when I was ashamed of him and I remember every time I bared my backside to his strap; I remember when he told me the facts of life and how we both started to laugh when he used the slang synonym for erection; I remember insisting that I was his favorite son. In every way I pursued what Joyce Carol Oates has called "the phantasmagoria of personality." Not to do so was to visualize my father wrapped in butcher paper, and that was simply unthinkable. It is memory, after all, that gives dignity to death.

3.

DIVISION III, MUNICIPAL COURT, Santa Monica, a hot Wednesday in August. I sit and read the transcript of a vice case. I learn how to charge fellatio to a restaurant in Marina del Key on a BankAmericard and that Greek is something other than a nationality and that the cover of a Chinese vice cop is rarely busted, because the girls never think that the fuzz will be Chinese. I learn that a "nurse call" is a John who wants an enema and that an outcall massage service called "Teenagers Who Are Terrific" offers, in outcall terms, the potential for a dynamite acronym. Department B, Superior Court, the sentencing of a prisoner convicted of multiple murders—life without possibility of parole. "He is to spend the rest of his days in prison, he is to die in prison." The judge's nasal voice is without inflection. "Society should never, be it sixty years from now, be forced to accept the risk of his presence." Department J, a family hearing: A psychiatrist testifies that a husband's masturbation fantasies were powered by his wife's infidelities. The wife is wearing a white dress, and she shapes her nails with an emery board. Department K, a custody hearing, and the tightroping of perjury:

Q. You bought cocaine for your wife?
A. No, I paid for the cocaine my wife bought.

I am drawn to the Santa Monica Courthouse the way some people are drawn to church. It is only a five-minute drive from my house, five minutes through a time warp back into the concepts of sin and retribution that were the underpinnings of my Catholic childhood. There in that antiseptic institutional pile just a few hundred yards from the sand and the sea and the Bain de Soleil I am exposed to a tapestry of transgressions scarcely imaginable to those Sisters of Mercy who were the moral arbiters of my youth, a tableau of sex and money and controlled substances, a world of the snortable, sniffable, smokable, shootable, and swallowable.

One rids himself quickly of a number of illusions in the Santa Monica Courthouse, in any courthouse. The first fancy to go is the immutability of truth. A courthouse is by definition a place where people lie; not to lie is to invite confinement in what one superior court judge calls "a structured setting." There is a presumption of perjury, and even that which is accepted as truth is pockmarked with distortion and self-interest. "I like the guy who says, 'Sure, I was in the store,' " a defense attorney tells me. " 'But there was no way that bitch could've recognized me with my mask on. It was a Batman mask. Who'd she think I was? Bruce Wayne? And I didn't have no shotgun. It was a twenty-two. If she says she can recognize me, she's blowing smoke up your ass, counselor.' " The attorney smiles. "That is an easy client to defend."

The next illusion to go is the principle of innocent until proven guilty. In the Santa Monica Courthouse, in any courthouse, the criminal justice system is lubricated by a presumption of guilt, the simple reason being that most criminal defendants *are* guilty.

The case backlog in every court is so huge that without plea bargaining the drains of justice would clog up irrevocably; the brokering of convictions is the Drano that keeps the system unclogged. There is little room for Perry Mason. Delay is the best defense, continuance the only strategy; memories fade, evidence goes flat, witnesses move away, address unknown; the case load backs up, nobody cares; and finally it is time to deal, to close the file. "The only cases that go to trial," a defense attorney repeats to me over lunch, "are the unimportant crimes of important people and the important crimes of unimportant people."

In Los Angeles County, the same district attorneys, the same public defenders are assigned to the same judge and the same courtroom every day. In this cozy atmosphere, the accused are like so many markers on a board. The players feel each other out, measure the worth of felon against felony. The haggling is like a Turkish bazaar. To a defense attorney, success is measured not so much by acquittal as by the kicking of a felony down to a misdemeanor, by the agreement that time served will be counted against time; victory is talking a jury in a trial's penalty phase into life without possibility of parole instead of cyanide tablets dropped into a pail of sulfuric acid. "You don't play the game," a former public defender told me. "You play the players." It is a totally hermetic world, a world in which the most rancid view of human behavior prevails, and I find it mesmerizing.

First there are the touches, the signatures that make each crime statistic human. In the morning, I come early to watch the arrival of the black-and-white bus with the mesh bars in the windows that the sheriff's office uses to transport prisoners from the county jail to the courthouse; the prisoners are shackled and wear denims stenciled "County Jail" and file to the lockup, where they wait until their cases are called. Most of the faces are black and brown, an implicit reminder of economic determinism: Crime is the cottage industry of the underprivileged; whites make bail. In the courtrooms, the accused begin to take on separate identities. A young white male cops a plea to possession. He stands before the judge holding a soccer ball under his arm; no mention is made of the ball. Same courtroom, next case. A show business coker, Gucci handbag

and blue suede loafers, no socks; case continued. A youthful black
pleads guilty to armed robbery in exchange for the dropping of a
murder charge; the quid pro quo is an agreement to testify against
the partner who had allegedly killed the attendant in the gas station they had stuck up together. As the bailiff leads him back to the
lockup, the youth blows a kiss to his mother and sister; sticking
from the back pocket of his denims I see a tattered paperback copy
of Richard Wright's *Black Boy*. A lawyer petitions the court for a
single cell in the county jail for his client, a pale redheaded teenager.
"A first offender," his lawyer whispers to me. "Fresh meat. Everyone wants a whack at him. He doesn't get a single cell, he'll get his
asshole stretched." Another black in jail denims; he wants both an
O.R. release and to dismiss his court-appointed attorney. "This case
is getting serious, Your Honor," he says. "I need me a real lawyer.
I get me on the street, I can get me some money." I think I would
not want to be on the street he gets it on.

It is like watching the ultimate game show, the game being life
itself. Every tactic is explored for advantage, even racism. I recall a
day I spent years ago with a public defender in Clark County,
Nevada. He had two black clients that day, one a prostitute who had
killed a trick, the other a man accused of stealing a number of checks
from a local NAACP office. The man's case was dismissed when the
lawyer claimed that, for a black, stealing from the NAACP was not
a robbery but a loan; the prostitute's case thrown out when he had her
testify that the John, in her words, "wanted me to satisfy his dog."

In the corridors of the Santa Monica Courthouse I meet the
woman attorney who one day had a professional burglar client
appearing in three different courtrooms on three different charges
under three different names, with no one the wiser. Over there is the
attorney from the Manson case who once put a hostile witness's
homosexuality on the record: "Let the record reflect that the witness
winked at my client." The man in the custom-made three-piece suit
with buttonholes on the sleeve is a former radical lawyer now defend-
ing a member of the Mafia. He was once the man you called if you
blew up Fort Ord or if you were a rock-'n'-roller caught with ninety-
seven pounds of blow. Every case that had a number at the end of it,
there he was; it was said that he thought the Indianapolis 500 was

an illegal detention case. "I never saw him when he wasn't wearing a blue work shirt and sandals," an attorney says, not without admiration. "Now he's representing the wiseguys."

I watch, I listen, I learn. Department 127, the daily calendar, Case No. B342076, 192.1 PC, one count. In the state penal code, 192.1 is manslaughter. The defendant had interfered in a domestic argument and killed a man who was beating up on a woman. She had been released on her own recognizance. "Her case will never get to trial," my guide says. I ask why. "Manslaughter is what you plead down to. You don't try manslaughter. If the D.A. is only charging manslaughter, he doesn't have a case." I begin to hear the undertones. I sit in municipal court after three drinks and a large lunch. I am the only spectator at the preliminary hearing. The district attorney has evasive eyes and seems uneasy about my presence. He wonders if I am a reporter. His eyes do not meet mine, and he mumbles something about the FBI and a potential for embarrassment. The drinks take hold and I begin to doze. An FBI agent testifies about an armed robbery at 1:15 A.M. on a quiet street in Beverly Hills. Nothing extraordinary here. But when the agent steps from the stand he and the district attorney whisper quietly. I realize I am under discussion. The FBI agent kneels next to me. He wonders if he might ask who it is I work for.

I am now wide awake. The victims of the armed robbery were in fact three FBI agents, one female, two male; one of the victims was the agent who had just testified. They had allegedly been stuck up by the two sullen blacks at the defense table. The three agents had been on a stakeout that had nothing to do with the two blacks. On the nation's business, as it were. The feds were embarrassed, and their embarrassment was a source of some quiet satisfaction in Division III. Not only had the myth of FBI invincibility been tarnished, but the agents had also shown some uncertainty in picking their assailants from a sheriff's lineup. Defense counsel bored in on this uncertainty. The suspect being staked out had in fact been arrested before the three agents came on duty. So they had gone to Lawry's and had a bottle of wine, and after that they spent a couple of hours in a bar behind Cedars-Sinai Hospital; the stickup occurred when they left the saloon. I suspect I could have conducted that cross-examination. How many drinks were consumed? Two hours in this bar and you just had coffee? I think I know now what it means to implant reasonable doubt.

When I think of the law, I do not think of Archibald Cox and Earl Warren. I do not think of Mr. Justice Cardozo or Mr. Justice Holmes. Theirs is a law of abstraction and beauty. When I think of the law I think of a morning in the Santa Monica Courthouse. I watch a judge sentence a man to two years in prison. The accused is just another hype, with a past—and probably a future—defined by a rap sheet. When sentence is passed, the defendant asks the judge if he will marry him before he is sent away. The bride is a Mexican woman, six months' pregnant with one front tooth missing. The bailiff and the public defender are the witnesses. The groom kisses the bride; the prosecutor and the public defender kiss the bride; even I kiss the bride. The judge says, "Don't write me in six months and say you want an annulment because you haven't consummated your marriage."

That is the law.

The Simpsons

[1994]

I.

IS THERE ANYONE out there who has not heard the facts, the factoids, the allegations, the half-truths, the untruths, the leaks, the smears, heard the e-mail jokes (hundreds of them, thousands, tasteless, it is always agreed, in all mitigating sanctimony, even as they are passed on: "Did you hear that O.J.'s signed a new contract with Hertz . . . he's going to be making license plates for them. . . . The bad news is O.J.'s going to prison, the good news is that Michael Jackson's taking the kids. . . . Did you hear O.J.'s last words to Nicole . . . your waiter will be with you shortly. . . . Rodney King told O.J., 'Good thing you didn't get out of the car, Juice . . .' "), heard the theories zipping along the communications highway, crisscrossing the Internet, hundreds of them, too, thousands, *vide* Lauren Swann to François Coulombe, Sunday, July 10, 1994, 10:04:13 AM ("Why was nothing else but a glove found at the back of the guest house? How convenient"), *vide* Joan Porte to Lauren Swann, Sunday, July 10, 1994, 2:23:19 PM ("Personally I think someone saw how easy it was to make Michael Jackson fall, and had it in for O.J."), the bloody butchery murders of Nicole and Ron (who in death achieved what O.J. earned in life, the true fame of not needing a last name for identification) a nirvana for conspiracy theorists, halcyon days, not since JFK and the grassy knoll, the three tramps, the single bullet, Zapruder frames 200 to 224.

Ninety-five million Americans in two-thirds of the nation's households tuned in on the longest, slowest chase in television history, a chase that no film director would dare stage. In the skies above, a squadron of telecopters recorded the event, while below A.C. Cowling's white Bronco, escorted front and rear by what appeared to be most of the police agencies in southern California, made its leisurely way north from the El Toro Y, up the Santa Ana, the Artesia, and the San Diego freeways, its stately choreography reminiscent of water ballets from M-G-M's old Esther Williams musicals.

"Wet she was a star," Esther Williams's producer once confided to me about his former meal ticket, and the same calculation could be applied to the passenger crouched in the back of Cowling's Bronco, cellular telephone and .357 Magnum at the ready, the possibility that he would blow his brains out a topic of endless speculation by anchormen and anchorwomen reporting on his hegira: in an open field, wearing helmet and pads, O.J. Simpson was a star. But that was long ago, and he would end that night in handcuffs, mugged and fingerprinted, a soon-to-be forty-seven-year-old man with a new identification in the Los Angeles County jail, Prisoner No. 4013970, charged in the arrest warrant with violating Section 187 (a) of the California Penal Code, to wit in count one that "Orenthal James Simpson . . . did willfully, unlawfully, and with malice aforethought murder Nicole Brown Simpson, a human being," and in count two that he "did willfully, unlawfully, and with malice aforethought murder Ronald Lyle Goldman, a human being."

❧

THE PROFESSIONAL ATHLETE is isolated early, anointed for the possibility of fame and fortune when still a child. In a recent interview in the Buddhist quarterly *Tricycle*, Phil Jackson, coach of the Chicago Bulls and a practicing Buddhist, said that ". . . in the seventh, eighth and ninth grades, eighty percent of these kids are noticed and given privileged lives. From then on, everything is paid for. By the time we get them, at age twenty, they've had maybe eight years of a programmed existence where everything has been spoonfed to them. They've got shoe people coming after them, sportswear people, agents, lawyers—they might have an entourage of five to ten people vying for their favor."[1] For the child athlete of color from a poor family, sports offer the best, and in many cases the only, opportunity to get out of harm's way.

The case history of Orenthal James Simpson was in no way original: a gang background, trouble with the law, truancy and grades so bad he was unable to get into college. Military service seemed worth trying. "I was gonna join the Marines and fight in Vietnam," he told an interviewer, "but . . . a friend came back from Vietnam missing a leg, and I thought I had to be *crazy* to go there."[2] He maneuvered his way into junior college and a draft deferment, and then entered the University of Southern California, won the Heisman Trophy as the country's best football player, and in 1969 was the first player chosen in the NFL draft.

The life of the professional athlete is an unreal, emotionally underdeveloped existence, lived at the frontier of instinct and reflex, where the difference between success and failure can be measured in microseconds; split vision, muscle memory, and hand-to-eye coordination are better refined than the vocabulary to explain them. That the athlete will never again do anything in his life as well as what he does at age twenty-five is a truth best left unstated. As long as he can perform, the athlete has an exemption from the realities of life; his physical skills will endure, and his every whim is a demand likely to be satisfied.

Sexual entitlement is a part of the package, as if the women who are drawn to him and his fame and his riches are just another bonus clause in his contract, a perk, like the suite on the road and the free rental car at his disposal. By the time he is thirty, he is professionally in decline, especially if like O.J. Simpson he is a running back with chancy knees. After sports, if he still manages to maintain his high profile, he is really famous for formerly being famous. It is a constantly diminishing psychic bank account on which to draw. He is too old to begin the kind of work that promises much reward, even if he were educated, qualified, and so disposed; chemical dependency is an expensive outlet, but rehab promises a possible profit center if a writer can be found to put its lessons in book form with the proper moral platitudes. Sports broadcasting and television huckstering allow some of the better known to trade on their names for a few more years, until a newer, fresher retiree appears. For other semi-solvent former stars, retirement becomes an endless treadmill of card shows, "fantasy camps" where aging fans pay to play ball against their childhood idols, celebrity golf tournaments, old-timers' games, and meet-and-greet paid appearances at the weddings, birthdays, anniversaries, and bar mitzvahs of strangers, every handshake rung up on a cash register, the sexual favor provided for the randy guest in the nature of a tip.

~

O.J. Simpson was one of the few retired athletes, and certainly the first black, to succeed in exploiting his retirement, becoming in the process more widely known than he ever was as a football player, known to a generation that had never seen him on a gridiron, a favorite of women as well as men who fantasized their own eighty-yard runs. He was the quintessential intimate stranger, the person we think we know because of his celebrity. He had the perfect marketable nickname—O.J., the Juice—he had been, in the terms of his profession, not merely good but great, and he had that smile like sunlight, the smile that must have masked, we can speculate now, how many scars from a childhood in San Francisco's Potrero Hill projects, how many volcanic eruptions of temper, how many racial affronts. Simpson was able to transcend color not through sports but through the marketplace, product endorsements, in particular the Hertz commercials. Corporate spokesmen normally have a short shelf life, but Simpson remained the public persona of Hertz for an almost incredible seventeen years, from 1977, when he was still a Buffalo Bills running back, to the night that Nicole Brown Simpson and Ronald Lyle Goldman were murdered.

The point of the Hertz campaign was a promise to speed the business traveler out of the airport, into his car, and on the way to his appointment. It was a nervy decision for Hertz to select Simpson as the surrogate for those white mid-level middle-class corporate managers whose lives revolved around airline hubs and the OAG Pocket Flight Guide. To see O.J. Simpson racing through an airport was at first both startling and witty, then routine and reassuring. He was always in a subdued suit and unthreatening tie, the uniform of middle management, unlike Magic Johnson and Michael Jordan, the other black endorsement megastars, who in their commercials were never far removed from a basketball or a jersey. "People identify with me, and I don't think that I'm offensive to anyone," Simpson says in the quickie paperback *O.J. Simpson: American Hero, American Tragedy*. "People have told me I'm colorless. Everyone likes me. I stay out of politics, I don't like to save people for the Lord."

With O.J. Simpson, white Americans could congratulate themselves with the spurious notion that they were colorblind, a conclusion made possible by Simpson's conversion of himself into a white man's idea of an acceptable black man. He bought a large house on a corner lot in Brentwood Park, where his neighbors included Michael Ovitz, the president of Creative Artists Agency, who is ritually described as "the most powerful man in Hollywood"; Gil Garcetti, the Los Angeles County district attorney, whose office will be prosecuting Simpson on two counts of murder in the first degree, the double murder counting as a special circumstance, which means Garcetti will have to decide if he will seek the death penalty for his neighbor; Richard Riordan, the mayor of Los Angeles; and, directly across the street, Stanley Sheinbaum, the political activist, former ACLU board member, and former president of the Los Angeles Police Commission.

~⌒∽

SIMPSON'S BLACK FIRST wife, Marguerite Whitley, the mother of his three children (the youngest of whom, Aaren, died after a swimming pool accident shortly before her second birthday), was dismissed, although it took a court order to get her out of the Brentwood house. Simpson lived the restless life of the retired upscale ex-jock: golf and high-stakes card games at the Riviera Country Club in Pacific Palisades, expensive fast cars, quick trips in search of the sun, corporate conventions, some discreet drug use. Surrounding him was the sort of entourage that regularly attaches itself to superannuated former athletes, rich white sports fanatics basking in the reflected warmth of his fame as he basked in the comfort of their wealth, and the kind of celebrity lawyers who like to hang with the celebrities they represent, sharing in the overflow of drugs and girls. The entourage became to Simpson in retirement what the Electric Company, his offensive line in Buffalo, had been in his playing days, protectors of the franchise, middle-aged schmoozers and hangers-on shielding the Juice from any bad news, letting him go on thinking, as he had his entire life, that should trouble ever arrive it could be handled.

~

JOHN CHEEVER LIKED staying in Brentwood Park when he visited Los Angeles, because, he said, it reminded him of Connecticut. As it happened, I lived in Brentwood Park for ten years, in a center-plan New England house on a lot with deciduous trees that seemed to shed their leaves not seasonally but whenever they got nervous. I was only a minute or so from O.J. Simpson's house and Gil Garcetti's house and Mike Ovitz's house and Richard Riordan's house; it was a neighborhood small enough so that everyone pretty much knew where everyone else lived, and had at least a nodding acquaintance with many neighbors. Brentwood is perhaps the most sedate of Los Angeles's West Side communities, the West Side being that part of the basin stretching from Beverly Hills to the ocean. Its residents are generally prosperous and liberal and it has a high concentration of the Jewish show business community who were not particularly welcome in the established rich sections of the city.

If less so than in Beverly Hills, Holmby Hills, and Bel Air, many of the older Brentwood Park houses come with pedigrees; on my old street, the director Rob Reiner lives in Norman Lear's old house, and in an earlier incarnation Norman Lear's old house was the house where Jane Fonda grew up. My neighbor across the street was the Brentwood Park Property Owner's Association link with the Los Angeles Police Department. She also always had an LAPD officer or two living in the apartment above her garage, a protective presence to her neighbors, and she put out the Brentwood Park crime report: "There are 3 male and 1 female latins who are good burglary suspects who have been seen apparently casing houses. White VW Bug—1967. California license plate X8YZ 06B1. Driver is a male latin with a tattoo on inside of right arm—female face with 'CARLOS' above it."

The center of local activity, one might even say its town square, is the Brentwood Mart, a ramshackle one-story collection of stalls, stores, and small businesses built around a small open courtyard. For the last twenty years, it has been presided over by the manager of The Book Nook, a tiny, perfect book store and magazine stand. The Mart is where the neighborhood gathers to read *The New York Times* and the movie trade papers, to sip espresso or a potassium cocktail (carrot juice, spinach juice, and two I can't remember) or go to the drugstore or eat ribs or fried chicken or get a haircut or hand-dipped chocolates, and to check out the community bulletin board for the entry requirements for the Malibu Kiwanis chili cook-off or the lost and found notices for neighborhood pets ("Found: Kitty Kat Mostly White With Light Brown Ears. Siamese Mix? Very Blue Eyes"). There was scarcely a day when some errand did not bring me to the Mart, and occasionally I would see O.J. Simpson in tennis clothes browsing at the Book Nook, where he got his *USA Today* and picked up the latest Jack Higgins or Clive Cussler novel.

∽

I MENTION THIS to point out that Brentwood is a genuine neighborhood, because when I read about it in the newspapers after the murders of Nicole Brown Simpson and Ronald Lyle Goldman, human beings, and the arrest of O.J. Simpson for committing those murders, the adjectives attached to it made it seem a contemporary sybaritic Sodom. "The fast lane life that flows along San Vicente Boulevard," *The New York Times* said in a profile of Goldman, going on about "trendy" Brentwood, with its "opulence and glamor," its "moneyed elite," "young models" and "local luminaries like Nicole Brown Simpson." In fact, there are two Brentwoods, the Brentwood north of San Vicente Boulevard with its single-family houses, high privet and oleander hedges, north-south tennis courts and heated pools, and the Brentwood south of San Vicente and east of Bundy, a considerably meaner and less homogenous place altogether, a condo district of high density "town houses," a local answer to affordable housing for the recently divorced with pre-nuptial agreements, the provisionally separated, and the not yet married.

The San Vicente "fast lane" where the young congregate is a diversified economy of gyms, tanning salons, bad restaurants, singles bars, cappuccino bars, and outlets for expensive sweatclothes and athletic shoes. Working out is a job category more satisfying than work or study; a firm body and tight buns are in the nature of character references. It is an area populated by the beautiful underemployed, would-be actors, actresses, and models, male and female, with portfolios of 8x10 glossies passing as curricula vitae; a gig as a waiter or waitress is only a temporary indisposition, with a free meal thrown in that can be worked off on a stair-master. One has the sense that many people one sees on San Vicente are just waiting to be discovered, the way Lana Turner was allegedly discovered at Schwab's drugstore in Hollywood, drinking a soda; the difference is in the expectation that the lightning of discovery will strike on the weight machines at The Gym or in the tanning room at Le Beach Club or while having a postworkout cappuccino at Starbucks. These are places, however, where no one but they go; it is as if they are trying out for each other, as if youth and beauty are constants to be squandered in pursuit of a lifestyle they do not wish to work all that hard to achieve.

It is a world in which Ronald Lyle Goldman was an easy fit. The late film director Sam Peckinpah once told me that the only Hollywood story worth making was one he called "The Third Man Through the Door." There is the star, Peckinpah said, there's the star's consort, and then there's the third man through the door, holding it open for the other two, the one whose face is blurred out in the publicity photographs. Ronald Lyle Goldman seemed the definition of the third man through the door. He was twenty-five, a college dropout from Illinois, his looks as gorgeously unexceptional as Nicole Brown Simpson's. What he wanted was never quite clear. He modeled once for Armani, he gave tennis lessons, he worked out on the machines at The Gym, and he waited table at Mezzaluna, a second-rate Brentwood restaurant elevated in the postmurder stories to a "hot spot." Sometimes he told friends he wanted to own a restaurant of his own, other times that if he had not "made it" (making it at what never precisely defined) by thirty, he would like to become a paramedic. It was a life not unpleasurably adrift, and so it might have remained, had Ronald Lyle Goldman not had the misfortune to meet Nicole Brown Simpson.

∼

WE KNOW NOW, as we always do in the aftermath of bloodshed, that the marriage of Nicole and O.J. Simpson prior to their 1992 divorce had been volatile, and occasionally violent. There were frequent 911 calls to settle domestic disputes, and in 1989 the Los Angeles city attorney filed a spousal battery complaint against Simpson after a fight on New Year's Eve. "He's going to kill me, he's going to kill me," she wept to the officers who answered her 911 call early that New Year's morning. They had found her hiding in the bushes outside her mock Tudor house on North Rockingham Drive, wearing only sweatpants and a bra; her eye was blackened, her lips cut and swollen, there were scratches on her neck, and bruises on her cheek and forehead. Simpson shouted angrily at the police that it was a "family matter . . . why do you want to make a big deal out of it," and sped away in his Bentley. Cooling down, and surely aware that she had no place to go offering the life to which she had become accustomed, Nicole refused to press charges. The city attorney, however, was not deterred. O.J. Simpson pleaded no contest to spousal battery and received the same light sentence that most first-time wife-beaters receive—a small fine, community service, and mandatory counseling. After sentence was imposed, the couple issued a joint statement: "Our marriage is as strong as the day we were married."

Or at least strong enough to stagger on for another three years. Simpson was a compulsive philanderer, while Nicole was without resources except for what she received by her husband's grace and favor; her father was also a beneficiary of Simpson's largesse, having been awarded a Hertz franchise at the Ritz Carlton Hotel in Laguna Niguel. There had of course been a prenuptial agreement that had taken seven months to negotiate, and under which, on August 20,

1985, Nicole had signed a quit claim to the house on North Rockingham, the major asset in O.J. Simpson's financial statement. In the divorce settlement, Nicole received a lump sum payment of $433,750 and $10,000 a month in child support for the two children of the marriage, daughter Sydney and son Justin. In his counterclaim to her divorce suit, Simpson stated: "Petitioner [Nicole] has done nothing but play, taking nice vacations, spending time exercising and entertaining, and being entertained."

At thirty-three, Nicole Brown Simpson was essentially returning to the life she was leading when she met her ex-husband sixteen years earlier, except that now she had a white Ferrari with the kind of vanity license plate that adolescents favor—L84AD8, which decodes into Late For A Date. Nicole Brown was scarcely more than a child herself when she met O.J. Simpson. She was seventeen, a homecoming princess at Dana Hills High School in the Orange County beach community of Monarch Point. Higher education was not an option she vigorously pursued. Tall and willowy, she worked as a boutique sales clerk, and then as a waitress at the Daisy, a Beverly Hills club; and it was there that O.J. Simpson, thirty years old, shakily married to his first wife, his football career just about over, fixed on Nicole Brown.

Since the mid-1960s, when my wife and I used to go there, the Daisy has been a notorious pickup spot for men with an itch. It is useful perhaps here to pause and consider the kind of young woman still in her teens who becomes the consort of a high-profile swinger half a generation older. What the child-women who make this choice bring with them is youth, a compliant disposition, a taste for the world's goods, and a minimal sense of their own identity. They are defined by the men they sleep with; sex is their primary vocabulary. O.J. Simpson divorced Marguerite Whitley, took Nicole Brown as his live-in mistress, and in 1985 married her. She had a personal trainer, a nutritionist, a fully staffed household, two children, an apartment on Manhattan's East Side, an oceanfront vacation house in Laguna Beach, holidays in Hawaii and Mexico, and skiing trips to Colorado. In actuality, however, she was chattel with a wedding ring, her security a 911 emergency number she had good reason to call often.

IN THE NEIGHBORHOOD of San Vicente Boulevard to which she gravitated with her children, Sydney and Justin, after the divorce, Nicole Brown Simpson still had the cachet of her married name; in this habitat of the young, the tan, and the beautiful she had the status of the second person through the door, and being close to her was as close as any of her new friends would probably ever get to fame. She jogged under the coral trees on the San Vicente median, turned up at The Gym and Starbucks, and oversaw the after-school activities of her children. She tooled around Brentwood in her Ferrari, sometimes letting Ron Goldman drive it, and at night she danced in local clubs. "She had just gotten it all together," her older sister Denise Brown told *The New York Times* after her death. "She was going to start her life over." Friends said she was enjoying her freedom, "becoming her own woman."

What form that independence would take, however, was uncertain. Simpson claimed that paternity gave him free access not only to the house he thought he was paying for, but *droit de seigneur* over the mother of his children as well. He and Nicole took vacations together, they "dated," there was an attempt at reconciliation. Other interludes were less placid. If Simpson was not exactly a stalker, he did make his ex-wife aware of his considerable and, to her and her friends, dangerous and obsessive presence. Once, according to unsealed grand jury testimony, he spied on Nicole through a window while she was having oral sex with a man she had been seeing. Last fall, during one of his high-pitched visits, Nicole was forced to make two more 911 calls. "He broke the back door down to get in . . ." she sobbed to the 911 operator. "He's fucking going nuts . . . He's going to beat the shit out of me." On the tapes, as if in some primal rage, Simpson could be heard screaming in the background about the earlier fellatio he said he had witnessed as his children were upstairs sleeping.

A black ex-athlete growing older ungracefully, tenuously living a white life on the limited visa of his contract as a television pitchman; his beautiful battered ex-wife trying at age thirty-five to start over after half a lifetime on someone else's tab; a waiter and unsuccessful male model uncertain whether to become a restaura-teur or a paramedic, collecting business cards from the men on whose tables he waited in case one might decide to invest in his dream restaurant: these were characters of considerable and ambiguous par-ticularity. With the events of June 12, however, when Nicole Brown Simpson and Ronald Lyle Goldman were found slashed and stabbed to death, and with the arrest of Orenthal James Simpson for killing them, all three lost whatever identity they had in the frantic search to find some larger meaning that would explain the crime. The story demanded a moral: youth wasted, promise denied, spousal abuse, domestic violence, the race card; show me a hero, F. Scott Fitzgerald jotted in his notebook, and I will write you a tragedy.

2.

IN LOS ANGELES, the case was an experience as uniting in its way as an earthquake. Serious people, unwilling to accept what on the face of it seemed to be the facts, offered theories, even to strangers in checkout lines and movie queues: it was straight, it was gay, it was the Colombians, it was the Mafia, it was the Klan, it was a setup, it was a drug deal gone bad. On *This Week with David Brinkley*, the panel seemed petulant that the country was absorbed by something other than what normally came out of Washington. For several Hollywood studios, the preliminary hearing with its captive audience was an opportunity for free TV time. Universal Pictures moved an 18-wheeler truck, with ads for its new release, *The Shadow*, plastered on both sides, to a spot out-side the courthouse where it would appear in live news coverage. "It boils down to this," an MGM executive told a reporter from the *Los Angeles Times*. "What's a studio to do when they've got close to 100 million viewers watching?"

I spent a day in a TV studio with two of the experts covering the hearing live for ABC; one was an old friend, Leslie Abramson, the attorney who defended Erik Menendez on the charge of murdering his parents and hung the jury, the other Robert Philibosian, one of

Gil Garcetti's predecessors as Los Angeles County District Attorney. From her car on our way to the studio, Ms. Abramson called her office to get her messages. There was one of interest: a caller who did not identify himself but who appeared to be a disgruntled LAPD officer. The caller said that the Robbery-Homicide detectives who went to the Simpson house on the night of the killings did not follow investigative procedures laid out in the LAPD police manual, and that a copy of the manual should be given to Robert Shapiro, who was leading the Simpson defense, to use during his cross-examination of the detectives. That an LAPD cop might go against his own in a case of this magnitude was a factor I had not considered, and I asked Ms. Abramson why a cop would snitch out other cops. Like everyone else in the LAPD, she said, he has an agenda. Such as? He might be an O.J. fan, she said, or he might not have been promoted, or he might just hate "the schmucks" in Robbery Homicide, because Robbery-Homicide detectives, Ms. Abramson said, exhibit an excess of "attitude" that is deeply resented by many uniformed officers.

If the hearing was serious business, it was also entertainment, and ABC's four-person legal team avidly examined the overnight ratings, which showed ABC outpacing the other two networks. In the tiny studio they shared, Ms. Abramson called Philibosian "Bobby," although in his dark suit and serious tie he did not seem the Bobby type. Off camera, the two commentators were biting about the cast of characters, especially Kato Kaelin, the dazed-looking part-time soft-core porn actor and full-time Simpson houseguest, whose licit and otherwise duties were a source of joyful speculation. When one of the detectives grew restive during cross-examination, Ms. Abramson said, "He's getting a little pissy." She knew the detective from other cases. "He doesn't like being confronted. He gets defensive." Philibosian was equally critical of prosecutor Marcia Clark. "She's got that smug little smirk on her face that doesn't play well to a jury." And later: "It's poor technique to ask multiple questions." On camera, none of the lawyers on any of the networks mentioned what they all knew, that the outcome of the hearing was pre-ordained: that no municipal court judge was going to take the heat for throwing the most spectacular murder case of the century out of court on a constitutional technicality, no matter how valid that technicality might be.

~

IT WAS A tabloid story, and even the most sober newspapers and newscasts handled it in a tabloid way, with an unexamined inflation of rhetoric. "Hero" and "tragedy" were debased coinage, as were "mansion" and "estate"; Nicole was always "beautiful" and "blonde," but Simpson, as Stanley Crouch pointed out in the *Los Angeles Times*, was never referred to as "handsome, brown, woolly-headed O.J." The phrase invariably hung on Simpson's defense team was "high-priced," as if the fees allegedly being earned were a guarantee of effectiveness. In fact, during the first days after the murders, Simpson's lawyers were almost amateurishly ineffective. Their first mistake was in allowing detectives to question Simpson without an attorney present. The explanation given by his first lawyer suggested that Simpson had relied on what he considered his celebrity exemption. For nearly thirty years, no one had ever told him what he did not wish to know, and he had the star's total faith in his ability to talk his way out of any unpleasantness, as if nothing he said could be held against him.

"Those statements are going to come back to haunt him," I was told by Johnnie L. Cochran, Jr., a former deputy district attorney and one of the best trial lawyers in Los Angeles. (It was Cochran, an African American, who took over the Michael Jackson case, and got it out of the headlines. One of his more successful specialties is handling plaintiffs in brutality cases against the LAPD.) I asked Cochran and several other criminal lawyers with wide experience in murder cases how they would handle a client who is so used to having his own way. In essence what they all said was this: You tell him, You were in handcuffs when I arrived, this is a death penalty pop, you could go to the gas chamber, and if you want to go downtown and talk to detectives without me, get yourself another lawyer. Then you tell the cops, Arrest him, take it to the grand jury, he's not speaking, you talk to me. You want a blood sample, get a court order.

Lawyer number one departed, to be replaced by Robert Shapiro, a Century City attorney with a roster of celebrity clients, including baseball players Darryl Strawberry and Vince Coleman; the singer Rod Stewart; Johnny Carson and F. Lee Bailey, both of whom he defended on drunk-driving charges; and Marlon Brando's son, Christian, for whom he plea bargained a ten-year voluntary manslaughter sentence after the young Brando shot his sister's lover to death in a drunken dispute. Spinning the media in celebrity cases was his stock in trade. Never call a homicide a "tragedy," Shapiro once advised in an article about handling the press, call it a "horrible human event."

Shapiro has never tried a capital murder case. "This is not the case to use as a learning experience," Cochran told me. By claiming right off that Simpson had an alibi—that he was at home when the murders were committed—Shapiro failed to observe, in the view of most defense attorneys, lesson number one. "You don't say a word unless you know all the facts," Cochran said. "If you say he had an alibi and the blood places him at the crime scene, then you're stuck with a bad alibi. If you open your mouth, you limit your options." Nor did Shapiro make clear to Simpson, I was told by a source close to the case, that if he were charged with special circumstance murder, or horrible human event, he could not get bail. When he was finally told, when it finally sunk in that he was looking at a seven-by-nine jail cell at least to the end of his trial, Simpson and A.C. Cowlings took off in the Bronco.

Perhaps the worst early mistake made by the high priced defense team, both in pitch and timing, was the public reading of Simpson's quasi-suicide note during the hours when he was a fugitive and prospective suicide in the back of Cowling's Bronco. Spin was a major part of the Simpson defense, but none of the spin doctors seemed to realize how maudlin, self-absorbed, ugly, and ultimately counterproductive the letter was. "At times," her spousal abuser wrote, "I've felt like a battered husband or boyfriend, but I loved her." Ronald Lyle Goldman received even shorter shrift: "I'm sorry for the Goldman family. I know how much it hurts."

The rest of the letter might well have been heard at a sports testimonial dinner, The Football Hall of Fame Honors O.J. Simpson: "Ahmad, I never stopped being proud of you. Marcus, you got a great lady in Catherine, don't mess it up . . . Skip and Cathy, I love

you guys." There was even a salute to his current girlfriend, Paula
Barbieri (who has parlayed her affair with Simpson into a photo feature in the October *Playboy*): "Paula, what can I say? I'm sorry I'm
not going to—we're not going to have our chance . . . I've had a
good life. I'm proud of how I lived. My mama taught me how to
do unto others . . . Peace and love. O.J."

∽

FOR GIL GARCETTI, the Simpson case seemed one that was all
downside, with no upside. First there was the embarrassment of
Simpson not voluntarily turning himself in to police—an alternative not generally available to a non-celebrity accused double murderer. "I want to say to the entire community—Mr. Simpson is a
fugitive from justice," Garcetti said in a public statement while
Simpson was on the run, his whereabouts still unknown. "If you
assist in any way, you are committing a felony. You will be prose-
cuted as a felon." There was in this warning an odd stridence that
led inexorably to its subtext: that Simpson might disappear into
black South Central Los Angeles and that the police would have to
go looking for him, with all the possibilities that scenario presented
for a riotous conflagration.

Simpson had not, in fact, led the kind of life that would have
drawn him naturally to South Central for camouflage. So assiduously
had he pursued racial neutrality that he had become estranged
from prominent elements of Los Angeles's black leadership. The
criticism was careful, but criticism nonetheless. "He might have
kept a stronger profile in helping the community of need," the Reverend Cecil Murray, of the First African Methodist Episcopalian
Church, told Lloyd Grove of *The Washington Post* after Simpson's
arrest. Of the city's black spokesmen, Murray is first among equals,
and black Los Angeles's unofficial liaison with the white establish-
ment. "O.J. lapsed in that regard." Among South Central's rank and
file, the lapse was forgiven as soon as telecopters picked up A.C.
Cowling's Bronco with its police escort. "They never thought of him
as black before," the "raptivist" Sister Souljah explained to a friend
of mine, "and when they saw him chased by all those cops, it was
the blackest thing he had ever done."

Over twenty black churches held prayer vigils for Simpson, and T-shirts inscribed "Turn The Juice Loose" were instant street-corner best sellers. The first polls showed that nearly three-quarters of the city's blacks had some degree of sympathy toward Simpson, as opposed to 38 percent of Anglo respondents, and 50 percent of Latino; according to a *Newsweek* poll in late July, 60 percent of blacks nationwide thought that Simpson was set up by a person or persons unknown. That the trial would be held in downtown Los Angeles insured that race would be an issue. "I hate to sound stereotypical," Cochran said, "but 30 to 40 percent of the jury pool downtown is minority, and most of that is African American."

Eleven days after the preliminary hearing ended, Cochran, Cecil Murray, and other African American leaders turned up the heat on Garcetti in a highly publicized two-hour meeting at the offices of the Urban League in the predominantly black Crenshaw District. Boxed in both by the leaders and by the geography of the venue, Garcetti felt compelled to give the absurd assurance that Simpson would be treated fairly, as if a fair trial was not a basic tenet of Anglo-Saxon law. Garcetti then moved on to a disquisition on fairness. "We're also interested in fairness to the victims," he added, "and interested in fairness, frankly, for the community as a whole." The leaders urged not only that the jury be racially mixed but also that the "death committee," or the eight senior deputy DAs who decide whether the office will seek the death penalty on any given case, be integrated, so as to no longer consist of eight middle-aged white males. The clear implication was that without such changes, blacks could perceive the proceedings against Simpson as unfair, upping the level of volatility.

The day after the meeting, Cochran himself joined the defense team; it was the best news Simpson had received since June 12. Lawyers specializing in DNA evidence were flown in from New York and at hearings late in August they vigorously challenged the prosecution's assertions that early DNA tests indicated that drops of blood found at the murder scene proved Simpson's presence at the site when the murders were committed. In their counterattack, the DNA specialists accused police analysts of sloppy lab work, and seized on every discrepancy relating to the number and descriptions of blood samples as showing a pattern of professional incompetence. At the same time, the defense accused prosecutors of playing fast and loose with the required disclosure of blood evidence. A defense strategy that no one would dare broach publicly began taking shape: if acquittal on grounds of reasonable doubt was impossible, Simpson's lawyers would try to hang the downtown jury, and then plea bargain. "Even if the jury consisted of the Buffalo Bills starting eleven and O.J. Simpson's mother," W. William Hodes, a professor of law at the University of Indiana wrote in a letter to *The New York Times*, "there is no possibility of an acquittal, and the defense is not trying to achieve one."[3]

                      ~

IT WAS A STRATEGY that presented Garcetti with another vexing problem (still unresolved at this writing): whether or not to seek the death penalty. There are nineteen special circumstances in the California penal code calling for a consideration of the death penalty, including murder of a law enforcement officer, murder by torture, murder committed during the commission of an ancillary felony, murder by bomb, and, as applicable in the Simpson case, multiple murder. The death penalty, however, is rarely sought in domestic homicide cases, even when there is more than one body. Of the more than 2,800 men on death row nationwide, according to the *Los Angeles Times*, only 34, or 1.2 percent, killed their wives.

    If Garcetti did not ask for the death penalty, however, many defense attorneys, including Leslie Abramson, whose client Erik Menendez is awaiting trial once again in a death penalty case, were prepared to claim that the district attorney was selectively charging. Some argued that Garcetti would be giving a break to a high-profile defendant, with a history of spousal abuse, and a nolo contendere plea for same, both because Simpson was a celebrity and because the district attorney was afraid of another riot should there be a conviction. Ms. Abramson noted that unlike Simpson, Erik Menendez has no prior record of violence, and a history of violence is one of the criteria for seeking the death penalty. But if Garcetti did go for the death penalty, he faced the difficulty of finding a jury that would sentence someone who has run through their living rooms for a quarter of a century either to the gas chamber or to death by lethal injection, the choice to be made by the condemned.

Even more vexatious for Garcetti is the public perception that his office is not very competent. Although it prosecutes 70,000 felonies a year, with a 93 percent conviction rate (most of which are plea bargains), the office, over the past thirteen years, has stumbled so repeatedly in high-profile trials that, as Garcetti admitted to the *Los Angeles Times*, "people are poking fun at us." For example, David Letterman. After the two Menendez juries hung, Letterman said: "I'm not sure I believe this, but a friend of mine out there told me he got out of a speeding ticket last week by telling the cops he was on his way to murder his parents."

There have been successes—the fraud conviction of S&L king Charles Keating and the murder conviction of the serial killer nicknamed the Night Stalker—but the flops get the attention, especially now with blanket television coverage the factor it has become. There was the Hillside Strangler case, which was so botched by the DA that the trial judge assigned the case to the attorney general of California. There was the McMartin case, in which the proprietors of a "preschool" were charged with hundreds of counts of sexually molesting dozens of children; the McMartin case, which should never have been brought in the first place, ended once in a hung jury, and after a second trial with an acquittal. There was the *Twilight Zone* case (in which the film director John Landis was accused of recklessly endangering the lives of three actors, two of them children, killed in a helicopter stunt he conceived and directed), which ended in the acquittal of Landis and his co-defendants. The cops who beat Rodney King were acquitted, and the blacks who beat Reginald Denny in 1992's LA Riots convicted only of lesser charges; the Menendez cases, described by prosecutors as a "slam dunk," ended in two mistrials.

Garcetti now faces a dilemma: a hung jury, a plea bargain, or a conviction on lesser murder or manslaughter charges will be regarded as still another flop. A murder one conviction, however, brings with it the possibility that Los Angeles might once again burn.

3.

IN THE END, it is likely that the Simpson trial will be just another diversion for a public with an insatiable appetite for diversion. While the concept that an accused person is innocent until proven guilty beyond a reasonable doubt is the bedrock of our criminal justice system, recent events have shown us that most Americans believe in it only selectively; it is an abstract idea that they feel should not necessarily apply to the Menendez brothers or the cops who beat Rodney King or to Orenthal James Simpson. More and more, "agendas" are what count. Gloria Allred and a consortium of women's groups, including both pro-choice and anti-abortion spokeswomen, sought, on behalf of Nicole Simpson, the same kind of audience with Garcetti that the black leadership had, in this case to demand that the district attorney seek the death penalty. One of the investigating detectives told a psychiatrist he left the Marine Corps because of "the Mexicans and the niggers"—and his lawyer has threatened to sue the defense attorneys, Simpson, and *The New Yorker*, where the charges were first printed, for circulating this and other allegedly racist remarks.

There were so many preposterous images on the periphery of the case that at times it seemed as if both the victims and the seriousness of the crimes against them were forgotten: Simpson and Kato taking O.J.'s Bentley to McDonald's for takeout just prior to the murders; the loyalist gofer, A.C. Cowlings, becoming a star on the Z-list party circuit (e.g., the Adult Films Dinner), even as prosecutors wrestled with how to deal with him, postponing indefinitely his indictment on charges of aiding and abetting a fugitive. This was the district attorney's way of squeezing Cowlings, so that the threat of future prosecution might deter him from testifying for Simpson—a risky assumption at best. Robert Shapiro installed an 800 line, ostensibly to help the Simpson defense team and also to buck up O.J. "Hello, this is the law offices of Robert L. Shapiro," the voice mail operator says. "Thank you for your call. If you have any information or evidence regarding the O.J. Simpson case, press 2 now. If you are an expert in a field relating to the O.J.

Simpson case and would like to offer your services, press 3 now. If you would like the address where you can send a letter of support to O.J., press 1 now. If you are seeking legal representation from the offices of Robert Shapiro, press 4 now." Taste prevailed, and "4" was quickly dropped.

Within days, according to Shapiro, the 800 line received 250,000 calls. The received wisdom was that the 800 line was a public relations ploy of doubtful benefit, but a New York homicide detective I know marveled at its tactical cunning. "It's a cop's nightmare," he said. "It means LAPD has to check out every lead, even the cockamamie ones. Let's say of the 250,000 calls, 249,000 are garbage, even 249,500. That leaves five hundred to check before the trial starts. No one has that kind of resources. Then at trial, the defense finds something not checked out; bingo, reasonable doubt."

ANY TRIAL IS a ritual, with its own totems. Calumny is the language spoken, the lie accepted, the half-truth chiseled on stone. The victims unable to speak for themselves will be put on trial and presented as co-conspirators in their own murders. It is well to remember that what we will read in the newspapers or see on television is not necessarily the same story the jury is hearing. Reporters covering a trial are less qualified than they sometimes think to comment on the way the facts admitted into testimony affect the collective mind of the jury. There are reasons for this. Reporters are privy to what the jury cannot hear. They have access to the lawyers, and to the conflicting spins of the adversarial system. They hear the judge's rulings on motions when the jury is out of the room. They have transcripts of the sidebar conversations between the bench and opposing counsel. Most of all, the reporters, with their excessive knowingness, are available to each other, refining and polishing a story by accretion, a narrative that may or may not tell the story of what actually happened. The stories the jurors eventually devise on their own proceed from a limited and narrowly defined set of facts. It is already accepted, by those who argue the pros and cons of the case on the television talk shows, that O.J.

Simpson has "lost in the court of public opinion." Perhaps he has, but he will be tried in a court of law, where an irreparably tarnished reputation is still not a capital offense.

NOTES

[1] *Tricycle*, Summer 1993, p. 94.

[2] Marc Cerasini, *O.J. Simpson: American Hero, American Tragedy* (Pinnacle Books, 1994), p. 56.

[3] W. William Hodes, letter to *The New York Times*, August 12, 1994.

STAR

BUCK

IN LATE MAY of 1951, when Willie Mays and I both were young, I drove to the Polo Grounds one evening to see the Giants play the Boston Braves. The reason for my outing was less to take in the ball game than to avoid a sociology exam. I was flunking sociology that spring—*Middletown in Transition* conflicted with what I then perceived as the pursuit of the good life—and at Princeton, where I was, in the words of my faculty advisor, "wintering," one could escape the tarnish of a failing grade simply by reporting sick, not taking the exam, and making up the credit in a later semester. And so as I took my seat in the upper deck behind first base, a doctor's certificate stating that I was being tested for incipient mononucleosis in my pocket, I felt only a sense of relief at having deflected the inevitable. I had no way of knowing that I was about to witness what was to be, in the circumscribed world of baseball, a historic event, the first major league home run of Willie Mays.

I had never seen Willie Mays until that night. He had reported to the Giants just three days before in Philadelphia after opening the season at Minneapolis, in the American Association, where in thirty-five games he had amassed seventy-one hits, knocked in thirty runs, was batting .477, and had hit one ball so hard in Milwaukee, it was said, that it had actually driven a hole through the outfield fence. The Giants were going nowhere. They had lost eleven of their first twelve games and were anchored in the second division. So vigorously did the Minneapolis citizenry protest at Mays's recall that the Giants placed advertisements in the local papers apologizing for the act. Willie Mays was twenty years old.

He had gone 0-for-12 in a series in Philadelphia and for this game, his first in New York, the Boston pitcher was Warren Spahn. "If you're going to guess when you come up to bat," Willie Mays said later, "might as well guess on the first pitch. And might as well guess fast ball is what he's going to throw." Mays guessed right. The first pitch Spahn threw was a fast ball that Mays hit into the darkness beyond the left-field roof.

That was 1951. The Giants lost the game that night 4-to-1 and in the newspapers the next morning there were stories of other home runs (Luke Easter hit one, as did Bobby Doerr and Ralph Kiner) and of more cosmic events: Mohammed Mossadegh was defying Sir Winston Churchill over the nationalization of the Anglo-Iranian Oil Company, Senator Robert Taft complained about the conduct of the MacArthur hearing before the Senate Foreign Relations and Armed Services committees, and Sergeant Claiborne W. Hodges captured 112 Reds as the 28th Division pushed into North Korea. There is something sad and dated about those headlines today as there was something precocious and unexceptional about a first major league home run in 1951. As I looked back at that first home run at the start of this season, fifteen years later, Willie Mays seemed to me a figure from some other time, more a memory of my own youth than the only man with a shot—a long shot to be sure—at the all-time record of 714 home runs set by Babe Ruth.

I had not seen him play in those fifteen years, seen none of the intervening five-hundred-odd home runs. Between him and Ruth stood only three men—Mel Ott with the National League record of 511 and Ted Williams and Jimmy Foxx with 521 and 534 respectively—all three of whom he seemed certain to pass this year. And so in much the same spirit as I had gone that night to the Polo Grounds (which sadly is no more), I flew to Houston to see Willie Mays in quest of a record, to see what that record meant to the man of thirty-five still living the dream of the boy of twenty.

⁓

THE GIANTS WERE staying at the Shamrock Hotel, itself a faded vestige of the $20-million folly that Glenn McCarthy had opened in the mudflats of southwest Houston on St. Patrick's Day in 1949, an opening which had drawn three thousand guests whose din drowned out the special radio broadcast of the event and who created a telephone emergency which was equaled in the records of Southwestern Bell only by the Galveston Flood of 1909. The hotel now seemed almost shabby and was taken over that afternoon in late April by the convention of the Texas Butane Dealers' Association. In the lobby, a tired girl in black tights, mesh stockings and a white ribbon which identified her as "Miss Friendly Flame" was passing out blue lollipops. "Blue for *bu*tane," she kept repeating wearily.

Shortly after four o'clock, Mays emerged from the elevator into the milling throng of butane dealers and their wives. As he picked his way across the lobby, a conventioneer in boots and Stetson who had passed most of the afternoon in the hospitality suite said loudly to his companion, "Who's the nigra?"

"That ain't no nigra," his friend said. "That's Willie Mays."

"Well, what do you know," the butane dealer said. "I gotta get his autograph." He tried to place his drink on the edge of a table, but it fell to the floor, splashing bourbon on the ankles of Miss Friendly Flame. Without looking back, he pushed after Mays, calling "Hey, boy . . ."

If Mays heard, he gave no notice.

He had come into Houston with 509 home runs, only two behind Ott's National League record and, with a good chance at least to tie it in the four-game series against the Astros, he was besieged by local sportswriters in the Giant dugout before the first game. With reporters he does not know, Mays is wary and slightly antagonistic. He never looked at his questioners, but kept his eyes fixed on the batting cage, where Houston was taking pregame hitting practice.

"Look," he said finally, "you writers are keeping closer tab on that record than I am. Me, I'm not antagonizing any pitchers by talking about it. If I get conscious of it, I'm afraid it'll jinx me. So ask me something else."

It was that strange diction of the professional athlete, in equal parts self-conscious, defensive and patronizing.

"What about the book, Willie?"

"What about it?" Mays said. His autobiography, ghosted by San Francisco novelist and sportswriter Charles Einstein, had just been published and in it Mays had discussed his disenchantment with former Giant manager Alvin Dark over Dark's allegation that Negro ballplayers were not as mentally alert as whites.

"Have you talked to Alvin about it?"

"There's nothin' to say," Mays said. "I said that in the book. Ain't you read the book?"

The sportswriter was apologetic. "Actually, no. But I've read a lot about it."

"I think you're just trying to see if I read my own book," Mays said. "Haven't read it and asking me all those questions about it."

"I thought I'd wait until it came out in paperback," the Houston writer laughed nervously.

"Don't do me no favors," Mays said.

The reporter quickly changed the subject. "Have you thought who'd play you if there's a movie sale?"

"Sidney," Mays said. "He's the only one got the right build."

"Sidney who?"

Mays stared at the questioner and after a moment said quietly, "*Poitier,* man."

The Giants were now taking hitting practice and Mays took a bat from the rack and stepped into the batting cage. He hit the first three balls thrown to him deep into the left-field seats. "Shoot," he said to no one in particular, "trying to find out if I read my own book."

As he left the cage, I introduced myself and said that I had seen his first home run in the Polo Grounds fifteen years before. He looked at me impassively and said nothing. Beside him, Giant coach Larry Jansen began to laugh.

"Buck," Jansen said (all the Giants call Mays "Buck"), "if everyone who's told you this past week they were in the Polo Grounds that night was actually there, that game must have drawn a hundred thirty-eight thousand people."

"I was thinking a hundred and fifty," Mays said.

I tried to strike up rapport in another direction. Knowing that Mays and his wife, from whom he is now divorced, had adopted a three-day-old baby in 1959, I told him that my wife and I had recently done the same.

"How 'bout that," Mays said wearily. Nothing further was volunteered.

The Giants were shut out that night and again the next afternoon in the first game of a day-night doubleheader. The only home runs were hit by Houston players and when they were struck, the message board which circles the outfield lit up in a tooting, blazing Western cartoon with fireworks, rockets, bomb bursts, snorting cattle, galloping horses, pistol-packing cowboys and ricocheting bullets. (A home run by a visiting player is greeted only by a ticking time bomb flashing "Tilt.") It occurred to me that the Astrodome was to the old Polo Grounds as Andy Warhol is to James McNeill Whistler, and as one with a strong sense of nostalgia, I found the display disconcerting.

Before the night game, the crowd was serenaded by the Kilgore Junior College Rangerettes. Dressed in red, white and blue cowgirl outfits, the Rangerettes resembled the chorus line in a Busby Berkeley musical. Waving flags and kicking their booted legs in a parody of the Rockettes, the girls swung into their finale, a neo-rock-'n-roll version of "God Bless America." In the Giant dugout, the players perused them like practiced flesh peddlers.

"Third from the end," one of the Giants said. "She's got that anxious look."

"Naw," said another. "Her legs don't quit."

"There's one there got her eyes on you, Buck."

Mays laughed and lifted his arms helplessly over his head.

"Buck thinks that's trouble he don't need."

The Houston pitcher that night was Robin Roberts. Now thirty-nine and in the last flickering twilight of his career, Roberts had won 281 games since he broke in with the Phillies in 1948 and was trying desperately to hang on until he won three hundred, a mark reached by only fourteen pitchers in major league history. His fast ball but a memory and armed only with guile and faultless control, Roberts held the Giants to one run in six innings and that run scored when the Houston shortstop dropped a pop fly. But with two outs in the seventh, and the score tied 1-to-1, Mays lashed a home run five rows deep behind the 406-foot sign in left field. When the ball was hit, Roberts's shoulders sagged and he did not bother to turn around to watch it go out.

"It wouldn't have brought it back," he said later in the Houston clubhouse after the Astros lost the game 2-to-1. He has a handsome, gentle face and lines of fatigue were etched around his eyes. "You been around as long as I have, you know when it's gone."

"How do you pitch to him, Robin?" a reporter asked.

Roberts took a long drink from a carton of milk before answering, as if wondering how many times he had been asked that question in the last eighteen years. "You move the ball in and out. If he guesses wrong, you got a chance. If he guesses right . . ." He shrugged.

"How many has he hit off you, all told?"

"Look, why don't you ask him?" Roberts said with a flash of impatience. "I just lost the game. He won it."

In the Giants' locker room, Mays could not remember exactly how many home runs he had hit off Roberts. "Four or five," he said. "He's been over in the American League a long time."

"That's the 241st game he's lost," a Houston writer said.

"He's won a couple, too," Mays said succinctly.

"I guess he didn't do too bad for a guy thirty-nine years old," the reporter persisted.

"Man, you got something against a guy getting old?" Mays said.

The next day—Sunday—Mays did not take batting practice, as he seldom does, now that he is older, when a day game follows a night game. Nor does he ever take fielding practice, again in an effort to conserve his energy. In the Giant dugout, the players, many of whom hate to fly, were talking about the National League's contingency plans to restock a ball club with players from other teams in the event of an air disaster.

"Hey, Buck," one of the Giants said, "I knew a guy hated to fly and would only take trains. Then he got killed in a train crash."

"What happened?" Mays said.

"A plane hit the train."

Mays shook his head and the dugout broke up in macabre laughter. Walking back into the Giant clubhouse, Mays had the trainer put an ice pack on his left hand, which was bruised and sore, causing him to lose control of the bat. As he soaked his hand, he listened expressionlessly while equipment manager Eddie Logan, who has been with the Giants since the days of Mel Ott, reminisced about Ott and the record.

"Ottie would have been glad it's staying with the Giants," Logan said.

"Haven't broken it yet," Mays said.

"It's only a matter of time, Buck," Logan said. "You ever seen him play?"

"Only in the newsreels," Mays said. "He was only a little guy. Don't know how he ever hit kicking out his foot like that." He took the ice pack off his hand and clenched his fist several times. "I guess that'll have to do it," he said.

It was another tough game. The Houston pitcher was Larry Dierker, a slender nineteen-year-old who was only four years old when Mays broke in with the Giants. Into the seventh inning, Dierker shut the Giants out, but tiring, he allowed a run and was relieved by right-hander Jim Owens. With two outs in the eighth inning and the Giants down a run, Mays came up with no one on. On the third pitch, he sent a drive crashing toward the left-field stands. He took two steps toward first base, then stopped and watched the ball as it disappeared into the crowd.

In the press box, a member of the Giants' party asked Judge Roy Hofheinz, owner of the Astros, to let loose the pyrotechnics on the message board, which had never before been lit up for a visiting player's home run.

"That one only tied the record," Judge Hofheinz said. "If he breaks it, we'll see."

Mays did not come to bat again.

The Giant clubhouse after the 4-2 victory was crowded with press and photographers. The celebration had all the spontaneity of an elaborately choreographed Japanese *No* drama. The festive postgame clubhouse seemed to exist only in the minds of reporters with deadlines to meet and headlines to match. Only when a camera was pointed at one of the players did he rouse himself from his torpor, smile animatedly, and say, as if by rote, that he would tell his grandchildren that he had seen Willie Mays tie the National League home-run record. Those players not being interviewed sat quietly before their lockers drinking beer and nibbling cold cuts, watching the reporters clustered around Mays's cubbyhole, as if wanting to point out to the press that this was only the twelfth game of the season, that there were 150 left, and that baseball was, after all, a business.

Mays sat in front of his locker, naked except for the uniform shirt he had put back on for the benefit of the photographers. Patiently he observed the ritual he had gone through so many times before.

"Were you thinking of Ott when you circled the bases, Willie?"

"No."

"What were you thinking?"

"Tie score."

A park policeman broke through the crowd to tell Giant manager Herman Franks, a portly, balding man who affects an air of permanent anger, that the fan who had caught the record-tying ball in the stands was at the clubhouse door. Franks eyed the fan suspiciously.

"A lot of foul balls went into the stands today," he said. "How do I know this is the one?"

"You don't," said the fan, a husky, barrel-chested brakeman from the Missouri-Pacific Railroad, who had driven 152 miles to the game from his home in east Texas. "You just gotta take my word for it."

"I'll give you fifty for it," Franks said.

The brakeman took the fifty dollars from Franks and carefully counted it to see if it was all there.

"Christ," Franks said, "he doesn't trust me."

An iced bottle of champagne had been sent down to the clubhouse and Franks popped the cork. Mays sipped a glass for the photographers and then passed it to one of the other players. A photographer asked Franks to pour some over Mays's head.

"Shit, not that picture again," Franks said disgustedly. "Don't you guys ever get any new ideas?"

With a pained look on his face, he asked Mays if he minded. Mays shook his head and dutifully submitted to the dunking.

It was a half-hour before Mays could finally get to the shower. When he emerged, the clubhouse was all but deserted. Someone asked him if he wanted the record-tying ball.

"Naw," Mays said. "It's Herman's fifty. Let him keep it. All it means to me is something else to dust."

It seemed certain that Willie Mays would hit his National League record-breaking 512th home run on San Francisco's ten-game home stand, and the Giants made plans for the event as if it were a diamond jubilee. A multitiered cake was baked with the number 512 embedded in the frosting with tiny silver sugar beads. One hundred dollars was earmarked for the fan who caught the record ball. In the photographers' booth at Candlestick Park, fifteen camera crews from local and network television moved in to record every move Mays made. From the Giant front office came an endless stream of arcane statistics: the first major league home run was hit by Ross Barnes of the Cincinnati Red Stockings off "Cherokee" Fisher of the Chicago Cubs on May 2, 1876; in running out his 511 home runs, Mays had trotted 183,960 feet around the bases, or 34.6 miles. A list was compiled of the thirty-one pitchers off whom Mays had hit five or more home runs (leading the parade, with eighteen, was Warren Spahn), and the homers themselves were broken down by day and night games, left-handed versus right-handed pitchers, by club, by date, by park. In the San Francisco papers, sports pundits, who reflect their city's almost maniacal resentment of all things New York, set out to prove that Mays's 511 home runs had actually traveled farther than Ott's, bulwarking their arguments not only with comparative fence distances but also with the variation between East and West Coast wind currents.

But then Mays and the Giants stopped hitting and the victory cake began to get stale.

Nine days passed. Atlanta, Cincinnati and St. Louis came and went without number 512 being struck. There was standing room only in the press box, and as the games went by, the headlines got bigger and the stories thinner. A rumor was investigated that the Braves had formed a pool on which one of their pitchers would serve up the record breaker. Outfielders were questioned as to how close to the fence they were when they caught long fly balls hit by Mays. Former National League batting champion Ernie Lombardi, who is now press box custodian at Candlestick Park, was interviewed about the number of home runs he had hit. "I seen on one of them bubble-gum cards it was a hundred ninety-seven, a hundred ninety-eight," Lombardi said. "Anyway less than two hundred." The theft of Giant president Horace Stoneham's Cadillac by a North Beach beatnik was duly recorded as was the death of a seventy-year-old retired Navy lieutenant commander who became Candlestick Park's first heart attack victim of the season on Senior Citizens' Day.

At the plate, Mays began to press and tumbled into a slump that saw him get only three hits in twenty-five at bats. Dogged at every step by photographers, it was an effort for him not to lose his patience.

"How can I not think of the record?" he snapped after a loss to the Braves. "You guys remind me of it every time I turn around."

Nor did four losses in five games improve Herman Franks's disposition. "Go ahead, just don't stand there," he growled at a reporter after a loss to Cincinnati. "Ask me something silly."

As if his slump were not enough, Mays was also hurting. With the Giants down 11-to-0 against the Braves, he was rested midway through the game more for artistic reasons than anything else. "It just wouldn't be right if Willie hit it in a game like this," said Giant public relations director Garry Schumacher. But the next day, with the Reds battering the Giants, he was removed from the game in the fifth inning with a cold and upset stomach. Though ordered to stay in bed, he showed up at the park the following afternoon shortly before game time and began getting dressed, only to have Franks send him back home again to rest.

"Sick as he was, he thought he could do something to help," Franks said.

"When will he be back in the lineup, Herman?"

"How the hell should I know?" Franks rasped. "Now I suppose tomorrow you'll say that Franks answered that in his usual grouchy style."

Mays was back in the lineup against the Cardinals on Friday night, with the cameras once again recording his every sneeze. But on Sunday, running out an infield roller, he stumbled over first base, wrenching his knee. As he limped from the field, someone in the photographers' booth yelled, "Strike the set." Before Mays was in the dugout, the camera crews were packing their equipment. An inning later, it was pointed out in the press box that last year, when Mays hit his personal high of fifty-two home runs, he had once gone twenty-two days without a homer. It was a statistic that cheered only the freelance television cameramen.

"I hope he never hits the sonofabitch," said one. "I get $82.50 every game I'm out here."

~

ON WEDNESDAY, MAY 4, ten days after Mays hit his record-tying home run and after tailing him around for two weeks, I found myself succumbing to the old sports page adage that no story is complete without either a child or a priest. I struck out with the child, but from a Jesuit friend I learned the name of the Reverend Peter Keegan, a curate at St. Cecilia's Roman Catholic Church in San Francisco and one of Mays's closest friends. I called on Father Keegan at St. Cecilia's rectory and was in luck. He had just come from lunch at Mays's home and told me that he had given him a pair of rosary beads and a St. Christopher's medal.

"For good luck," I said. Even as I said it I realized that I too had become a student of the memorabilia of a nonevent.

"Well," Father Keegan said, "actually it's his birthday Friday. But it won't do any harm and if it works I suppose you could call it a good-luck charm."

"Did you talk about the record?"

"I said he's been pressing and told him he was going to hit it tonight."

"What did he say?"

"He said 'I hope so, Father.' "

That night, shortly before the game with the Los Angeles Dodgers, I asked Mays if he was wearing his talisman. He stared at me suspiciously.

"The medal," I said.

"How did you know about that?" Mays said.

I told him I had seen Father Keegan that afternoon.

"Man," Mays said, "you guys are really following me around."

The Dodger pitcher that evening was Claude Osteen, who had not thrown a home-run ball in 96 2/3 innings. Twice Osteen struck out Mays, each time making him look bad. But in the fifth inning, with two outs, Osteen threw Mays a high change-up. With seemingly only a flick of his bat, Mays sent a drive arcing in a high parabola over the right-field fence. As he circled the bases, Candlestick Park erupted. Whistling, cheering and stamping their feet, the crowd interrupted the game for five minutes and twice brought Mays from the dugout to doff his cap with the chant, "We want Willie."

The rest of the game was an anticlimax. In the Giant clubhouse, television cables were strewn all over the floor and floodlights burned down on Mays's locker. Someone kicked over a carton of fan mail, littering Mays's cubbyhole with letters. Interviewed on two postgame shows (throughout one of which he called the sportscaster by the wrong name), Mays did not arrive in the locker room for twenty minutes after the game ended. As he entered, Franks whispered to him that the boy who had caught the record-breaking ball was asking $1,000 for it.

"He wants a thousand, he can keep that mother," Mays said.

For nearly half an hour, flashbulbs popped and microphones were pushed into Mays's face, as reporters and newscasters elbowed each other out of the way. Occasionally tempers flared. "Just wait a goddamn minute," a reporter shouted at one broadcaster. "I was asking him a question."

"What did you feel, Willie?"

"Relief," Mays said.

"What do you want to do now?"

"I just want to get the hell out of here and go home, that's what I want to do."

"Give us a smile, Willie."

"I don't have no more smiles, fellows," Mays said. "I am just smiled out."

Only once did Mays seem genuinely amused. That was when a newscaster from ABC's *Wide World of Sports* pumped his hand and said, "Willie, you are a great credit to the game of baseball."

"Why, thanks, man," Mays said.

Almost as an afterthought, the cake with the 512 lettered on it was wheeled in front of Mays's locker. Mays cut into it for the photographers, but the cake was by now so stale that it crumbled like a tenement under the wrecker's ball. He held a piece in front of his mouth, then threw it back on the plate when the photographers left. No one else touched it.

When the crowd finally thinned, Herman Franks, wearing nothing but a shirt, shower clogs and his Giant cap, pulled up a stool in front of Mays's locker. Puffing on a cigar, Franks said, "Now you can relax until you get seven hundred and something."

"Shoot," Mays said. "There's Williams and there's Foxx and then it's going to start all over again. Ain't that right?"

"No," Franks said. "You've got a breeze now for five years."

"I hope you're right," Mays said tiredly.

No one knew better than Mays the odds against his catching Ruth. "I'm thirty-five now," he said. "I'd have to average forty a year to catch up with that guy. I don't think I can do it."

He wrapped a towel around his middle and plodded slowly into the shower. The cameras were gone and the flashbulbs were no longer popping. The newsreel cables had been removed and the clubhouse was almost empty. On the bulletin board was chalked a message: "Plane leaving for St. Louis Friday morning, 8:15, TWA flt. 162. Please be at airport 7:45. Arrive St. Louis 1:40."

"POET OF RESENTMENT"

[1997]

❧

I.

IN THE PREFACE of his ghostwritten autobiography, *I Never Had It Made*, published in 1972 two days after he died at the age of fifty-three, enfeebled by diabetes and nearly blind, Jackie Robinson wrote, "Money is America's God, and business people can dig black power if it coincides with green power." Twenty-five years after his death, fifty years after he broke major league baseball's color bar against black players in 1947, honored in this anniversary year of that event from one end of the country to the other, his Brooklyn Dodger uniform number 42 retired by order of the baseball commissioner's office, never to be issued to another major leaguer (the twelve players currently wearing it—many black, in honor of Robinson—may keep it until the end of their careers), Jackie Robinson has been embraced by green power.

During Robinson's ten-year big league career, from 1947 to 1956, player salaries were so low that most major leaguers, except for those on the highest pay scale, worked during the off-season to supplement their incomes. Baseball's reserve clause kept players tied to their franchises, as if they were plantation labor, to be sold or dealt away as their owners saw fit. With no free agency, there were no agents, and players were forced to deal directly with owners whose sole negotiating tactic was take it or leave it. Robinson's highest salary was $42,500, less than half that earned by Ted Williams or Joe DiMaggio. Sports marketing, except for cigarette advertising, was in its infancy. Players with a little money to invest usually plowed it into modest retail establishments, such as a liquor store (Robinson's teammate Roy Campanella had one in Harlem) or a bar and grill, often fronting these enterprises for the kind of dicey partners who attach themselves like limpets to professional athletes, sucking funds from the unwary and inexperienced. The economic muscle flexed by such one-name black superstars as Michael (Jordan), Junior (Ken Griffey, Jr.), and Tiger (Woods) was still in the faraway.

~

IT IS DOUBTFUL that Jackie Robinson could ever have imagined that in his fiftieth anniversary year he would rival Michael, Junior, and Tiger as America's top-drawing sports marketing personality; Michael and Junior were children when he died, Tiger not even born. Handling the merchandising and advertising deals for Robinson's widow, Rachel, and the rest of his family is an agency that specializes in marketing dead personalities in and out of sports (Joe Louis, Babe Ruth, Secretariat, Oscar Wilde). Coca-Cola has put out commemorative Robinson bottles, Wheaties uses his picture on three different cereal boxes, McDonald's his likeness on tray liners. Nike and Apple feature him in television commercials, and there are Robinson bats, computer games, key chains, jerseys, medallions, plaques, mugs, T-shirts, and 12-inch Robinson busts ($29.99). On the Internet, suppliers list e-mail addresses where vendors can order Robinson memorabilia in bulk.

Even the United States Mint hopped on the bandwagon, designing 100,000 gold coins to celebrate Robinson's accomplishments on and off the field ($200 each), and 200,000 silver coins ($35 each), a portion of the proceeds going to the Jackie Robinson Foundation, which supports educational and leadership programs for minority youth. And although Princeton professor Arnold Rampersad says he maintained editorial control over his encyclopedic new biography,

Jackie Robinson, Rachel Robinson retains what Professor Rampersad calls "a piece of the action."[1]

It is interesting to conjecture what Jackie Robinson might have thought of the more vulgar displays of green power (Professor Rampersad calls them "regrettable"), and especially the connection of his name to Nike, whose chairman, Philip Knight, collects docile superstar athletes the way a big-game hunter collects trophies. That Nike's sneakers and other athletic products are largely manufactured in third-world sweatshops by poorly paid people of color, often children, is a development about which Michael, Junior, and Tiger, each a superstar of color with a long-term multimillion-dollar Nike contract, have maintained what might most charitably be called a discreet silence. One does not have to read very far in Rampersad's biography to guess how Robinson would have reacted to Philip Knight's child labor sweatshops. He had the nature of a common scold, he was a world-class injustice collector, and his inability to keep his mouth shut even when it might better serve his interest was legendary. In the end, his interest would always be something other than a Nike contract, and Philip Knight's beneficence.

∼

HIS NAME WAS Jack, not Jackie, Jack Roosevelt Robinson, the youngest of five children born in 1919 to an illiterate, philandering Georgia sharecropper and his wife. Mallie Robinson, Jack's mother, had a sixth-grade education, a considerable achievement for a black girl in turn-of-the-century rural Georgia, and the good sense to leave her husband Jerry in 1920 for southern California, where she had relatives in Pasadena. The star athlete in the family was Robinson's older brother, Mack, who won a silver medal to Jesse Owens's gold in the 200-yard dash at the 1936 Berlin Olympic Games. After the Olympics, Mack Robinson returned to Pasadena, where he could only get a job as a night-shift street sweeper, a task he performed while provocatively wearing his USA Olympic jacket.

Such attitude ran in the family. Jack Robinson was a middling student who had a problem with authority; on his elementary school grade transcript, an official noted his likely future occupation as "Gardener." His passport away from gardening was athletics. Football, basketball, baseball, track, tennis—whatever the sport, Robinson excelled, and as he progressed from high school to Pasadena Junior College to UCLA, his fame grew, usually referenced on the sports pages by his color. Jack became "Jackie," the "dusky flash," a "dark-hued phantom of the gridiron," "a soft-spoken, dark-skinned kid with a flash of illuminating white teeth." At UCLA, track was his best sport (he won an NCAA broad jump title), basketball his second best (he twice led the Pacific Coast Conference in scoring), football his third (as a wingback he averaged 11.4 yards a carry); baseball was his poorest (his batting average was .097).

Trouble did not avoid him, nor did he go out of his way to avoid it. As an undergraduate he twice had altercations with Pasadena police officers that he thought racially instigated, and each time he spent a night in jail, escaping serious penalty because he was an athlete. "He would flash angry in a heartbeat," a black UCLA football teammate said of him, and the reputation stuck. His rough edges were somewhat smoothed by Rachel Isum, a UCLA student he married in 1945 after a five-year courtship. Trained as a nurse, Rachel Robinson was as steely in her quiet way as her husband; if he took no prisoners, she took no grief, either from him or from Jim Crow. She once broke their engagement when he ordered her to quit the Nurse Cadet Corps, and after they were married she would intentionally drink at White Only water fountains in the South and use White Only rest rooms.

Robinson was drafted early in 1942, and took basic training at Ft. Riley, Kansas, where he became close friends with heavyweight champion Joe Louis. They were an oddly matched pair. Louis was unlettered, a white man's idea of a good black man, and an inveterate womanizer; Robinson was college-educated (always on the verge of flunking out of UCLA, from which he never graduated), his antennae delicately tuned to pick up any racial slight real or imagined, and he was something of a prig (although during one hiatus in his engagement to Rachel he managed, according to his service record, to pick up a dose of the clap). "I'm sure if it wasn't for Joe Louis," Robinson would later say, "the color line in baseball would not have been broken for another ten years."

In the army there was also a color line that Robinson and other black applicants to officer candidate school found difficult to cross. Secretary of War Henry Stimson, the prototype of WASP rectitude, stated his objections bluntly: "Leadership is not imbedded in the negro race yet and to try to make commissioned officers to lead men into battle—colored men—is only to work a disaster to both." The war's pressing manpower demands ultimately forced the lowering of the bar, and Robinson was accepted at OCS, even though a chronically arthritic right ankle limited his duty options. Commissioned a second lieutenant, he was transferred to Camp Hood, Texas, where in the summer of 1944 he was again involved in a racial fracas. Ordered to move to the rear of a bus at Hood, Robinson refused, as local Jim Crow laws did not apply on a military post. Voices were raised, expletives bandied, MPs called, the word "nigger" used or not used depending on the source. Skittish higher commanders saw the case as "full of dynamite," but Robinson was still charged with insubordination and failure to obey an order from a superior officer. Brought before a court-martial, he was acquitted on both counts. Four months later, one suspects to the army's enormous relief, his arthritic ankle won him an honorable discharge "by reason of physical disqualification."

He had few prospects, beyond a tentative $300-a-month offer from the Kansas City Monarchs in the Negro National League. It had been five years since Robinson last played baseball, that season he batted .097 at UCLA, but he managed to make the 1945 Monarch team, even hitting .345 if the Negro League's notoriously unreliable statistics are to be believed. But he had little in common with his hard-living, hard-drinking, hard-loving Monarch teammates. He "seemed to be from another world," Rampersad writes, "a world of colleges, California, and a troubling familiarity with white people."

⁓

WERE IT NOT for Jackie Robinson, Branch Rickey would be remembered, if at all, as a Bible-thumping midwestern Methodist windbag who neither played baseball on Sundays when he was a mediocre catcher for the St. Louis Browns and the New York Highlanders, nor attended games on the Sabbath as a baseball executive.

As general manager of the St. Louis Cardinals, he established a model minor league farm system, but ignored racism; St. Louis was Jim Crow country, where blacks were not even permitted in the grandstand at Sportsman's Park. Then, in 1942, Rickey moved to the Brooklyn Dodgers as general manager and part owner, and quietly began looking for a Negro player to integrate the major leagues.

Rickey's motives were both pragmatic and idealistic: here was a situation in which it might be possible to both make money and do the right thing, "to intervene," as Rampersad somewhat extravagantly writes, "in the moral history of the nation." Needing a cover story that would allow him to scout the Negro Leagues without arousing suspicion among the more overtly racist owners, Rickey said he wanted to put together a black team, the Brooklyn Brown Dodgers, to play in Ebbets Field when the Dodgers were on the road, and give the franchise a new revenue source. After the fact, not everyone would give Rickey full marks for seeing the moment and seizing it, in part because he could be so insufferably superior. "I knew him for what he was," Walter O'Malley, Rickey's former Dodger partner, would later tell the journalist Roger Kahn. "Rickey's Brooklyn contract called for salary plus a percentage of the take, and during World War II the take fell off. It was then Rickey mentioned signing a Negro. He had a fiscal interest."[2]

If there was some truth in O'Malley's mean-spirited remark, the fact remains that Rickey did what no else was willing to do. Other owners made excuses: Negroes were happier in their own league, none were qualified to play in the majors, white players would revolt. However shrewd a judge of talent Rickey was, Robinson seemed an unusual choice as his trailblazer. He was not the best player in the Negro League, or even on the Monarchs. He had a weak arm, an arthritic ankle, and little power (in the bandbox ballparks of his era, he never hit more than nineteen home runs, while his Dodger teammates regularly hit thirty or forty). He was also old for a first-year player—twenty-seven—and most importantly he had never suffered racial indignity without lashing back.

What Rickey intuited, however, was that Robinson of all the black players, many more skilled than he, had both the character and the historical vision to understand what it meant to be first, and what the cost of failure would be. It was prescience of a high order. Rickey laid out every possible racist scenario, from beanballs, to spikings, to the ugliest epithets, and told Robinson that to retaliate was to lose, and jeopardize the future for other black players. In his autobiography, Robinson remembered Rickey saying, "I'm looking for a ballplayer with the guts not to fight back." Robinson accepted the terms, and signed a contract with the Dodgers' Montreal farm club. The reaction of white players, Rampersad notes, was summed up by Bob Feller, the Cleveland pitching ace. Robinson, Feller said, was a football player "tied up in the shoulders [who] couldn't hit an inside pitch to save his neck. If he were a white man, I doubt they would consider him as big league material." Ironically, Feller and Robinson were both elected to baseball's Hall of Fame in the same year, 1962.

In Montreal, Robinson quickly became the "Colored Comet." There were incidents—he was called "nigger" and "snowflake" and once an opposing player threw a black cat onto the field, shouting, "Here's your cousin"—but he deflected every insult, avoided every argument. With all the racial distractions, he still won the International League's batting title with a .349 average; Brooklyn was the necessary next stop.

Around the National League, however, a rebellion was simmering, one far more extensive than previously thought, according to the ESPN documentary, *Breaking the Line*, produced to mark the legacy of Robinson's career in the fiftieth anniversary year of his joining the Dodgers. In Robinson's own clubhouse, a claque of Southern teammates petitioned the front office to keep him off the club, a mutiny put down in a middle-of-the-night tirade by the manager, Leo Durocher. But elderly contemporaries of Robinson told ESPN that other clubs were ready to strike; they were waiting only for word from the Dodger insurgents. Economic self-preservation scuttled the conspiracy; baseball players in 1947 were working stiffs, not all that much better paid than the rest of the population, and they could not risk possible suspension and loss of a salary.

For his first two years with the Dodgers, Robinson followed Rickey's injunction, keeping both his tongue and his cool in the presence of unrelenting pressure and abuse, both verbal and physical.

It was a nastier game fifty years ago than it is today; pitchers knocked batters down as a matter of course and baserunners slid with high spikes; Robinson's color only made him a more frequent and opportunistic target. His game was built on speed and quickness, talents less valued in baseball once Babe Ruth made the home run the ultimate weapon, and it baffled and infuriated opponents. He could drop a bunt on a dime, and drive pitchers to distraction with his baserunning harassment. His skills finally won a grudging respect; he could play, and that was a quality even more admired by his teammates and opponents than his willed Gandhian self-control.

2.

BY 1949, THERE were only five blacks in the major leagues, and only three teams (the Dodgers, the New York Giants, and the Cleveland Indians) were "integrated," but there was no turning back, even though scouting reports would still read (about Red Sox pitching prospect Earl Wilson): "a well-mannered colored boy, not too black, pleasant to talk to, well-educated, very good appearance."[3] That year, Robinson's natural ability was finally allowed to fuse with his natural competitiveness and hostility, and he won both the National League batting title and the league's Most Valuable Player award. But perhaps the most significant event of his season was an invitation to appear as a friendly witness before the House Committee on Un-American Activities.

What prompted the invitation was a comment at a peace conference in Paris by Paul Robeson, who said it was "unthinkable," considering America's racist history, to expect that Negroes would fight for their country against a Communist enemy. For HUAC, Robeson's longstanding flirtation with left-wing causes made him the ideal bad black, and Robinson, playing a white man's game, the ideal good one. Robinson was uneasy about the invitation to testify, but in the end it was an offer he could ill refuse; he was, as Rampersad says, "firmly anticommunist," and he had honorably served as a commissioned officer "whose patriotism had survived his court-martial."

In a statement carefully drafted by the executive director of the

Urban League, Robinson said Robeson's contention seemed "silly," but he never denied Robeson's central allegation that American racism was pervasive. Blacks were "stirred up" before communism arrived, he said, and would be "stirred up long after the party has disappeared—unless Jim Crow has disappeared by then as well." For many blacks, Robinson's appearance before HUAC made him seem like a "handkerchief head," but white America was unequivocal in its praise. "Quite a man, this Jackie Robinson," the New York *Daily News* editorialized, unwittingly making him seem, like Earl Wilson, "a well-mannered colored boy." He was fêted by, among others, the Catholic War Veterans, the Rotary Club, the Veterans of Foreign Wars, and the Freedoms Foundation. Robinson had become an icon.

∽

IT IS THE icon rather than the ballplayer who has been remembered this anniversary year, along with tales that embellish the iconography. No account is complete without mention of Robinson's relationship with Pee Wee Reese, the white Kentucky-born shortstop who would not join the boycott of his new teammate that was proposed by other Dodger Southerners. In these tales, Reese is always Huck to Robinson's Jim. During one game, when Robinson was the object of particularly vicious racist abuse from the other club, Reese walked over from shortstop and put his hand on his teammate's shoulder, a gesture that tacitly sent a message to the league that Robinson now and forever was a Dodger.

That story has become part of the Robinson canon. Its problem, as Rampersad astutely points out, is that no one, including Robinson, who did not even mention it in a quickie 1948 autobiography (*Jackie Robinson: My Own Story*), can remember where or when it happened, and what actually took place. Was it in Cincinnati or Boston? 1947 or 1948? Did Reese touch Robinson or just talk to him? In some variation, the incident did occur, but as memories falter and eyewitnesses depart the living, it is the most ennobling version that is carved into lore, to be repeated as gospel by those not present and perhaps not even born at the time. "When the legend becomes fact," as a character says in the John Ford film, *The Man Who Shot Liberty Valance*, "print the legend."

For the baseball addict, the best Robinson statistics are found not in the literature about him but on the Internet. The Brooklyn Dodger Web page chronologically lists every time Robinson stole home (in what inning and against what pitcher), and also every time he got caught stealing home (twelve times versus nineteen successful attempts; other sources say he stole home twenty-two times). On the Web, one can find Robinson's lifetime batting average against every other National League team, both at Ebbets Field and on the road (over the course of a ten-year career, he hit best at Forbes Field in Pittsburgh, .342, with an on-base percentage of .438).

～

ROBINSON APPEARS ALMOST indifferent to his baseball accomplishments. In *I Never Had It Made*, his years with the Dodgers take up only sixty-two pages of a 275-page book, and seem largely cribbed from the clips. Only occasionally is there any sense that without baseball, and the fires it stoked, there would have been no icon. Freed from Branch Rickey's strictures, Robinson became what Stanley Crouch calls a "poet of resentment," in much the same way that Charlie Parker and Miles Davis were. Robinson was the first black athlete outside boxing who could publicly display his acrimony toward the white world. But where Joe Louis was advised never to smile when he knocked out a white opponent, Robinson reveled in rubbing it in. "This guy didn't just come to play," Leo Durocher said of him. "He come to beat you. He come to cram the goddamn bat right up your ass."[4]

As a ballplayer, Robinson had more in common with the surly and volatile Chicago White Sox superstar Albert Belle than the burnishers of his memory are willing to admit. He played like a black Ty Cobb, give no quarter, take none. Rage fueled him; he needed adversaries the way most people need friends. Even Rickey was not spared his tongue; he complained that Rickey conducted contract negotiations in a way that was "pure plantation." Robinson was a vicious bench jockey, not above speculating about an opponent's sexual inadequacy. In Milwaukee, warming up before a game, he suddenly fired the ball into the Braves dugout at pitcher Lew Burdette, who he claimed was baiting him. Later, far from apologizing, he said, "I wanted to hit him right between the eyes."

At Ebbets Field, after Giants pitcher Sal Maglie knocked him and a teammate down, Robinson deliberately bunted toward first base, trying to entice Maglie to cover the bag so he could run over him. Maglie wisely let his second baseman Davey Williams cover, and Robinson crushed him with a shoulder block; on film, it looked like a freeway accident, the 200-pound Robinson knocking the 160-pound Williams flat. Robinson made no excuses; Williams should have got out of the way, he told reporters, and anyway he was trying to hit Maglie.[5] In a similar incident forty years later, when Belle, playing payback the way Robinson might have, dropped a Milwaukee infielder with an elbow after getting hit by a pitch, he was fined by the league and vilified by the sporting press.

Robinson saw racism in every brushback pitch and every umpire's call that went against him. Walter O'Malley was a particular villain, because of the power play he had used to force Rickey out as a Dodger co-owner. "I was one of those 'uppity niggers' in O'Malley's book," Robinson wrote in *I Never Had It Made*, when O'Malley's real sin was that he was not as solicitous of Robinson as Rickey had been. Nor did Robinson mask his disdain for the new Dodger manager, Walter Alston, who had to deal with the reality that Robinson's career was running down. More and more he was seen as a pop-off, using his fading athletic eminence as a pulpit to speak out on black issues. He criticized the Yankees for not having a black player, and owners for not challenging Jim Crow laws at Florida spring training camps.

A number of white reporters (and a few blacks) complained that he was becoming a "crusader," "a soapbox orator," a "rabble-rouser," "an enemy of his race" who was not showing proper gratitude for the chance he had been given. For Robinson, that kind of gratitude was for Stepin Fetchit. He had moved his family into a lily-white neighborhood in Stamford, Connecticut, and was condescending toward his black teammates, who were not that crazy about him either. They were "really nice," he wrote to Rachel Robinson, "but I don't believe they would make an evening very entertaining."

No professional athlete likes to admit that he has played too long. There is too much money involved, rarely enough saved, and there is the eternal hope that age has not withered skills. The sad fact was that by the end of the 1956 season, Robinson was old, overweight, and over the hill. By effort of memory and will, he was still occasionally the Man, but he had, in his last two seasons, missed eighty-six games and batted in only seventy-nine runs. No sentimentalist, O'Malley traded him to the Giants for a small amount of cash and an undistinguished left-handed relief pitcher. Robinson, however, had the last laugh; he retired, and sold *Look* magazine exclusive rights to the story for $50,000, or $7,500 more than his highest Dodger salary.

3.

RETIREMENT IS PURGATORY for the former sports star. The world outside organized sports is unforgiving. Robinson had an exploitable name, and if he was, as Rampersad writes, "a loose cannon," he was also, in the words of Martin Luther King, "a sit-inner before sit-ins, a freedom rider before freedom rides." There was never a want of promoters hoping to capitalize on his fame, but his business ventures were generally underfinanced and badly managed— a Harlem clothing store, several different fast-food investments, an insurance company, a real estate development scheme for low-income housing. When Chock full o'Nuts, a chain of inexpensive New York coffee shops, hired Robinson as vice-president for personnel at a salary of $30,000 a year, it turned out to be a figurehead job for which he had minimal qualifications; most of the company's employees were black, and it was the hope of the firm's president that Robinson's management presence would slow down any effort to unionize.

Which, in fact, it did. Nominally Robinson was a Republican, but the only issue that really engaged him was civil rights. Off and on in his retirement, he signed his name to a ghosted newspaper column that allowed him to comment on the issues, and as usual he did not hesitate to speak his mind. He became a kind of national nag, forever firing off letters and telegrams and pronouncements to the White House and to lesser politicians, who listened earnestly even if they did not heed his advice. "A true friend is one who speaks the truth," Hubert Humphrey responded after Robinson had taken him to task for some malfeasance, "and I always look upon Jackie Robinson as a true friend."

This was the kind of nonsense politicians can spout in their sleep, and the trusting Robinson usually took them at their word. The politicians knew his value: Jackie Robinson was a perfect photo opportunity. Richard Nixon curried his favor early, and to the dismay of many blacks, Robinson backed him in 1960 against John Kennedy. The Kennedy campaign responded to his attacks with a Sal Maglie–type political beanball; Robinson, Robert Kennedy declared in a radio interview, "used his race to defeat a union shop" at Chock full o'Nuts. Over the years, Robinson's enthusiasm for Nixon would waver ("I do not consider my decision . . . in 1960 one of my finer ones," he wrote in his autobiography) but in one high period, after receiving a plaque signed by the Nixons, Robinson responded by dispatching them twenty-four pounds of Chock full o'Nuts coffee.

HE LIVED THE restless life of the retired jock. There were awards and dinners and celebrity golf tournaments and holidays on the cuff, and too many planes and too many cities, in his case usually connected with civil rights fundraisers, protest marches, sit-ins, and visiting the sites of bombed-out black churches and other outrages. By the mid-Sixties, however, Robinson's health was failing. His hair had gone almost snow-white, and diabetes was slowly crippling him. As Robinson had supplanted Joe Louis as the defining black American, so he was now being supplanted by a younger generation of more militant blacks. Increasingly he was becoming, if not irrelevant, then behind the curve of black thinking, something of an Uncle Tom to younger agitators.

"Old Black Joe, Jackie Must Go," was a refrain now heard on the streets of Harlem. Malcolm X mocked him for toadying to white mentors—first Branch Rickey, then Richard Nixon, then Nelson

Rockefeller (Robinson had enlisted in Rockefeller's gubernatorial campaign). For Robinson, the great integrator, black separatism was incomprehensible. The revolution "now demanded a new image," Rampersad writes. "Gone was the ideal of patient suffering; gone, too, was the underlying ideal of an integrated America. . . . Power was the great goal; and justice demanded an element of retribution, or revenge."

Retribution was foreign to Robinson's thinking. Nor did he understand why Martin Luther King made Vietnam almost as much an issue for blacks as racial injustice. Robinson supported the war in Vietnam on the grounds that America with its faults was still his country, and his country was at war. But he also supported Muhammad Ali's refusal to be drafted. When Ali said, "No Viet Cong ever called me 'nigger,' " this was a sentiment Robinson could understand. Ali, he wrote, "has won a battle by standing up for his principle." He also defended the black American medal winners at the Mexico City Olympics who gave a black power salute when the national anthem was played, for which they were stripped of their medals.

Such independence did not go unnoticed by J. Edgar Hoover, whose FBI regularly checked up on Robinson after Rickey signed him in 1945, mainly because he was mentioned approvingly in the *Daily Worker* and other left-wing journals; the FBI file was updated even at the height of his Republicanism. After Richard Nixon was elected president in 1968, John Ehrlichman ordered an FBI check after Robinson supported the right of the Black Panthers to speak out, although he vigorously disagreed with their agenda.[6] Attacked by blacks, he was also attacked by whites. "It is surely time to put an end to the mischievous national habit of taking seriously this pompous moralizer," William F. Buckley, Jr., wrote after Robinson had criticized Nixon's 1968 Southern strategy, "who whines his way through life as though all America were at Ebbets Field cheering him on against the big bad racist St. Louis Cardinals."

At home in Stamford (a community Mr. Buckley also called home), there was a problem. His oldest son, Jackie Jr., suffered in the glare of his father's fame. Silence and recrimination marked their relationship. Uninterested in athletics or academic study, Jackie Jr. joined the army and shipped out to Vietnam, leaving a pregnant girlfriend he chose not to marry; their daughter was Jack and Rachel Robinson's first grandchild. Jackie Jr. returned from Asia a junkie. Growing up in a white environment left him feeling neither white nor black. In the most heartbreaking moment of Professor Rampersad's book, Jackie Jr. tells Rachel Robinson, as she recalls in her unpublished papers, that his younger brother David could not be a *faux* whitey as he tried to be, that he must learn to talk the black talk, dance the black dance.

Jackie Jr.'s rehab failed; there were more drug-related arrests, more rehab. The turmoil of the Sixties tormented Robinson in the same way it tormented other men of his generation. He understood neither his child nor why his wife insisted on working (Rachel was a psychiatric nurse and an assistant professor at Yale's School of Nursing) nor his own place in a mutable world. In 1971, Jackie Jr. died in an automobile accident; his brother David took his advice and lives on a farm in Tanzania. Sixteen months after his son's death, nine days after he was honored by major league baseball at the 1972 World Series, Jack Roosevelt Robinson died of a heart attack and complications from diabetes.

～

PROFESSOR RAMPERSAD, IN *Jackie Robinson*, leans toward the hagiographical. He seems to have read everything written (or ghost-written) by and about Robinson, and he is protective, nonjudgmental. Although his is not an official biography, Rachel Robinson appears in its pages as very much the keeper of her husband's flame. However filtered, it is a great story, and a sad one. Unlike Michael Jordan and Tiger Woods, Jackie Robinson never tried to convert himself into an acceptable black man. Seven years before *Brown v. Board of Education*, before Rosa Parks, before Martin Luther King, he accomplished what was thought unthinkable—the integration of major league baseball. It would not have succeeded if Webbo Clarke, who integrated the Washington Senators in 1955, had been first; or Bob Trice, the first black on the Philadelphia Athletics; or Bill Greason, the first on the Cardinals.

A chronic complainer, sensitive as a carbuncle, Robinson, one feels, might have been a trial to know or team with. In the making of a national myth, however, his complications have been revised into virtues; even the banal is seen as uplifting. Robinson, Rampersad tells us, liked to settle in "a cozy club chair where he read his beloved newspapers and magazines." We similarly learn that he cooked breakfast on weekends, "with waffles and pancakes his specialties." This celebration of the ordinary only diminishes Robinson. He was a literary creation as much as an athletic or political one: granted an opportunity for greatness, he did not blink, but in the anniversary year of that opportunity, it is the familiar litany of the hero's uncomplicated righteousness that prevails on the websites and in the newspaper special editions. The inscription on Robinson's gravestone reads: "A Life Is Not Important Except In The Impact It Has On Other Lives." Greeting card sentiment. A more appropriate inscription is found in his preface to *I Never Had It Made*: "I cannot stand and sing the anthem. I cannot salute the flag. I know that I am a black man in a white world."

NOTES

1. *The Washington Post*, April 4, 1997, and *The Washington Post* website, www.washingtonpost.com.

2. Roger Kahn, *The Boys of Summer* (1972; reprinted by HarperCollins, 1987), p. 426.

3. Quoted in *Breaking the Line*, ESPN.

4. Roger Kahn, *The Boys of Summer*, p. 393.

5. *The New York Times*, *New York Herald-Tribune*, and *Sunday News*, April 24, 1955.

6. *Breaking the Line*, ESPN.

Birth of a Salesman

FOR THIRTY-FIVE YEARS, David Halberstam, an unsilent member of the Silent Generation, has contemplated America and its place in the world, casting his eye on big subjects—Vietnam, global economics, race, mass media, and the 1950s. Like Graham Greene, who, between his weightier fictions on sin and salvation and the transgressions of Pax Americana, published the tidy thrillers he called "entertainments," Halberstam intersperses his eight-hundred-page baggy monsters with diversions of his own. His subject is always sports—the 1949 American League pennant race (*Summer of '49*), scullers questing for a place on the 1984 Olympic team (*The Amateurs*), the 1964 World Series between the New York Yankees and the St. Louis Cardinals (*October 1964*), and the troubled 1978–1979 season of the NBA's Portland Trailblazers (*The Breaks of the Game*).

Writing well about sports is as difficult as writing well about sex. In sports, the confluence of the 1989 Oakland vs. San Francisco World Series and the Loma Prieta earthquake notwithstanding, the earth rarely moves. Today, because of television, reporting on who won and who lost is a penny short and a day late; on a single Saturday in February, nineteen men's and women's college basketball games, and one NBA game, were televised in the New York area. There were also two championship boxing bouts, two NHL hockey games, skiing and figure skating championships, a soccer match, two golf tournaments, harness and thoroughbred racing, and two track meets. With so much action immediately available onscreen, the written report conveys only what one has already seen, if not live, then on the late-night news wrap-ups and the highlight shows, with instant replay, clever cutting, multiple angles, slo-mo, super slo-mo—plus trash talk, hoop hanging, styled home run trots, and end-zone dirty dancing.

On top of this, the sports wire is supplemented by all-sports-all-the-time sports radio, where hosts like "Mad Dog" Russo on New York's WFAN encourage fans who call in to bring their vitriol to a splendid boil; the blood lust these callers direct at athletes, coaches, managers, referees, umpires, and owners who have incurred their displeasure seems on the level of the musings of the nation's Trench Coat Mafias. Inevitably, sportswriters feel the need to compete with the fevered callers and the mad dog hosts who set the tone of sports commentary. The felicitous phrase and the graceful sentence, never an abundant commodity on the sports pages, have given way to the sodden, uninventive invective of sports radio. "Gutless" and "yellow" are adjectives of choice, "choke" a predicate for any losing situation, and "phonies," usually gutless and often chokers, populate the sporting scene. Indeed the self-image of many contemporary sportswriters seems to depend on maintaining that were it not for sports, athletes would be pumping gas, if they were not sticking up the gas station.

Sports sections, like the sports franchises they cover, have become dominated by stars. The reason is economic; the only ads that appear in most big-city sports pages—any issue of the *Los Angeles Times*, for example—are for cures for impotence, baldness, and hair loss, for retail computer outlets and for auto tire discounters. Big-ticket advertisers—for sports gear and equipment—get more bang for the buck on sports television. But in a time of declining revenues, editors go for star sports columnists; the sports pages are the most-read section of the newspaper, and the columnists are the panzer commanders of the circulation wars. By a multiple of several times, star sports columnists are the most-read and highest-paid writers on a newspaper, earning salaries as high as $500,000 a year.

There are too many columns and too little space, Pete Hamill, who edited both New York tabloids, the *Post* and the *Daily News*, told me; this is a circumstance that encourages cutthroat competition among the columnists, and no abiding loyalty to their papers. When a tabloid sports star sees him for lunch, a top editor at *The New York Times* confided to me, he knows that the columnist is using the putative interest of the *Times* (whose own columnists do not earn in the half-million-dollar range) as leverage to bump or renegotiate his contract.

SOME SPORTSWRITING STARS have become, in Calvin Trillin's memorable phrase about TV's Sunday political pundits, sabbath gasbags, exchanging zingers on ESPN and laughing uproariously at each other's bad jokes. With only a few exceptions the sports column has become a glum business, all performance and attitude, a venting of ego intended to counterbalance the weight of athlete fame and money. What separates David Halberstam from most other writers about sports is that as a Pulitzer Prize winner[1], a best-selling writer, the recipient of sixteen honorary degrees, and one of the most indefatigable reporters of his generation, he suffers no ego deficit in relation to his star and superstar subjects. Nor is he envious of their celebrity and material success. He genuinely likes them, and especially enjoys the company of those he calls "lifers," the scouts, trainers, and assistant coaches whom fame and riches have passed by, but whose life remains the game. He tells us that the father of Phil Jackson, Michael Jordan's last coach on the Chicago Bulls, was an evangelical minister in North Dakota, and that Jackson grew up in a church whose parishioners spoke in tongues, so that it was not a remarkable stretch when, as an adult, he became a practicing Buddhist.

Sports for Halberstam reflect American society, a society in which race remains the insoluble issue. White America sees the playing field, where athletes of color dominate in skill and generally predominate in numbers, as validation of the comforting illusion that the nation is color-blind. This is an illusion that Halberstam subjects to constant examination in his sporting entertainments, first in *The*

Breaks of the Game (1981), which is among the best books I know of about professional sports in this country, an exploration not only of a basketball team coming apart at the seams, but of race and money and community.

Race was also a factor in Halberstam's *October 1964*. He writes that after the signing of Jackie Robinson by the Brooklyn Dodgers, and his resulting stardom, the National League actively sought out the best young black players; between 1953 and 1962, nine of the league's ten Most Valuable Players were black. In the American League, the attitude was different. "I don't want you sneaking around down any back alleys and signing any niggers," he quotes Yankee general manager George Weiss warning his top scout, who, when he worked for the Dodgers, had enthusiastically endorsed Robinson; the American League's first black MVP, in 1963, was Yankee catcher Elston Howard. To Halberstam, the 1964 Series was a clash between the two cultures: the Yankees with one black starter (Howard) lost to the Cardinals, who had four, plus the terrifying (because of the brushback pitch he threw without hesitation at hitters of whatever racial persuasion) future Hall of Fame pitcher Bob Gibson, who won three games.

For *The Amateurs*, Halberstam took up single sculling so that he might learn to appreciate the physical torment his emotionally volatile rowers experienced for what in the end was no treasure and scant acclaim, only the personal satisfaction of competition and possible selection for the 1984 Olympic team.[2] Dispassionately, he recorded the relationships among the competitors in the tryouts and the training camps, where suspicion, dislike, envy, and distrust threatened the occasional fragile comity and where, never far below the surface, there lurked the possibility of mutiny against the coaches. For these oarsmen, winning one for Old Glory was not the first order of business; it was Yale vs. Harvard, East Coast strength vs. West Coast technique, or at its most primitive, you're not as good as I am.

~

HALBERSTAM RETURNS TO basketball and to race in *Playing for Keeps*, the story of Michael Jordan's career and his final season with the Chicago Bulls. When *The Breaks of the Game* was published in 1981, Halberstam had noted the cracks that were beginning to show in the social and economic architecture of professional athletics. What interests him eighteen years later is the way in which those fissures widened to the point where they essentially forced the aging edifice, and the old ways in which business was done there, to collapse. Michael Jordan was not alone responsible for the structural changes, but his arrival on the pro basketball scene, and in a more important sense on the national economic stage, supplied the last and loudest trumpet that blew the walls down.

Jordan is perhaps the most successful athlete in history, a figure known in any corner of the globe where one has access to a television set. Pelé, the Brazilian soccer genius, had the same kind of recognition except in America, where the sport has never caught on commercially. In athletic talent, Jordan had only one equivalent, an athlete himself in a way, and one every bit as gifted as he—Mikhail Baryshnikov. Each seemed to find a way to conquer gravity, to slip "the surly bonds of earth," as John Gillespie Magee's World War II poem celebrating the idea of flight had it. Jordan was Air; there was something magical about the nickname, more magical even than "Magic." Of course he has published his own memoir—*For the Love of the Game: My Story*. Like Jordan himself, it seems more a product than a book, its prose a pottage of cliché, sermon, self-adulation, and self-righteousness, set off by glorious photographs and trick typography in a dazzling number of hues, fonts, and sizes, often centered for maximum effect.

IF THERE IS ONE PLAYER I WOULD HAVE LIKED TO
PLAY AGAINST IN HIS PRIME
IT WOULD HAVE BEEN
Jerry West.

And did he feel sorry for friends such as Charles Barkley and Patrick Ewing when he played against them?

NO.

Where did he never find comfort?

IN THE SPOTLIGHT.

In the face of such modesty, Halberstam wisely does not concentrate heavily on Jordan's airiness, focusing more on the business and sociological infrastructure of basketball than on the game and its fluid floor rhythms. Twenty years ago the sport was perceived as too black and too tainted with drugs. CBS was broadcasting few games, and in many major venues the 1980 NBA championship series between Julius Erving's Philadelphia 76ers and Magic Johnson's Los Angeles Lakers was only carried on late-night tape delay. As a medium for advertising, the NBA ranked, said one league executive, "somewhere between mud wrestling and tractor pulling." There was even talk, Halberstam writes, of "splitting the season into two sections to heighten fan interest and, to counter the claim that players did not play hard for forty-eight minutes, of awarding a point in the standings to a team every time it won a quarter."

The arrival of Magic Johnson with the Lakers and Larry Bird with the Boston Celtics was the first step in turning the NBA into an economic colossus. Theirs was a natural rivalry, starting at the NCAA final the previous spring when Johnson's Michigan State team beat Bird and Indiana State. One was white, one was black, one played for the Celtics, the NBA's most storied franchise, the other for the show-time Lakers, Magicalized into Hollywood's team; at Laker games, it seemed as if Jack Nicholson in his courtside seat by the home bench got more TV face time than the lesser players. In all, Bird and Johnson matched up in three NBA finals, the Celtics winning the first, the Lakers the next two; the alchemy of these two superstars changed the NBA story line from color, cocaine, and rehab to the intimacy and acrobatic movements of the pro game, with its no-look passes, slam dunks, three pointers, and triple doubles.

~

ALMOST EXACTLY COINCIDENTAL with, and in long-range economic terms more important than, the NBA debuts of Johnson and Bird was the launch, that same autumn of 1979, of an all-sports twenty-four-hour national cable television network out of a bare-bones office in Plainville, Connecticut. The enterprise was called the Entertainment Sports Programming Network, ESPN for short. It was an idea, says Halberstam, that began "a giant explosion of the sports world in America and an even greater one in the internationalization of sports." With $10 million of seed money from Getty Oil, ESPN was a bargain basement operation at first, with only 1.4 million potential subscribers, but it caught on, as Halberstam writes, by giving hard-core fans "a sports fix each night." College basketball was its first big score, one with a beneficial and unforeseen long-range side effect; via ESPN, college stars became household names even before they were drafted by the pros, which worked to the network's advantage when it began to broadcast NBA games in 1982.

Two years later, David Stern, who had been the league's counsel, became NBA commissioner and Michael Jordan was drafted by the Chicago Bulls, another coincidence of timing that created a union as significant as that of Johnson and Bird. In the 1980s, America exported more fast food, soft drinks, footwear, sports paraphernalia, music, movies, and sports than it did automobiles and industrial products, and Stern saw his charter as forging a partnership between this relaxed side of corporate America and the NBA. For television broadcasts, "he wanted the best of America's heartland companies as his sponsors," Halberstam writes. "He wanted companies such as Coke and McDonald's, signature companies of the postwar nation. If they came aboard, so would everyone else." They did. Basketball became the signature sport of the new cultural imperialism, in part because the sneakers worn by NBA players were its signature product; football cleats and baseball spikes were eliminated as too special for mass marketing, and with sneaker companies battling over signing young stars as soon as they were drafted, the NBA was the beneficiary.

Television supplied the medium, and Jordan broadcast the message. He was the perfect messenger, more skillful than anyone who had ever played the game, articulate, intelligent, and, of importance to fat-cat advertisers, physically beautiful. He was also brilliantly managed by his agent, David Falk, who, when Jordan signed a sneaker contract with Nike, demanded advertising guarantees, and subsequently both a Jordan shoe line and a Jordan apparel line. The Air Jordan commercials he did for Nike (directed by Spike Lee) turned him "into a dream," Jordan admitted. To the international youth culture that bought the products of the new imperialism, Jordan's color was irrelevant. He became the first all-purpose entertainment superstar, yet he understood that the longevity of the role depended on his remaining pure as a basketball player. "He sold Nike sneakers if you wanted to jump high, Big Macs if you were hungry, first Coke and then Gatorade if you were thirsty, Wheaties if you need an All-American cereal, and Hanes underwear if you needed shorts," Halberstam writes. "He sold sunglasses, men's cologne, and hot dogs. Mostly he sold himself."

～

WITH JORDAN, THE NBA began promoting players rather than teams, the sizzle as well as the steak, selling entertainment instead of just a game. It was rock-and-roll with tall people, dancing girls, strobe lighting, luxury boxes, and Jumbotron screens on which the fans could watch the game and themselves. To basketball purists, this was heresy. "There is no 'I' in the word 'team,'" one of Jordan's Chicago coaches told him, to which Jordan quickly replied, "There is in the word 'win.'" In Bulls' owner Jerry Reinsdorf and general manager Jerry Krause, Jordan had the foes he always seemed to need to stoke his competitive fires. In *My Story*, his text states:

THEY WERE BUSINESSMEN.
THEY WERE NOT SPORTSMEN

and goes on:

THEY MADE BUSINESS DECISIONS AND BASKETBALL
JUST HAPPENED TO BE THE
BUSINESS.

Halberstam is unsparing about the often poisonous relations between Jordan and his bosses, Reinsdorf and Krause, particularly

Krause, a skilled evaluator of basketball talent. He was also short, overweight, aggressively unlikable, and Jewish, a perfect lightning rod for Bulls management and its almost 100 percent black labor force. Putting Krause out front as the players' primary target was the way Reinsdorf played the game. As sketched by Halberstam, Reinsdorf, a real estate promoter, has all the charm of a Dickensian villain as painted by Lucien Freud. Bullying came naturally to him. Unlike most NBA owners, he did not want the ego boost that association with athletes brought; a personal connection would only cede leverage to agents and their clients.

Reinsdorf saw his players essentially as men not as smart as he was, whose weaknesses he would not hesitate to exploit at the bargaining table. He knew that athletes, fearful of career-ending injuries, wanted guaranteed long-term contracts, which of course were less costly to ownership than a series of short-term contracts for a healthy and increasingly productive player would prove to be. He perceived, Halberstam writes, that Jordan's negotiating weakness was his desire to protect his corporate image, that he was wary of holding out or demanding to renegotiate, which he thought would make him look like just another "spoiled contemporary athlete."

Playing this card, Reinsdorf was able to sign Jordan to an eight-year contract for approximately $3 million a year—a steal when compared to the salary of the NBA's other top stars, none of whom could match his abilities on the court. By the end of that contract, Jordan was earning many times his Bulls deal in outside income, but his relationship with management had permanently curdled. When crossed, Jordan could become nasty, and Krause became the object of his nastiness. "Jordan was skilled at verbal blood sport," Halberstam writes, ". . . mature and very tough mentally, and he had a certain high, professional coldness that allowed him to turn on his emotions as he so chose and to use his rage as an instrument."

Rage did not inhibit his game. In his thirteen years with the Bulls, Jordan led them to six NBA championships, won the league scoring title ten times, and retired with the highest career points per game average—31.5. His only failure was the disastrous time-out he took in 1994 to play minor league baseball, where he learned that hitting a curve ball was harder than hitting a jumper from the

top of the key; the public embarrassment, and the unconcealed glee
it unleashed in many sports columns, was an assault on Jordan's considerable capacity for hubris. It was a career misstep that only
increased the distance that Jordan kept from the print media. He
was a creature of television, and TV reporters, "hungry for access,"
Halberstam says, "became as much ambassadors from their networks
to him as journalists." His retirement just before the current season beatified him as the greatest basketball player ever, although
Larry Bird offered a sly demurral. "Is he the greatest?" Bird asked,
then answered, "He's in the top two."

~

FORTUNE MAGAZINE ESTIMATED that Jordan had generated $10
billion in revenues for the game, the broadcasters, and his corporate
partners; in 1996, his income in salary and endorsements was $78
million, and his only rival as a global celebrity was Princess Diana.
As the epitome of the entertainment culture, Jordan avoided con-
troversy and racial characterization as elements that could only
taint his carefully nurtured image. "Being black in America is like
having a second full-time job," Arthur Ashe once said, but it was
a job Jordan preferred not to undertake. He represented a different
generation of young blacks, many of whom, like himself, had been
denied little because of their race.

In 1990, when asked to publicly support Harvey Gantt, a black,
who in a close race was contesting Jesse Helms for the U.S. Senate
seat in North Carolina, Jordan, a native North Carolinian and former star at the University of North Carolina, declined, saying that
Republicans bought shoes, too. Then at the 1992 Olympics in
Barcelona, where Reebok was the official sportswear supplier, Jordan, because of his Nike association, initially refused to wear gear
with the Reebok logo. He and the other players with Nike deals
finally relented, but at the medal ceremony after the American basketball team won the gold, he draped an American flag over his
shoulder to hide the Reebok logo on his uniform. Unlike Ashe,
Muhammad Ali, or Jackie Robinson, who had not only athletic skill
but an appreciation of history and the courage to confront it, Jordan

was uncomfortable as history's point man, and seemed to regard himself instead as the first citizen of Nike Town. His contribution to the racial dialogue was at best an oblique one, that of showing a reluctant corporate America, in Halberstam's words, "that a stunningly gifted and attractive black athlete could be a compelling salesman of a vast variety of rather mundane products."

Because of the Jordan impact, today's high draft choice enters the NBA combining the attraction of both rock star and basketball player. Many are surrounded by a posse of hangers-on whose only real function is to make the highly paid player's consumption even more conspicuous; the new ethic of team sports, says Miami Heat coach Pat Riley, is "the disease of more." Shaquille O'Neal signed with Orlando, Halberstam writes, "as a full-service entertainment conglomerate," with a sneaker deal, a Pepsi deal, and record and movie deals. In Jordan's league salaries have climbed 2,500 percent since 1978. Coaching a modern NBA team, one coach said, is like dealing with twelve corporations rather than twelve players. With increasing frequency, high schoolers like Kevin Garnett of the Minnesota Timberwolves and Kobe Bryant of the Lakers bypass college and sign contracts worth tens of millions of dollars before they are twenty.

~

A RETIRED SUPERSTAR will spend more than half his life being known primarily as the star he formerly was. For his myth to survive, the icon, if he is Michael Jordan, must look busy and keep moving, another day, another city, another meeting, another venture, another award, another dinner, another photo shoot, another commercial, another golf tournament, another withdrawal from the carefully husbanded account of celebrity—an upmarket and successful Willy Loman. In *The Washington Post* last February, Kevin Merida described a post-NBA Jordan event, at a middle school in the District to announce a national grant program for teachers, known as "Jordan Fundamentals." The time allocated was two and a half hours. Jordan entered the school via a back door and spoke to none of the security or custodial staff. Nor did he speak to the teachers or to the crowd outside. He autographed one basketball and one photograph. The photograph was photocopied for distribution to students, and the school was promised a thousand T-shirts for being the site of the photo op.

One can find a further hint of Jordan's future in *The Best American Sports Writing of the Century*, which Halberstam edited, and for which he wrote an introduction. The two best pieces in the book—Gay Talese on Joe DiMaggio and Richard Ben Cramer on Ted Williams—are each about athletes in their lonely silent seasons. There is Williams in the Florida Keys, profane, aware of his failures as husband and father, and having a hell of a good time. And there is DiMaggio, seldom anywhere for long, keeper of his own flame, a flame kept burning more brightly than it might have, perhaps, by Paul Simon in his song "Mrs. Robinson":

> *Where have you gone, Joe DiMaggio,*
> *A nation turns its lonely eyes to you.*

To which DiMaggio answered, when Simon introduced himself to him in a restaurant: "I just did a Mr. Coffee commercial. . . . I haven't gone anywhere."

In his introduction to *Best American Sports Writing*, which was finished some months before DiMaggio's death, Halberstam acknowledges the special quality of the ballplayer, but challenges the sentimental legend that would be revived when DiMaggio died. The man behind the legend, Halberstam says, was

> self-absorbed . . . , suspicious, often hostile, often surly, and largely devoid of charm. By and large those who were close to him . . . tended to be sycophants, people whose principal importance came from their proximity to him.

Good fortune has always trailed Michael Jordan. As age overtakes him, and as memories fade and newer and younger superstar pitchmen supersede him on the advertising and entertainment circuit, it is likely that his well-developed pride and his considerable wealth will preserve him from selling his autograph to strangers at card shows. Perhaps he will find his own Paul Simon, who will celebrate the autumn of his years. Where have you gone, Michael Jordan? To which he might reply, I just did

A NIKE COMMERCIAL.

Notes

[1] I met Halberstam in 1962 when he was *The New York Times*'s man in Vietnam, on the way to his Pulitzer. As *Time* magazine's Far East writer, stationed in New York, I had flown into Saigon more or less as a day tripper to get the "feel" of the situation— a week or so was all that *Time*'s editors thought a writer with New York wisdom and the availability of Washington expertise needed to catch the lay of the land, and to set straight the local reporters whom my editors thought had gone native. That Halberstam was able to overlook this impertinence, and that I recognized it as such, made for a friendship that has persisted to the present.

[2] Halberstam still sculls. At some point, a film producer asked if I had any interest in making *The Amateurs* into a screenplay. I saw no visual way of explaining why the rowers endured the pain. One could show the boats skimming through the water, and buckets of sweat, and muscles and tendons stretched into cords, but why they did it seemed unfilmable. It was suggested that a Halberstam surrogate would try to discover why, but then it would become a movie about a reporter and not his subject, generally a bad idea.

STAR!

[2004]

I.

GAVIN LAMBERT WAS the first person in the movie business my wife and I met when we moved to Los Angeles in 1964. It was at a small outdoor Sunday lunch in Beverly Hills given by my brother and sister-in-law, both peers in Hollywood's version of Debrett's. There were six of us, the fifth and sixth being Gavin and his New York literary agent, Helen Strauss, who was also my wife's book agent. Gavin had careful, hooded, missing-nothing eyes, spoke so softly that one could hardly hear him, and looked, as he does to this day, as if he were trying to suppress a laugh and only half succeeding. He was gay, but hiding in the closet was something actors did, not an expatriate English writer who had come out at age eleven. In his wonderfully indirect memoir, *Mainly About Lindsay Anderson*, Lambert described reporting for conscription as an Oxford undergraduate during World War II, when pederasty was still a criminal offense in England. "I decided to dress and behave with the utmost normality," he wrote, "except for painting my eyelids gold."

After Oxford (and rejection by the military), he edited *Sight and Sound*, turning what he called a "terminally boring" English film magazine into a precursor of *Cahiers du Cinéma*, offering poisonous reviews along with serious contributions by Carl Dreyer, Jean Renoir, Josef von Sternberg, and Lindsay Anderson, a friend of Gavin's since public school and Oxford, and as formidable a critic as he was later to become a stage and film director. Gavin worked for a while as an assistant to, script doctor for, and part-time lover of the director Nicholas Ray. Moving to California, he wrote *The Slide Area*, seven connected stories about Hollywood's marginal and downsized fringe, modeled on Christopher Isherwood's *Goodbye to Berlin*, and was nominated for an Academy Award for his screenplay (shared with T.E.B. Clarke) of *Sons and Lovers*.

In the years since we met, there have been numerous scripts and ten more books, including the novel *Inside Daisy Clover*, *On Cukor* (a series of conversations with the director George Cukor that is as stimulating about film as *Hitchcock Truffaut*), and *GWTW*, about the making of *Gone With the Wind*, which is dedicated to my wife and me. Now, with *Natalie Wood: A Life*, he has found an almost perfect subject, his friend Natalie Wood, the star of *Inside Daisy Clover*, perhaps her best film role (with a screenplay by Lambert). She was a movie star out of a post–Joan Crawford, pre–Julia Roberts age—promiscuous, insecure, talented, irrational, funny, generous, shrewd, occasionally unstable, and untrusting of anyone who would get too close to her—except for a Praetorian Guard of gay men.

2.

Natalie Zacharenko—Natalie Wood—was born of parents, Maria Stepanovna Zudilov and Nikolai Stepanovich Zacharenko, who never would have met were it not for the Russian Revolution. The Zudilovs, Lambert writes, were haute bourgeoisie, rich from the father's soap and candle factories in southern Siberia. When Red units roaming the countryside began executing suspected tsarists, the family set in motion its plan for flight, with jewels and money sewed into their clothes so that they could bribe their way to safety. As they were leaving their country house, the family discovered Maria Zudilov's oldest half-brother hanging from a tree; it was a display of revolutionary justice that left six-year-old Maria with a lifelong tendency to convulsive outbursts, often merely as a means of getting her own way. The Zacharenkos were pro-tsarist but poor; Nikolai Stepanovich's father had worked in a chocolate factory and died in the streets of Vladivostok, fighting the Bolsheviks. His widow escaped to Shanghai with her three sons, and eventually the sons made their way to Canada, then into the United States, and finally to San Francisco.

The Zudilovs settled in the Manchurian city of Harbin, where they became leading members of the large Russian exile community there, with a Chinese cook and a German nanny and ballet lessons for the daughters. Maria had a highly developed erotic sense, and when she was seventeen, she managed to get herself secretly married and pregnant—or vice versa; the child of that union was Natalie Wood's older half-sister, Olga.

Outside its Russian enclave, Harbin was seething with civil and martial unrest—Reds fighting Whites, street demonstrations by underpaid Chinese workers, and a festering Chinese nationalist movement whose xenophobia was directed at the exiles. Shortly after Olga's birth, Maria's husband, Alexei Tatuloff, left for San Francisco, promising to bring his wife and daughter when he found work. It was 1930, a bad time to emigrate to America. Jobs were scarce. Still, after a year spent unloading ships on the waterfront, he was able to summon his wife and daughter to join him.

On Maria's arrival in San Francisco, her husband had a suggestion—a ménage à trois with his current girlfriend. Maria turned the offer down, but having hardly any other choices, she stuck with Tatulov, moving in and out of a series of mean, small apartments where Russian exiles camped. It was her husband who introduced her to Nikolai Zacharenko, a stevedore he had met on the docks. Nikolai was now Nick Gurdin, hard-drinking, semi-employed, and fervently tsarist. At best a feckless wife and mother, Maria had an affair with Gurdin while also quietly conducting an on-again, off-again romance with a Russian-born officer on the Matson Line. Ultimately she and Tatuloff divorced, and when she married Nick Gurdin, she was again pregnant, not by him but by the Matson officer. A daughter was born on July 20, 1938. Her birth certificate listed her name as Natalie Zacharenko, but she was called Natasha Gurdin.

~

NATASHA GURDIN'S CHILDHOOD effectively ended the day her mother marched her onto the location of a sentimental Don Ameche movie, *Happy Land*, that was shooting an exterior parade sequence in Santa Rosa, outside San Francisco. Depositing her five-year-old daughter onto the lap of the flabbergasted director, Irving Pichel, whom she had never met, she whispered, "Make Mr. Pichel love you." Natasha did. Pichel gave Natasha a piece of business to do and a reaction shot—she was to drop an ice cream cone and then cry (the reaction was ultimately cut from the final film). He also told Maria that he would be shooting another picture in Los Angeles, in which there might be a part that Natasha could test for. On this slim reed of encouragement, Maria moved the family to Los Angeles. She had always been a fantast, at times claiming her mother had Romanov connections and had married beneath her, at others that she was a foundling raised by Gypsies who taught her to tell fortunes and then abandoned her on a Siberian steppe. In her daughter she saw the ticket to the life she had dreamed about, thought she deserved, and would have had except for the accidents of history—like the Russian Revolution.

Natasha won the part in the second Pichel movie, *Tomorrow Is Forever*, and also a new name—Natalie Wood—bestowed on her by the movie's producers as a gesture to their friend Sam Wood, who had directed Gary Cooper in *Pride of the Yankees* and Ronald Reagan in *King's Row*, but who is perhaps best remembered for relentlessly rooting out Communist influences in Hollywood films and writing, with Ayn Rand, a manifesto of filmmaking don'ts, including "*Don't* Glorify Failure"; "*Don't* Deify the Common Man"; "*Don't* Smear the Free Enterprise System, Success, and Industrialists."

Shepherded by her mother, Natalie Wood became a professional daughter, the onscreen child of Orson Welles, Barbara Stanwyck, Gene Tierney, Margaret Sullavan, Irene Dunne, Joan Blondell, Bette Davis, and Maureen O'Hara. She was happier on a movie set than anyplace else, and since Nick Gurdin was often unemployed and often drunk, her family's most reliable source of income as well.

Her mother taught her to distrust everyone, especially children at school and other child actors. Gigi Perreau, a slightly younger contemporary at one studio school, remembered receiving notes from Wood that said, "*I'm* going to be a star, but *you're* not." Sometimes Nick Gurdin found work as a studio carpenter, but Natalie's mother instructed her never to acknowledge him if he came on the set; she was talent, he was crew, and any sign of affection between daughter and father would embarrass her co-workers.

Natalie's every move was photographed, a documentation of a happy childhood as comprehensive as it was false. She was a poster child for the American Cancer Society, and with her breakthrough movie, *Miracle on 34th Street*, won honorary membership in the Polly Pigtails Club plus a trip to New York to appear in the Macy's Thanksgiving Parade. Her mother was her shadow. "By supervising Natalie's publicity, especially in relation to her family background," Lambert writes, "Maria succeeded in fabricating a persona (former ballerina, exemplary mother) for herself, and Natalie felt obliged to validate it." As Natalie's guardian, she was able to get a clause into her daughter's contracts guaranteeing her a stipend of a hundred dollars a week for overseeing Natalie's fan mail. Her daughter's roles were interchangeably forgettable. In Paul Newman's film debut, *The Silver Chalice*, Lambert notes, "Natalie (with fourteenth billing) played Helena, a teenage slave girl who grows up to become Virginia Mayo."

⁓

ADOLESCENCE WAS A minefield for child actresses, and puberty and breasts best unacknowledged. Most of them were unable to cross over from kid sister parts to grownup star roles, where they could be the object of desire or even co-conspirators in sexual license (as long as it did not go unpunished). Shirley Temple failed, as did Peggy Ann Garner and Margaret O'Brien; they lacked either the will or the talent or had left so lasting an impression as child stars that the idea of having sex with them seemed akin to child molestation. Only Elizabeth Taylor and Natalie Wood were able to cross that no man's land, Taylor because she was so beautiful, Wood because at sixteen she played the female lead opposite James Dean in what became a great American cult film, Nicholas Ray's *Rebel Without a Cause*.

Looked at today, *Rebel* seems dated, a relic, but it spoke to a generation of the disaffected young, a Sixties movie made in 1955, with death, drag races, and switchblade knife fights. It was also rich with sexual idiosyncrasy and tension, reflecting its offscreen combinations. Even before she was cast, Wood had begun her first serious affair, with Ray himself. Many times married, constantly trolling for women, and occasionally men, Ray, Lambert writes, resembled "an aging Heathcliff." Much of the cast was equally ambiguous sexually; James Dean was bisexual, as were Nick Adams and Sal Mineo. And Wood, with Ray's complaisance, was also sleeping with Dennis Hopper, who was acting in his first credited part. It was Hopper who best captured the rigidly structured, moment-to-moment spirit of studio-dominated Hollywood. "I never had a friend like Natalie again," he told Lambert. "She was a very important part of my life until we lost touch after I left Warner's."

~

IN 1962, NATALIE WOOD made the cover of *Life* magazine, in those days a certificate of stardom. The most striking image in the multipage layout was a photograph of an impeccably groomed Wood sitting at an enormous conference table in the offices of the William Morris Agency, surrounded by a covey of middle-aged (and older) lawyers, agents, publicists, accountants, and financial planners, all focused on the professional care and maintenance of a twenty-three-year-old actress barely five feet tall and weighing less than a hundred pounds. "You get tough in this business until you get big enough to have people to get tough for you," she once said. "Then you can sit back and be a lady." Already a gilt-edged property, she had won an Oscar nomination for *Rebel Without a Cause*, starred in *Splendor in the Grass* (gaining another Oscar nomination) and *West Side Story*, both big hits, and had recently completed *Gypsy* (her singing voice was dubbed in both musicals).

In films like *Inside Daisy Clover*, *Love with a Proper Stranger*, *This Property Is Condemned*, and *Splendor in the Grass*, Lambert writes, Wood played "outsiders, at odds with convention and/or their families. But as winner or loser, Natalie remained vulnerable, and when she survived it was always at a cost." These "lost girls," as

Lambert calls them, had an across-the-board appeal, to men and women, to the macho and to the sexually ambivalent. Like all great movie actors, Lambert says, she performed "with a minimum of 'acting.'" Less was always more—a look, a silence, a slight movement of head or hand.

In the Hollywood manner, she had also married (at nineteen) and divorced; her husband was the actor Robert Wagner, whom everyone called "RJ." Wagner was what the studios used to call "a perfect first husband." He was eight years older, in the business (a friend of Tracy, Bogart, and Bacall), solvent, and not a troublemaker (the proof: his longtime and very quiet romance with Barbara Stanwyck, who was old enough to be his mother). That the two might have had nothing in common was irrelevant. Theirs was a romance made for the fan magazines; Wagner had proposed by leaving a diamond and pearl ring in a champagne glass, inscribed with the words "Marry me."

They were Hollywood's happiest couple right up to the moment the marriage foundered. It was for the usual reason: conflicting careers, his going south, hers headed for the stratosphere. Rage, drink, and infidelity were unmentionable side issues. Before the divorce, Wood decided to see a psychiatrist but, ever the star, she insisted that the analyst first be checked out by her publicist. Her instructions, the publicist would tell Lambert, were straightforward: "Tell that son of a bitch not to fuck with my talent."

She had a battalion of lovers up and down the Hollywood rank structure—officers, NCOs, enlisted men, straight, bisexual, gay. Warren Beatty, Steve McQueen, Frank Sinatra. Nicky Hilton, Elizabeth Taylor's kinky, abusive, and alcoholic first husband, a practicing Catholic, as Lambert reports, who kept a handgun, pornographic pictures, and rosary beads on his bedside table. Jerry Brown represented politics; Jerome Robbins, her gay co-director on *West Side Story*, proposed marriage. "Her serious affairs always ended for one of two reasons," Lambert writes. "They were exciting, as in Warren's case, but offered no security; or they offered security, but were not exciting enough." Meeting Beatty by chance sometime after their breakup, Wood went home and overdosed on Seconal. Under an assumed name, her doctor and her secretary checked her into a hospital, where she had her stomach pumped. Her agents were summoned, and when they arrived at the hospital they got right to the point—*The Great Race*, the picture she was shooting at Warner's: "If she pulls through," her doctor was asked, "what are the chances she can make it to Warner's by 6:30 A.M. Monday?" Wood, however, had already made the star's decision, insisting on being released the next day so she could make her Monday call. "I'll get by," she told her secretary. "There aren't any closeups scheduled."

3.

MY WIFE WORE Natalie Wood's clothes before we actually became friendly with her. Natalie gave the clothes to The Colleagues, a Los Angeles charitable organization of rich, largely show business–connected women, who held an annual sale for unwed mothers in which they sold off their expensive previous year's couture creations. My sister-in-law, a Colleague, was a friend of Wood's, and although it was contrary to the sale rules, she would put aside Natalie's contributions for my wife, who was as slight as she was. My wife remembers "a white Saint Laurent evening dress, a water-colored satin Galanos evening dress, and a yellow wool bouclé coat by Edith Head that had been part of Natalie's wardrobe for *Love with a Proper Stranger*." The price was right—ten to twenty dollars an item.

"We don't go for strangers in Hollywood," Cecelia Brady says in *The Last Tycoon*. Outsiders like my wife and me had to be thoroughly vetted before receiving passports into that closed community, usually via a network of acquaintances. Gavin Lambert was a friend of ours, as were Natalie's secretary, a writer named Mart Crowley, and a dancer named Howard Jeffrey, a confidant who was quite possibly the funniest man I have ever known (and later an AIDS victim). Natalie was like a hen mother for what she called her nucleus; she paid for Crowley's analysis in order to get him dried out and back to work; it was during this period that he wrote his play *The Boys in the Band*, the first theatrical super hit with openly gay characters, in which the most memorable role was the Howard Jeffrey surrogate. Toward her "nucleus," however, Natalie could sometimes be demanding. One year at the San Francisco Film Festival, where she was being honored,

Crowley, who had accompanied her (as had Lambert), was entertaining a trick in his hotel room when she burst in on them, wearing a nightgown, drunk and out of control. "You're not good enough for my friend," she screamed at the startled young man, then upset the table full of sandwiches and cake that Mart had ordered for the youth.

She had married a second time, an English agent named Richard Gregson, and had her first child, a daughter called Natasha. The marriage lasted until she discovered that Gregson was having an affair with her new young female secretary; she threw him out that day, refusing to accept his excuse that it was "just a fling." A year later, she remarried Wagner, and a year after that, they had a daughter, Courtney. It was as if second time lucky, two veterans of the Hollywood marital, sexual, and professional wars were now contented, at peace. Motherhood was the part she was playing now, and she gave herself over to it as completely as she had given herself over to stardom. She had worked steadily since she was four years old, and although she considered scripts and plotted career moves, she in fact did not make a picture between 1969 and 1975.

We would see Natalie and RJ occasionally at dinner or at parties, usually when we were in the company of one of the nucleus. She was fun to be with and extremely perceptive. She was also as acute about the business of Hollywood as anyone we knew, aware of her own worth and the worth of everyone else, and understood money the way a French bourgeoise did. Like most people in the movie industry, she was an enthusiastic gossip; she not only knew where all the bodies were buried, but under how much dirt.

I asked her once what it was like being a child star, and she replied, "They took care of you," *they* being the studio. The studio—whichever one was employing her—was more protective of her, or of their investment in her, than her parents were. When Nick Gurdin killed a pedestrian in a drunk-driving accident, the studio was able to bury a manslaughter charge and get his penalty reduced to a six-month suspension of his driver's license with no jail time. But of course in shielding the actress from the demands of real life the studio left her with the sense that anyone who got too close to her would ultimately want something from her; only the men in the nucleus were exempted from this suspicion.

In the late 1970s, my wife and I flew to San Francisco to meet with the Wagners about a screenplay idea a producer friend of ours and theirs wanted us to pitch to them. Nothing came of the meeting, but at a waterfront dinner in Sausalito, we became aware of a subtle change in the ecology of their lives. After his movie career crashed, RJ had turned to television, and had become a major TV series star, making an immense amount of money (they were in San Francisco because he was on location). In the restaurant and outside afterward, people would ask for his autograph or to have their pictures taken with him and only then seemed to recognize her.

She was working sporadically, and had not had a hit since 1969, with *Bob & Carol & Ted & Alice*. (She had done the picture for a fraction of her fee, but had made $3 million from her share of the profit.) With her daughters in school, the career urge had returned, and with it the tensions and accusations and the wandering eye that seemed to fall on her leading men. "Swishing her tail," she would call it, and claim it was innocent, but it caused alcoholic eruptions in the marriage. The parts she was offered were generally in junky movies like *Meteor* (1979)—a science-fiction thriller with cheap special effects—that promised little hope for a big-screen comeback, and as she approached forty, her best work was in television; she and RJ did *Cat on a Hot Tin Roof* with Laurence Olivier as a kind of caricature Big Daddy, and she played (very effectively) the Deborah Kerr part in a six-hour miniseries of *From Here to Eternity*, with William Devane in the Burt Lancaster part.

~

IN 1981, SHE agreed to play the lead in an improbable sci-fi film called *Brainstorm*, opposite Christopher Walken. From the start, there was trouble. Although he had made many pictures, Walken had the New York stage actor's disdain for film acting, and if this dismissiveness made RJ angry, it found a receptive listener in Natalie, who had agreed to play her first theatrical part, in the venerable potboiler *Anastasia*, about the Romanovs' putative (and fraudulent) surviving daughter. Wagner was convinced she and Walken were having an affair, as were the members of the nucleus, and Walken made no effort to allay the suspicions. "She was," Lambert writes, "disturbed, overmedicated, and attracted to him." Over Thanksgiving, the *Brainstorm* company had a break, and despite the charged suspicions, the Wagners invited Walken to spend the holiday with them on their boat at Catalina Island, off Los Angeles.

The weekend was a disaster, Lambert writes, an alcohol-fueled free-for-all during which RJ and Natalie quarreled incessantly. The first night, Natalie took the dinghy ashore to escape and slept in a motel; back onboard the next day, a patina of amity returned. "The undertow is very strong today," Natalie wrote in her daybook, the first of the last two entries she made while on the boat; the last was "This loneliness won't leave me alone." That night, the drinking and emotional outbursts again boiled over. RJ was angry with Natalie and with Walken, who "kept encouraging Natalie to pursue her career as an actress, to follow her own desires and needs." Intoxicated, Natalie went up on deck. It was some time before RJ missed her. Hours later her body was found miles from the boat, floating face down on an ocean swell.

What happened will probably never be known. Everyone was too drunk, the two survivors assaulted by guilt and memories best forgotten. The speculation about that night was scurrilous. Walken and Wagner each made two statements to authorities. There are some contradictions in their accounts, but they are only about the timing of events, and Lambert believes the discrepancies are the result of nothing more sinister than excessive drinking, poor memory, and "the natural desire of both men to protect their own and Natalie's privacy." Walken has never publicly mentioned the weekend since. Natalie Wood was forty-three years old.

～

HER FUNERAL WAS by invitation only, with valet parking, and paparazzi hanging over the walls of the Westwood Memorial Park, where Marilyn Monroe was also buried. Maria Gurdin was quietly moaning, her last bow as Natalie's mother. Richard Gregson had flown in from England, and he and RJ stood with their daughters, Natasha and Courtney. It was a fearsomely hot day, and Hollywood's nobility and yeomen had turned out in force. After the brief Russian Orthodox service, my wife and I dropped by the Wagner house to pay our respects. In the absence of a hostess, Elizabeth Taylor greeted every guest as they came through the door, clasping each to her substantial bosom and intoning mysteriously, "I am Mother Courage." In the living room, the family Sinatra—Frank, his first wife, Nancy, their children, Tina, Nancy, and Frank Jr.—had commandeered a couch, and they sat silently, arms folded, as if they were at a funeral in Palermo. There was one mesmerizing moment when the sound seemed sucked out of the room: the arrival of Christopher Walken, who strode the length of the house, looking neither right nor left, and went out into the garden.

Wagner gave Lambert unconditional access to Natalie's diaries and notes; no topic was out of bounds, no friend asked not to cooperate, no approvals or any preliminary reading of the manuscript sought. He talked at length to Lambert about the drinking and the rages and the fears, his and hers. It is the access and the freedom from having to dissimulate or resort to innuendo that give *Natalie Wood* its power and its grace. She was a movie star, from probably the last period when stars were still icons and not like other people, and she made all of stardom's stops—multiple lovers, marriages, substance abuse, suicide attempts, some serious, some not. If she was a victim of changing times, she was neither unaware of it nor unamused by it. When she had to play the star, Lambert writes, she would say it was time to "put on the badge," and put it on she did, with a jade cigarette holder, expensive clothes, "coordinated" jewelry, perfect hair and makeup.

Lambert's special gift is the ability to understand perfectly both the star and the complicated child woman. In death, she was still putting on the badge. When she was in the mortuary, Sydney Guillaroff, for decades the senior hair stylist at Metro, was asked to prepare Natalie's hair. He "brought along a fall he had created for Ava Gardner, whose hair was almost exactly the same color," Lambert writes. "He shampooed Natalie's hair by hand, blow-dried it, then began very carefully to comb the front over Gardner's fall."

That was stardom.

CRITICAL

PAULINE

[1973]

❧

SOME FACTS: A year or so ago I was asked to review Pauline Kael's *Raising Kane,* an arrogantly silly book that made me giggle and hoot as much as any I had ever read about Hollywood. But because I had a picture coming out later that year and because Ms. Kael is the film critic of the *New Yorker,* my worst instinct prevailed and I passed on the assignment. It was an ignoble thing to do, and thus when, shortly before the same picture was released, I was asked to review Ms. Kael's new book *Deeper into Movies,* I agreed, on the condition that I could review her entire oeuvre. A few weeks later, that picture opened in New York and Ms. Kael disliked it as thoroughly as I had *Raising Kane.* That, for those who wish to get off here, is the record.

In fact, I met Ms. Kael once and found her enormously engaging. It was at a party at my agent's house in New York on Academy Award night. She was perched in front of the television set, a tiny, birdlike woman in a Pucci knockdown and orthopedic shoes, giving the raspberry to each award. William Friedkin was a "corrupt director," Gene Hackman would be "ruined" by his Oscar. There was a refreshing directness about her. "Who are you?" she asked me. I told her. "I liked your book," she said. The book was called *The Studio,* and was a nonfiction account of a year in which I had the run of Twentieth Century-Fox. "Where's Joan?" she asked. "I want to meet her."

I was not wild about introducing Ms. Kael to my wife, Joan Didion. She had despised Joan's novel, *Play It as It Lays* (Wilfrid Sheed had reported her reading it aloud derisively on the beaches of Long Island), as she was later to despise the film made from the book, and Joan in turn had hammered Kael over the years, suggesting among other things "vocational guidance." They circled each other warily, Ms. Kael from the Napa Valley, my wife from the Sacramento Valley, and they hit upon their rhythm—Valley talk. They talked about ranches and pickups and whiskey on the floorboards and the Silverado Trail, two tough little numbers, each with the instincts of a mongoose and an amiable contempt for the other's work, putting on a good old girl number. It was a funny act to watch and I liked her.

I even liked talking to her about movies. In general, I like fewer films than she does, but arguing opinions about movies is like arguing about God, politics or sex, a stimulating but ultimately windy exercise. With that rather substantial caveat, I often find Kael enjoyable to read. She is as passionate about movies as anyone who has ever written about them, and it is from this passion that all her other virtues derive. She is funny, quirky, bright, encyclopedic, healthily mean-spirited, combative, malevolent, contentious and often right. She is also often ludicrous, and this too derives from that same passion. At times she seems less a critic than a den mother, swatting her favorites gently when they get out of line, lavishing them with attention, smothering them with superlatives for their successes. How was one to react to her contention that the opening of *Last Tango in Paris* was a cultural landmark comparable to the first performance of *Le Sacre du Printemps*? Such maternal excess scars her work, and worse. In her rhapsodies to the stylish and efficient potboilers of the young Coppola and the boyish Spielberg, her search for cosmology in the entertaining rubbish of *Jaws* and *The Godfathers,* Kael exhibits a passion so sexual in its underpinning that it becomes embarrassing.

If Kael looks better than she actually is, it is in no small part due to the quality of the competition. The nature of the film critic is to pump himself up. One critic's cant is another's Kant; the game is less one of taste than of ego and exhibitionism. It is exhibitionism, however, at a dispiriting level. One does not set out in life to become a movie critic; it is where one ends up. A truce is made with life, an armistice with ambition: it is far easier for the manqué litterateur to explain why he has not made a movie than why he has not written a book. Stanley Kauffmann, erstwhile actor, editor, playwright, drama critic, filmmaker, novelist—a Renaissance failure, as it were—is smarmy, Judith Crist unreadable, the news-magazine reviewers would-be screenwriters with an eye for the main chance. John Simon has limitless venom, but he sprays it around so indiscriminately that it becomes antitoxic and he rather sweet. And what can one say about a man who ruts after fame so promiscuously that he debated Jacqueline Susann on television and allowed himself to be interviewed for the woman's page of the *New York Times* as Daniel Ellsberg's wife's former boy friend? How perverted the lust for celebrity when one can portray oneself publicly as the Eddie Fisher of the Pentagon Papers.

Which leaves Kael. Reading her on film is like reading Lysenko on genetics—fascinating, unless you know something about genetics. The Rosetta Stone of her work is *Raising Kane,* which combines the Herman Mankiewicz–Orson Welles shooting script of *Citizen Kane* with a commentary by Kael on the making of the picture. *Raising Kane* reads as if it were not so much written as chattered in a movie queue by one of those film buffs who has seen everything and understood nothing. It is a pastiche of morgue clips, selective interviewing and gussied-up gossip speciously fobbed off as film erudition. It abounds in lists of old movies—*The Moon's Our Home* and *He Married His Wife* and *Easy Living* and *Midnight* and *Mississippi* and *Million Dollar Legs*—that seem dropped in only to impress the muddleheaded: if she has seen that many films she must be getting at something. The ploy belongs to the idiot savant, and recurs constantly in Kael's work; she needs only the faintest cue to swing into *She Done Him Wrong, I'm No Angel, Top Hat, Swing Time, The Lady Eve*—usually by way of showing them superior to the latest Fellini or Resnais.

Raising Kane is also suffused with that protocol of banality that flourishes west of Central Park—Hollywood the Destroyer. In the case of Herman Mankiewicz, it was not true; he flowered in Hollywood as he never had in New York. In the case of other writers, it is ridiculous. There is first of all the assumption that if these writers had not been working for Sam Goldwyn or Irving Thalberg they would have been writing *Moby Dick* or *Long Day's Journey into Night.* Then there were the writers who were not destroyed—Faulkner, Hellman, O'Hara, Behrman, West, Kaufman—writers who took the money and ran. The writers who fell apart in Hollywood would have fallen apart in Zabar's; the flaw was in them, not the community, but this is hard for the determinist movie critic to accept.

All this was by way of decorating Kael's thesis that Herman Mankiewicz was at least equally responsible with Welles for *Citizen Kane.* What seems to bother Kael is Welles's contention that "cinema is the work of one single person." There in a nutshell is the auteur theory, a theory that seems designed to inflate the already swollen vanity of film directors while enraging just about everyone else. Perhaps if the auteur theory were less Frenchified and more in the American grain, it might be more acceptable. The chairman of the board theory, say, or the senior partner theory. All it means is that someone is in charge, and that someone, that senior partner, is generally the director. I do not think that Kael would dispute the notion that there is not a page in *The New Yorker* that does not reflect the personality, taste and interests of its editor, William Shawn, even though he rarely writes a word that is in it. This, of course, is what Welles meant, as anyone who has ever worked on a film would understand. Unless one is courting disaster, the final choices must ultimately reside in the hands of one man. Read the script of *Citizen Kane* and see: ten directors could have shot it word for word; nine would have botched it, the tenth was a genius.

In her zeal to show Welles as a thief stealing credit from Mankiewicz, Kael has indulged in some highly suspect, not to say slovenly, reporting. As Peter Bogdanovich pointed out in *Esquire,* Kael simply ignored any indication that Welles had anything to do with the script of *Citizen Kane,* despite evidence that his participation was, to say the least, active. That is the way the Pentagon operates; the government has no monopoly on the selective truth.

But it is when Kael gets into the actual filming of *Kane* that she becomes particularly inane. "There's the scene of Welles eating in the newspaper office," she writes, "which was obviously caught by the camera crew, and which, to be a 'good sport,' he had to use." I thought I was hallucinating the first time I read that sentence, and now, every time I break it down and parse it, new questions arise. Where was the camera? Were Welles's meals usually lit? Was it his habit to dine in the middle of a setup? When did the crew have its own lunch break? Did the crew usually stand discreetly out of camera range and watch Welles gobble? Was Welles a noted "good sport"? Is Pauline Kael trying to tell us that *Citizen Kane* was cinema verité?

It is this implacable ignorance of the mechanics of filmmaking that prevails in all of Kael's books. Yet she is never called on it. The reason, of course, is that her audience knows even less of these mechanics than she does, and professional film people do not wish to incur her displeasure by calling attention to it. She seems to believe that films are made by a consortium of independent contractors—the writer writes, the cutter cuts, the actor acts, the cameraman photographs. In effect she is always blaming the cellist for the tuba solo. She cannot seem to get it through her skull that if Conrad Hall shoots that "fancy bleak cinematography" she so despises, it is because his director, Richard Brooks, wants it. To be sure, the error is not Kael's alone. Few critics understand the roles of chance, compromise, accident and contingency in the day-by-day of a picture. One prominent critic evoked Eric Rohmer when a scene in a picture on which I worked was filmed entirely as a reaction shot. The reason for the reaction shot was that we were behind schedule, the location had to be abandoned and the actor in the scene showed up too drunk to say his lines.

The entire process of directing eludes Kael. She perceives it as flashy "technique" and tricky "camera angles," which quite rightly she considers the last refuge of the charlatan. She understands what writers do, but she thinks they do it alone: she cannot seem to understand that good directors direct the writer the same way they direct the actors or the cameraman. Generally they pick their projects and hire their writers. I cannot imagine Kael sitting down with William Shawn after seeing a movie and discussing what they are going to say about it, but that is what a story conference is all about. When Kael talks about the screenplay of *Sunday, Bloody Sunday* being successful because scenarist Penelope Gilliatt kept her "self-respect as a writer," she's talking gibberish. If a writer is not in control in the story conference and behind the camera and in the cutting room, if there is another writer banging away on the set, as there was on *Sunday, Bloody Sunday,* "self-respect" is beside the point. Robert Benton and David Newman, the scenarists of *Bonnie and Clyde,* may, as Kael says, "be good enough to join that category of unmentionable men who do what directors are glorified for." That is a very nice compliment, but it does tend to glide over the really unmentionable Robert Towne, who rewrote *Bonnie and Clyde,* as well as the picture's producer, Warren Beatty, and director, Arthur Penn, who hired and guided him through the rewrite.

This insensitivity to the way movies are made eventually corrodes Kael's real virtues. "Coherence and wit and feeling" are what she most wants to see in a film. Almost alone among the major critics she sees "escapism" as a "function of art," and, "in terms of modern big city life and small town boredom, it may be a major factor in keeping us sane." Most invigoratingly, she has postulated a theory of movies as "trash art," an idea, considering the maniac economics of the movie business, that may be the only viable way to view the form. So far, so good. But with the years, Kael's crotchets have become rigidified. By temperament out of the Preston Sturges 1930s, she seems almost an exile in the sixties and seventies. Anomie, acidie and alienation are personally repellent to her. She often complains of pictures that make her feel "slugged and depressed," and bingo, we are into *Million Dollar Legs* again. She eviscerates Fellini, Resnais and Antonioni for their concern with the morally languid upper-middle class (that she liked *L'Avventura* seems almost an exercise in aberrant behavior). Part West Side radical, part populist Western xenophobe, she sniffs out fashionable "anti-Americanism" like a lady from the DAR, and God help the trendy foreigner or American living abroad (e.g., Richard Lester, who directed *Petulia*) who she thinks is spitting on the flag.

Kael makes rather casual use of the word fascist. Sam Peckinpah's *The Straw Dogs* is a "fascist work of art" and action pictures in

general are "better suited to fascism . . . than to democracy." About
The Great Waldo Pepper, she writes: "I can't tell if Americans will like
this movie, but I think Hitler would have drunk a toast to it." This
is sleazy, a crotchet that needs a biopsy, "fascism" used in the way
Joe McCarthy tossed around "Communism" a generation ago. "If
thought corrupts language," George Orwell wrote, "language can
also corrupt thought."

What seems eccentric or idiosyncratic in the course of one Kael
review or even one Kael book finally becomes alarming over six
books and some seven hundred reviews. She is fluent in the more
evasive verb tenses, e.g., "M-G-M's lawyers *must have taken* a dim
view of this. A smaller company . . . *might have encouraged* him." After
a little of this fishiness, one begins to smell the taint in Kael's
famous style, with all its spontaneity and populist energy. The
style begins to seem, based as it is largely on parenthetical innuendo
and cleverly buried qualifiers, less energetic and spontaneous than
merely shifty, and quite calculated. When Kael tells us that
"Jean Renoir is the only proof that it is possible to be great and sane
in movies, and he hasn't worked often in recent years," we are
meant to infer that Renoir's greatness and sanity render him unem-
ployable. In fact, Renoir is almost eighty and an invalid. And when
she tells us, about Sidney Lumet doing *The Group,* that "it's doubtful that he ever read any Mary McCarthy," we are meant to read
"doubtful that he ever" as "certain that he'd never." Rich with
subjunctives, slippery with "presumably's," it is a rancid technique; others less charitable than I might—to borrow a verb tense
from the progenitrix—even call it dishonest.

And even I might go that far when it comes to Kael's creative
viewing. In her review of *Jeremiah Johnson,* she wrote: "When the
Crows, recognizing Jeremiah's courage, end their war against him,
and the chief gives him the peace sign, Jeremiah signals him back,
giving him the finger." Not in the print I saw he didn't—Robert
Redford returned the peace signal—and when I checked with the
director's office I was told that no scene was ever written or shot in
which Jeremiah gave the Crow the finger. But the imaginary finger was necessary for Kael to make her point. "In that gesture," she
wrote, "the moviemakers load him with guilt for what the white

Americans have done to the Indians, and at the same time ask us to laugh at the gesture." *Jeremiah Johnson,* she concluded, seemed to have been made "by vultures." Perhaps it was only reviewed by one.

When language degenerates, what is it worth? Like the reporter who sits in the hotel bar and fashions energetic and colorful dispatches about street life in the far country, Kael counts on a reader who will accept her version as filed. Here a little fudging about the temple bells, there a description of the parrot bazaar too picturesque to pass up, never mind that the parrot bazaar is shuttered. Robert Redford giving the finger to the Crow, Orson Welles stealing a credit, who will ever know the difference? What is regrettable is that not too many of Pauline Kael's readers will, and what is more regrettable still is that Pauline Kael knows it.

CRITICAL

[1987]

HERE IS WHY writers should never respond to their reviews. In 1969, I published a book called *The Studio.* The review in *Time* was generally enthusiastic, except for a comment that I had used a word wrong. The word was "vicissitudes," and the reviewer said I was the sort of writer who thought "vicissitudes" was classier than "ups and downs." I used to work at *Time,* and I am familiar with what Calvin Trillin, another *Time* alumnus, calls "the old *Time* yutz," that jab in the ribs that says to the alumnus, Don't get too big for your britches now that you're publishing books, buster, we knew you when. I should have let it go—I used the word I meant to use and the review was favorable—but instead I wrote not to the reviewer but to the magazine's managing editor, Henry Anatole Grunwald, formerly my editor and later editor in chief of all the Time Inc. publications. Henry was born in Austria and is full of Middle European charm and savoir faire and killer instinct. "Dear Henry," I wrote sweetly, "Actually I don't blame you for this, because English is after all your second language." As sallies go, not bad, but not as good as Henry's reply. *"Lieber Johann,"* his letter began, and continued to its conclusion, in German.

In their single-minded self-absorption, writers have a tendency to think that criticism is peculiar to their line of work. One night several years ago, I put this proposition to a federal judge and to my brother-in-law, who is CEO of a major corporation. I said they had never been called "slime," as I once was in a counter-cultural newspaper. Words, they answered, only words, words that had no substantial effect on my ability to make a living. As opposed, my brother-in-law said, to that one bad quarter that could make him liable to being fired by his board. As opposed, the federal judge said, to having every ruling and every decision subject to reversal either by the Ninth Circuit or the United States Supreme Court.

In fact, when I was younger, I used to think that reviews really mattered; they were the writer's board, his appelate court, the final arbiter of his professional worth. Now, after nine books and five movies, I reckon that I have been reviewed some four thousand times and find that idea egregious nonsense. Of those four thousand reviews, only the tiniest fraction had any commercial or critical relevance. Outside the major metropolitan areas, many reviewers tend to rewrite jacket copy or the publisher's press release or even to steal a notice from a big-city newspaper. Let me give an example: in the daily *New York Times,* Christopher Lehmann-Haupt once reviewed a novel by my wife; a month or so later the exact same notice appeared verbatim in the Sunday book review of a paper in the Pacific Northwest, under the byline of that paper's book editor. And it was a pan, no less, which did seem to stretch the limits of propriety.

One never gets inured to reviews, but scar tissue does form. In the first place, reviews are always disappointing, even when laudatory. I remember a scene in Frederic Raphael's *Glittering Prizes* in which the author read his reviews—generally good—before breakfast, then had to face the day; that's all there was, there was nothing more. This is because there are two separate aspects to the writer's life: writing, which, however painful, is always rewarding, if only to prove to the writer that he can still do it; and being published, which, no matter how lavish the praise, is for the writer only wasting time until he gets back to work. In the second place, only an amateur believes his negative reviews, because then he has to believe the good ones as well, and it is even more pernicious to believe that you are the latest literary wunderkind than it is to believe you are slime.

One does, however, have to suppress the urge to cross-examine one's attacker. In *Reading Myself and Others,* Philip Roth calls unmailed letters to reviewers "a flourishing subliterary genre with a long and moving history, yet one that is all but unknown to the general public." The best advice is to forget it, and novelists, Roth says, "generally do forget it, or continually remind themselves that they ought to be forgetting it during the sieges of remembering." I remember once waking in the dead of night, and in the privacy of my bedroom accusing a woman reviewer of having a face like a dirt road, a face from which, I knew, every zit and pit had been removed in its book jacket and publicity representation by the miracle of airbrushing and retouching, not to mention the sordid demands of vanity. An aggressive reaction, to be sure, and not even a response (except indirectly) to an indictment of me; rather it was predicated on a single observation in the course of a review in which my wife's foot was held to the fire. "My charity does not naturally extend itself," the reviewer had written archly, "to . . . someone who has chosen to burden her adopted daughter with the name Quintana Roo." Up to that moment, I had fastidiously supposed that one's children were off limits, and that whether a child was natural or adopted was not an aspect of one's talent against which points might be scored. In any event, my daughter Quintana, then thirteen, was so burdened by her name that she was already negotiating, in anticipation of her driver's license three years hence, for the vanity license plate QROO.

When attacked, it is also comforting to consider the slings and arrows endured by other writers. In the darkest days of World War I, George Bernard Shaw published an antiwar pamphlet, "Common Sense and the War," which elicited an infuriated response from a public ready to accuse him of treason and worse. "The hag Sedition was your mother, and Perversity begot you, Mischief was your midwife, and Misrule your nurse, and Unreason brought you up at her feet," a playwright named Henry Arthur Jones wrote in an open letter to Shaw. "No other ancestry and rearing had you, you freakish homunculus, germinated outside of lawful procreation." Of another writer it was said that his "muse is at once indecent and ugly, lascivious and gawky, lubricious and coarse." And again: "You might strike out of existence all that he has written, and the world would not be consciously poorer." Yet again: "an American writer who . . . attracted attention by a volume of so-called poems which were chiefly remarkable for their absurd extravagances and shameless obscenity, and who has since, we are glad to say, been little heard of among decent people." The target of this opprobrium was Walt Whitman, the volume *Leaves of Grass*; the names of most of his accusers are for their sake blessedly lost to memory, or if remembered at all, only as risible footnotes in the Whitman biographies.

There is another reason it is useless to complain: in a way a critic almost never can, the writer knows where "the dry rot" (as Graham Greene once felicitously called it) of a book is actually located, knows all the tricks he used trying to calk it. For all the animus to which a writer is occasionally exposed, I can recall only once being told by a critic something I did not already know about a book of mine. The critic was John Leonard, then of *The New York Times,* and he mentioned to me at a party that he had wanted to review my novel *Dutch Shea, Jr.* because it was so predicated on class hatred. He was absolutely right, but until that moment I had never been aware of it; I wish he had reviewed the book and expanded on that idea, even though he never told me if he liked it or not.

Leonard also told me he knew that in that same book I had taken a gratuitous whack at him and three other critics (although I never named them), in a scene where the protagonist, as he contemplates suicide, watches the *Dick Cavett Show.* I had actually seen this show, and listened while Leonard and the other panelists talked endlessly about the state of American letters. One panelist was a reviewer whose work, all self-promoting butch and blather, I detested, a sentiment I was sure was reciprocated, although to the best of my knowledge he had never reviewed me in the regional journals and the house organ of Euro-trash where he held forth on literature. As my potential suicide watched the show he mused that the unnamed reviewer "looked like Queen Victoria . . . sadly, badly, desperately in need of a diuretic, Naturetin K for bloat." And on and on in similar vein; suicide deferred, although ultimately not even a subsequent and still uncredited appearance by the Victoria clone on yet another PBS show in the novel's last scene could stay the gun my protagonist placed in his mouth, the Empress of India lookalike prattling onscreen even as the trigger was pulled.

Writers are prone to this sort of thing. When he was an editor at the *Partisan Review,* Delmore Schwartz was once unflattering about a short story submitted him by Calder Willingham. In his novel *End as a Man,* Willingham settled accounts by calling a whorehouse Hotel Delmore, later telling a friend of Schwartz that the choice of the name had been deliberate, adding however that he would not have used it had not "Delmore" been so "exactly right from an artistic point of view." Another novelist I know took aim at a daily reviewer for *The New York Times,* an indefatigable ladies' man whose girls seemed to get younger as he got older. The novelist created a scene in a novel just so the reviewer could walk through it unnamed but unmistakable to those who knew him, giving the author a chance to comment on the reviewer's sexual proclivities. And I suppose the ultimate payback came when a writer I know, infuriated by a bad notice, met the reviewer's wife at a party and with malice aforethought seduced her. I might add that the writer in question is my only source for this story.

There are writers who claim not to read their reviews—Saul Bellow comes to mind. The critic Anatole Broyard once scolded Bellow for this stance, saying he might learn something from his critics. What Broyard actually meant, of course, was that Bellow might learn something from the caveats of Anatole Broyard, *maître* to *maître,* as it were, a very slick form of self-aggrandizement. In any event, it scarcely matters if you read your bad reviews, because your friends will tell you what they say anyway. What, after all, are friends for? A few years ago in New York I saw a headline in a hotel magazine stand: JOHN LAHR PUNCTURES THE DIDION-DUNNE BALLOON, and inside there was a caricature of my wife and me. Better a balloon punctured, I thought, than never a balloon at all, and I neither bought the magazine nor read the piece. I had also written enough pieces like that myself to know a dirty little secret: whatever the author's disavowals, whatever his claim to be acting in the service of literature, he is writing for an audience of one— the object of his disaffection—and for that audience of one not to read it is his Zen triumph.

By the time I returned home to Los Angeles, however, I had already received seven copies of Lahr's puncturing, including two from my mother-in-law, mailed in separate envelopes, as if she only trusted the U.S. Postal Service to deliver one of every two pieces of mail. Sticking to Zen principles, I still have not read it, but via friends and family clucking over the unfairness of it all I was made aware ("Why would he say that you are . . .") of each of the sins for which Mr. Lahr claims that my wife and I should do penance. None of them surprised me much; since the late 1970s, we have been a cottage industry for Mr. Lahr, who has detailed our shortcomings, either singly or in tandem, four times by my account, updating the bill of particulars with each new book. I should be flattered. In at least one instance, Mr. Lahr has shown himself to be a very acute critic of fiction, in that he seems to have abandoned the writing of novels, a discipline in which he demonstrated no discernible gift. Before he became preoccupied with our general inferiority, he did write two novels and sent advance copies of both, each accompanied by a flowery personal entreaty for favorable comment, this before he had sharpened the pin with which to puncture the balloon.

This is not to argue that Mr. Lahr has no right to change his mind (or to imply that the failure to produce jacket quotes caused him to do so). There is, however, a preemptive-strike school that says if I attack you, then you can't attack me, with a statute of limitations that never seems to run out. A district attorney I know calls this the intellectual's version of extortion. One way around this kind of blackmail is to declare an interest. I once reviewed a book by Pauline Kael after she shredded a movie I had written. I disliked her work even before that review (she was, by the way, on the money about the movie in question), indicated in my first paragraph her prior dislike of the picture, and then wrote, "That, for those who wish to get off here, is the record."

Some years later, in *The New Republic,* Henry Fairlie unloaded on one of William F. Buckley's collections of columns, *Right Reason.* In the course of taking Mr. Buckley rather strenuously to task, Mr. Fairlie noted that among the pieces was "an ad hominem attack on me, notable mainly for its misinformation," then continued his bombing run. Mr. Buckley's response was to buy an advertising page in *The New Republic,* where he reprinted in full the charge sheet Mr. Fairlie had mentioned. Mr. Buckley makes a habit of that sort of reply, although usually less expensively. I was less infatuated with his *Overdrive* than he thought I should be, and he responded to *The New York Review of Books* (where my piece appeared) with a letter in which he detailed the people and publications who liked *Overdrive* more than I (Louis Auchincloss, Lance Morrow, and *People*), made an obliquely humorous reference to Salvadoran death squads, considered the failures and repetitions of my own work, and, finally, delivered the kayo punch: "Dunne begins his review by reporting that he and I have had a 'fitful' correspondence over the years. . . . But you see, those notes, while perhaps addressed to the couple, were really directed to his wife, who, of the two, was my friend."

I suspect the reason for this tick is that Mr. Buckley is an enthusiastic dilator on the defects of others, and in my experience enthusiastic dilators are considerably less enthusiastic when someone dilates upon them—"dilate" being Mr. Buckley's verb, from *Overdrive.* He seems not to understand the basic ecology of the literary life, that if you are not sometimes attacked, then you cannot be very good, the attack itself a certification of worth, whether it be Norman Podhoretz on John Updike or Irving Howe on Philip Roth; *vide* also the attacks on Whitman and Shaw. Better to bask in the glow of being one of the world's best fast writers, a gracefully Delphic encomium Mr. Buckley once received from Kurt Vonnegut, and one that has always seemed to me on the level of being called the world's best premature ejaculator, the pleasure enjoyed in inverse proportion to the pleasure given.

Ultimately it is a waste of time to reply directly to your critics; to do so is only a public acknowledgment that the shot hit home, and that your feelings are hurt. What it comes down to is this: Would I rather do what I do, as imperfectly as my harshest critics say I do it, or what they do, as perfectly as they think they do it? The question needs no answer. Only once do I claim to have had the last word with a critic, and that in a way he never knew. The reviewer was John Simon, he who in his quest for the brass ring has made a reputation for himself mainly by lingering on what he perceives as the physical shortfalls of the actresses he sees on stage and screen. The last time I saw Mr. Simon he was having dinner in the billiard room of a thirty-four-room apartment on Park Avenue. Honesty compels me to report, in the interests of those actresses whose tinny voices and pendulous breasts and flabby muscle tone he has maligned, that a giblet of quiche decorated his primary chin, and his teeth, all too visible as he ate, seemed the product either of bad dentistry or a stagnant genetic pool.

Mr. Simon has sampled every dish on the buffet of hustle, from elitism to language to being the spokesperson for one of Claus von Bülow's discarded mistresses. Language was the rack on which he had me stretched this time, in a column he wrote about a piece I had done on movie reviewers, one of whom coincidentally was Mr. Simon himself. Mr. Simon's scrutiny was sufficiently rigorous to have my friend Calvin Trillin send the following letter:

> Dear John Gregory—As one who has looked to you for guidance in these matters, I was naturally distressed to read in John Simon's column that your grammar and syntax are, to use the vernacular, not worth a shit.
>
> Yours,
> Calvin.

As it happened, Calvin's letter arrived in the same mail as a profit check from a very bad but very successful movie I had once helped to write. The check was, if I recall correctly, in the amount of $264,000. I took the check and Calvin's letter and Xeroxed them together on the same piece of paper. Then I mailed this Xerox back to Calvin by return post, with four words typed on the bottom: "Dear Calvin—Fuck syntax."

A STAR IS BORN

[1991]

❦

PHILLIPS, JULIA, film producer; b. Bklyn., April 7, 1944; d. Adolph and Tanya Miller; grad. Nicolet high sch.; B.A. Mt. Holyoke, 1965; m. Michael Phillips (div.); 1 dau., Kate Elizabeth. Former prodn. asst. McCall's Mag.; later textbook copywriter Macmillan Publs.; editorial asst. Ladies Home Journal, later asso. editor; head Mirisch Prodns., N.Y.; founded (with Tony Bill and Michael Phillips) Bill/Phillips Prodns., 1970; films include Steelyard Blues, 1973, The Sting (Acad. award for best picture of yr.) 1973, Taxi Driver (Palme d'or for best picture), 1976, The Big Bus, 1976, Close Encounters of the Third Kind; dir. Estate of Billy Buckner, 1974. Recipient Phi Beta Kappa award for ind. work, 1964. Mem. Acad. Motion Picture Arts and Scis. Democrat. Home: 2534 Benedict Canyon Beverly Hills CA 91210 Office: 1201 Producers 2 Columbia Pictures Colgems Square Burbank CA 91505.

Who's Who in America
40TH EDITION
1978–1979

THOSE WERE THE last days when Julia Phillips seemed to have the world on a string, dancing to her tune, the Oscar for *The Sting* and the follow-up successes of *Taxi Driver* and *Close Encounters* not yet consigned to ancient history, the final days before cocaine and freebasing and dealer boyfriends and hanger-on boyfriends and gigolos and too many insults and too many enemies and too little money and too much back taxes and lawyers and suicides and lousy advice and bad deals and rotten men finally took their toll. I knew her in those days, and she was then and is now the quintessential pain in the ass, which in an odd way is the source of her sometimes considerable, more often infuriating, charm.

We were her neighbors in Trancas, at the outermost edge of the Malibu, the older gentile couple in the house on the palisade. The first time we had Julia and her husband Michael to dinner, she got drunk (blaming it of course on the size of my drinks—actually drink; it was one Bloody Mary). She threw up in the bathroom, then checked out the prescriptions in the medicine cabinet, "the most thrilling medicine cabinet I had ever seen, every upper, downer, and in-betweener of interest in the *PDR*, circa 1973." All prescribed (in vain) for the migraine headaches with which my wife and I were both afflicted, but to a junkie it is comforting to think everyone else is a junkie, too. The next day my wife sent her some chicken soup to get her through the hangover. "*Shiksa* chicken soup," Julia called it, ready with a putdown even in extremis.

A few years later when Julia and Michael were noisily breaking up, and equally noisily getting back together again, they came by the house one day for a script meeting about a novel of mine they were interested in making into a movie. She was heavily into drugs by that time, which only exacerbated her pointlessly aggressive style, a style compounded by a voice that could cut metal. Unfortunately when I am confronted, I have a tendency to push back in kind, especially when someone not a writer tries to tell me what I had actually meant when I wrote something. We sparred edgily, with what I would like to think was a certain amount of humor, then suddenly she got up and left, alone, for what she said was another appointment.

Later that morning I received a call from Michael, in marriage, marital discord, and now in divorce always enormously protective of Julia. He said that she was not used to having people talk to her that way, and that I would have to apologize. What way? I said. I did not think that our conversation had gone beyond the bounds of normal script conference give-and-take, but Michael insisted that an apology was in order. So against my better judgment I did call her at home, and she in her tropistic way began to push and I in my tropistic way pushed back and one escalation led to another, until finally I told her to go fuck herself and hung up. Later that same day I sent her flowers; at the least I thought that the apology I sent with the bouquet would allow me the last word. Not quite. Many years after, she told me the real reason she had left our house that day was not because of our argument but because she had a date down the beach with a novelist with whom she had been having an affair, and who not coincidentally was as heavy into the blow as she was.

~

WITH SOME OF the punctuation missing, and without the post-script, these are two of the less racy stories Ms. Phillips now tells in her first book. Masquerading in its Library of Congress catalog listing as autobiography, *You'll Never Eat Lunch in This Town Again* is in fact the prototype of the classic big Hollywood novel. Most books about Hollywood (I could even argue all), especially those ostensibly based on autobiographical fact, are essentially fiction, so selectively are they recalled and filigreed and their sets dressed. Like most show people, Ms. Phillips tends to prefer, and with reason, anecdote to fact. Facts are unforgiving, but anecdote is essentially selfaggrandizing. Nuance and subtext are purged in the interest of placing the subject in the most favorable light. In this context, truth is an acceptable casualty. The plot never varies. The protagonist, whether it be Monroe Stahr or Julia Phillips, is always presented as the nobler citizen brought down not by his or her own faults or hubris or misdeeds, but by the philistines and the pharisees in charge, to whom this finer sensibility must pay professional obeisance. Billy Brady, Cecilia's father, was Monroe Stahr's demon, "with a suspiciousness developed like a muscle" and little more "than a drummer's sense of a story." For Julia Phillips, the ogres are names for the most part unknown outside the Hollywood community, "Mike Ovitz, Jeff Katzenberg, and Mark Canton," three whom she blames "for the decline of the movies." These three, and their clones, she poses darkly, are responsible "for the real poverty of vision abroad in the land." Vision, of course, is what the protagonists of these fairy tales always have.

It is well to remember that Hollywood, for all its presumed sophistication, is a small company town where all the mills manufacture the same product. Because they know little of the larger world, the toilers in these factories, the people who actually make the movies, tend to confer totemic wisdom on the most ordinary of the community's citizens (Mike Who, Jeff What, Mark What's-His-Name; the names are interchangeable, and indeed are constantly changing) only because they run the company stores. The public is a co-conspirator in this lust for the mundane. Agents today are written about in *Vanity Fair*, leading one to wonder who has ever heard of Ron Meyer or Ed Limato except Tina Brown, and why it is that their ministrations to Cher and Mel Gibson take up so many column inches.

Such micro-inspection encourages self-importance. Just last year I sat at a table in a restaurant in Los Angeles with a studio executive who the previous year had been compensated in the amount of tens of millions of dollars (a figure verified by his company's annual report). The host of the small dinner party (seven people) was a man with several billion of his own dollars and several billion more family dollars. Throughout dinner, the multimillion-dollar-a-year CEO never shut up, while the billionaire never opened his mouth or took his eyes off the executive during the evening-long soliloquy. (The executive's wife could not seem to understand how I had been invited to dinner. A quick whisper: Did I know the billionaire in New York? Yes. Socially? Yes. In Hollywood, as in all rigorously structured colonial societies, the social *faux pas* of inviting a writer to dinner is rarely made; it is an invitation to anarchy.) It seemed not to occur to the executive that for all his forty or fifty million dollars a year in salary and ancillary compensation, he was to the billionaire still just someone else's employee, however highly paid, however the local industry gentry hung on his every word.

It should also be remembered that Hollywood is a men's club that has always treated women cruelly. Even actresses as honored as Sigourney Weaver and Meryl Streep complain constantly that they are paid but a fraction of what their male counterparts are paid. Nor are they allowed, in their professional lives, to age gracefully, as male stars are; on the screen, men grow older, women grow old. If to prolong their star life, actresses yield to the demands of modern cosmetic surgery, too often the disquieting result is to make them look like quinquagenarian and anaphrodisiacal nymphets. Non-actresses fare little better. Women screenwriters are always being promised a chance to direct, if they will only cut their screenplay price, but the no man's land between promises made and promises kept is littered with the bodies of women who believed.

For women with no negotiable talent, who wish "to work in film" or to produce (that refuge for the untalented), the options are even more limited, and coarse. In the Industry, they are commonly called "development sluts." Meaning those young women with looks (the overweight need not apply nor those with moles), drive, and no discernible talent to whom the studios sometimes give a housekeeping fund for an office and a secretary, and some "development money" to work with would-be or never-will-be screenwriters whose primary virtue is that they are not in the Writers Guild, and therefore not eligible for minimums or benefits. Occasionally a screenplay might develop, perhaps even a picture put into production, by which time the developer has been removed from the project (via a clause in the boilerplate of the contract she has never bothered to read) and was setting up still another office paid for by yet another studio, all the while realizing but never quite admitting (in her quaint Spanish-style apartment off Laurel Canyon with the *Rolling Stone* posters on the walls and the Chianti bottle candles and the high-tech sound system and in the garage the BMW 315 whose payments she could not quite manage) that the reason she was being sponsored by her economic and professional betters was that occasionally she make herself available to scratch the itch of someone more important on the pecking order.

～

JULIA PHILLIPS MANAGED to avoid this particular circle of hell because she arrived in Hollywood with a husband, a few contacts from a series of low-level magazine and movie jobs in New York, and private means large enough to allow her and her husband both to option film projects and to rent a house at the beach that was a perfect place to call in those social markers that in the movie industry are always professional as well. She also arrived with a full cargo of emotional freight, most of it rather shopworn—there was an adored scientist father, a not-so-adored mother, and a younger male sibling to whom she appears to have stopped talking somewhere along life's highway.

She was the sort of bright child that, in her telling, parables were always seeking out. In a Brooklyn grade school she claims to have learned two life lessons: "1) Something about me invites accusation. Best to be rigidly honest as I am likely to be suspected anyway. 2) Friends will turn on you." The perfection of this prepubescent Thatcherian formulation is presented without hint of irony. Ms. Phillips's idea of rigid honesty, moreover, usually tended to draw attention to herself. Given oysters in a restaurant when she was four, she proclaimed loudly that they tasted like snot. Such precocity was encouraged, and in fact is a propensity Ms. Phillips has never lost, but while precociousness in a four-year-old is occasionally appealing, the practice, when it continues into middle age, can become tiresome.

~

THE PHILLIPS' MOVE to California, in the early 1970s, corresponded almost exactly to that time when the guard was changing in Hollywood. Henry Hathaway was still directing pictures with John Wayne, and Hal Wallis was producing them, and Chasen's was still the restaurant to go to on Sunday night, at least if you were seated at à banquette just inside the door. The Phillips' house in Malibu became a magnet for youthful (and generally talented) Hollywood have-nots desperate to become haves. Weekends one could usually find Steven Spielberg and Brian de Palma wandering outside their house just down the beach from ours, and Martin Scorcese and Al Pacino and Robert De Niro and Paul Schrader and Jill Clayburgh and Margot Kidder and David Ward and the Phillipses' soon-to-be-ex-partner, Tony Bill. None of them was yet quite famous, all of them were ambitious, and like heat-seeking missiles they sought each other out, their egos locking onto each other so fiercely that Sunday afternoons at the beach were like exercises in Top Gun training. David Ward wrote *The Sting*, Paul Schrader *Taxi Driver* and an early script of *Close Encounters of the Third Kind*; Spielberg directed *Close Encounters* and Scorcese *Taxi Driver*, with De Niro starring. As it turned out for the Phillipses, three consecutive hits, both critically and commercially; seldom has "networking" paid off so handsomely.

It seems to be Ms. Phillips's contention that this was a new guard, and she was on the point, taking movies in a direction they had never been taken before. It was also a time when, as the writer-director Nora Ephron recently remarked, women felt that "to get ahead in Hollywood they had to say 'fuck' and 'shit' a lot in meetings." The style came naturally to Ms. Phillips. She seemed to see herself as the ugly duckling at the party, and her every instinct was to inflict the first hurt. She was always ready to erupt with rage and hostility, the reasons for which she is never able to clarify in 573 pages. Her style was confrontational, tending invariably to denigration.

She was also an injustice collector, who seems never to have forgotten a slight, real or imagined, and she goes out of her way not only to settle scores but to create new bogeypersons ("bigger tits and fatter lips, from which hardly ever a clever word is uttered," she says for no apparent reason of the generation of Hollywood women that followed her). She pauses over every physical flaw, every wen and every excess pound, and she seems to credit and comfort herself that because the human contract is a sham, a higher honesty than others practice (and by others, she usually means men) compels her to do so. I am not convinced, however, that calling someone a "slob," or a "fat slob," or "dirty looking" or "priapic," or describing a group of producers as having faces "that looked like female privates" amounts to anything other than an adult example of the four-year-old sensibility that said oysters tasted like snot.

As long as success followed success, however, this was considered wit. *The Sting* won the Academy Award in 1974, and the first profit check its producers shared was $4.3 million, which made Julia Phillips just about the funniest person in town. *Taxi Driver* followed, more or less produced by Michael Phillips, and then *Close Encounters*, Julia's project. It is always difficult to explain exactly what a producer does, but in the case of Ms. Phillips (and all successful producers), the main task is to act as a heat shield between the director making the picture and the studio providing the money; this means getting more money, and justifying the increase in the budget with studio executives, at both of which tasks she was adept. Ms. Phillips was always considered "a good meeting"; she fought hard and was richly fluent in the lingua franca of badrap in which most of the business of Hollywood is conducted. Nor was her ego ever in short supply. "I am a spotter of trends," she writes portentously, although what trends she spotted she never makes entirely clear.

Like all producers, she considered herself a writer, a better writer in fact than the screenwriters she usually hired, and tended to confuse "pitching," that is, tossing out ideas in a story conference, with the act of writing itself. Hers was a mind activated by a thousand such story conferences; she pitched, the writer caught. In her mind, the writer, fellow coker, and putative paramour she calls by the pseudonym "Grady Rabinowitz" (because he obviously refused to sign a release) once told me, pitching was the important part; writing the screenplay was only an incidental afterthought.

With *The Sting*, Ms. Phillips now had the means to finance what had become a ravenous cocaine (and later freebase) habit. Her marriage broke up, and as her behavior became more erratic, she was fired, at Spielberg's insistence, from day-to-day participation in the production of *Close Encounters*. No matter. Like all cokers, she believed she functioned better when she was flying, and like all cokers she also had a million ideas a minute, although she was sometimes less than discriminating about where they came from. She seemed to think the director Sam Peckinpah had given me an idea I was working into a novel (actually Sam had an off-the-cuff idea about how he might make a movie from a book of my wife's), and then appropriated the idea herself (and in her version gets it hopelessly garbled) and tried to persuade various studios to put development money into it. From a player she had degenerated into a hustler, "taking meetings" about ephemeral projects and scorning proposed production deals as if she were still important, in one case because her financial sponsors would not build her a personal office bathroom, where she could snort in private.

About the meetings, we learn little other than how awful the people were with whom she had to meet, how fat and stupid and ugly and what their sexual peculiarities were and how wanting they were in their performance of same, and finally how contaminated their motives when they finally passed on her pictures. We also get a rather too extensive look at the wardrobe she wore to these meetings: ". . . my green Alaïa leather suit . . . hightoppers and a Joseph Tricot miniskirt . . . my gold Harriet Selwyn blazer with matching vest and an old pair of poison-green Krizia pants. . . ." She moved her dealers into her house ("I have always depended on the strangers whose kindness I purchase," she writes with an awkward bow to Tennessee Williams), which allowed her to get her cocaine wholesale, but also brought her an extra ration of violence. One tried to strangle her, another aimed an automatic rifle at her and her daughter; the gun-toter made her pregnant; she freebased right up to the moment of the abortion. At last she was prevailed to check into a rehab at the Mayo Clinic. It did not take; in the three months after she got out, she blew $120,000 on coke. Finally, she had the ultimate Hollywood comeuppance; she was fired by her business manager. "We service rich people," he told her, "and you are no longer a rich person."

～

CARELESS WITH HER own life, Ms. Phillips is equally careless in the writing of it. Names are casually misspelled, both those of professional acquaintances (the director John Milius becomes "Jon") and also others belonging to the world outside Hollywood (the Nobel Prize–winning physicist I. I. Rabi, a friend of her parents, thus becomes "Raabe"); characters are introduced by only a first or only a last name, and no other identification, as if being known by her is benediction enough. To a *Los Angeles Times* interviewer, Ms. Phillips recently asserted that she had "a rigidly trained mind . . . I'm always being told about my incredible memory." If by "incredible" she means "not credible; unbelievable" (definition 2, *The Random House Dictionary of the English Language*) then perhaps: for example, my wife and I are presented at a party we did not attend, complete to kisses and false congratulations, and when I read her the entry in our day book that proved we were not there, she asked if she could keep us as part of the *mise en scène* anyway.

On finishing *Lunch*, one is tempted to regard it only as a one-woman Masada trip. But with a certain devious skill, Julia Phillips has created of herself something far more calculating, perhaps even pernicious, a Hollywood fabulist in the great tradition perfected by Louise Brooks. As with all successful fantasts, Ms. Phillips has the gift of keeping the focus on herself. She is never peripheral; in her own mind, in every situation, she is always the sun around which the world as she sees it revolves, spreading not only light but also heat. Like Brooks, Ms. Phillips perceives herself as the last principled person, if not in the world, then at least in the Hollywood community that first rewarded her, however fleetingly, with fame, fortune, and awards, and then, in her elaborately gerry-built construct, abandoned her because she was more honest and more uncompromising than the rest of the community, with its tainted history of tainted accommodations, could in fact accommodate.

For Ms. Phillips this is an entirely comforting, and even an engaging myth, predicated as it is on fantastical assumptions of moral superiority. Even addled by drugs, she presents herself as a woman of a higher order of sensitivity and perception than those whose scorn she has now attracted, and the taking of the drugs is only one further proof of this superiority: "My theater is one where I never take gifts and I always pay in cash," she writes. "I have established this snobbery of never letting any of my dealers feed my nose out of their stash. If such a thing is possible, I command their respect." As evidence of an elevated moral position, this is demented.

In the theater of her imagination, Ms. Phillips sees herself as a truthteller, brutally frank to the point of self-destruction, when in fact so much is concealed in her book that there is little in this truthtelling that is not shaded to her ultimate advantage. While admitting to willful self-indulgence, she proceeds to convert it as a kind of quirky iconoclasm, to her individualism writ large. Calling attention to shortcomings in such a way that the reader is meant to congratulate her for her honesty in so doing absolves her of the shortcomings themselves. She thus becomes less a real person than the product of her own fevered sensibility, constantly reinventing herself as circumstances and her own psychic need dictate.

The prevailing wisdom in Hollywood is that Julia Phillips *will* never eat lunch there again, at least in the sense that lunch is working. (Not, however, because of this book; her bridges were already burned; for years she has been yesterday's news.) But the fact is that whatever her pretentions and however evasive and indifferently written *You'll Never Eat Lunch in This Town Again* is, its enormous sales (a number one best seller with a $640,000 reprint sale) indicate that she did tap into something. I propose that its success has nothing to do either with its rather dubious gossip or its tawdry sexuality, but with something far more basic. The movie industry, as already mentioned, is a boy's club, and women deeply resent it. "I still maintain that if I had been a man I would have been protected for the genius work I'd done," Ms. Phillips said in a recent interview. Strike "genius work" and she may be right; contemporary Hollywood has always looked less benignly on the malfeasances of women than it has those of men, who routinely get second, third, and fifth chances whatever their felonies, addictions, aberrations, drug tirades, or sexual depredations, and usually without risk of social ostracism or loss of a window table at Spago.

It is entirely consistent with this boys' club ethic that most of the Hollywood attacks against *You'll Never Eat Lunch in This Town Again* have been led by men, whereas Industry women, especially young women, while acknowledging the book's various and unpleasant faults, respond to it in the same way much of the local Los Angeles citizenry responded to the Rodney King videotape: it exposes something they know in their bones, something that represents the reality of their own class situation. Self-serving though she may be, Julia Phillips is only saying what they feel. I doubt that it was her intention, but Ms. Phillips has in fact written a book about class, an inferior class. Women in Hollywood rank even below screenwriters, and that is about as inferior as you can get.

PHILIP DUNNE (NO KIN) was another Malibu neighbor. The son of Finley Peter Dunne, he went to St. Bernard's in New York, Middlesex, and Harvard, arriving in Hollywood in 1930, and a job (at $35 a week) at the old Fox Studios, where his charter was to give scripts a "Harvard slant." In his thirty years at Fox, Dunne was twice nominated for an Academy Award; he also directed ten pictures, and in 1962 won the Laurel Award for lifetime achievement in screenwriting ("more for longevity than for literary excellence," he noted wryly in his 1980 autobiography *Take Two*). *How Green Was My Valley* won the Academy Award for best picture in 1941 (over, it should be noted, *Citizen Kane*) and four other Oscars, including best director for John Ford (over, it should be noted again, Orson Welles). Dunne's script was also nominated, one of the picture's ten nominations, but it lost out to Sidney Buchman and Seton I. Miller's adaptation of *Here Comes Mister Jordan*.

His polished and expert screenplay is published in *How Green Was My Valley*, but what gives this short book its impact is Dunne's graceful and witty accompanying essay, only twenty-five pages long, about what it was like to work in Hollywood in the days of the moguls. Every studio in that era had its own character, and Fox was known as "the writers' studio," its character molded by Darryl E. Zanuck, out of Wahoo, Nebraska, and as a young man in Hollywood the author of the *Rin Tin Tin* screenplays. On the Zanuck assembly line, writers wrote and directors directed; writers were responsible only to Zanuck and were discouraged from visiting the set, while only a select handful of directors were ever permitted to offer script suggestions. They were given a completed script, and told to shoot it as written; Dunne, in fact, never even met several of the directors charged with shooting his screenplays. "I can best describe [Fox]," he writes, "as a strict but benevolent imperium, with Zanuck, no Caligula or Nero, its all-powerful Augustus." Notice he does not say that Augustus has a face like female private parts.

Other studio staff writers had failed to make a usable script out of Richard Llewellyn's novel before Zanuck finally offered the assignment to Dunne. When he read the other scripts, he asked Zanuck what had prompted him to buy the novel in the first place, and only then was sent the book to read. To direct, Zanuck had borrowed William Wyler from the Goldwyn studio; Wyler was an old friend of Dunne's, and one of the few directors in Hollywood Zanuck would allow to have a hand in the writing. Wyler and Dunne went to Lake Arrowhead and worked out a script. But Wyler's reputation for extravagance had scared off Fox's New York money people, and he departed the project. Enter John Ford, another old friend and Irish drinking companion of Dunne's. "Like many of the upper class," Dunne writes of Ford (quoting Hilaire Belloc), "he liked the sound of broken glass."

Dunne takes *How Green Was My Valley* through production, post-production, and release. His essay ends at a special performance of the picture in 1972, shown at the Director's Guild for the dying John Ford, who had picked it as his favorite of the hundred or more films he had directed. It is a poignant ending for an elegant essay. To Philip Dunne, working at the writers' studio was as good as Hollywood could get. I confess to not sharing his enthusiasm for Ford's pictures (and he had several quarrels of his own with Ford's direction of *How Green Was My Valley*) and while I share his distaste for the pretensions of most film directors of the *auteur* school, I also think he tends to scant the director's contribution. Still, if you wish to learn how pictures were made in the age of the moguls, read Philip Dunne; if you wish to learn how mischief was made in the seventies and the eighties, read Julia Phillips.

Your Time Is My Time

[1992]

I.

TIME WAS A glorious place to work in the years that I was there, from 1959 to 1964. I was twenty-seven when I was hired, and an ignoramus, vintage Princeton '54, with a degree in history (I had written my senior thesis on Lord Lothian, the Cliveden Set's house Christian Scientist, an appeaser, and later British ambassador to Washington at the time of the destroyer for bases deal, and never cottoned to the fact that he was also, as *Time* in those days would have it, Nancy Astor's great and good friend). I got my job because a woman I was seeing on the sly, Vassar '57, was also seeing George J.W. Goodman, Harvard '52, a writer in *Time*'s business section who was later to become the author and PBS economics guru "Adam Smith." Goodman, I was informed by Vassar '57, was leaving *Time* for *Fortune*, which meant that if I moved fast there was probably a job open. I applied to *Time*'s personnel man, a friend, Yale '49, and was in due course interviewed by Otto Fuerbringer, Harvard '32, and *Time*'s managing editor. The cut of my orange and black jib seemed to satisfy him, and the $7,700 a year I was offered more than satisfied me, and so a few weeks later I went to work as a writer in the business section, although I was not altogether certain of the difference between a stock and a bond, and had no idea what "over the counter" meant.

The *Time* (and the *Life* and the *Fortune*) of those years was pervaded by a kind of Protestant entitlement and arrogance (no matter that I was an Irish Catholic; I felt spiritually brevetted a Protestant), an arrogance often spectacularly unearned (as in my case), or earned largely in the city rooms of the *Harvard Crimson* or the *Yale Daily News* or the *Daily Princetonian*. A corporate hubris prevailed, a confidence in ourselves, and in our place in the world. However misplaced this confidence, there was a verbal *esprit de corps*, a sense of purpose founded on the conviction that every Tuesday *Time* would give the educated man (the educated woman was considered so minor a factor that the magazine would not hire women writers; women on the staff could only aspire to be researchers, the *Time* equivalent of domestics) a review of the previous week's events presented with some political rigor and intellectual brio.

∽

THERE WAS NO pretense to objectivity; *Time* had a partisan Republican point of view, and if it was one not shared by many of its gentrified Ivy Leaguers, few felt the compulsion to quit. The excessive compression led to what became known as *Time* style, often ludicrous, easily parodied, but rich with possibilities for veiled and not so veiled innuendo; one wonders how many great and good friends were so identified over the years. Perhaps *Time*'s most prophetic contribution to journalism, however, was the importance it attached to "soft news," the back-of-the-book news that was rarely reported in the daily papers, weekly digests of what was happening in science and medicine and art and education and in the press. We were amateurs for the most part, inspired amateurs in some cases, discoursing easily on the brushstrokes and color schemes of Bernard Buffet one week and on the financial restructuring of the Malaysian economy planned by Tunku Abdul Rahman the next, and few were ever the wiser.

The first piece I wrote for *Time* was an obituary of oilman Sid Richardson, of whom I had never heard until the day he died. On that first closing night, and all the rest of the closing nights during my tenure, waiters from the Tower Suite, on top of the Time-Life Building, rolled in buffet carts with beef Wellington and chicken divan and sole and assorted appetizers and vegetables and desserts. There was wine, French and domestic, and an elderly *Time* factotum, once said to be a superior foreign correspondent but by then a burnt-out case, was in charge of dispensing the liquor, and did so in prodigious quantities. Hotel rooms were available for those sub-urbanites who had missed their last train, or would so claim to their wives when in fact all they wished was an adulterous snuggle with a back-of-the-book researcher, Radcliffe '58 or Smith '47. For those who lived in town and who were working into the small hours, there were limousines to take us home, Carey Cadillacs for most, but I secured a company charge account at Buckingham Livery, which only used Rolls-Royces, and when I turned in my expense accounts no one objected. It was not journalism, but it was fun, and through constant practice, four or five stories a week, one did learn to meet deadlines and write to space, and with an infusion of curiosity even to learn a little about the world.

∼

HENRY LUCE WAS still around, a spectral presence to those of us in the lower editorial orders, so sure of himself and the Protestant hegemony (a legacy as the son of a Presbyterian missionary in China, albeit one with enough wherewithal to send his son to Hotchkiss and Yale) that he ordained this to be "The American Century." Among ourselves, we called him "Luce," and envied those higher up on the food chain who referred to him as "Harry," and we woundered if we would ever reach such eminence, or impertinence. Luce had formulated a doctrine of Church and State, with Church the editorial staff and State those on the business and publishing end. Between Church and State there was to be perfect separation, and we monks and nuns of the Church believed in our bones that the editor-in-chief enjoyed papal infallibility to which the State must always defer. As long as Luce was alive, the Church was indeed *prima inter pares*, but with his death this was a cross that the State was increasingly unwilling bear, the cross upon which the Church, and Time Inc., were ultimately nailed.

Within the one true editorial church, however, there were schisms, the most nettlesome to *Time*'s all powerful managing editors being the independence of the News Bureau, which ostensibly was part of their domain. While the magazine's chief of correspondents was nominally subordinate to the managing editor, he and he alone, by Luce's fiat, hired and fired the reporters who staffed *Time*'s foreign and domestic bureaus, and it was to him they were responsible, not to the managing editor; the better the reporters, the more insidious the challenge to the managing editor's dominion. Since *Time* was an editor-driven magazine, what the managing editor did not dominate he did not entirely trust, and damn the facts.

Theodore H. White, a Luce favorite, discovered this truth in the late 1940s when Luce did not believe his dispatches from China that corruption within the Kuomintang would bring about the defeat of Chiang Kai-shek and victory for Mao Tse-tung. White left; Mao won; Luce was unrepentant. In my years, Otto Fuerbringer questioned the integrity and abilities of the late Charles Mohr, another Luce favorite, a superior journalist and relentlessly nonideological war correspondent who as early as 1962 was reporting from Saigon that the war in Vietnam was at best a questionable and at worst a no-win proposition.[1] Mohr finally quit and went to *The New York Times*, where he covered so many wars so well he earned the reputation of being something of a soldier *manqué*.

⁓

EVEN WITHOUT BYLINES, and even with their files rewritten by editors with partisan views often at war with what was seen on the ground, the correspondents, in the 1960s, were the magazine's stars, its true professionals, and this was in no small way the doing of Richard M. Clurman, *Time*'s chief of correspondents. Clurman "upgraded the news service," David Halberstam wrote in *The Powers That Be*, "building what became . . . one of the great journalistic stables in the world. . . . He could offer his reporters good jobs, good— very good in those days—pay, [and] unusually generous expense accounts."[2] Clurman was in every way antithetical to what the *Time* catechism calls, with beguiling and unexamined pomposity, the "*Time* culture," which basically meant its Ivy League fiefdom of gentlemen amateurs, every week expert in a new directory of the world's data base. He was a Jew who went to the University of Chicago and had theatrical connections—his uncle was the theater director and critic Harold Clurman—and he had once worked at *Commentary*.

Clurman was fiercely protective of his reporters, and they in turn were fiercely loyal to him, although not immune to mocking his well-documented pretentions. His home telephone, it was reported, had as many buttons as the alphabet; and when he visited his troops in the field it was claimed he always booked two first-class tickets so he would not be bothered by the plebs, or would have a place to offer any personage on board worthy of his company. "There are worse sins," one of his admiring former reporters, Yale '57, said recently, "than self-importance." To this day Clurman drops names as easily as Darryl Strawberry drops fly balls. After I left *Time*, I ran into him once in the lobby of the Mark Hopkins Hotel in San Francisco and mischievously left messages for him with the hotel operator—Mr. Clurman, please call John Sherman Cooper, you know the number; Mr. Clurman, call U Thant, use the private line—confident that he would return every call even as he suspected he was being had.

As journalist and executive, Clurman stalked *Time*'s corridors of power for what he calls "twenty gratifying and exhilarating years." Remembering everything and forgetting nothing, including a few grudges, he is uniquely qualified to report on the abortive merger between Time Inc., and Warner Communications, Inc., and the subsequent (after the merger was challenged in the courts by what was then the Gulf + Western Corporation and afterward became Paramount Communications, Inc.) forced leveraged buyout of WCI by Time. If Clurman is overly romantic, even moony, about the old *Time* culture, he is bracingly mean-spirited about the confederacy of dunces who sold that culture down the river to the corporate riverboat gambler, Steven J. Ross, chairman and chief executive officer of WCI. What gives *To the End of Time* its engaging nastiness is Clurman's account of the way Ross, in every way legally, picked the pockets of Time's dim senior executives, and the gold from the corporation's teeth.

2.

In fact, Henry Luce's death in 1967 all but preordained *Time*'s demise as an independent entity. Whatever one might think of Luce's vision, he did have one, and one that was shared, in large part, by his own designated heirs apparent, Hedley Donovan and Andrew Heiskell, respectively Pope of the Church and Chief of State. After the retirements of Donovan and Heiskell, however, *Time* passed to a generation of tough-guy managers who had never known Luce well enough to call him Harry, or if they did, only hesitantly, and who did not share his passion for print. They were bean counters, from finance and circulation and ad sales departments, and because the corporate profit centers were increasingly in television and cable systems and forest products they were never entirely comfortable sharing power with the editor-in-chief, as had been laid down in the corporate by-laws by Hedley Donovan, and ratified by the board of directors. According to the Donovan Charter, the editor-in-chief reported directly to the board, and not to the CEO, and was entirely reponsible for the contents of the magazines. He was, moreover, assured membership on the board, and could intervene in business practices "if publishing activities seemed to conflict with editorial standards."

Heiskell's successor as CEO was J. Richard Munro, once publisher of *Sports Illustrated*, and a former marine sergeant wounded three times during the Korean War. As Time's president and chief operating officer, Munro had chosen Nicholas J. Nicholas, Jr., Andover- and Princeton-educated, the son of a career US Navy submarine officer. Nicholas was instrumental in getting Time's television operations off the ground, and as he climbed the corporate ladder his efficiency in cutting budgets earned him the name "Nick the Knife" within the company; less flatteringly, the head of one investment banking house recently characterized him to me as "that little shit in elevator shoes."

Munro was so unsentimental about *Time*'s publishing heritage that he canceled his mentor Heiskell's free (and tiny) grace-and-favor office in the Time-Life Building and made him put up $50,000 a year in rent and secretarial services; and then later, when the executive offices were scheduled for redecoration Munro suggested that the portraits of Luce, Heiskell, and Donovan be removed. When Heiskell threatened to protest to the board, Munro backed down. Nicholas was displeased. "Who is Andrew Heiskell?" he asked. "Andrew was the latest guy to come along. Hedley Donovan was the number-two editor-in-chief. We're now into number four. Big deal. Give me a break." One may tax Henry Luce for many things, but never, I expect, for being so vulgar as to say, "Big deal, give me a break."

⁓

IN TRUTH, *TIME* has become all but irrelevant in the years since Luce died, a dentist's office magazine more often bought than read, except in those few foreign places where access to what is happening is not readily available. A weekly newsmagazine is an oxymoron in an age of television news, the national edition of *The New York Times, USA Today*, and, most importantly, Ted Turner's twenty-four-hour Cable News Network. What *Time* provided was less news than a kind of racy presentation—"Shortly after two o'clock one day last week . . ."—a tarty take on what its readers already knew. Once the jewel in Luce's crown, *Time* was seen by its new managers as just another rhinestone. "*Time* culture" notwithstanding, Munro called *People* and *Sports Illustrated* "the huge engines that drive" the magazine division; a 1988 *People* cover on Princess Diana made more money in one issue than *Vanity Fair* made all year, and *SI*'s annual swimsuit edition is a cash cow. In other words the *Time* culture was about gossip and cleavage.

Not that *Time* and *Life* and *Fortune* had lost any of their pretensions. A few years ago, when I was living in Los Angeles, *Time* began preparing a cover story on California, and I was contacted by a reporter in "Bevedit," as its LA bureau was always called (because it is located in Beverly Hills), and asked what "changes" I had discerned in the state. "Since when?" I asked. "Since *Time*'s last California cover," he answered.

A few years earlier, my wife had signed a contract to do a column for *Life* in spite of my admonitions that writing in such an editor-dominated environment was like being nibbled to death by ducks. What won her over was the promise made to her by the late George

Hunt, then *Life*'s managing editor: "There's a world in revolution out there. We can put you in Prague tomorrow, Moscow the next day, Peking when we can get you in. You can do that, or you can stay home and find a babysitter." She signed the contract, but then George Hunt retired, and to the enormous relief of all concerned, she quit after nine columns, never having got to Prague, Peking, or Moscow (and being turned down when she asked to go to My Lai the week the massacre story broke; she did however get to Santa Monica and to Hermiston, Oregon). The last straw was when Hunt's successor said to her, "Why can't you find the little guy doing a good job and give him a pat on the back?"

~

DURING THE 1980S, Time's once sure touch in starting new magazines faltered. Millions were spent in launching something called *TV-Cable Week*, which was meant to be a direct competitor to Walter Annenberg's *TV Guide*; *TV-Cable Week* was a humiliating folly, and was closed down in only five months. The dreadful *Entertainment Weekly* staggers along, while other ventures died aborning. Overseeing new magazine development, Henry Anatole Grunwald, the Viennese-born former managing editor of *Time* and Donovan's successor as editor-in-chief (as well as, an article of faith at *Time*, the company's house intellectual), tried not to leave too many fingerprints on these failures, in part by patronizing Munro, his supposed corporate superior. An assiduous Everyman who coached a suburban Little League team, Munro was given to peanut butter and Big Macs, and until he saw *Batman* after the merger had not seen a movie in ten years. "I don't take Dick to the opera," Grunwald said, "and he doesn't take me to the ballgame."

Among the troops, there was a certain gallows humor about Time's inability to start profitable new magazines; one tongue-in-cheek in-house flyer listed "Six Stages of New Magazine Development: 1) Exultation 2) Disenchantment 3) Confusion 4) The Search for the Guilty 5) Punishment of the Innocent 6) Distinction for the Uninvolved."

For their part, Munro and Nicholas talked big and thought small. In 1985, Ted Turner, badly in need of money, offered Time a half interest in CNN for $300 million. Munro hid when Turner showed up at the Time-Life Building; one of his advisers said Turner "wasn't a Time Inc. type. He drinks too much, spends money crazily, and chases women." CNN is now worth $5 billion, and in a marvelous irony Turner was chosen *Time*'s 1991 Man of the Year.[3] Warren Buffett, the legendary Omaha corporate investor who had major holdings in both The Washington Post Company and Capital Cities/ABC, fared no better. Knowing how fearful Munro and Nicholas were of a hostile takeover, Buffett offered to buy enough Time stock to make the company invulnerable to a takeover by putting that stock into the equivalent of a non-voting trust. In spurning this offer, Nicholas was as usual tough instead of smart. "What does he bring to the party?" he asked about Buffett, who had the courtesy not to ask the same question about him. Buffett, Munro said in retrospect, "was a couple of steps—not surprising—ahead of where we were. Boy, if he'd come across two years later, we would have been terribly interested." For Munro to say that Buffett was only a couple of steps ahead comes close to being libel.

∽

IT WAS, IN fact, a libel suit against *Time* by Israeli defense minister Ariel Sharon that effectively ended Luce's doctrinal separation of Church and State. In its issue of February 21, 1983, *Time* published a story on the findings of Israel's Kahan Commission, which had investigated the massacres in the Palestinian refugee camps at Sabra and Shatila after the assassination of Lebanon's president Bashir Gemayel. *Time* claimed access to an unpublished Appendix B of the Report and from this claimed authority for printing the allegation that Sharon "reportedly told the Gemayels that . . . he expected the Christian forces to go into the Palestinian refugee camps. He also reportedly discussed with the Gemayels the need to take revenge for the assassination."

As an old *Time* writer, I immediately spotted, in two consecutive sentences, the weasel-word "reportedly," the *Time*-honored hedge against the possibility that the facts in a given sentence might not hold up to reasonable scrutiny. Sharon sued. Although Munro and the publishing side wanted to settle, it was Henry Grunwald's call

as editor-in-chief, and Grunwald elected to fight the suit. Thomas
Barr, who headed the Cravath, Swaine and Moore legal team defend-
ing *Time* against Sharon, was the kind of bullying advocate who, in
taking a deposition, without a judge present, would try to rattle
opposing counsel by calling him "Sonny" and offering such inter-
jections, on the record, as "Horseshit" and "Jesus Christ." Once he
suggested that a Jewish lawyer's inability to take depositions on
Rosh Hashana was "a dodge," a remark that would perhaps pass
unnoticed in the Protestant preserves of Meadowcroft Lane in
Greenwich, where, according to his entry in *Who's Who*, Barr cele-
brates the Christian holidays.[4]

Time's case rested on the testimony and reporting of David
Halevy, the correspondent who claimed to have seen Appendix B.
In 1980, the magazine had put Halevy on probation for a questionable story on Menachem Begin's reputed failing health, a story
for which *Time* had to issue a grudging retraction. (In deposition,
Time tried to conceal the results of its investigation of Halevy and
even that any investigation had taken place, "to a point," as Renata
Adler noted in *Reckless Disregard*, "very near the borderline of legal
ethics." Asked if he recalled the contents of Halevy's personnel file,
Time's chief of correspondents, Richard Duncan, who had conducted the investigation and should have known the file intimately,
swore under oath: "No, I do not."

In his deposition and on the stand, Halevy was incapable of keeping his story straight. Even those *Time* witnesses who had put Halevy
on probation now went out on a limb to vouch for his bona fides, to
the horror, it turned out, of many of his colleagues who had worked
with him in the field, but who felt constrained, out of loyalty to their
employer, from giving a public and honest evaluation of his trust-
worthiness. In its verdict, the jury found *Time*'s story a) defamatory
b) false of the facts and c) without malice; because of the absence of
malice, it was therefore not per se libelous. But in an extraordinary
amplifying statement, the jury put its distaste for *Time*'s behavior on
the record by saying that David Halevy had "acted negligently and
carelessly in reporting and verifying the information."

"We won, flat-out and going away," Thomas Barr insisted. But
Time's board was not so sure that either the magazine or the

corporation could afford many such victories, not to mention the ridicule the story and the lawsuit directed at *Time*'s editors, writers, and fact checkers. "You could have all this horseshit you wanted about church and state," one director said. "But directors can be sued and you can't adopt an absolute philosophy like that." Close to retirement, and about to be named US ambassador to Austria by the Reagan administration, Grunwald appointed *Time*'s managing editor Jason McManus, a former Rhodes scholar, as his heir. The Sharon experience, however, impelled a number of directors to vow that McManus would be the last editor-in-chief automatically put on the board, and also led to the rewriting of the Donovan Charter so that McManus and his successors would in the future report to a corporate superior on the publishing side. The State had finally succeeded in subordinating the Church, and it was the State that now began listening to the courting song of WCI's Steven J. Ross, a song that a rock group recording on one of WCI's labels might call "Synergy."

3.

STEVEN J. ROSS, like Jay Gatsby, is his own best invention. He was born in Brooklyn, the son of an oil-burner salesman who changed his name from Rechnitz to Ross and at the first opportunity moved his family to less parochial surroundings in Manhattan. Ross's entry in *Who's Who* is a scant six lines, and what is between the lines has been concocted largely from whole cloth by Ross himself and public relations men with imaginations equally as vivid as his own. He joined the navy at seventeen in June 1945, and claims today that his deafness is the result of his ship, the USS *Hopping*, a destroyer escort turned into high-speed transport, participating in amphibious landings in the Pacific theater; in fact, Clurman notes that after digging up his service record, Seaman 1/C Ross spent only seven days of his year-long navy tour at sea, two days from Norfolk to Charleston, and five from Charleston to Green Cove Springs, Florida, where the *Hopping* was decommissioned.

On the GI Bill, Ross went to Paul Smith's, a junior college near Lake Placid with courses in "forestry," "hospitality," and "resorts management," the perfect school for someone whose closest friends claim has never read a book and who pronounces the name of *Madame Bovary*'s creator as Flow Bert. In a touch-football game at college, Ross broke his arm. With the gloss of time, this broken arm is alleged to have been fractured while Ross was a rookie defensive end for the Cleveland Browns; the Browns have no record that Ross ever tried out for the team.

One of his teachers at Paul Smith's remembers that even then Ross was a wizard with numbers, but a Jewish boy with a fantast's memory from a jerk-water junior college was not exactly what Wall Street recruiters were looking for, especially the tonier Jewish firms like Salomon Brothers and Kuhn, Loeb. Ross took a job as a stockboy on Seventh Avenue, and had graduated to salesman of men's slacks and bathing suits when, at twenty-six, he married the daughter of a man who owned a chain of funeral parlors. Offered a job at his father-in-law's Riverside Funeral Home on Manhattan's Upper West Side, Ross was smart enough to see possibilities that existed beyond the grave. "I learned about people in the funeral business," he told Connie Bruck of *The New Yorker*. "It's a service business. You service people in an emotional time—you learn about their needs, their feelings."[5] For Ross, grief was also opportunity. "I negotiated my first deal for [him] on the back stairs of Campbell Funeral Home," Felix Rohatyn of Lazard Frères told Connie Bruck, "while a funeral was going on in the front."

In his own way, Ross was as much a visionary as Luce, because only a visionary could have figured out how to parlay stiffs into a multibillion-dollar communications empire. Funeral homes had limousines; to keep the limos working between funerals, Ross branched into limousine rental. From car rentals, it was an easy jump into parking lots, via the Kinney Service Corporation, named after Kinney Street, around the corner from the company's first office in Newark. The downside of parking lots was the people who ran them, and it was from Kinney that Ross was first tarnished with the mob taint that he has never entirely lost. "Parking is a rough business," Felix Rohatyn mused to Connie Bruck. "Did some people's relatives have unsavory connections? Probably. Did some people who worked for Steve wrongly assume he would do certain things?

Probably. But did *he* know? I just don't believe he did." This is probably as qualified a character reference as one can get.

Ross simply could not pass up a deal, and he bought and sold companies as if business was a giant monopoly game. Using what Clurman calls "an array of stock swaps, acquisitions, successes, failures, spinoffs, warrants, mergers, buy-outs, tax write-offs, trades or whatever deal device was handy," Kinney became a conglomerate of 160 different entities, including dry-wall partitions, comic books, plumbing contracting, data processing, newsstands, a New Jersey bank, hospital cleaning and window washing; within Kinney the funeral parlors were called "our permanent parking division." In 1967, Ross acquired the Ashley Famous Artists talent agency, and with the Ashley Famous foothold in show business soon acquired Warner-Seven Arts, the ruin of Warner Bros., in its time one of the great motion picture companies. Movies offered live bodies instead of dead ones, movie star live bodies, and glamour instead of grief. Ross began to spin off all his unrelated companies to concentrate on the movie business, and its ancillary appurtenances in the record and cable TV industries. With its dubious connotations, the Kinney name was banished and the new company reincarnated as Warner Communications Inc.

～

ROSS DIVORCED HIS first wife, and married the Daisy Buchanan of his dreams, Amanda Mortimer Burden, stepdaughter of CBS's William Paley ("Brooklyn meets Park Avenue," said Paley, at a wedding fete), and when she left him sixteen months later, he segued into a third marriage with the woman he had abandoned for his trophy second wife. At the upper echelons of WCI, life was sweet; salaries were huge, stock options plentiful, and when one executive wished to redecorate his office suite, the price of $700,000 was not seen as excessive. Ross's own annual recompense was between ten and twenty million dollars, and his personal barber trimmed, blowdried, and combed his immaculate corona of white hair every day. WCI maintained four Gulfstream corporate jets, a Hawker Siddeley, and three helicopters, and there was a fully staffed vacation house in Acapulco for executives and favored movie and recording stars stocked with $24,000 worth of tennis shoes in every size and color. In his own New York office, Ross kept between $60,000 and $90,000 in cash that he variously claimed was gambling winnings (on which he never paid taxes, he told the IRS, because his losses "netted out" his winnings every year) or, in another version, the money was used to keep a mistress in baubles when he was between marriages.

～

THERE WAS, HOWEVER, a large cloud over the corporation which evoked the memory of those people who were said to run parking lots. In the early 1970s, WCI made a $250,000 investment in the Westchester Premier Theater, in Westchester County outside New York. Soon Liza Minelli, Diana Ross, Linda Ronstadt, and Johnny Carson were playing there to standing-room-only audiences. Frank Sinatra was also a headliner, but when *Life* ran a photograph of Sinatra in his Westchester dressing room with Carlo Gambino, Jimmy "The Weasel" Fratianno, and Paul Castellano, who was later hit, allegedly on the orders of John Gotti, in front of a midtown Manhattan steakhouse, it was a preview of the kind of trouble Westchester would present to WCI and indirectly to Ross himself. Within two years of its opening, and for all its big stars and full houses, Westchester filed for bankruptcy, and was finally torn down.

The Westchester venture attracted federal prosecutors, and they followed a trail of kickbacks, skimming, and $220,000 worth of bribes right to Ross's office door. Charges were brought, and Ross named an unindicted co-conspirator, although Ross's lawyers were able to stop this information from being made public in order to avoid what they called "pre-trial publicity." A number of second-tier thugs were sent to jail, and one of Ross's closest associates, Jay Emmett, in return for a light sentence, blamed everything on a minor WCI accountant, who then refused to give up Ross as the federal attorneys wanted. As part of his plea bargain, Emmett wore a wire to tape a conversation with Ross, but took the precaution of warning him about the wire beforehand, which was not exactly what prosecutors had in mind.

"Greater love hath no man," said a mutual friend of both Ross

and Emmett, "than one who would secretly tell you he would be
wired by the Feds when he next talked to you." As per his contract,
WCI advanced Emmett his $700,000 legal fees; the convicted
accountant was subsequently hired to do tax work for clients fun-
neled to him by Ross's own chief financial adviser. Hoping to put
the case behind them, WCI's board hired Michael Armstrong, a
criminal lawyer, to conduct his own independent investigation of
the Westchester affair, but his 663-page report was hardly the
ringing vote of confidence Ross might have desired. On the topics
of fraud and bribery, the Armstrong Report concluded, "our concerns about Ross' credibility have prevented us from reaching any
definite conclusions about his possible involvement."

Although the Armstrong Report was buried, the Westchester
case hovers over Ross, as Connie Bruck wrote, "like an unappeased
spirit"; it is, said one WCI director, his Chappaquiddick. But for
Ross, out of sight was out of mind, and he looked for new fields to
conquer. "Synergy" was the new corporate buzzword, the inter-
locking of compatible interests—movies and magazines, TV and
cable, hardware and software, et cetera and so forth. (In the OED,
synergy is defined as "combined or coordinated action of a group of
bodily organs, of nerve centers or muscles, etc.") In the corporate
debasement of language, synergy was essentially just a new upmarket word for greed, a rationale for allowing the big to get bigger,
usually on an international scale. Ross wanted to synergize, and so
did Munro and Nicholas, and in the end they were no match for a
man who kept $24,000 worth of sneakers in a vacation pad.

4.

NOT ALL OF Time's directors were enamored of Ross as The Gentleman Caller, or as fearful as Munro and Nicholas of a hostile
takeover. "If all you want to do is make money by whatever means,"
said board member Arthur Temple, who with his family had once
been the largest stockholder in Time Inc., "let's just open a string
of whorehouses across the country." Most of the board, however, suffered from what Clurman calls "terminal indifference," and were

content to go along with Munro, Nicholas, and Gerald Levin, Nicholas's exact contemporary and blood rival in the executive suite. Their discussions with Ross were conducted in great secrecy, with Time code-named "Tango" (as in, "It takes two to . . .") and Warners "Wonder" (as in "wonderful"). Time's twelve outside directors knew Ross only distantly, if at all, and after negotiations began, only one took the trouble to meet privately with him. Although they were aware of the Armstrong Report, neither the board nor key Time executives asked to see it; it would have been "embarrassing" to Ross, one said, and another added, "Steve is such a sensitive soul." Munro said it all: "If I'd read the Armstrong Report, it may have told me some things that were a little less than positive about Steve. But to me it was kind of ancient history. That was then. This is now . . . Let's make this goddamn deal happen."

Since Munro was contemplating retirement, the key to Time's acquisition of WCI was, from his point of view, that Nicholas serve as co-CEO with Ross, to succeed him in five years, and that such a succession could only be changed by a two thirds vote of the combined board. To show his troops that Time was not being hustled, Munro even dusted off the sanctity of Church and State, which under his stewardship, at least in the board room if not with the self-deluded editorial staff, had been relegated to the status of heresy.

For months Ross bobbed and weaved with Time's negotiators; although he recognized that Time was acquiring Warner's, he did not explicitly wish to have it admitted, WCI being his creation as much as Time was Luce's. At last a deal was cut, but when Munro and Nicholas arrived at Ross's immense Park Avenue apartment to announce the merger, Ross tearfully backed away. The sticking point this time was the succession. Ross's tears softened the resolve of Munro and Nicholas, who were now totally dazzled by the prospects of global synergism. At every juncture, they and Time's board caved in, until finally a succession agreement was ratified that junked the two-thirds rule, and while it stipulated that Nicholas would take over as sole CEO in five years, Ross was to remain as chairman of the board for ten, and as an adviser for five years after that; Ross's $14 million annual compensation would continue, and

Time would immediately let him cash in $125 million in accumulated stocks, rights, and benefits.

As a lagniappe of their own, Munro, Nicholas, Levin, and McManus also received whopping new stock options, although their salaries stayed "only" in the million-dollar range. Blinded by Ross's tears, neither Nicholas nor Munro seemed to realize that what they had negotiated was for Nicholas to become a highly paid copilot who could at any moment be fired by a simple majority of a board dominated by WCI. "Ross is absolutely good to his word," Nicholas blustered when it was suggested that his was perhaps a less than perfect situation. The good word, it should be said, of someone who claimed to have been a defensive end for the Cleveland Browns. No one agreed more about the value of Ross's word than Steven J. Ross himself. "I signed it in blood," he said. "It was a matter of honor with me. My word is my word."

~

ON JASON MCMANUS'S instructions, *Time* did not run a story the week of the biggest media merger in history because he did not wish to be "a shill for the deal," and hoped instead to write a tasteful and discreet editor's letter about it for the following week's issue. How McManus would have finessed *Time*'s high-minded pieties about the RJR-Nabisco takeover just three months earlier ("A Game of Greed" ran the cover line) in writing about Ross he did not say. *Newsweek* covered the merger as if it was the discovery of a cancer cure, and then in an advertisement gave *Time*'s absent journalism a very public finger: "We stay ahead of the competition, even when the competition is the story."

McManus and his deputies went into contortions to justify their decision. "You're not going to give us this integrity shit, are you?" asked McManus's number two in replying to one complaint, as if the integrity shit was not what *Time* was supposed to have been about, and what led Theodore White and Charles Mohr to depart when theirs was questioned.[6] On the editorial floors, McManus's decision was seen as the perfect metaphor for the role the magazines would have in Time Warner Inc., and he did not help his case when he tried to explain the benefits of the merger to the editorial staff, whose Newspaper Guild unit was negotiating a new contract with *Time*, which was offering only 3 or 4 percent wage increases. Pressed about the huge executive compensation packages, including his own million-dollar deal, with stock options on top, McManus said, with an absence of irony noticeable for someone who had once been a published writer of fiction, "We journalists didn't get into this business for the money."

Munro and Nicholas had no trouble with the deal, and in fact were so pleased with themselves that they wrote George Bush to announce the merger on specially designed stationery bearing both their names, patting themselves on the back for a deal in which essentially no money changed hands and no crippling debt was incurred. What the merger announcement had done, however, was to put Time in play. Waiting for the final papers to be signed, it lined up $5 billion in emergency financing, and also paid a group of banks $5 million not to help anyone who might attempt a hostile takeover. This last move is called "bankmail," and is defined by one economics professor as "using shareholder money to bribe a bank not to finance a lucrative tender offer to shareholders."

That Time was willing to ladle out so much protection money only proved to Gulf + Western's Martin Davis how ripe the company was for a hostile takeover before the merger was approved. To this corporate shark, Munro was a guppy, and he was also certain that whatever Ross's assurances to the contrary, he would never willingly pass the baton to Nicholas. Martin Davis's major claim to fame, after succeeding the late Charles Bluhdorn as G+W's CEO, was that he had driven both Barry Diller and Michael Eisner from Paramount Pictures, the G+W film studio they had made so hugely successful, in so doing making each rich beyond his dreams— Diller through his holdings at Twentieth Century Fox, where he next hung his hat, Eisner by way of his at Disney. With his glasses and hesitant chin, Davis might be taken for an accountant—one who always looks as if he had just tasted something unpleasant— and perhaps in compensation he takes pride in being known as "the toughest boss in New York," one with a history of verbally abusing people who work for him; at an off-the-record editorial luncheon given him at *The New York Times*, the name of one of his equally aggressive division managers was mentioned, and Davis, I am told by an editor who was present, offered to "trot him over on a leash."

Three months after the proposed Time Warner merger was announced, Davis (who by that time had changed G+W's name to Paramount Communications) made a hostile bid to Time stockholders in the amount of $175 a share, 40 percent over market price, $10.7 billion in all. Time employees, whose equity was largely tied up in the company's pension and profit sharing plans, began pricing holiday houses in Tuscany. Munro and Nicholas, however, knew that if Davis and Paramount took over, their days as executives were numbered, and so they prepared for a long, vicious fight.

To Munro and Nicholas, Davis was "a liar" and "a son of a bitch," and when Davis tried to reach Munro on the telephone, Munro reverted to the Marine Corps parade ground lingo of his youth by ordering his secretary: "Tell him to go fuck himself." Time hired Kross and Associates, an international private detective agency, to dig up dirt on Davis, and even asked Kross to check if a business reporter for a rival publication was sleeping with a Paramount executive; Kross had a higher sense of propriety than Time, saying it would look bad for an organization with Time's putative journalistic credentials to order an investigation into the sex life of a reporter. It should also be said, as Clurman notes, that Time had never ordered a similar investigation into the checkered history of Steven J. Ross. What Time had not seen fit to mention, however, Paramount did, dredging up the Westchester Theater affair, racketeering charges by associates, and allegations of insider trading by Ross. Time, Paramount said in a legal brief, imperiled "its journalistic integrity by going into business with a company which in the recent past has been the subject of criminal investigations, prosecutions and in some cases convictions."

When Davis bumped his tender offer to $182, and then to $200, smarter Time stockholders cashed in, including some holding options at $13 a share. Davis's bid ended any idea of Time's peacefully merging its assets with WCI, since Time's shareholders would not vote for a merger with Warner if they could have $200 a share from Davis. Time would now have to buy Warner's, in the process taking on the huge debt incurred by buying out WCI stockholders, and also dashing the hopes of those Time shareholders, including most of its employees, who thought they had latched on to a bonanza. The "most important revisions," Clurman writes,

> involved paying more than a billion dollars to Ross and Warner employees and stockholders, as well as potential millions in new stock options. Time Inc. employees got no cash, although its top trio of executives [Munro, Nicholas, and Levin] got new contracts and millions in income for the rest of their lives. The value of the stock that Time employees held dropped to almost one-third ($66) of its pre-merger high ($182). The mid-level Time Inc. employees and stockholders would have to wait for the "long term" to realize any financial benefits from the deal.

Because both Time and Paramount were incorporated in Delaware, the Delaware chancery court had to rule on the conflict-ing offers, and in July 1989 decided in favor of Time. The decision saddled the new Time Warner Inc. with billions of dollars in debt, but Ross came away with what compensation experts said was the biggest payout ever made to an executive in a public company— $193 million, plus at least 1.8 million new stock options, and long-term bonuses that could reach hundreds of millions more over the fifteen-year term of his contract. Perhaps coincidentally, Ross's seventy-nine-page contract referred to him as the "Executive," while Nicholas in his contract was called "Employee"; however acci-dentally this language was arrived at, it did dispel any doubt that might have existed about who was in charge. Dissatisfied though he might have been at his contractual designation, Nicholas did have a first-class ticket on the gravy train; his new contract prom-ised a package in the fifty-million-dollar range, while Munro, Levin, and McManus, in their new contracts, would divvy up tens of millions more between them.

Justifying the deal, Munro sounded like the drill instructor as cheerleader. "What the fuck do they mean, Warner wins?" he asked. "Time Warner Inc. wins. Everybody wins. There's this mentality out there of the scorekeeper. It always comes out in the press as 'Nick the prick. Dick the dummy. Steve the hustler'—that Ross is smarter than we are. No. We won—both companies. Don't those assholes out there understand that? We *all* won." In the Time cafeteria, the employees had a firmer grip on reality. They knew who won, and more importantly that they had not; when Munro stopped by for lunch, they booed him.

5.

WHAT HAPPENED TO Time Warner after the deal was ratified was like waiting for a computer virus to kick in; it was going to happen, but unlike the Michelangelo virus, one did not know exactly when. Realizing his bona fides were questioned on the magazines, Ross romanced writers and editors with flowers and notes ("Love, Steve" was how they ended, even to people he might not recognize if he saw them), and if someone expressed a liking for a particular wine served at lunch, he might receive a case the next day. But while Ross played sommelier, the accountants were at work. In the fall of 1990, the magazine division announced a 10 percent across the board budget cutback, with a forced reduction of 600 jobs on all the magazines, including fifty editorial jobs on *Time*. "It's now part of the way we do business," Nicholas told protesting magazine staffers; he then neatly shifted the blame for the layoffs to McManus and the head of the magazine division.

For his part, McManus was reinterpreting the *Time* culture in a manner suggesting Vidkun Quisling was now in charge, and order had to be preserved. Senior editorial staff were put under three-year renewable contracts, and in them, McManus himself wrote muzzling provisions prohibiting managing editors from criticizing Time Warner, its affiliates, or subsidiaries even after they left the company, at the risk of losing their severance or retirement benefits. Ross questioned the wisdom and the necessity of this extortionate clause, but was overridden by *Time*'s directors. The editors professed not to mind, even though McManus did not have the clause in his own new contract, nor did Warner executives have it in theirs. "The contract . . . assures me I'll get three years' pay if I'm fired," *Time* managing editor Henry Muller said. "If they're willing to give me three years' pay, I didn't bother with the criticism clause." This is the language of a brothel; an empire built on words—whatever one thought of the words—had passed to people threatened by words and for whom words seemed to have no meaning.

～

"STEVE IS A good guy," Nicholas had said of Ross in the honeymoon period. "Absolutely good to his word." "My word is my word," Ross had agreed. So much for words. In late February, Nicholas was ousted by Ross in a palace coup while on a skiing vacation with his family in Vail. His firing, as such it was for all the fulsomeness of his letter of resignation, and Ross's equally fulsome reply, went unmourned in the corridors of *Time*, its editors and writers eternally hopeful that his successor, and each successor's successor, would perhaps be the new Sun King. That the current *Time* really has no distinctive place in contemporary American journalism was a fact that few wished to face, and the redesign promised by its current managers (*Time*'s third redesign in fourteen years, with the target date Memorial Day or sooner) seems only a further attempt to keep abreast of magazine fashion, as if *Time* had become just another journalistic couture house.

The reasons for Nicholas's departure really did not matter. Pick one, all, or a combination: Nicholas and Ross had a fundamental disagreement on how to retire Time Warner's debt; Ross had prostate cancer, and Nicholas used the actuarial tables to whisper against him: *le roi est mort, vive le roi*; Gerald Levin positioned himself as Ross's man at *Time*, and plotted against Nicholas, his old foe, for the best of corporate reasons, like Brutus; J. Richard Munro, retired but still a voice on the board, put his finger to the wind and turned on his former protégé. Although company PR men said Ross's condition was improving as a result of his chemotherapy treatments, and that he would return soon to the corporate wars, the twin prospects of Ross's mortality and Nicholas as his successor did not sit well with the board whatever Nicholas's contract stipulated. Nicholas was soon gone, rich in benefits, destitute in reputation.

Although his book was finished months before Nicholas was fired, Clurman was prescient in predicting the inevitable outcome, wrong only in that he had not expected the corporate bloodletting to happen so quickly. He is not the most graceful of writers, too often apt to fall into the fancy flourishes of *Time* style ("The barge was . . . loaded to her gunwales with a gourmet's selection of fine wines and viands tended to by a betoqued French chef"). But *To the End of Time* is a fascinating book, ugly only because it is such an ugly story of a particularly ugly period in American business. Its final irony, one that Clurman cannot quite bring himself to say explicitly, perhaps from a residual allegiance to his former employers, is that in the land of Lilliput that Time has now become, Steven J. Ross seems a giant.

NOTES

1. I was the writer charged with tailoring Mohr's Vietnam cables for the magazine. His last file, in the fall of 1963, began, "The war in Vietnam is being lost," and in that vein I wrote the story, while quite convinced that Mohr's gloomy, and accurate, prescience would not survive the editing process. I was right. The story was entirely rewritten by my senior editor, and then edited by Fuerbringer to the point of saying that the war was not only winnable, but that there was already light at the end of the tunnel. I left *Time* a few months later.

2. Dell, 1986, p. 502.

3. *Time* ultimately acquired a 20.5 percent stake in CNN, but with only 10.5 percent voting power.

4. The details in this paragraph come from *Reckless Disregard* (Knopf, 1986) by Renata Adler and from "New Grub Street" in my book *Crooning* (Simon and Schuster, 1990).

5. Connie Bruck, *The New Yorker*, January 8, 1990, p. 67.

6. To his credit, the deputy editor, Gilbert Rogin, a gifted short-story writer and former managing editor of *Sports Illustrated*, later amended his words by saying, "I have a general hostility to appeals to journalism as if it were some kind of religion."

DEATH OF A
YALE MAN

[1993]

🦋

I.

IT SHOULD BE said at the outset that Calvin Trillin and I have been friends for over thirty years. It should further be said that I once dedicated a book to him and his wife, Alice, and that he, somewhat more problematically, dedicated a book to me. Or to be more precise, included in his novel *Floater*—loosely based on our days together at *Time*—what he called a "Claimer" (as opposed to "Disclaimer"): "The character of Andy Wolferman is based on John Gregory Dunne, though it tends to flatter." When I asked Mr. Trillin how his portrait of the pathological gossip Wolferman might in any way have been flattering, he said, "I made you Jewish."

Since he left *Time* in 1963 to write, at the invitation of *The New Yorker*'s late editor William Shawn, about the integration of the University of Georgia (a three-part article that became his first book, *An Education in Georgia*), Mr. Trillin has been the quintessential *New Yorker* writer, the author of approximately three hundred bylined pieces, casuals, and stories, so many that neither he nor the magazine is able to come up with an exact count. For fifteen years, from the late 1960s to the early 1980s, he reported every three weeks on some aspect of the American scene, traveling to most of the country's major cities and to rural venues and crossroads as diverse as Gees Bend, Alabama, New Glarus, Wisconsin, Mamou, Louisiana, Locke, California, Lander, Wyoming, and Biddeford, Maine.

~

HUMAN INTEREST HAS never been his game. "I wasn't interested in doing what is sometimes called Americana—stories about people like the last fellow in Jasper County, Georgia, who can whittle worth a damn," he wrote in the introduction to *Killings*,[1] titled appropriately after sixteen murders he had written about over the years. "I didn't want to do stories about typical or representative Americans. . . . I didn't do stories that could be called 'Boston at Three Hundred' or 'Is the New South Really New?' "

What did interest Mr. Trillin was what Edith Wharton called the underside of the social tapestry where the threads are knotted and the loose ends hang. His America is informed more by Sherwood Anderson than by Garrison Keillor; he is attracted to stories about people who behave if not exactly badly then certainly not well, with the result that many of his pieces, especially when they are read one after another (as in *Killings*), appear to be drawn from a deeply conservative reserve that seems at times almost melancholic. The prose is spare and unadorned, like a tree in late autumn stripped of its leaves; it is without ego—in his reporting the pronoun "I" almost never appears—and without tricks. Of course making it seem without tricks is the biggest trick of all.

His curiosity, like his wanderlust, is prodigious. Picking a jury in Brooklyn. A General Motors stockholders meeting in Detroit. A Yale-educated former philosophy professor turned private detective in California. A homosexual Methodist minister in Colorado. An American Legionnaire and his hippie daughter in Kansas. A one-shot antelope hunt in Wyoming. The way Frankie Lymon and the Teenagers were done out of their share of a hit single called "Why Do Fools Fall in Love," this last a dazzling tale of chicanery, villainy, criminality, and venality by an assortment of thieves, liars, crooks, and racists who make the similarly predatory Flatbush brothers, the music promoters in Spike Lee's *Mo' Better Blues*, seem like benign humanists.

The pertinent detail in the social weave rarely escapes him. "It's a matter of honor with an Italian hit man not to touch anything," he quotes a homicide detective saying on the subject of murder. "Cubans rob the guy as part of the deal—the price plus what he's carrying." His tone is usually conversational, at times seeming to come almost from an oral tradition. He begins a piece in his collection *American Stories*[2] about a Louisiana woman's fight with a lawyer in a state agency over whether her parents should have been identified as "white" or "colored" on her birth certificate in this deceptively simple way: "Susie Guillory Phipps thinks this all started in 1977, when she wanted to apply for a passport. Jack Westholtz thinks it started long before that."

Like Murray Kempton, Mr. Trillin tries to find something good to say, however recherché, even about those who have violated every clause of the human contract. "Even people who assume all criminal lawyers to be part fixer," he wrote of a high-flying, seven-times-married Miami Beach criminal attorney found shot to death in his car, "refer to Harvey St. Jean as a gentleman." And of a lupine music promoter: "Morris Levy was a seventh-grade dropout from the Bronx who eventually became one of the most powerful figures in the record industry. . . . He was a friend, and occasionally a business partner, of mobsters; he was also the Man of the Year at United Jewish Appeal dinners, and a planter of forests in Israel." The ludicrous holds particular appeal. The late Harvey St. Jean, he wrote, had lived at a private club "where the average age of the residents was forty," and then added the local computation of that average: ". . . a sixty-year-old guy and a twenty-year-old broad."

～

CALVIN TRILLIN'S RENOWN, however, resides less with the range and the acuity of his reportage than with the public perception of him as a humorist, one who appeared thirty-three times on *The Johnny Carson Show*. It was true that he always appeared on the final segment, known in the trade as the author's ghetto, after Robin Williams or Cher had departed, except on one occasion when, he claims, he was followed by a harpist. Still it was thirty-three times, meaning he was asked back not just to hawk a book but because

Carson thought he was funny. He has a humor column that is syndicated in seventy-five newspapers (the columns have been collected in four books), and every issue of *The Nation* carries a piece of his political doggerel, as in his adieu to George Bush:

> *Farewell to you, George Herbert Walker.*
> *Though never treasured as a talker—*
> *Your predicates were often prone*
> *To wander, nounless, off alone—*
> *You did your best in your own way,*
> *The way of Greenwich Country Day.*
> *We wish you well. Just take your ease,*
> *And never order Japanese.*
> *May your repose remain un-blighted—*
> *Unless, of course, you get indicted.*[3]

Although he has lived most of his adult life in New York, Mr. Trillin's humor has little of the city's sharp Jewish edge; it is less ethnic, even deracinated (in public if not in private), more gentle and ironic, reflective of his Midwestern roots. Food is a continuing preoccupation, less classic cooking than egalitarian regional food, the food of catfish festivals and pizza kings and crab boils. He seems to have visited every fast food and barbecue restaurant in America, and collected his impressions in three books, *American Fried*, *Third Helpings*, and *Alice, Let's Eat*, the titles speaking volumes about the kind of cuisine he favors. Along the way he has also found the time to write three short novels; he once told me he only wrote novels at his summer house in Nova Scotia, making it sound as if fiction was a summer work project, something so unimportant it could only be done in Canada.

2.

ONE FEBRUARY MORNING in 1991, Calvin Trillin tells us, he spotted a headline on *The New York Times*'s obituary page: ROGER D. HANSEN, 55, PROFESSOR AND AUTHOR. Roger Hansen, known to Mr. Trillin as Denny, had been a friend and classmate at Yale. His obituary was short, without a photograph. "Roger D. Hansen, a professor of international relations at Johns Hopkins University's Nitze School of Advanced International Relations in Washington, was found dead at the home of a friend in Rehoboth Beach, Del. . . . Dr. Hansen took his life by inhaling carbon monoxide, the police in Rehoboth Beach said. Colleagues at Johns Hopkins . . . said he had a severe back ailment that had required major operations."

There is nothing like the unexpected death of a friend to make one aware of one's own mortality, and to call absolutes into question. Denny Hansen was one of those college golden boys on whom life's honors were meant, as if by predestination, to be lavished. Denny Hansen was a scholar—magna cum laude and Phi Beta Kappa. Denny Hansen was an athlete—a varsity swimmer. Denny Hansen was a BMOC—a member of DKE, the Elizabethan Club, the senior society Scroll and Key, a Rhodes Scholar. *Life* magazine and its star photographer Alfred Eisenstaedt had covered Denny Hansen's Yale graduation under the headline, "A Farewell to Bright College Years." A year after his Yale graduation, *Life* did a follow-up of Denny Hansen, the Rhodes Scholar: "Man of Eli at Oxford." It was an article of faith among Denny Hansen's friends in the Yale class of 1957 that Denny Hansen would one day be elected president of the United States. A future president was not meant to be found lying on the floor of a locked garage in Rehoboth Beach, with the ignition of his Honda turned on and the gas pedal held down by a book and a frying pan. A future president was not meant to kill himself because of a bad back. A future president was meant to have more than a three-sentence obit listing no known survivors.

∽

REMEMBERING DENNY IS a contemplation on the nature of friendship, and a contemplation as well on Calvin Trillin's own life and attitudes, and on the attitudes of his—and my—generation. That it is so unexpectedly personal is what helps make *Remembering Denny* so sad and so moving. Mr. Trillin is the most private of men, and for as long as I have known him he has regarded the public self-examination practiced by so many writers (including my wife,

Joan Didion, and myself), the filtering of facts through a personal prism, as an indulgence not to be countenanced. His considerable wit has always acted as a baffle against introspection; since Yale, as he admits in this book, he has also deliberately crafted himself as someone who never takes anything seriously, thus giving himself a means of deflecting the inquiry of others.

Denny Hansen's death caught Mr. Trillin at a fallow moment in his relations with *The New Yorker*. He belonged to the era of William Shawn, and while he maintained a civil discourse with Shawn's successor, Robert Gottlieb, he remained a Shawn man (to this day he refers to him as "Mr. Shawn"). He was only sporadically represented in the magazine and increasingly he played the humorist's rather than the reporter's card. He conceived two limited-run, off-Broadway solo shows, *Calvin Trillin's Uncle Sam* in 1988, and two years later *Words, No Music*, both deadpan free-association monologues about the state of the nation, and its foibles. "Mary had a little lamb," he remembered as the jingle of a restaurant he once visited in Owensboro, Kentucky. "Why don't you have some, too?" Both a trustee of the New York Public Library and a member of the Yale Corporation, he worked indefatigably on behalf of each institution, appearing as master of ceremonies or after-dinner speaker at countless fundraising events, his timing honed on Carson and on stage, his routines as smooth and polished as old stones (the tuxedo he bought at J. Press as a Yale student and was still wearing into the late 1980s is one I heard on more than one public occasion).

It was fun, but it was not reporting, and Mr. Trillin was too good a writer not to know, however ignoble the urge, that in the suicide of Denny Hansen there was writer's gold. "I wanted to know more about Denny," he writes.

> Poking around other people's lives is nothing new for me, of course—I've done that for a living for a number of years—but ordinarily the people in question are strangers. . . . I suppose I had begun to wonder whether back in the fifties, when we had been under the impression that we were more or less in control of our futures, we might have made up a life for Denny to live.

A life that already in death suggested parallels with that of Christian Darling, the burnt-out case in Irwin Shaw's "The Eighty-Yard Run," whose only psychic capital was the shining moment in a college football game now only dimly remembered, an account he had long since overdrawn.

～

THE MEMORIAL SERVICE was held in Washington, and it was as if Denny Hansen's Yale classmates and his colleagues at Johns Hopkins School of Advanced International Studies were talking about two people who were hardly even nodding acquaintances. To the surprise of his classmates, the Yale "Denny" had become in his professional life "Roger." The Yale eulogist remembered that Denny Hansen's "years at Yale were unambiguously happy times, and [that] he seemed to personify the mythical Yalies of fiction, the Dink Stovers, the Frank Merriwells"; it was as if he was trying to guide the mourners past the unpleasant fact of suicide, and past their failure to register any hint of turmoil in the Denny Hansen they knew. The Hopkins speakers were more measured, recalling a Roger Hansen who, while the brilliance of his foreign policy analyses was never in question, was not ". . . always . . . easy and pleasant . . . to deal with . . . Roger could be and often was a prickly and indeed difficult colleague. . . ."

To Denny's classmates, the Hopkins speakers were remarkably ungracious, and they thought it was "pissant" for one of them to mention that his last book, on American foreign policy in the 1970s, had failed to find a publisher. After the service, the Yale contingent gathered to drink and brood and to talk about why he had chosen to be alone and cut off from friends who still claimed to revere him; most of his Yale classmates had not seen him in years, and when they did make a date Denny Hansen usually canceled at the last minute or stood them up. Nor was he in touch with his family; the papers he left at his death indicated that he did not even know if his mother in California was alive or dead. Finally they reluctantly considered the subtext they had all decrypted in the bleak *Times* obituary. "Until the day Denny died," Mr. Trillin writes, "it had never occurred to me that he might be gay. . . . For me, Denny was in a compartment in my mind that had to do with Yale in the fifties, and there simply weren't any gay people in the compartment."

~

LIKE DENNY, A.K.A. Roger Hansen, Calvin Trillin was a member in good standing of what became known as The Silent Generation, those of us born in the years between Franklin Roosevelt's first election and the end of World War II, too young to remember the indelible first-hand experiences our parents had of the Depression and the economic dislocations of the 1930s, too young as well to serve in, and be shaped by the war, but too old to have to make the decisions forced on the following generation by the social dislocations of the sixties, decisions on race and Vietnam and gender and sexual identification. "We were white males," Mr. Trillin writes, who "came of age at a time when the privileged position of white males was so deeply embedded in the structure of the society that we didn't even think much about it." To go along, we went along. (To my eternal shame, I wrote on my entrance essay to Princeton that I wished to go there to meet "contacts" who might help me in later life.) It was naturally expected that our generation would one day produce a president (if not Denny Hansen, then someone else); it is entirely fitting that the only presidential candidate from that emotionally and socially constipated silent generation was Michael Dukakis.

Both Denny Hansen and Calvin Trillin were beneficiaries of the transition begun at Yale before World War II to change the university gradually from what its former president Kingman Brewster labeled "a finishing school on Long Island Sound" into a place that better reflected the demographic and regional composition of the country at large. This transition, Mr. Trillin writes, was "a sort of *apertura* to the yahoos," middle-class white high-school boys from the Midwest and West. With perhaps less enthusiasm, the outreach even included Jews, although until the late 1960s Yale had the lowest percentage of Jews in the Ivy League, a figure, Mr. Trillin notes, that "remained suspiciously consistent from year to year."

Where Denny Hansen had traveled to New Haven from Sequoia Union High School in Redwood City, California, Mr. Trillin came from Southwest High School in Kansas City, the son of a grocer, ultimately a well-to-do grocer, who at age two, and named Avrom Trilinski, had arrived with his parents in Galveston from near Kiev. Trilinski became Trillin, Avrom became Abe, and the family settled in St. Joseph, Missouri. In a household where he spoke Yiddish with his parents, and learned English with a Missouri twang, Abe Trillin somehow found a copy of Frank Johnson's *Stover at Yale*, and it so impressed him that although he never went to college himself, and was not yet married, he vowed one day to send a son there. That son (after a first daughter) he named Calvin, "because he believed . . . that it would be an appropriate name for someone at Yale." In fact, neither Abe nor Edyth Trillin could ever bring themselves to call him Calvin, and to this day he is called "Bud" by everyone he knows, save out of sheer perversity by my wife and myself.

Abe Trillin is a spectacular character, "a shy man, who was particularly uncomfortable talking about personal matters, and to the best of my knowledge, we never actually had a long heart-to-heart about anything." This reticence is shared by his son, who in the book never mentions either Abe's given or Americanized first and last names, referring to him only as "my father." The money for Yale Abe Trillin saved from a rebate paid by a bread company for prompt payment of its bills and the prominent display of its products. There was, of course, no corresponding bread fund to send his daughter Sukie to Wellesley or Radcliffe; in Abe Trillin's Jewish ethic, as in my family's Irish Catholic one, daughters were meant to marry, the sooner the better, and an Ivy League education would be wasted on wives and mothers.

For his father, Mr. Trillin says, "the most important reason for Yale's existence" was "to turn the likes of us into the likes of them. . . . He wanted us to have the same opportunities." Abe Trillin was not unaware of the probable cost of this transformation. "In the fifties," his son writes,

> it was common for a young man like Denny or like me—someone whose grandparents had been immigrants and whose family hadn't been to college—to be sent away to places like Yale by parents who realized that they were putting a distance between themselves and

their son forever. . . . I know that my father was aware of this from the start, because after he died my mother told me so, not without a touch of resentment.

⁓

MR. TRILLIN CLAIMS he arrived at New Haven never having heard of Dostoevsky or Greenwich, a bit of hyperbole I tend to doubt, but if it is true then his father must have approved at how quickly his son learned, and became one of "them." He was a reporter on, and as a junior was elected chairman of, the *Yale Daily News*, he was an addition to stag lines at eastern coming-out parties, he was celebrated as a campus wit and college personage who was tapped, as were Denny Hansen and thirteen other class wheels (although it would have been bad form for them to think of themselves as such), by Scroll and Key. The idea of entitlement went unchallenged. "Weenie" was the cruel Yale term of opprobrium for those classmates who did not buy into or catch onto the undergraduate meritocracy. A chemistry major was seen as the definition of a weenie, someone "beyond the pale," someone who worked too hard, who played in the band rather than heeling for the *News*, who did not attend Tap Day because he knew the senior societies would overlook him.

Among those who were tapped, it was agreed that the senior societies such as Skull and Bones or Scroll and Key were models of democracy, because each mixed fifteen seniors, one of whom might be a star lacrosse player, another the alto in the Whiffenpoofs, a third the editor of a humor magazine, without reference to whether they "got to Yale by family tradition or bread-company rebate. . . . It also meant that absolutely everyone was being judged." By the standards of the entitled tappees, of course.

⁓

THE SUBJECT OF Ivy League undergraduate entitlement is one Mr. Trillin and I have argued fiercely about. Like his father, he had bought into the idea of a Yale diploma as a passport into the larger world of "them," the world of affairs and decision-making. For the entitled, the idea of failure was not supposed to exist, which is why the death of Denny Hansen was so confusing to him. Only weenies were supposed to settle into a life of mediocrity and oblivion. In our arguments, I always mention two of my Princeton contemporaries, both of whom were considered the New Jersey equivalent of weenies (as indeed was I); one became a rapacious corporate raider preying mercilessly on those who so judged him, another a scholar with an international reputation. In the Yale construct, however, a weenie would always be a weenie, one of life's eternal chemistry majors; little allowance was made for a separate path after college. The intangible called leadership asserted itself then or never. "There was also an assumption," Mr. Trillin writes, "that the society was ours to lead and that preparing what amounted to a leadership class made good sense."

What a leadership class is prepared to do, of course, is maintain its own power by preserving the status quo. At Yale, in those years, the biggest potential threat to the status quo was the possibility of the college admitting women. As chairman of the *Yale Daily News*, Mr. Trillin stood foursquare with the leadership class in opposition. "Oh save us!" he wrote in a fiery editorial. "Oh save us from the giggling crowds, the domestic lecture, the home economic classes of a female infiltration. . . . In the changing of an institution's traditions, where is the line between what is justifiable and what is so extreme that by its exaction the institution no longer exists? . . . We who shudder at the thought of the type of women Yale would admit— we must stand guard together."[4] Time, however, worked its changes; both his daughters, Class of '90 and Class of '93, turned out to be the type of women Yale would admit.

3.

"WHOM THE GODS wish to destroy," Cyril Connolly once said, "they first call promising." It was as if the gods had Denny Hansen in mind. He defined promise, although no one in Yale '57 could exactly explain why, except to mention what Abe Trillin had called "his million dollar smile," as if the smile was a bankable commodity, and not—Connolly again—an enemy of promise. His friends, for obscure and largely unexamined reasons, had made up not so much a life as an exaggerated fantasy for him to lead, and wittingly or unwittingly he was a co-conspirator in their plan. In this context, it seemed entirely appropriate for *Life* to cover Denny Hansen's graduation weekend. How *Life* happened to choose him, however, could be construed as a parable of the charade that was Denny Hansen's post-college life.

The idea had initially been floated at *Life* by someone from Amherst, Mr. Trillin discovered as he rummaged through Denny Hansen's past, but the magazine, either because it forgot the source or because it thought Yale had more glamour, asked Yale's publicity department rather than Amherst's to submit some names. The Yale administrator who made the selections was an old grad and Scroll and Key man with the Wodehousian nickname "Totty." Loyal to Keys, Totty naturally wanted a Keys man as the representative of the new broad-based democratic Yale, and in Denny Hansen thought he had the perfect candidate, a scholar athlete and Rhodes nominee from a western high school.

In what passed as fair play, Totty also sent along to *Life* a second possibility, a football player out of Skull and Bones named Ackerman. It is suggested that Totty only picked Ackerman because his name sounded Jewish (he was, in fact, Dutch), and that *Life* would therefore shy away from him. Several years before, the magazine had done a feature on a Wellesley weekend, and in it had run a photo of a father and daughter named Goldstein, the upshot being that on the eastern college grapevine Wellesley was said to have been cast as a "Jewish school." Denny Hansen was thus anointed by default, perhaps colored by a touch of anti-Semitism. And his bright college years became a burden that he might have escaped had he only been a weenie, and not the repository of so many unredeemed hopes.

~

HIS WAS NOT a bad life, just marked-down from the expectations of his million-dollar smile. The day he left New Haven, he moved into a world where there were people as smart or even smarter than he, tougher and more sophisticated, people who knew that a spread in *Life* on a college senior was not an accolade but just another disposable story in a magazine with pages to fill every week. His star did not shine at Oxford nor did it later at Princeton's Woodrow Wilson School, where a professor said he seemed to want to "start at the top." Denny became Roger; Roger's ambition was to enter the foreign service, but he was turned down, "a serious setback," Mr. Trillin says, "when he seemed to have lost the momentum of his youth." The reason he initially gave was a chronic and painful back problem; in a subsequent version he cited a difficult psychoanalysis. Even later he would claim that the prominent father of an American friend at Oxford had written the State Department and accused him of being a homosexual, a charge he called preposterous. The accusation, Mr. Trillin writes, "confirmed his secret fears that the life of limitless possibilities supposedly open to him could never really be."

Roger worked as a Senate aide and for a planning council, but he seemed to be running in place as friends and classmates were getting assigned to important embassies, or becoming partners in good law firms, or bureau chiefs and editors for major newspapers and magazines. Trying journalism, he struck out at NBC News both in Washington (he was fired after he called his boss "a horse's ass") and in Cleveland (the best a Cleveland contemporary who subsequently made it to the network could say about him was that he was "better educated than anyone else in the newsroom"). Not ten years out of Yale, he was already assessing himself and his future with a cold eye; he told his analyst that he could not deal with authority, that his expectations were unreasonably high, and that he was afraid of becoming a homosexual.

Only once did he have a real chance at the brass ring. During the Carter administration, he was appointed to the White House National Security Council; it seemed an opportunity to make up for his rejection by the foreign service, but he lasted only seven months. "His strength . . . was talking about policy," Mr. Trillin quotes a friend as saying, "and then he had a chance to make policy and he just couldn't." His field was the third world, not exactly a front-burner subject at the height of the cold war, one which a colleague said only "interested ex-hippies and women who are worried about babies with diarrhea." The brief experience in the

White House was another blow to an already battered self-confidence. At Yale reunions (which he did not attend), none of his classmates talked any more about his being president; many could not even remember who he was.

~

AT FORTY-ONE, Roger Hansen accepted a professorship at the Johns Hopkins School of Advanced International Studies, but with only one book published—*The Politics of Mexican Development*, highly praised and little read except by professionals in the field—his most productive years of scholarship seemed in the past. He was unable to get along with many of his Hopkins colleagues, Mr. Trillin was told, no longer saw old friends, and was so overly punctilious and judgmental that to disagree with him was to risk being dismissed as corrupt, or the object of "sudden explosions and vituperative letters." While some foreign policy professionals generously saw him as "neurotic but no more than most people," his superior on a project sponsored by the Council on Foreign Relations was unequivocal: "He was impossible to work with." His views on what was moral or immoral, principled or unprincipled, were rigid—but also subject to sudden change. "Denny may have in the last few years of his life," Mr. Trillin notes sadly, "got to the point at which people winced when they saw him approaching." Bitterness became the norm. "They wanted at a minimum Henry Kissinger," he said of the people who had endowed his chair at Hopkins, "and they got me."

So far as Mr. Trillin was able to find out the only person who became close to him was a woman Trillin calls Carol Austin, with whom Roger Hansen seems to have had a platonic, "agonizingly chaste" relationship lasting ten years. If Carol Austin was in one way Roger Hansen's "cover," she was more importantly his only human contact, a one-woman surrogate family replacing the one in Redwood City he had so deliberately cast aside, as if family and past were stains to be rubbed out. "He was not a compromising personality," Carol Austin recalled for Mr. Trillin. "He couldn't seem to learn that people may be good people even though you disagree with them on this or that." Finally, to Roger Hansen's distress, she broke off the relationship, and to his further distress later married. "I suppose," Mr. Trillin writes, "that Denny hung on to the possibility of marrying Carol Austin as his chance to live what we had all been brought up to think of as a normal life."

Pain was now his constant companion. "Three rounds of back surgery . . . have resulted in a lost decade, and a mental state bordering on clinical depression," he wrote to a friend early in 1990. "Also temporarily lost in the process has been the capacity to write—the concentration has just not come back." This incapacity doomed the book he had more or less abandoned anyway, on Nixon's foreign policy. Nor could his doctors adjust the levels of his pain-killing and anti-depressant medications. To his psychiatrist, he would talk about the constant pain, about the rages he could not seem to channel, about his homosexuality.

According to *The Blade*, a gay Washington paper which to the chagrin of his Yale friends printed an obituary, Roger Hansen "enjoyed dancing" at local clubs. Intermittently he lived with a young man who after a couple of years moved to California. Another younger gay friend told Mr. Trillin that he had tried to teach Roger "how to act, how to dress. 'Don't wear those pants. Don't worry if you're in a bad mood and you went to the bar and nothing happened.' " But for those in The Silent Generation, "the theology of heterosexuality," as Andrew Kopkind has written, "offered the only hope of earthly salvation." However Roger Hansen might have wished to distance himself from this faith, he never learned to operate effectively, according to the friend who had been his mentor, in "what amounted to a subculture with its own customs and rules and hierarchies."

Increasingly he was alone, isolated, both a prisoner and a casualty of artificial expectations. Faced, with still another operation that would place him in a body cast for months, apparently uncomfortable with his inability to come out except selectively, his level of accomplishment less than that to which he aspired, and to which he might have thought, at least in the beginning, he was entitled, Roger Hansen began to consider the ultimate alternative. Months before the end, with a chilling attention to detail, he began to compose the suicide note he left to be found after he died. "I'm in a lot of pain and will not consider further back surgery," he wrote. "The probabilities of any surgical relief are too marginal for me to hang on and suffer any more. When the pain becomes unbearable, I will take my own life. I will do so with regret, and with the feeling that there are no other viable options." On New Year's Day, 1991, he took an overdose of pills but succeeded only in becoming semicomatose for a few days. A month or so later, he borrowed the weekend house a gay friend kept in Rehoboth Beach.

～

THE MORE MR. TRILLIN investigated Denny/Roger Hansen's life and death, the less certain he became of the verities he had accepted since Yale. He finds it hard to explain why he and the meritocracy of Yale '57 invested so much in Denny Hansen as a symbol, when his most obvious attraction seemed to be that he was not a weenie, but was visibly clubbable, a perfect fit for their rather primitive idea of public acceptance. As he probed both into Denny Hansen's life and his own, Mr. Trillin began at last to question the odious concept of weenie. "Are we fairly represented by the person who told me in 1970 that if the undergraduates had no word for weenie they were all weenies?" he writes. "Some of us have changed, of course, but speaking as someone who takes it for granted that some of the people whose company he most enjoys must have been weenies in college, I know that those distinctions we made as adolescents will never quite leave us."

Doubt was now factored into the entitlement equation. "The common feeling about people my age," Mr. Trillin notes, "is that somehow the rules got changed in the middle of the game." Talking to Andrew Kopkind, a friend of thirty-five years, he became painfully aware of how the casual smart remark about homosexuality could have created distance between them. "When we called somebody a fairy," he recalls with almost palpable regret, "we just wanted to say something mean." They remain friends, but he understands why Kopkind and the man with whom he has lived for the past twenty years "spend most of their time with people they met post-Stonewall—people whose friendship was not embedded in a different era, before the rules changed."

The rules did change, the ground did shift, and it is in this shift that Mr. Trillin has found his most profound subject. He allows at the end of this book that he does not know why Denny Hansen killed himself. He allows that after years of looking into other people's lives he has concluded that even the oldest friends are unknowable. He describes visiting a young man who had lived briefly with Denny Hansen in the 1980s, and referring to himself as an old friend. "Roger would have said that you didn't know him at all," the young man said. "I couldn't agree with you more," Calvin Trillin said.

It would seem that no one really knew Roger Hansen. His estate was valued at more than three quarters of a million dollars. He left his Hopkins pension to Carol Austin, who except for one chance meeting he had not seen in ten years, and the balance to Yale University.

NOTES

1. Ticknor and Fields, 1984.

2. Ticknor and Fields, 1991.

3. *The Nation*, January 25, 1993.

4. *Yale Daily News*, September 29, 1956.

REGARDS

we are not unaware that sometime in the not too distant future we face a moment that only those of us who are adoptive parents will ever have to face—our daughter's decision to search or not to search for her natural parents.

I remember that when I was growing up a staple of radio drama was the show built around adoption. Usually the dilemma involved a child who had just learned by accident that it was adopted. This information could only come accidentally, because in those days it was considered a radical departure from the norm to inform your son or daughter that he or she was not your own flesh and blood. If such information had to be revealed, it was often followed by the specious addendum that the natural parents had died when the child was an infant. An automobile accident was viewed as the most expeditious and efficient way to get rid of both parents at once. One of my contemporaries, then a young actress, was not told that she was adopted until she was twenty-two and the beneficiary of a small inheritance from her natural father's will. Her adoptive mother could not bring herself to tell her daughter the reason behind the bequest and entrusted the task to an agent from the William Morris office.

Today we are more enlightened, aware of the psychological evidence that such barbaric secrecy can only inflict hurt. When Quintana was born, she was offered to us privately by the gynecologist who delivered her. In California, such private adoptions are not only legal but in the mid-sixties, before legalized abortion and before the sexual revolution made it acceptable for an unwed mother to keep her child, were quite common. The night we went to see Quintana for the first time at Saint John's, there was a tacit agreement between us that "No Information" was only a bracelet. It was quite easy to congratulate ourselves for agreeing to be so open when the only information we had about her mother was her age, where she was from and a certified record of her good health. What we did not realize was that through one bureaucratic slipup we would learn her mother's name and that through another she would learn ours, and Quintana's.

From the day we brought Quintana home from the hospital, we tried never to equivocate. When she was little, we always had Spanish-speaking help and one of the first words she learned, long before she understood its import, was *adoptada*. As she grew older, she never tired of asking us how we happened to adopt her. We told her that we went to the hospital and were given our choice of any baby in the nursery. "No, not that baby," we had said, "not that baby, not that baby . . ." All this with full gestures of inspection, until finally: "That baby!" Her face would always light up and she would say: "Quintana." When she asked a question about her adoption, we answered, never volunteering more than she requested, convinced that as she grew her questions would become more searching and complicated. In terms I hoped she would understand, I tried to explain that adoption offered to a parent the possibility of escaping the prison of the genes, that no matter how perfect the natural child, the parent could not help acknowledging in black moments that some of his or her bad blood was bubbling around in the offspring; with an *adoptada,* we were innocent of any knowledge of bad blood.

In time Quintana began to intuit that our simple parable of free choice in the hospital nursery was somewhat more complex than we had indicated. She now knew that being adopted meant being born of another mother, and that person she began referring to as "my other mommy." How old, she asked, was my other mommy when I was born? Eighteen, we answered, and on her stubby little fingers she added on her own age, and with each birthday her other mommy became twenty-three, then twenty-five and twenty-eight. There was no obsessive interest, just occasional queries, some more difficult to answer than others. Why had her other mother given her up? We said that we did not know—which was true—and could only assume that it was because she was little more than a child herself, alone and without the resources to bring up a baby. The answer seemed to satisfy, at least until we became close friends with a young woman, unmarried, with a small child of her own. The contradiction was, of course, apparent to Quintana, and yet she seemed to understand, in the way that children do, that there had been a millennium's worth of social change in the years since her birth, that the pressures on a young unmarried mother were far more in 1966 than they were in 1973. (She did, after all, invariably refer to the man in the White House as President Nixon Vietnam Watergate, almost as if he had a three-tiered name like John Quincy Adams.) We were sure that she viewed her status with equanimity, but how much so we did not realize until her eighth birthday party. There were twenty little girls at the party, and as little girls do, they were discussing things gynecological, specifically the orifice in their mothers' bodies from which they had emerged at birth. "I didn't," Quintana said matter-of-factly. She was sitting in a large wicker fan chair and her pronouncement impelled the other children to silence. "I was adopted." We had often wondered how she would handle this moment with her peers, and we froze, but she pulled it off with such élan and aplomb that in moments the other children were bemoaning their own misfortune in not being adopted, one even claiming, "Well, I was almost adopted."

Because my wife and I both work at home, Quintana has never had any confusion about how we make our living. Our mindless staring at our respective typewriters means food on the table in a way the mysterious phrase "going to the office" never can. From the time she could walk, we have taken her to meetings whenever we were without help, and she has been a quick study on the nuances of our life. "She's remarkably well adjusted," my brother once said about her. "Considering that every time I see her she's in a different city." I think she could pick an agent out of a police lineup, and out of the blue one night at dinner she offered that all young movie directors were short and had frizzy hair and wore Ditto pants and wire glasses and shirts with three buttons opened. (As far as I know, she had never laid eyes on Bogdanovich, Spielberg or Scorsese.) Not long ago an actress received an award for a picture we had written for her. The actress's acceptance speech at the televised award ceremony drove Quintana into an absolute fury. "She never," Quintana reported, "thanked *us*." Since she not only identifies with our work but at times even considers herself an equal partner, I of course discussed this piece with her before I began working on it. I told her what it was about and said I would drop it if she would be embarrassed or if she thought the subject too private. She gave it some thought and finally said she wanted me to write it.

I must, however, try to explain and perhaps even try to justify my own motives. The week after *Roots* was televised, each child in Quintana's fifth-grade class was asked to trace a family tree. On my side Quintana went back to her great-grandfather Burns, who arrived from Ireland shortly after the Civil War, a ten-year-old refugee from the potato famine, and on her mother's side to her great-great-great-great-grandmother Cornwall, who came west in a wagon train in 1846. As it happens, I have little interest in family beyond my immediate living relatives. (I can never remember the given names of my paternal grandparents and have never known my paternal grandmother's maiden name. This lack of interest mystifies my wife.) Yet I wanted Quintana to understand that if she wished, there were blood choices other than Dominick Burns and Nancy Hardin Cornwall. Over the past few years, there has been a growing body of literature about adoptees seeking their own roots. I am in general sympathetic to this quest, although not always to the dogged absolutism of the more militant seekers. But I would be remiss if I did not say that I am more than a little sensitive to the way the literature presents adoptive parents. We are usually shown as frozen in the postures of radio drama, untouched by the changes in attitudes of the last several generations. In point of fact we accept that our children might seek out their roots, even encourage it; we accept it as an adventure like life itself—perhaps painful, one hopes enriching. I know not one adoptive parent who does not feel this way. Yet in the literature there is the implicit assumption that we are threatened by the possibility of search, that we would consider it an act of disloyalty on the part of our children. The patronizing nature of this assumption is never noted in the literature. It is as if we were Hudson and Mrs. Bridges, below-stairs surrogates taking care of the wee one, and I don't like it one damn bit.

❧

OFTEN THESE DAYS I find myself thinking of Quintana's natural mother. Both my wife and I admit more than a passing interest in the woman who produced this extraordinary child. (As far as we know, she never named the father, and even more interesting, Quintana has never asked about him.) When Quintana was small, and before the legalities of adoption were complete, we imagined her mother everywhere, a wraithlike presence staring through the chain-link fence at the blond infant sunbathing in the crib. Occasionally today we see a photograph of a young woman in a magazine—the mother as we imagine her to look—and we pass it to each other without comment. Once we even checked the name of a model in *Vogue* through her modeling agency; she turned out to be a Finn. I often wonder if she thinks of Quintana, or of us. (Remember, we know each other's names.) There is the possibility that having endured the twin traumas of birth and the giving up of a child, she blocked out the names the caseworker gave her, but I don't really believe it. I consider it more likely that she has followed the fairly well-documented passage of Quintana through childhood into adolescence. Writers are at least semipublic figures, and in the interest of commerce or selling a book or a movie, or even out of simple vanity, we allow interviews and photo layouts and look into television cameras; we even write about ourselves, and our children. I recall wondering how this sentient young woman of our imagination had reacted to four pages in *People*. It is possible, even likely, that she will read this piece. I know that it is an almost intolerable invasion of her privacy. I think it probable, however, that in the dark reaches of night she has considered the possibility of a further incursion, of opening a door one day and seeing a young woman who says, "Hello, Mother, I am your daughter."

Perhaps this is romantic fantasy. We know none of the circumstances of the woman's life, or even if she is still alive. We once suggested to our lawyer that we make a discreet inquiry and he quite firmly said that this was a quest that belonged only to Quintana, if she wished to make it, and not to us. What is not fantasy is that for the past year, Quintana has known the name of her natural mother. It was at dinner and she said that she would like to meet her one day, but that it would be hard, not knowing her name. There finally was the moment: we had never equivocated; did we begin now? We took a deep breath and told Quintana, then age ten, her mother's name. We also said that if she decided to search her out, we would help her in any way we could. (I must allow, however, that we would prefer she wait to make this decision until the Sturm und Drang of adolescence is past.) We then considered the possibility that her mother, for whatever good or circumstantial reasons of her own, might prefer not to see her. I am personally troubled by the militant contention that the natural mother has no right of choice in this matter. "I did not ask to be born," an adoptee once was quoted in a news story I read. "She has to see me." If only life were so simple, if only pain did not hurt. Yet we would never try to influence Quintana on this point. How important it is to know her parentage is a question only she can answer; it is her decision to make.

All parents realize, or should realize, that children are not possessions, but are only lent to us, angel boarders, as it were. Adoptive parents realize this earlier and perhaps more poignantly than others. I do not know the end of this story. It is possible that Quintana will find more reality in family commitment and cousins across the continent and heirloom orange spoons and pictures in an album and faded letters from Dominick Burns and diary entries from Nancy Hardin Cornwall than in the uncertainties of blood. It is equally possible that she will venture into the unknown. I once asked her what she would do if she met her natural mother. "I'd put one arm around Mom," she said, "and one arm around my other mommy, and I'd say, 'Hello, Mommies.' "

If that's the way it turns out, that is what she will do.

FRACTURES

[1976]

I HAD INTENDED, when I began this piece, to write about *The Mary Tyler Moore Show.* I spent an afternoon in Studio City watching the run-through of the 147th segment to be filmed since the show first went on the air seven years ago. I made the requisite notes about the fastidious professionalism of my friends Jim Brooks and Allan Burns, who created the series in 1970 and have become very rich writing and producing it ever since. I noted the terminal ennui that sets in after seven years, an ennui that has led Mary Tyler Moore and her organization to make the unprecedented decision to take the show off the air voluntarily at the end of this season. I read all the clips about Mary Tyler Moore and grew irritated at the lust of interviewers to ferret out flaws we would accept without question in children or lovers. "Chain-smokes." "Reserved in front of strangers." "Private." "Disciplined." "Whim like steel." (She sounded like a winner to me, and in the parlance of my father-in-law, who spends a lot of time around crap tables, "only the winner goes to dinner.") I meant to talk about the social and professional chasm that exists in Hollywood between movie and television people, with television on the ghetto side of the tracks. And I intended to write about my mother, who was in many ways the quintessential *Mary Tyler Moore* viewer, a strong, tough, funny woman with an eminently rational view of the human condition. In 1972, she changed her mind in the polling booth and voted for George McGovern, whom she detested, because she did not think anyone deserved to get beaten as badly as he was going to be, especially by Richard Nixon. Even in the intimidating presence of death, she never lost her sense of humor. "One good thing you can say about dying," she told me shortly before she did, "I won't have to read about Patty Hearst anymore."

In other words, I didn't have much. It was an honorable idea for a column. Serious. Not very interesting. Which was why breaking my elbow seemed a godsend.

A natural disaster, a domestic crisis—such are the secret yearnings of a writer with an idea he doubts will work. My house was burgled twice and the two resulting pieces netted me a lot more than the burglars got. I can recall one columnist who eked three columns out of his house burning down, one on the fire, a second on the unsung dignity of fire fighting, and a third on his insurance adjuster and a long view on the charred artifacts of a lifetime. So avid for material is your average columnist that once, when my daughter caught my wife and me in flagrante delicto, I seriously wondered if there was a column in it. (As it turned out, only a column mention.) And so, as I lay in my driveway, pain radiating up and down from the bulge on my elbow that was obviously a broken bone, my immediate thought was that I was saved from bidding adieu to Mary Tyler Moore.

It was my third break. I worked my first, a collarbone, into a backgrounder for the *Kingswood News*; I was eleven and the *News* was my school newspaper. I never used my second, a broken toe; how does a grown man confess, without sounding deranged, that he kicked his bathtub in a rage after reading the sports pages about a dispute between Alvin Dark and Charlie Finley? As material went, this third break would have been better had I done it in the classic Hollywood manner, punching out a producer or director (and I had several candidates in mind, including at least one woman), or à la Walter Wanger plugging Jennings Lang in his south forty after a parking-lot dispute over Joan Bennett. (Actually I was in a parking-lot dispute a couple of years ago. It was the day before Christmas at a liquor store in Malibu and I honestly don't know how it started.

As I picked myself up off the asphalt, my opponent was getting into a dusty pickup with Oklahoma plates along with a girl who called him "Lew Bob.") Alas, this break seemed to offer little opportunity to exhibit grace under pressure. Indeed the only note of fashion I could introduce was that I was wearing Gucci loafers, which may or may not have been the reason why I slipped and fell in my driveway while bringing up the garbage.

I was trundled to a hospital that looked like a rainy-day set for a beach movie. The people in the emergency room reminded me of a remark by the late Johanna Mankiewicz Davis, who once said not only were there no blacks in Malibu, there were no brunettes either. Everyone there seemed to be blond and wearing a wet suit and there was sand all over the floor. Surrounded by these clones, it occurred to me that I was acting out an episode of *The Mary Tyler Moore Show.* All around were scalps wounded by flying surfboards and there I was, less the sardonic Lou Grant than the self-absorbed Ted Baxter, trying to imply that the garbage pail I had been heading for was in the vicinity of the Banzai Pipeline.

Instead of saying farewell to Mary Tyler Moore, I found myself trapped in what seemed an endless segment, playing all the parts, my dignity constantly assaulted by a phantom laugh track. I had not anticipated, even as my arm was wrenched to a right angle and encased in a cast from shoulder to fingertips, the constant pain. The X-rays showed the ulna fractured (already I was putting on airs: other people's bones were "broken"; mine was "fractured") in three places and it felt as if someone were playing snooker with the three errant bone chips; at times I was sure that I could feel the muscles atrophying. Unable to shave, I vowed to grow a beard; my wife gave her permission only if it made me look like the survivor of a plane crash in the Andes and not like someone who drove a Mercedes. A friend suggested I run up and down the sidelines at the Dallas Cowboys training camp in Thousand Oaks, drinking Gatorade and pretending I was on the injured reserve list. My daughter attempted to divert me by showing me the dollhouse she had built on three bookshelves in her bedroom. The dollhouse had one living room, one dining room, one kitchen, one bathroom, one bedroom and one projection room. "Most people," she explained, had projection rooms.

My disposition, fragile at the best of times, was not improved by the Internal Revenue Service, which claimed a payment was past due, even though we had the canceled check. No entreaty, not even a photocopy of the canceled check, could deflect the IRS computers from totting up interest and attendant penalties. Finally I typed out a note with my good left hand: "Re Yrs July 26th: Fuck you. Strong letter to follow." The feds replied almost by return mail: "We are glad to tell you that with the additional information you submitted, we are able to reduce your penalty to $0.00."

With sleep impossible, I became a walking compendium of lines from all those old Joan Crawford movies that show on television at four in the morning. "Do you like music?" Conrad Veidt asked her in *A Woman's Face*. Joan pounded away at the Steinway, not a hair of her pompadour out of place. "Some symphonies," she replied, "most concertos." It was better than Demerol. Unable to work, I busied myself taking a cram course for the New York transit patrolman's civil-service examination. I flunked Proportions and Work Schedules but received a perfect score on Judgment and Accidents. I never asked why we had this New York transit patrolman's cram course lying around the living room. Maybe it was because we had no projection room.

An advertisement invited me to hire "PARTY PEOPLE. Naked Bartender. Fighting Couple. Et cetera." The mail offered a chance at a "gold mine . . . that has no parallel in the history of the written word," an opportunity to look at a transcription of an interview with Jesse James. This interview was taped in 1949, when Jesse was 102. The throb in my elbow made me impatient with the news from Chowchilla and Entebbe, Beirut and Belfast; I was drawn to humbler datelines, more eternal verities. An acre of plastic burning out of control in Santa Fe Springs, a process server in East Los Angeles nearly strangled when a servee grabbed and twisted his puka-shell necklace, a Bible station in Washington using the Scriptures to announce numbers payoffs. Each story reminded me of the first editor I ever had. "Nuns and midgets, that's the ticket," he used to say. "The story tells itself if it's got nuns and midgets."

For all those weeks in a cast, my life seemed an interminable story conference about the comic possibilities of fractures; it lacked only that perfect pitch for the ridiculous that came so easily to Mary Tyler Moore's writers. The whole experience of the broken elbow gave me more insight into the success of *The Mary Tyler Moore Show* than attending a week of production meetings would have. I watch the high-decibel confrontations on which most television shows turn and wonder whatever happened to quiet desperation. But for seven years, *Mary Tyler Moore* has looked at the mundane—the broken-elbow level of life—and found in it not only comedy but a measure of dignity as well. I remember the show when Mary implied she was taking the pill. My mother, a devout Catholic, asked me if she had heard correctly.

I nodded.

"Then it must be all right," my mother said.

Memories of a
Left Fielder

[1977]

THIS IS MY last season. This is the year I hang up my spikes and give my glove to a children's hospital and take off the white uniform with the blue number 90 on the back—there's a story on how I was assigned a number that high, but I'll get to it later—and shake hands with Nobe Kawano, the clubhouse boy (it's funny calling Nobe a boy; he's older than I am), and probably with Tommy LaSorda, although as far as I'm concerned, Walter Alston will always be *the* manager of the Dodgers (I remember last year when Allen Malamud of the *Herald-Examiner* said Walt was out of touch with us players and should quit, and Walt called Malamud "fat," which under the circumstances probably was not the smartest thing for the Skip to have said, but as facts go, it was more accurate than anything you're likely to see in the *Examiner* on any given day) and walk out of the Dodger clubhouse for the last time. That's right, I am packing it in. I suppose there'll be a "day" for me—the last home stand against Houston—and I suppose if we make it into the play-offs and the series my retirement will be postponed, but what happens in October happens. All I know is that in 1978, I will no longer be in left field for the Los Angeles Dodgers. I am sick of the travel and I am sick of the aggravation, and now LaSorda sits me down against certain right-handers. Bleep that, say I. There's never been a pitcher born I couldn't hit; you can look it up—I'm .303 lifetime against Seaver, and him and Marichal and Gibson are the three best I ever hit against, not a petunia in the bunch, and in case you're interested, I'm .297 lifetime against Marichal and .316 against Gibson. So that's it, goodbye, Charlie, sayonara, Old John is calling it quits. . . .

It may come as a surprise to some readers to learn that I have been the regular left fielder for the Dodgers, in both Brooklyn and Los Angeles, for the last thirty-five years. At any given time, my actual tenure in left field has only been for some fifteen or twenty of those thirty-five years, for as I grew older in my nonuniformed life, I kept pushing up the date of my rookie year from 1942 to 1947 to 1953 and finally to 1958. In my frivolous life, I write the odd book or the odd film for the likes of Pacino or Streisand, but that is strictly a Clark Kent or Bruce Wayne cover. No literary friend has ever penetrated my double life (it would, after all, be rather difficult for Joan Didion to accept the fact that for the last fifteen years she's been sleeping with a five-time National League batting champion), although twice on the field I nearly blew my cover with an unthinking reference to belles lettres. The first was in the old Forbes Field in Pittsburgh, when I told Jim Gilliam one day that what I liked about Red Smith's sportswriting was the particular undulating rhythm of his sentence structure. Jim just looked at me for a while and finally he said, "I got to take infield." From that day to this we've never had much to say to each other beyond "His fast ball tails away" or "His curve ball breaks straight down" or "Attaboy" or "How to go." The second time was in Oakland during the '74 series. I saw Roger Angell before the third game and told him that reading him on baseball was like reading Trollope on mid-Victoriana—you both, I said, understand the social architecture. I never saw anyone look so surprised, I suppose it had never occurred to him that a left fielder with a pulled hamstring (I still hit .337 that year, even with no leg hits because of the hamstring) might have read the Palliser novels.

There will be some who will suggest that I suffer from a serious schizophrenia, that fandom has skidded across the county line into a dangerous and perhaps committable fantasy. So be it. I just happen to love the Dodgers in more ways than Elizabeth Barrett loved Robert Browning. When I was a very young boy I believed that I personally controlled the destiny of the Dodgers, that the team's won-lost record was determined by my manual transgressions of the sixth commandment. In 1944, when the team finished in seventh place and lost ninety-one games, I was convinced that my palm would become hirsute and that I would grow no taller than a jockey. Nearing six feet and rampantly, even ostentatiously, carnal, I stopped equating the supine with sin; the 1963 season was bliss itself—ninety-nine wins and a four-game sweep of the Yankees in the series.

Oddly enough, I find my occasional forays into the Dodger clubhouse infinitely sad. I have now reached the age where I see these young athletes in various stages of undress not as boys of summer but as the car dealers of the not too distant future, the insurance salesmen, pitching coaches, beer distributors—men of autumn, in other words—the more fortunate among them paunchy panelists on *Hollywood Squares.* The diamond is fantasia, the locker room a real world where a pitcher discusses how to apply K-Y jelly to the private parts of a Philadelphia groupie, and the manager in the middle of a losing streak tells a sportswriter that there are two things everybody has one of—an opinion and an asshole. There is an autographed picture of Frank Sinatra in the manager's office and three photos of Don Rickles; the message board blinks A DODGER STADIUM WELCOME TO JILLY RIZZO. In fantasy, however, the mystery remains. In the major league of the mind, Pete Rose does not pose for Jockey shorts, two weighted bats over his shoulder, his basket encased in a pair of camouflage green Metre Brief International Skants. Can Chrissie Evert for Feminique be far behind, or Johnny Bench for Detane, the Climax Control for Men? Who will step up for Prelude 3, the new dual-intensity vibrator, or Texture Plus with Pleasure Dots?

Nor, as it happens, am I much of a student of the sports pages. A quick look at the box score, a computation of batting averages on my pocket calculator, and that is it. Although from April to October I regard my time in front of a typewriter as much a front as Clark Kent's chores on the *Daily Planet,* a certain residual professionalism makes me look with distaste upon the Quintus Slides of the local sporting press. A year or so ago, I was at Dodger Stadium one Sunday when a man and his son leaped from the stands and the father tried to burn an American flag in center field. Rick Monday, then of the Chicago Cubs, now the Dodgers' center fielder, raced from his position, grabbed the flag from the arsonist and was saluted on the message board: RICK MONDAY YOU MADE A GREAT PLAY. The firebug, one William Errol Thomas, Jr., thirty-seven, unemployed, was arrested, given the choice of a $60 fine or three days in the slammer, served the time and disappeared. I personally find flag burning stupid and always, as it most certainly was in this case, counterproductive: Monday was named grand marshal of Chicago's "Salute to the American Flag" parade and was honored for his deed at baseball banquets throughout the winter; the photograph of him rescuing the flag was a poster given to fans at Dodger Stadium on Flag Day this year. "If he's going to burn a flag, he better not do it in front of somebody who doesn't appreciate it," Monday told writers. "I've visited enough veterans' hospitals and seen enough guys with their legs blown off defending that flag."

The Dickensian irony of Monday's statement was unremarked upon by the sporting press. It is seldom if ever mentioned in the sports pages that while the magnates of baseball have an almost mystical devotion to the flag, this devotion, during the Vietnam war, did not extend to volunteering their athletes to get shot in defense of it. The military history of the major leagues during Vietnam was essentially a history of National Guard weekends and evening reserve meetings, a kind of legal draft dodging that carried with it credentials of patriotism denied those who bugged out to Canada. Robert James "Rick" Monday, Santa Monica High School, '63, Arizona State, '67, six feet three, 195 pounds, was not paid a bonus of $104,000 to get his ass shot off in Nam; a tour or two of VA hospitals passed for service in the boondocks. I do not mean to be harsh on Monday, only on that Captain America persona concocted in the press box; he was only another of his generation, too aware to enlist in a war where niggers got killed and greasers and rednecks, not graduate students or bonus babies. What grievance sparked William Errol Thomas, Jr., was impossible to discover in the sports pages, let alone what bargain he had struck with his draft board. Not long ago, more than a year after the fact, I tried in vain to find him. I went to the criminal courts building and pulled the record on Case No. 31-543367. Thomas, William Errol, Jr., Viol. Sec. 602 (J), P.C., one year probation, not to enter Dodger Stadium during probationary period. No personal information. His attorney in the public-defender's office said that Thomas was an American Indian, a transient living out of the back of his car. The Department of Motor Vehicles yielded no information as to his whereabouts, nor did the registrar of voters, nor the Veterans Administration. The Bureau of Indian Affairs in Phoenix could not help, nor could the Navajo Area Office in Window Rock; the sixth office I tried at the Pentagon said it would take a month to discover whether Thomas, William Errol, Jr., had ever done a hitch in the military. The absence of Thomas's name from the bureaucracy's computer printouts seemed to speak more volumes than the tedious saga of Captain America, but these volumes will never be read in the sporting green.

It is because of such temporal matters that I rarely sit in the press box at Dodger Stadium. Better to wander alone through the grounds at 1000 Elysian Park. One Thousand Elysian Park Avenue—has any ball yard ever had a more evocative address? Even the best way to get there is through a time warp, down Sunset Boulevard, through Silver Lake and Echo Park. This is Philip Marlowe country, where the detritus of the 1940s radiates from every crumbling bungalow; peeled gold lettering on a second-floor window summons pedestrians to LEARN THE RHUMBA. Then left up that Angeleno Champs-Elysées at the top of which stands Walter O'Malley's Arc de Triomphe. I make the trip fifteen or twenty times a year, always by myself; alone in Elysium I am not burdened by nonbelievers who would question my lifetime batting average of .34973, which rounded to the nearest decimal gives me a b.a. over the last twenty years of .350. On the bulletin board in my office, there is pinned a ragged piece of paper on which are printed my stats since 1958. (When I first joined the Dodgers in 1942, I always intended to retire in twenty years; an eraser changes the twenty-year span every spring.) During the off-season, I ravage *The Baseball Encyclopedia* for pertinent figures. I am first in lifetime doubles with 800, seven ahead of Speaker, and second in triples with 301, after Wahoo Sam Crawford. I've never been much of a home-run hitter (nineteen is my high in the bigs;

I average fourteen or fifteen a season), but ten times I accounted for at least 200 runs a season—that's RBIs plus runs scored, minus home runs (because homers are included in both RBIs and runs). Gehrig did that thirteen times; Ruth, eleven; Jimmy Foxx, nine; Charlie Gehringer, eight; Willie Mays only did it twice. Speed was always my game. The doubles and triples tell you that, and the 724 lifetime stolen bases (eight years, more than fifty); you walked me and I was as good as on third. Of course, what everyone talks about are the ten years with over 200 hits (once more than Cobb, twice more than Rose) and the two years in a row I hit over .400 (me, Cobb and Hornsby are the only ones ever to do it twice in a row, and no one has even hit .400 since Teddy Ballgame in 1941; my license plates are 403 JGD and 405 JGD in case you're wondering what my b.a. was those two years), but you know what I'm proudest of? The year I hit in 135 out of the 156 games I played, and for consistency, I'd put that against Joe D. and his fifty-six-game streak.

But those are only numbers, and numbers don't tell you about the good times, or the bad. I suppose you could call my contract battles with Walter O'Malley epic. They were never over money, but over the First Amendment: Walter did not like the idea of my writing books in the off-season and I was such a militant supporter of Marvin Miller and the Players' Association that he thought I was a Red. I always was one to speak my mind and the only two words Walter liked to hear a ballplayer say were "Yes, sir." It was my big mouth that got me my number 90. I was eighteen when I joined the Dodgers, a bonus baby, and I couldn't be farmed out, and Jackie Robinson didn't think much of bonus babies and insisted I be given a bat boy's number, and I said to him, "Listen, fella, the day you can hit as good as number ninety is the day you start pissing holy water." I shouldn't have said it, but of course I was right, and the number 90 has become as much of a trademark as Red Grange's 77.

It hasn't been a bad life, but the pulled hamstring has become chronic and I've got a novel coming out in October, and while I might come back next spring, it's time to start the rest of my life. I've given my farewell address a lot of thought, and this is what I'm going to say on my day, that last home stand against Houston:

"... And now it is time to say goodbye...."

(The 56,000 people in Dodger Stadium will cry as one, "NO!")

"... It is not an edifying spectacle to see a grown man cry, but bear with me ..."

("NOOO, NOOO ...")

"... I have worn this uniform for twenty years. I am a Dodger; I always will be a Dodger...."

(Sandy Koufax and all my teammates of the last thirty-five years will be weeping along the third-base foul line.)

"... Thank you for these twenty years, thank each and every one of you ... thank you ... thank you ... and goodbye."

Eureka!

[1978]

❧

I.

I MOVED TO California on the fifth day of June 1964. I can be very specific about the date: I had to swear to it in a legal deposition, signed and witnessed and admitted into evidence in Civil Court, City of New York, in and for the County of New York, as an addendum in the case of *New York Telephone Company, Plaintiff,* vs. *John Gregory Dunne, Index No, 103886/1964.* The charge against me was nonpayment of a bill from New York Telephone in the amount of $54.09. The record of the proceeding, Index No. 103886/1964, noted that a subpoena had been issued ordering me to court to answer the charge, and a process server, fully cognizant, as the record shows, that his "statements are true under the penalties of perjury," swore under oath that he had served me with said subpoena on July 7, 1964, in person at my residence, 41 East 75th Street, City of New York, County of New York. The case of *New York Telephone Company, Plaintiff,* vs. *John Gregory Dunne* was heard on July 24, 1964, and in due course I was found guilty as charged, fined $5 plus $9 in court costs and $1.16 in interest on the unpaid bill, making the total default $69.25. A warrant was also issued for my arrest for failure to answer a court order, namely the subpoena allegedly served on July 7, 1964.

Sometime later that summer, the papers pertaining to Index No. 103886/1964, Civil Court, City of New York, in and for the County of New York, were forwarded to me at my new home in Portuguese Bend, California, a peninsula protruding into the Pacific Ocean on the southwestern tip of Los Angeles County. The equilibrium of my first western summer was upset. The sealed crates containing the records of my past were drawn from storage and opened. A check of my bank statements confirmed that the bill from New York Telephone had been paid on time, the evidence being a canceled check, No. 61, dated March 23, 1964, drawn in the amount of $54.09 on the Chase Manhattan Bank, Rockefeller Center Branch, and paid to the order of the plaintiff, the New York Telephone Company. Witnesses attested that I had not been out of Los Angeles County since my arrival on the fifth of June, making it difficult for the process server, whatever his affirmations that his statements were "true under the penalties of perjury," to have served me with a subpoena on the Upper East Side of Manhattan on July 7. I engaged Carmine DeSapio's attorney and on his instructions sent this information to the president of the New York Telephone Company, copy as well to Mr. John McInerney, Clerk of the Civil Court, City of New York, in and for the County of New York. By return mail I received a letter from the president of New York Telephone apologizing for the unfortunate error, saying that the judgment had been vacated and that copies of the vacating order as well as his letter of apology had been put in my file. I was so warmed by this prompt recognition of corporate error that I immediately wrote back the president of New York Telephone, copies to Mr. Frederick Kappel, chairman of the board at AT&T, and to Mr. David Rockefeller at the Chase Bank, and told him to do something carnally improper to himself.

~

AND SO I was in California, on the lam, as it were, from the slam. Manifest Destiny, 1964. What was western expansion, after all, but a migration of malcontents and ne'er-do-wells, have-nots with no commitment to the stable society left behind, adventurers committed only to circumventing any society in their path. For eight years on the Upper East Side of Manhattan, I had been a have-not and a malcontent. I dreamed of being an adventurer. When I was twenty-five, I had put up $100 to buy a piece of an antimony mine in Thailand. I was not sure what antimony was, but I saw myself in riding boots and a wide-brimmed hat in the jungles of Siam. There was a whisper of opium and there were women always called sloe-eyed, wearing *ao dais* and practiced in the Oriental permutations of fellatio. The daydream, of course, was compensation for the reality I was then living. I was a traffic clerk in an industrial advertising agency, little more than a messenger in a Brooks Brothers suit and a white buttoned-down shirt and a striped tie, taking copy and layouts for industrial toilet fixtures to the client in the Bronx. At night I tried to write a novel titled *Not the Macedonian.* The first line of the novel—the only line I ever wrote—was "They called him Alexander the Great." Not, of course, the Macedonian. My Alexander was a movie director. In Hollywood. I had never met a movie director, I had never been in Hollywood. For that matter, I had never been west of Fort Carson, Colorado, where I had spent the last three months of a two-year stint as a peacetime Army draftee. Nor had I ever told anyone, least of all the girl I was then supposed to marry, that my fashionable address in New York's silk-stocking district was a rooming house, populated by men who had been beaten by the city. One roommate was a lawyer from South Carolina who had failed the New York Bar exam three times and was afraid to go home. Another was a drunk who had been out of work for eleven months. The owner-landlord of this townhouse between Madison and Park packed four people to a room, each at $56 a month, and day and night he prowled the corridors and stairwells looking for transgressions of his house rules. Once he threatened to evict me for tossing Q-Tips in the toilet, another time for violating the food protocols. His kitchen was run on a nonprofit honor system; a price list was posted (2¢ for a saltine, 5¢ for a saltine with a dab of peanut butter, 7¢ for a saltine with peanut butter and jelly, etc.) and the tenant was expected to tot up his expenses on a file card. Snitches reported to the owner-landlord that I had been negligent in the accounting of my nightly inhalation of Hydrox and milk. My only defense was rapture of the snack. I threw myself on his mercy and was sentenced to permanent loss of kitchen privileges.

Each day I scoured the "Apartments to Share" column in the *Times* real-estate section, but it was not until a man in a green-flocked apartment on East Fifteenth Street told me there was only one bed in his flat that I realized the meaning of the phrase in the ads, "Must be compatible." I haunted the sleazy one-room employment agencies along Forty-second Street and up Broadway, looking for a better job. I felt that if I only broke through to $75 a week it would be the first step to the cover of *Time.* In the evenings I concocted resumés, listing jobs I had never held with references from people I had never met. The most elaborate fiction was the invention of a job on a daily newspaper in Colorado Springs. During my service at Fort Carson, I had noted that this paper did not give its reporters bylines and so I bought up enough back issues at the out-of-town newsstand on Times Square to create for myself an unbylined city room background. The employment agents were impressed. Except one, a man with rheumy eyes and dandruff flaking down on his shiny blue suit. Even now I sometimes awake with a start remembering that awful day when he told me he had checked out one of my *soi-disant* Colorado references, who reported that he had never heard of me.

I can say now what I dared not say then: I was a jerk.

⁓

In time, however, my nonexistent job on the city desk of the Colorado Springs newspaper helped me find employment with a trusting trade magazine, an opportunity that I later parlayed into a five-year sojourn on *Time.* There I learned discipline, met deadlines and became adept at dealing with the more evasive transitions, the elusive "but," the slippery "nevertheless," the chimerical "on the other hand." I also learned that the writer on a news magazine is essentially a carpenter, chipping, whittling, planing a field correspondent's ten- or twelve-page file down into a seventy-line story, in effect cutting a sofa into a bar stool; in the eyes of his editors, both are places to sit.

Since days in *Time*'s New York office are counted as enhancing one's world vision, I became, after three years, the magazine's Saigon watcher, even though I had never been there. In 1962, I persuaded my editors to pay my way to Indochina, my alleged sphere of expertise, where I fornicated for five weeks and in what now seems a constant postcoital daze floated to the nascent realization that the war beginning to metastasize in Vietnam was a malignant operation. It was a difficult induction to explain to my editors back in New York. A whore in Cholon did not seem much of a source, notwithstanding the brother she claimed was in Hanoi, from whom, in her text, she received periodic messages over an RFD route I suspected was not sanctioned by President Diem or Archbishop Thuc. It was just a feeling. I had the feeling when I monitored a conversation about Swiss bank accounts over drinks at the Cercle Sportif in Saigon, an abstract discussion punctuated by long silences, the simple question, "Do you favor Lausanne?" seeming to carry an absurd consignment of symbolic freight. I had the same feeling when I flew around the countryside for a few days with a four-star U.S. Army general from MACV. The bases he dropped in on reminded me of Fort Bliss or Fort Chaffee from my own Army days. The latrines were spotless, whitewashed stones lined the pathways between tents and the young volunteer American officers wore starched fatigues and spit-shined boots and their hair was clipped to the skull two inches over the ears. There were graphs and maps and overlays with grease pencil notations, and after every briefing there was coffee and optimism, but no American officer in whatever section we happened to be visiting could explain why the roads were not secure at night. Losing control of the roads at night was the nature of the war, the general said. He seemed to think this a reasonable explanation and stressed that the plans and procedures of his command were "viable"; I learned new and ambiguous meanings for the word "viable" during my short stay in Vietnam. A Turk nicknamed Cowboy had a less ambiguous expression. Cowboy was a former colonel in the Turkish air force who, after being declared redundant and forced into premature retirement, had signed on with the CIA for the Bay of Pigs. At $2,000 a month he was working off that contract in Vietnam, hedge-hopping over the hills to avoid ground fire, summing up what was happening in the jungles below in two words: "All shit."

Cowboy carried no weight in the Time-Life Building. Briefed at the Pentagon, lunched at the White House, my editors saw the light at the end of the tunnel; they thought my sibylline meanderings the pornography of a malcontent. In the ensuing religious wars about Vietnam that rent *Time*, I sided with the doubters in the Saigon bureau and asked to be relieved of the Vietnam desk. My penance was reassignment to the Benelux portfolio, along with responsibility for the less doctrinaire capitals of Western Europe—a beat that encompassed by-elections in Liechtenstein, Scandinavian sexual mores and Common Market agricultural policy. "How small," I wrote, "is a small tomato?" I became sullen, a whisperer in the corridors. I did not get an expected raise, a short time later I married, a short time after that, still a malcontent, not yet a have, I quit my job. Ignorant of the impending posse from the New York Telephone Company, the adventurer routed himself to California.

Eureka, as the state motto has it: "I have found it."

I had found it.

2.

WHAT I FOUND first was culture shock. Imagine: an Irish Catholic out of Hartford, Connecticut, two generations removed from steerage, with the political outlook of an alderman and social graces polished to a semigloss at the Hartford Golf Club. Imagine a traveler with this passport confronting that capitol south of the Tehachapis called El Pueblo de Nuestra Senora La Reina de Los Angeles. My wife was a fifth-generation Californian and was in a sense returning home (although her real home was the equally impenetrable flatland of the Central Valley), but to me it was a new world: *the* new world. I watched Los Angeles television, listened to Los Angeles radio, devoured Los Angeles newspapers trying to find the visa that would provide entry. "Go gargle razor blades," advised a local talk show host pleasantly; it was a benediction that seemed to set the tone of the place. Dawn televised live on the Sunset Strip: a minister of the Lord inquired of a stringy-haired nubile what she liked doing best in the world. An unequivocal answer: "Balling." Another channel, another preacher. This one ascribed the evils of the contemporary liberal ethic—my own contemporary liberal ethic, as modified in generations of smoke-filled rooms—to one "J. J. Russo." It was some time before I apprehended that the Italianate "J. J." was in fact Jean-Jacques Rousseau. In a newspaper I read of a man living on the rim of Death Valley who walked alone out into the desert, leaving behind a note that he wanted to "talk to God." God apparently talked back: the man was bitten by a rattlesnake and died.

Fundamentalism, the Deity, the elements—those familiar *aides-mémoire* that titillate the casual visitor to the western shore. I did not need a pony to find the immediate subtext of banality and vulgarity. It took a long time, however, to learn that the real lesson in each of those parables was to quite another point. Los Angeles is the least accessible and therefore the worst reported of American cities. It is not available to the walker in the city. There is no place where the natives gather. Distance obliterates unity and community. This inaccessibility means that the contemporary de Tocqueville on a layover between planes can define Los Angeles only in terms of his own culture shock. A negative moral value is attached to the taco stand, to the unnatural presence of palm trees at Christmas (although the climate of Los Angeles at Christmas exactly duplicates that of Bethlehem), even to the San Andreas fault. Whenever she thought of California, an editor at the *New York Times* once told me, she thought of Capri plants and plastic flowers. She is an intelligent woman and I do not think she meant to embrace the cliché with such absolute credulity; she would have been sincerely pained had I replied that whenever I thought of New York I thought of Halston and Bobby Zarem. (My most endearing memory of this woman is seeing her at a party in New York, as always meticulously pulled together, except that the side seam on her Pucci dress had parted. The parted seam was the sort of social detail that marked her own reportage, which had a feel for texture absent in her *a priori* invention of a California overrun with plastic greenery.) "I would love to see you play with the idea of California as the only true source of American culture," she wrote my wife and me, fellow conspirators, or so she thought, in her fantasy of the western experience. "I mean, what other state would have pearlized rainbow-colored plastic shells around its public telephones?"

Notice "plastic," that perfect trigger word, the one word that invariably identifies its user as culturally superior. When I arrived in California in 1964, the catch words and phrases meant to define the place were "smog" and "freeways" and "kook religions," which then spun off alliteratively into "kooky California cults." Still the emigré, I referred to my new country as "Lotusland"; it was a while before I realized that anyone who calls Los Angeles "Lotusland" is a functioning booby. In the years since 1964, only the words have changed. California is a land of "rapacious philodendron" and "squash yellow Datsuns," Marion Knox noted on the Op Ed page of the *New York Times*; seven months in the Los Angeles bureau of *Time* seemed to Ms. Knox an adventure in Oz. "Angel dust." "The 'in' dry cleaner." "Men in black bathing suits, glossy with Bain de Soleil." (Perhaps a tad of homophobia there, a residual nightmare of Harry's Bar in Bloomingdale's.) "The place of honor at . . . dinner parties," Ms. Knox reported, "is next to the hotshot realtor." I wonder idly whose dinner parties, wonder at what press party do you find the chic hairdresser and the hotshot realtor. I also think I have never read a more poignant illustration of Cecelia Brady's line in *The Last Tycoon:* "We don't go for strangers in Hollywood."

In *Esquire,* Richard Reeves spoke of "ideas with a California twist, or twisted California ideas—drinking vodka, est, credit cards, student revolts, political consultants, skateboards . . ." An absurd catalogue, venial sins, if sins they be at all, some not even Californian in origin. Ivy Lee had the Rockefeller ear before the term "political consultant" was invented, not to mention Edward Bernays and Benjamin Sonnenberg, who were plugged into the sockets of power when normalcy was still an idea to be cultivated. And what is est after all but a virus of psychiatry, a mutation of the search to find one's self, passed west from Vienna via Park Avenue, then carried back again, mutated, on the prevailing winds. (Stone-throwing in glass houses, this kind of exchange, a Ping-Pong game between midgets, est on one coast, Arica on the other, vodka drinking in California, Plato's Retreat in Manhattan, lacquered swimmers on the Malibu, their equally glossy brothers three time zones east in Cherry Grove.) The trigger words meant to define California become a litany, the litany a religion. The chief priests and pharisees attending the Los Angeles bureaus of Eastern publications keep the faith free from heresy. A year ago a reporter from *Time* telephoned my wife and me and said that the magazine was preparing a new cover story on California; he wondered if we had noticed any significant changes in the state since *Time*'s last California cover.

Still they come, these amateur anthropologists, the planes disgorging them at LAX, their date books available for dinner with the hotshot realtor. They are bent under the cargo of their preconceived notions. "The only people who live in L.A. are those who can't make it in New York," I once heard a young woman remark at dinner. She was the associate producer of a rock-and-roll television special and she was scarfing down chicken mole, chiles Jalapenos, guacamole, sour cream, cilantro and tortillas. "You cook New York," she complimented her hostess. "Mexico, actually," her hostess replied evenly, passing her a tortilla and watching her lather sour cream on it as if it were jam. Another dinner party, this for an eastern publisher in town to visit a local author. There were ten at dinner, it was late, we had all drunk too much. "Don't you miss New York?" the publisher asked. "Books. Publishing. Politics. Talk." His tone was sadly expansive. "Evenings like this."

The visitors have opinions, they cherish opinions, their opinions ricochet around the room like tracer fire. The very expression of an opinion seems to certify its worth. Socially acceptable opinion, edged with the most sentimental kind of humanism, condescension in drag. "Why can't you find the little guy doing a good job and give him a pat on the back?" as the managing editor of *Life* once asked my wife. Little people, that population west of the Hudson, this butcher, that baker, the candlestick maker, each with a heart as big as all outdoors. Usually there is a scheme to enrich the life of this little person, this cultural dwarf, some effort to bring him closer to the theater or the good new galleries. Mass transit, say. I remember one evening when a writer whose expertise was in menopausal sexual conduct insisted that mass transit was the only means of giving southern California that sense of community she thought it so sadly lacked. I did not say that I thought "community" was just another ersatz humanistic cryptogram. Nor did I say that I considered mass transit a punitive concept, an idea that runs counter to the fluidity that is, for better or worse, the bedrock precept of southern California, a fluidity that is the antithesis of community. She would not have heard me if I had said it, for one purpose of such promiscuous opinionizing is to filter out the disagreeable, to confirm the humanistic consensus.

He who rejects the dictatorship of this consensus is said to lack "input." Actors out from New York tell me they miss the input, novelists with a step deal at Paramount, journalists trying to escape the eastern winter. I inquire often after input, because I am so often told that California (except for San Francisco) is deficient in it, as if it were a vitamin. Input is people, I am told. Ideas. Street life. I question more closely. Input is the pot-au-feu of urban community. I wonder how much input Faulkner had in Oxford, Mississippi, and it occurs to me that scarcity of input might be a benign deficiency. Not everyone agrees. After two weeks in California, the publisher of *New York* magazine told Dick Cavett at a party in New York, he felt "brain-damaged." Delphina Ratazzi was at that party, and Geraldo Rivera. And Truman Capote, Calvin Klein, Charlotte Ford, George Plimpton, Barbara Allen with Philip Niarchos, Kurt Vonnegut, Carrie Fisher with Desi Arnaz, Jr., Joan Hackett and Arnold Schwarzenegger. I do not have much faith in any input I might have picked up at that party.

3.

California is not so much a state of the Union as it is an imagination that seceded from our reality a long time ago. In leading the world in the transition from industrial to post-industrial society, California's culture became the first to shift from coal to oil, from steel to plastic, from hardware to software, from materialism to mysticism, from reality to fantasy. California became the first to discover that it was fantasy that led reality, not the other way around.

—WILLIAM IRWIN THOMPSON

PERHAPS IT IS easiest to define Los Angeles by what it is not. Most emphatically it is not eastern. San Francisco is eastern, a creation of the gold rush, colonized by sea, Yankee architecture and Yankee attitudes boated around the Horn and grafted onto the bay. Any residual ribaldry in San Francisco is the legacy of that lust for yellow riches that attracted those early settlers in the first place. Small wonder Easterners feel comfortable there. They perceive an Atlantic clone; it does not threaten as does that space-age Fort Apache five hundred miles to the south.

Consider then the settling of southern California. It was—and in a real sense continues to be—the last western migration. It was a migration, however, divorced from the history not only of the West but of the rest of California as well, a migration that seemed to parody Frederick Jackson Turner and his theory on the significance of the frontier. In Turner's version, the way west was not for the judicious—overland, across a continent and its hard-scrabble history. Those who would amputate a past and hit the trail were not given to the idea of community. Dreamers or neurotics, they were individualists who shared an aversion to established values, to cohesion and stability. A hard man, Turner's western wayfarer, for a hard land.

The settlers of southern California traveled the same route across the Big Empty—but on an excursion ticket. By the mid-1880s, the frontier, as Turner noted, was for all intents and purposes closed, the continental span traced by a hatchwork of railroad lines. Where there were railroads, there was murderous competition, and when in 1886 the Santa Fe laid its track into southern California, it joined in battle with the Southern Pacific for the ultimate prize, the last terminal on the Pacific shore, a frontier of perpetual sunshine where the possibilities seemed as fertile as the land. The rate wars between the Santa Fe and the Southern Pacific denied sense. From the jumping-off points in the Missouri Valley, fares to southern California dropped from $125 to $100, and then in a maniacal frenzy of price-cutting to twelve, eight, six, four dollars. Finally on March 6, 1887, the price bottomed out at one dollar per passenger, one hundred copper pennies to racket down those trails blazed by the cattle drives and the Conestoga wagons, to cross that blank land darkened by the blood of the Indian wars.

What the railroads had essentially created in southern California was a frontier resort, a tumor on the western ethic. Bargain basement pioneers, every one a rebuke to Turner's hard man, flooded into southern California, 120,000 of them trained into Los Angeles alone by the Southern Pacific in 1887, the Santa Fe keeping pace with three and four trainloads a day. In such a melee, where personal histories were erased, the southland was an adventurer's nirvana. Land speculators preyed on the gullible, enticing them with oranges stuck into the branches of Joshua trees. But even when the land bubble burst, the newcomers stayed on, held captive by the sun, the prejudices and resentments of their abandoned life, the dreams and aspirations of their new one, cross-fertilizing in the luxuriant warmth.

And still they came, a generation on every trainload. If New York was the melting pot of Europe, Los Angeles was the melting pot of the United States. It was a bouillabaisse not to everyone's taste. "It is as if you tipped the United States up so all the commonplace people slid down there into southern California," was the way Frank Lloyd Wright put it. In *Southern California Country,* Carey McWilliams replied gently to Wright: "One of the reasons for this persistent impression of commonplaceness is, of course, that the newcomers have been stripped of their natural settings—their Vermont hills, their Kansas plains, their Iowa cornfields. Here their essential commonplaceness stands out garishly in the harsh illumination of the sun. Here every wart is revealed, every wrinkle underscored, every eccentricity emphasized."

Expansion, McWilliams noted, was the major business of southern California, the very reason for its existence. The volume and velocity of this migration set the tone of the place. From 1900 to 1940, the population of Los Angeles increased by nearly 1,600 percent. Everyone was an alien, the newcomer was never an exile. In an immigrant place where the majority was nonindigenous, the idea of community could not flourish, since community by definition is built on the deposits of shared experience. The fact that the spectacular growth of Los Angeles exactly coincided with the automotive age further weakened the idea of community. Where older cities, radiating out from a core, were defined and limited both by transportation and geography, Los Angeles was the first city on wheels, its landscape in three directions unbroken by natural barriers that could give it coherence and definition, its mobility limited only by a tank of gas.

The newness of Los Angeles—it is, after all, scarcely older than the century—and the idea of mobility as a cultural determinant lent the place a bumptiousness that was as appealing to some as it was aggravating to others. In a word, southern California was different, and in the history of the land, what is different is seldom treasured. Exempt from the history of the West, the cut-rate carpetbaggers who settled in the southland could adopt the western ethic and reinterpret it for their own uses. The result is a refinement of that ad hoc populism that has characterized California politics in this century, an ingrained suspicion of order, the bureaucracy of order and the predators of order. It is a straight line from Hiram Johnson to Howard Jarvis, and when Jerry Brown intones, "Issues are the last refuge of scoundrels," he is speaking in the authentic voice of a state where skepticism about government is endemic.

This attitude toward politics, as well as southern California's particular and aggressive set toward the world, could be dismissed as a sunstroked curiosity as long as the region remained a provincial and distant colony, and so it did remain until World War II. Even with the steady infusion of people and ideas and capital, southern California had almost no industrial base until the war. There was plenty of technological know-how—Los Angeles was the first city in the country to be entirely lit by electricity—and even before the turn of the century there was a sense that the city's destiny did not lie in divine guidance from the Atlantic. "The Pacific is the ocean of the future," Henry Huntington said then. "Europe can supply her own wants. We shall supply the needs of Asia."

Cowboy talk: there was no industry to supply the needs of Asia. Agriculture dominated southern California (Los Angeles until 1920 was the nation's richest agricultural county) and the population boom had spawned an improvised ancillary economy of the most demeaning sort. It seemed a region of maids and clerks, of animal hospitals and car dealerships and roadside stands, of pool services and curbstone mediums. "Piddling occupations," James M. Cain wrote in 1933. "What electric importance can be felt in a peddler of orange peelers? Or a confector of Bar-B-Q? Or the proprietor of a goldfish farm? Or a breeder of rabbit fryers?" In this service economy, Hollywood was the ultimate service industry—it required no raw materials except celluloid, which cost little to ship either as raw stock or finished film—but its payroll was enormous and from 1920 to 1940 it gave southern California a simulated industrial base. In 1938 the movie industry ranked fourteenth among all American businesses in gross volume, eleventh in total assets.

And then came the war. The figures tell the story. In an eight-year period, 1940 to 1948, the federal government invested $1 billion in the construction of new industrial plants in California, and private industry kicked in $400 million more; industrial employment rose 75 percent; Los Angeles alone juggled $10 billion in war production contracts. These were just numbers, however, as ephemeral as any wartime figures. What was important was the technological scaffolding propping up the numbers. As Carey McWilliams points out in *The Great Exception,** California "unlike other areas . . . did not *convert* to war production, for there was nothing much to 'convert'; what happened was that *new* industries and *new* plants were built overnight." "New" is a word that often takes on a suspect connotation when applied to California, but here were new plants untainted with the technological obsolescence afflicting so many older industries in the East. New processes using the new metals and new chemicals indigenous to California. New industries, such as aerospace and computers, which were mutually dependent, and in the case of aerospace particularly suited to the geography and climate of southern California, a place where hardware could be tested on the limitless wastes of the Mojave 365 days a year.*

In effect the war allowed southern California to find a sense of itself. The self discovered was not particularly endearing. Think of Frederick Jackson Turner's hard man, glaze him with prosperity, put him in sunglasses and there you have it—a freeway Billy the Kid. There was an extravagance about the place, a lust for the new, and it was this lust that allowed southern California to capitalize on the technologies of the future, to turn its attention away from the rest

---

* It should be noted here that McWilliams's two books, *Southern California Country* and *The Great Exception,* are essential to any study of California. I think they are great books, not only because I am now and often have been in McWilliams's debt, but more importantly because they are cool and informative, history as literature in every sense.

of the nation, from the bedrock of history itself. The boom years made Los Angeles an independent money mart, no longer an economic supplicant, its vision west across the Pacific to Japan and Australia, toward those frontiers envisioned by Henry Huntington; look if you need proof at the Yellow Pages and those branch offices in Tokyo and Sydney. To some the lusts of southern California seemed to lead only to venereal disease. "Reality . . . was whatever people said it was," J. D. Lorenz wrote in *Jerry Brown: The Man on the White Horse.* "It was the fresh start, the self-fulfilling prophecy, the victory of mind over matter. In a land without roots, reality was image, image replaced roots, and if the image could be constructed quickly, like a fabricated house, it could also be torn down quickly." It is part of the fascination of southern California that it would enthusiastically agree with Lorenz's screed. Better the fresh start than roots choking with moral crab grass, better the fabricated house than the dry rot of cities, better mind over matter than a paralysis of will.

Prosperity stoked the natural bombast of the southern California frontier. Los Angeles, that upstart on the Pacific, looked back on the eastern littoral with a cool indifference that bordered on contempt. See what community got you, it seemed to say; what good are stability and cohesion if their legacy is the South Bronx? Economic independence, coupled with that western urge to be left alone, made southern California in some metaphoric sense a sovereign nation, Pacifica, as it were, with Los Angeles as its capital. And here is the other negative that defines Los Angeles: it no longer regards itself as a second city.

The history of nationhood is also largely the history of a nation's single city—that London, that Paris, that New York (with Washington as its outermost exurb) where politics, money and culture coalesce to shape a national idea. Every place else is Manchester or Marseilles. The claim of Los Angeles to be the coequal of New York could be dismissed as the braggadocio of a provincial metropolis except for one thing. Los Angeles had Hollywood, the dream factory that is both a manufacturer of a national idea and an interpreter of it. Hollywood—the most ridiculed and the most envied cultural outpost of the century. Think of it: technology as an art form, an art form, moreover, bankrolled and nurtured by men who, in Louis Sherwin's surpassing remark, "knew only one word of two syllables and that word was 'fillum.' " At times I admit a certain impatience with Hollywood and all its orthodoxies. I hear that film is "truth at twenty-four frames a second" and wonder if any art has ever had a credo of such transcendental crap. Try it this way: "truth at sixty words a minute." But that is a factor of age and taste. When I was an undergraduate, the trek of the ambitious and allegedly literate bachelor of arts was to the East; to be heard, one was published, and the headquarters of print was New York. Now that trek is a trickle. The status of image has usurped the status of type. The young graduates head west, their book bags laden with manuals on lenses and cutting, more conversant with Jewison than with Joyce, almost blissfully persuaded that a knowledge of *Dallas* and *San Francisco, Casablanca* and *Maracaibo* is a knowledge of the world at large.

It is this aspect of the Hollywood scene that eastern interpreters fasten upon. Zapping the vulgarity is less demanding than learning the grammar, the grammar of film, and by extension the grammar of Los Angeles, and of California itself. In the beginning, there was the vulgarity of the movie pioneers, many of whom were from Eastern Europe. No recounting of that era is complete without referring to those early movie moguls as former "furriers" or "rag merchants." It was an ethnic code, cryptological anti-Semitism. For furrier read Jew. No, not Jew; the Sulzbergers were Jews, and the Meyers; these unlettered rag-traders were nothing but ostentatious, parvenu sheenies, and there was always a good giggle in the Goldfish who changed his name to Goldwyn. I think of the Marxist critic who in the space of a few thousand words spoke about Josef von Sternberg, who "spurns as canard the rumor that he was born Joe Stern of Brooklyn"; about Mervyn Leroy, of whom "it is rumored that his real name is Lasky"; and about Lewis Milestone, "whose actual name is said to be Milstein."

It was easier to laugh than it was to examine the movie earthquake and its recurring aftershocks, easier to maintain that Los Angeles's indifference to the cultural heritage of the East was evidence of an indigenous lack of culture. But the lines had been drawn, the opinion media of the East versus the Western image media of movies and television, and the spoils were the hearts and minds of America. This country had always been defined by the East. Everything was good or bad to the extent that it did or did not coincide with the eastern norm; the making of cultural rules, the fact of being the nation's social and cultural arbiter, imbued confidence. The movies were a severe shock to that confidence, all the more so because those images up there on screen did not seem to have an apparent editorial bias. "The movies did not describe or explore America," Michael Wood wrote in *America in the Movies*. "They invented it, dreamed up an America all their own, and persuaded us to share the dream. We shared it happily, because the dream was true in its fashion—true to a variety of American desires—and because there weren't all that many other dreams around."

The opinion media and the image media—each has an investment in its version of the American myth, each a stake in getting it wrong about the other. To the opinion media, southern California is the enemy camp, and their guerrilla tactic is one of deflation. In their version, the quintessential native was born in Whittier and carries the middle name Milhous. Apostates and quislings are spokesmen: the refugee from Long Beach, now a practicing Manhattan intellectual, who reports that life in Los Angeles is the life of a turnip; the film director who curtsies to his critical constituency and says that if Solzhenitsyn lived in L.A., he would have a hot tub and be doing TM. Hatred of New York is seen as an epidemic. "What do you hate (or dislike) about New York City?" begins a letter from *New York* magazine. "We are asking a number of persons . . ." *Esquire* finds this hatred, and Woody Allen in *Annie Hall*. It is a kind of negative boosterism that I find infinitely depressing. "As a well-known New York hater, you . . ." It was a correspondent from *Time* on the telephone. (*Time* again: its Los Angeles bureau is a Sun City for corporate remittance men.) I told the *Time* man that while I was gratified at being described as "well-known," I did not know how I had achieved the reputation of "New York hater." He admitted it was not from anything I had ever written. Nor anything I had said;

we had never met. Nor anything he had heard secondhand. I persisted: how had I achieved that dubious reputation. "You live here," he said finally.

The call troubled me for a long time. If I had not thought much about New York's financial crisis (the actual reason for the call), I certainly took no pleasure in its plight (the assumption of my caller). It just never crossed my mind. And there it was, the canker, the painful sore of reciprocity: Los Angeles was indifferent to New York. It was the same indifference that for decades New York had shown, and was no longer showing, to the rest of the country.

4.

The splendors and miseries of Los Angeles, the graces and grotesqueries, appear to me as unrepeatable as they are unprecedented, I share neither the optimism of those who see Los Angeles as the prototype of all future cities, nor the gloom of those who see it as the harbinger of universal urban doom. . . . It is immediately apparent that no city has ever been produced by such an extraordinary mixture of geography, climate, economics, demography, mechanics and culture; nor is it likely that an even remotely similar mixture will ever occur again.

—REYNER BANHAM,
Los Angeles: The Architecture of Four Ecologies

"THE FREEWAY IS FOREVER" was the slogan of a local radio station the summer I arrived in California. Here was the perfect metaphor for that state of mind called Los Angeles, but its meaning eluded me for years. Singular not plural, *freeway* not *freeways,* the definite article implying that what was in question was more an idea than a roadway. Seen from the air at night, the freeway is like a river, alive, sinuous, a reticulated glow of headlights tracing the huge contours of a city seventy miles square. Surface streets mark off grids of economy and class, but the freeway is totally egalitarian, a populist notion that makes Los Angeles comprehensible and complete. Alhambra and Silver Lake, Beverly Hills and Bell Gardens, each an exit, each available. "The point about this huge city," observed

Reyner Banham, "is that all its parts are equal and equally accessible from all other parts at once."

Driving the freeway induces a kind of narcosis. Speed is a virtue, and the speed of the place makes one obsessive, a gambler. The spirit is that of a city on the move, of people who have already moved here from somewhere else. Mobility is their common language; without it, or an appreciation of it, the visitor is an illiterate. The rear-view mirror reflects an instant city, its population trebled and retrebled in living memory. Its monuments are the artifacts of civil engineering, off-ramps and interchanges that sweep into concrete parabolas. There is no past, the city's hierarchy is jerry-built, there are few mistakes to repeat. The absence of past and structure is basic to the allure of Los Angeles. It deepens the sense of self-reliance, it fosters the idea of freedom, or at least the illusion of it. Freedom of movement most of all, freedom that liberates the dweller in this city from community chauvinism and neighborhood narcissism, allowing him to absorb the most lavish endowments his environment has to offer—sun and space.

The colonization of Los Angeles has reduced the concept of space to the level of jargon, to "my space" and "your space." Space is an idea. I do not think that anyone in the East truly understands the importance of this idea of space in the West. Fly west from the Atlantic seaboard, see the country open up below, there some lights, over there a town, on the horizon perhaps a city, in between massive, implacable emptiness. The importance of that emptiness is psychic. We have a sense out here, however specious, of being alone, of wanting, more importantly, to be left alone, of having our own space, a kingdom of self with a two-word motto: "Fuck Off." Fly east from the Pacific, conversely, and see the country as the Westerner sees it, urban sprawl mounting urban sprawl, a vast geographical gang-bang of incestuous blight, incestuous problems, incestuous ideas. People who vote Frank Rizzo and Abe Beame or Ed Koch into office have nothing to tell us. It is, of course, simple to say that both these views from the air are mirages, but even a mirage proceeds from some basic consciousness, some wish that seeks fulfillment. What, after all, is community? Space in the West, community in the East—these are the myths that sustain us.

WHEN I THINK of Los Angeles now, after almost a decade and a half of living not only in it but with it, I sometimes feel an astonishment, an attachment that approaches joy. I am attached to the way palm trees float and recede down empty avenues, attached to the deceptive perspectives of the pale subtropical light. I am attached to the drydocks of San Pedro, near where I used to live, and to the refineries of Torrance, which at night resemble an extraterrestrial space station. I am attached to the particular curve of coastline as one leaves the tunnel at the end of the Santa Monica Freeway to drive north on the Pacific Coast Highway. I am attached equally to the glories of the place and to its flaws, its faults, its occasional revelations of psychic and physical slippage, its beauties and its betrayals.

It is the end of the line.

It is the last stop.

Eureka!

I love it.

REGARDS

[1985]

IT WAS 1960, or maybe 1961, the winter, when I first became aware of Barry Farrell. I was a floater at *Time* magazine. A floater is a writer, usually a new young writer, who floats from section to section each issue, sitting in for the regular who is sick or on vacation. I was writing sports that week, and the lead piece in the section was going to be on a West Coast college basketball team, U.C. Berkeley, if memory serves. Now: I happen to detest basketball—bounce ball, Red Smith called it, an attitude that sums up my own—and I was looking forward to the assignment with low dread. The reporter on the piece was not even a staff correspondent but a stringer attached to *Time*'s San Francisco bureau, another cause for alarm. I waited all day Wednesday—filing day for the back of the book—for the file; nothing came in. Thursday A.M., still nothing. Thursday afternoon, nothing. I was in a rage. Then at dinnertime, the first take, More TK. I read; the fury abated. The file was—there is no other word for it—stylish. Not facts—six foot eleven, 19.7 ppg., 2.3 steals, 6.1 assists, that sort of thing—but an appreciation, a love of the game of basketball, a sense of its subtext and the fluid interplay of its personalities so lucidly explained that it almost made me rethink my own antipathy to the sport. There was nothing I had to do except trim to fit. The cable went into that week's magazine virtually as filed—and what a rarity that was at *Time*. I did not even know the name of the stringer until I hit the tag at the end of the file: "Regards, Farrell."

Regards, Farrell. Rarely have two words so perfectly summed up a single human being. Barry Farrell passed through life bestowing his regard as if it was a benediction, a kind of sanctifying grace. Of course he was hired by *Time* as a regular correspondent, and in due course he moved to New York as a staff writer for the magazine. It was there that we became friends, and we remained so until he died nearly twenty-five years later. Writers do not make easy friends of one another; they are professional carpers, too competitive, mean-spirited, and envious for the demands of lasting friendship. With only occasional lapses from grace, Barry and I were an exception to this rule.

How do you describe a friendship of a quarter of a century? You can't really. There is only a blur of images, shards of memory, and with each memory an angle of distortion, my psychic light meter adjusting differently than someone else's. Physical impressions first. He was tall and somewhat stooped, as if to compensate for his height, bearded, strawberry blond with jug ears, and the most extraordinary eyes, the eyes of someone who had seen too much, too many violations of the human contract. The first story he ever covered, as a young police reporter for the *Seattle Post-Intelligencer*, was a homosexual suicide, and then not so much a hanging as an accident, a homosexual who had strung himself up to increase the pleasure of onanism, and then had slipped during climax. Orgasm and strangulation, the ultimate death trip, and an exposed limp dick mocking the authorities who had to cut the body down: A few stories like that and the capacity for surprise is soon lost. I once told him he had the look of a Graham Greene priest; he had heard too much in confession, his pitch for evasion and deceit was too perfect. And yet always he was ready to absolve; it was not for him to cast the first stone.

Women loved him. He was that rare writer who looked the way a writer should look. I remember once seeing him standing at the elevator at *Time* wearing a trenchcoat and smoking a Gauloise (another wonderful affect, as was the occasional joint he would sometimes puff while in conference with the managing editor, confident in that innocent time that the editor would think it only some particularly noisome foreign tobacco he had picked up on his travels). He was on his way to France to romance a movie star. Forget that the movie star in question had romanced half the Western world; he was the first person I had ever known who had been in the feathers with an eminence of the silver screen. I envied his panache, and I wanted to cheer.

He was stylish, but there was so much substance beneath the style. Those eyes, the voice—Barry was that rare person who talked in complete sentences, every sentence perfectly parsed, plural predicates for plural subjects, no dangling participles, every clause modifying what it was supposed to modify, "that" never confused with "which"—people trusted him, they told him things they would never tell another reporter. Barry was a great chronicler of the city, any city. He liked cops and coroners and city hall bureaucrats, and to him they would confide the most appalling tales of municipal mendacity. The hostility between the homicide squads of the two police agencies in Los Angeles—the sheriff's office and the LAPD—was a situation made for him. He would imply to the LAPD homicide cops that the sheriffs thought they were no good, nothing more than traffic cops in polyester double knits, and then tell the sheriffs the LAPD thought they were firemen with police badges, with the result that both squads could not wait to tell him about the bone-headed screwups in the other's murder investigations.

Vietnam, the Middle East, Latin America—wherever Barry went, first for *Time,* then for *Life,* then on his own, his method was the same: never trust the official version, hang around, persevere, work the telephone, anticipate, and of course take advantage of, the unexpected. The spook he caught in a lie was a source of rare value—someone he then did not have to believe. He was a tenacious questioner, never deflected, following a kind of quiet Jesuitical logic, a holdover from the Catholicism he had long since abandoned, one that allowed him to illuminate dark corners. "Is Gary well hung?" he suddenly asked a jailhouse snitch about the stoolie's former cellmate, Gary Gilmore; it was a startling question, posed without judgment, perfectly evoking a world without women where any member, any orifice might offer opportunity for sexual release. Prison aristocracies intrigued him; "bum bandit" was the term he coined for a cell-block sexual imperialist, and he studied the bum bandits and the punks and all the subcategories in between with the eye of an anthropologist.

The cruelties of life did not pass him by. His two-year-old son was killed, electrocuted in a freak household accident, and his first marriage fell apart. His daughter Annie lived with her mother, adored and too rarely seen. Then marriage again, to Marcia, and after a time they adopted Joan, named after my wife. He left the warm embrace of the Time-Life Building and moved back to California and the freelancer's life. In retrospect, it was probably a mistake. Barry always had difficulty making deadlines—remember that first file he sent me—he needed some kind of corporate whiphand, and the possibility of a paycheck withheld. In the freelance world, his passion for perfection—the perfect word, the perfect image, the perfect example—led to pieces being a week late, then a month, two months, a year. He needed one more fact, there was someone in Reno, a whore in Salt Lake, a narc hiding out in Miami, this will nail it down, another trip was scheduled, another deadline postponed. Happiness was a motel on the Utah sand flats, interviewing Gary Gilmore on Death Row through a filter of lawyers; it was the obstacle that obsessed him, and the adrenaline and the ingenuity needed to overcome it, and if his Gilmore interviews only provided the subsoil out of which grew Norman Mailer's *The Executioner's Song*, what the hell, he would get back to his own work later, this was a moment in history not to be missed. Mailer had him pegged:

> Someone was always dying in his stories. Oscar Bonavena getting killed, Bobby Hall, young blond girls getting offed on highways in California. One cult slaying or another. He even had the reputation of being good at it. His telephone number leaped to the mind of various editors. Barry Farrell, crime reporter, with an inner life exasperatingly Catholic. Led his life out of his financial and emotional exigencies, took the jobs his bills and his battered psyche required

him to take, but somehow his assignments always took him into some great new moral complexity. Got into his writing like a haze.

Pure Norman, true Barry. I would give Barry the Philistine's argument: Finished is better than good. He did not listen, could not heed.

And yet. It was in this period that his best work was done. He and Marcia and Joan lived in a small house in Hollywood, and God, it was fun to go there for dinner. There were actors and NBA basketball players and writers and defendants and vice cops and lawyers and every kind of oddball—I remember one sweet old woman with a wooden leg who designed turn-on clothes for the hookers who worked the legal Nevada whorehouses, outfits with little heart-shaped openings framing the pubic symphysis—a little dope and a lot of booze. He was also teaching now, nonfiction writing, first at U.C. Santa Barbara, and then at colleges around Los Angeles, both to earn a little money and because he genuinely enjoyed it. He did not have students so much as disciples, acolytes who hung on his every word; he was E.T. as whiskey priest, bringing them communiqués from a world they could not believe existed.

Every morning, precisely at 9:15, he and I would talk on the telephone; a natter, he would call it. He had usually been up all night; he was always trying to find the best time to work, some schedule that would allow him to crack his writing block. In the background, I could hear the noises from the mean streets outside his Hollywood office, the wailing sirens and the voices of the dispossessed floating up through the open window. The New York and Los Angeles newspapers would be read by then, and with ribald shrewdness he would give me a close textual exegesis of the morning's news. I would often tell him I wished a tape-recording device could be implanted under his skin to record his conversation, those beautiful sentences, throwing out its tape at the end of the day. That, I said, would solve his writing block. His private life was becoming more untidy: he could not write and drank; he drank and could not write. He looked terrible. And then one day it happened—a minor automobile accident, a stroke, and a massive heart attack; none of the medical attendants on the scene knew which had occurred first.

For six months he lay semicomatose in a Veterans Administration hospital not five minutes from my house in Los Angeles. Finally he died. I cannot hear the telephone ring at 9:15 anymore without a frisson. It will not be Barry.

"He has an enthusiasm for tragedy," he once said about a noxious self-dramatizer who had done him harm; I had never heard anyone so effortlessly eviscerated; a simple declarative sentence in six perfectly chosen words; if only writing came so easy. So many times in the years since his death something has happened and he is the only person I wanted to call, the only one who would intuitively understand what was on my mind, what stuck in my throat. Perhaps that is how to define friendship. "Regards, Farrell." Regards, Barry. Regards, regards, and love.

"Lunch w/JE [my publisher]—showed her 1st 3–4 pp RWB." And thus began four years at the factory.

What civilians do not understand—and to a writer anyone not a writer is a civilian—is that writing is manual labor of the mind: a job, like laying pipe. Although I had not written a word, I had in fact thought a great deal about the novel I was meant to be writing over the course of the preceding year. I knew what the first sentence was going to be, and I also knew the last—it is a peculiarity of mine that I always know the last sentence of a book before I begin. That last sentence I intended to be a line of dialogue, either "No" or "Yes," with the penultimate line its reverse, either Yes or No, not in dialogue. It was the six or seven hundred pages between "When the trial began, we left the country" and "No" (or "Yes") that seemed a desert I could not irrigate.

I also knew the book would have a first-person narrator, largely because I had never used one before. The narrator I had in mind was the narrator of Ford Madox Ford's *The Good Soldier,* a commentator on events and actions, some not even witnessed, others at best only dimly understood, events and actions that in my case the narrator would have to reconstruct through letters and diaries and videotapes and secondhand accounts and Freedom of Information files and whatever else came to mind. "You'll be sorry," my wife, who is also a novelist, said when I told her my plan, and how right she was.

That summer of 1982 I did go to Central America, and I saw the possibilities for a section of the book I would not address for another three and a half years; my notes for the trip were twice as long as the section that eventually appeared in the manuscript. In September, I cleared away all other commitments and began concentrating on the book full-time. By the summer of 1983, I had completed 262 pages—and none of it seemed to work. Individual scenes played, but the narrative did not hold together. Narrative, I should explain, is not plot. Plot is "The queen died, the king died"; narrative is "The queen died, the king died of a broken heart." (I would like to claim that definition as my own, but it is a loose translation of E. M. Forster by way of Vladimir Nabokov.) Because one has written other books does not mean the next becomes any easier. Each book in fact is a tabula rasa; from book to book I seem to forget how to get characters in and out of rooms—a far more difficult task than the non-writer might think. Still I went to my office every day. That is the difference between the professional and the amateur. The professional guts a book through this period, in full knowledge that what he is doing is not very good. Not to work is to exhibit a failure of nerve, and a failure of nerve is the best definition I know for writer's block.

In August 1983, I put the manuscript aside and traveled to France and England, armed with my tattered copy of *The Good Soldier,* which by then went everywhere with me, not so much a book to read as a talisman to hold and touch. I was also accompanied by a photocopy of an interview Philip Roth had given *The New York Times* in 1977. "My own way," Roth had said, "seems to be to write six months of trash—heterosexual trash usually—and then to give up in despair, filing away a hundred pages or so that I can't stand, to find ten pages or so that are actually alive." The despair of another writer is enormously reassuring to one who thinks his own despair is unique.

Back home, I started all over again on page 1, circling the 262 pages like a vulture looking for live flesh to scavenge. I knew the problem. The narrative was too constricted; it was like a fetus strangling on its own umbilical cord. The time span of the book was eighteen years, ranging from California to Vietnam to Central America, from the radical politics of the 1960s to Hollywood in the '80s, and I knew I was moving uneasily among these venues. Knowing the problem, however, is not the same as solving it. The second draft, which I began in euphoria in the fall of 1983, I abandoned seventy-two pages later, again on the outskirts of despair.

I was now in 1984, having worked steadily for nearly two years with almost nothing to show for it except a file box full of pages with typing on them. To clear my head I wrote a long piece for *The New York Review of Books* about a septuagenarian former Hollywood Communist who had come out of the closet of his past, as it were, disguised as a prizewinning young Mexican novelist. I also needed money if I was ever going to finish this damn book, and I agreed to write the screen adaptation of Norman Mailer's novel *The Deer Park.* The fee was simply too high to pass up, and even with taxes and the commissions of agents, lawyer, and accountants deducted, my wife and I would have enough to keep us for approximately another two years.

Death had also intervened. "When the trial began, we left the country," I had written that spring of 1982. Five months later my niece was murdered, and when her killer came to trial in Los Angeles the following summer, my wife and I indeed did leave the country. "I do not understand people who attend the trials of those accused of murdering their loved ones," I had continued in those three or four pages I had shown my publisher at The Four Seasons half a year before any of this happened. "You see them on the local newscasts . . . I watch them kiss the prosecutor when the guilty verdict is brought in or scream at those jurors who were not convinced that the pimply-faced defendant was the buggerer of Jimmy and the dismemberer of Johnny." I wondered for several years if I should retain those lines in the final manuscript, should I ever complete it; in a slightly altered version I did. There, with all its emotional baggage, was the obscenity of coincidence.

On New Year's Day 1985, I began *The Red White and Blue* for the third time. This time it went well from the start. The two failed previous drafts yielded nuggets I had not been able to find before. Those first three or four pages I had written in the spring of 1982 became, in the spring of 1986, the last five pages of a 700-page novel; pages 44–46 in the second draft became pages 304–307 in the third. Slowly the book began to open up. In a churchyard in the Cotswolds, I found the name of a nineteenth-century churchwarden, Bentley Innocent; I immediately gave his surname to a character of my own. On that same trip, the English novelist Bruce Chatwin told me about a *papeterie* on Rue de l'Ancienne Comédie in Paris that was the only place left in the city that sold the notebooks he and I both favored; I set a scene there. In the papers of a dead friend whose literary executor I had become, I found an instruction sheet from the Nevada Department of Prisons on how to operate "a lethal gas chamber" for an execution and how to clean it when the job was completed. ("After each execution, sinks, plugs, pot and entire inside of cabinet should be washed down with warm water and a detergent. Add 2 ounces of agua ammonia to each gallon of water. . . .") Here was a perfect example of bureaucracy gone mad; it went into the manuscript. "Let's get the cows to Abilene," the producer of *The Deer Park* had said when the delivery of the screenplay was delayed; into the manuscript.

I devised stratagems and inside jokes to relieve the clock-punching tedium of a book that was building by only a page or a page and a half a day. I named someone after a character in one of my wife's earlier novels; a corpse received a name I have now used in four books. Because I believe scores are made to be settled, I settled a couple of scores in a way that only the person against whom the score was being settled would ever recognize, if indeed that person ever read the book. In my last novel, I had some gratuitous sport with Peter Jennings, the ABC anchorman, and when a friend of his asked how I could be beastly about someone I did not know, I replied, "Never be rude to a stranger, because the stranger may turn out to be a novelist with a long memory."

January 5, 1986, the first Monday of the new year: I now had 493 pages of *The Red White and Blue* completed. In the next three months, I worked seven days a week, taking only one day off during that entire stretch, seldom going out at night. This was the magic time that made up for the previous three and a half years of toil and anxiety and suicidal depression. It is like a dream sexual experience. Everything seems to work; the chance encounter, the overheard remark in a restaurant feed into the next day's material, opening up possibilities you had never considered. In three months I wrote 230 pages; in the last two weeks alone, ninety-two. On Sunday, April 6, at 2:19 in the afternoon, I wrote the last sentence: "No."

The book took two months short of four years to write, with another year spent taking notes and thinking about it. In the course of those four years, this is what I also did: I wrote three pieces for *The New York Review of Books* and a second screenplay, an adaptation of Carlos Fuentes' *The Old Gringo,* a meditation by Carlos (a good friend) on what happened to Ambrose Bierce when he went down to Mexico to die. The screenplay, without me, is in another stage of development, but from a biography of Bierce I would not otherwise have read I did get the book's epigraph: "History is an account, mostly false, of events, mostly unimportant, which are brought about by rulers, mostly knaves, and soldiers, mostly fools." Other than these interruptions, only the book. Four years, 1,400 days, 710 pages; prorated, it amounts to half a page, 125 words, a day. Put that way, not much to show for four years. But that is the writer's life. You write. You finish. You start over again.

CODA

THE PARIS REVIEW
INTERVIEW

[SPRING 1996]

THE FIFTH OF six children, John Gregory Dunne, the son of a prominent surgeon, was born in Hartford, Connecticut in 1932. He went to school at Portsmouth Priory (now Abbey) and on graduation moved on to Princeton, graduating from there in 1954. To please his mother he applied to the Stanford Business School, but changed his mind (if not hers) and instead volunteered for the draft. He served for two years in the army as an enlisted man, his overseas service spent with a gun battery in Germany. He speaks of his years at the Priory (where the monks were "very worldly") and in the army as being far more valuable than his time at Princeton. "In the army I was exposed to people I would not otherwise have known. I learned something about life."

Back in the States after his service, Dunne worked briefly in an ad agency (he was fired), then with the magazine *Industrial Design*. In 1959 he went to *Time* magazine and worked there until 1964, the year he married the author Joan Didion. Since devoting himself to his own work, Dunne has written a number of novels, including *The Red White and Blue, True Confessions, Dutch Shea, Jr., Vegas* and *Playland* and two nonfiction books, *Harp* and *The Studio*. He and Didion together have written over twenty screenplays, seven of which have reached the screen, including *The Panic in Needle Park, Play It*

As It Lays, A Star Is Born, True Confessions, Hills Like White Elephants, Broken Trust and, most recently, *Up Close & Personal*.

At present the couple lives in a large sunny apartment on New York's Upper East Side. One is struck by how neat and ordered everything is—no sense of confusion, files in neat piles. The floors throughout the apartment are bare, polished. The considerable library is in order: the fiction titles only fill the shelves of the master bedroom.

Both have workrooms. When the pair works on a screenplay, each does a separate draft, and then the two meet, sitting opposite each other at the desk in John's workplace where they thrash out successive drafts. Here too are mementos of their work together. Photographs taken on the set of various movies. A large police map of the streets of Los Angeles covers one wall. Authentic, it was used on the set of *True Confessions*—little black dots across its surface where crime-scene pins were once struck. On the opposite wall, a more serene scene: a blown-up photograph of Joan Didion, standing in the shallows of a quiet sea and holding a pair of sandals. Many photographs are of their daughter, Quintana Roo (named after a state in Mexico), now the photo editor at *Elle Decor* magazine. A recent addition in the workroom is a photograph of Quintana and Robert Redford, the costar, with Michelle Pfeiffer, of the newly released *Up Close & Personal*.

The interview that follows is a composite—partly conducted at the YMHA before a packed audience, partly at the Dunnes' home on the East Side, with a written portion about the novel *Playland*, added by the author himself.

INTERVIEWER

Your work is populated with the most extraordinary grotesqueries—nutty nuns, midgets, whores of the most breathtaking abilities and appetites. Do you know all these characters?

JOHN GREGORY DUNNE

Certainly I knew the nuns. You couldn't go to a parochial school in the 1940s and not know them. They were like concentration-camp guards. They all seemed to have rulers, and they hit you across the knuckles with them. The joke at St. Joseph's Cathedral School in Hartford, Connecticut, where I grew up, was that the nuns would hit you until you bled, and then hit you for bleeding. Having said that, I should also say they were great teachers. As a matter of fact, the best of my formal education came from the nuns at St. Joseph's and from the monks at Portsmouth Priory, a Benedictine boarding school in Rhode Island where I spent my junior and senior years of high school. The nuns taught me basic reading, writing and arithmetic; the monks taught me how to think, how to question, even to question Catholicism in order to better understand it. The nuns and the monks were far more valuable to me than my four years at Princeton. I'm not a practicing Catholic, but one thing you never lose from a Catholic education is a sense of sin, and the conviction that the taint on the human condition is the natural order.

INTERVIEWER

What about the whores and midgets?

DUNNE

I suppose for that I would have to go to my informal education. I spent two years as an enlisted man in the army in Germany after the Korean War, and those two years were the most important learning experience I really ever had. I was just a tight-assed upper-middle-class kid, the son of a surgeon, and I had this sense of Ivy League entitlement, and all that was knocked out of me in the army. Princeton boys didn't meet the white and black underclass that you meet as an enlisted draftee. It was a constituency of the dispossessed—high-school dropouts, petty criminals, rednecks, racists, gamblers, you name it, and I fit right in. I grew to hate the officer class that was my natural constituency. A Princeton classmate was an officer on my post, and he told me I was to salute him and call him sir, as if I had to be reminded, and also that he would discourage any outward signs that we knew each other. I hate that son of a bitch to this day. I took care of him in *Harp*. Those two years in Germany gave me a subject I suppose I've been mining for the past God knows how many years. It fit nicely with that Catholic sense of sin, the taint on the human condition. And it was in the army that I learned to appreciate whores. You didn't meet many Vassar girls when you were serving in a gun battery on the Czech border and were in a constant state of alert in case the Red Army came rolling across the frontier. As for midgets, they're part of that constituency of the dispossessed.

INTERVIEWER

You once said you only had one character. Is that true?

DUNNE

I've always thought a novelist only has one character, and that is himself or herself. In my case, me. So at the risk of being glib, I am the priest in *True Confessions* and the criminal lawyer in *Dutch Shea, Jr.* I've certainly never been a cop or a priest or a pimp lawyer, but these protagonists are in a sense my mouthpieces. I like to learn about their professions, which is why I so much like doing nonfiction. I'm a great believer in the novelist being "on the scene," reporting, traveling, meeting all sorts of people. You do nonfiction, you get to meet people you would not normally meet. I'm not a bad mimic, and I can pick up speech cadences that I would not pick up if I didn't hit the road.

INTERVIEWER

Do you think novels have a life of their own?

DUNNE

Before I began writing fiction, I thought that was nonsense. Then I learned otherwise. Let me give you an example. In *The Red White and Blue,* I started off thinking the protagonist would be the Benedictine priest, Bro Broderick. I realized rather quickly that he could not be, but that I was stuck with him as a character. He never really came to life until I finished the book, and went back and inserted his diary, which he had left in his will to the Widener Library at Harvard. Then for three hundred pages or so, I thought the leading character was the radical lawyer Leah Kaye, because whenever she appeared on the scene the book took off. Then when

I got to page five hundred of this seven-hundred-fifty-page manuscript, I realized *she* couldn't be the leading character because she had not appeared in over two hundred pages. It was only then that I realized that the narrator, who was the only survivor of the three major protagonists, would have to be the leading character. So novels *do* take charge of the writer, and the writer is basically a kind of sheepdog, just trying to keep things on track.

INTERVIEWER

Can you say something about the germination of a book?

DUNNE

I think any time a writer tells you where a book starts, he is lying, because I don't think he knows. You don't start off saying, "I'm going to write this grand saga about the human condition." It's a form of accretion. When my wife and I were in Indonesia in 1980 or 1981, we ran into this man who had been a University of Maryland extension teacher during the Vietnam War. He was stationed at Cam Ranh Bay. These GIs would go off in the morning in their choppers, and when they'd come back at night—if they were lucky—he would teach them remedial English. I made a note of it in my notebook, putting it away, because I knew this was a really great way to look at the Vietnam War, and it turned up in *The Red White and Blue.* When I am between books, I am an inveterate note taker. I jot things down mainly because they give me a buzz. I like to go to the library and take a month's newspaper, say August, 1962, and read through it. You can find great stuff in those little filler sections at the bottom of a page. Then, when it comes time to start writing a book, I sort of look through the stuff and see if any of it works. I also write down names. If you have a name, it can set someone in place. I have a great friend in California, the Irish novelist Brian Moore. We were having dinner one night, and Brian said that when he was a newspaperman in Montreal, a local character there was named Shake-Hands McCarthy. I said, "Stop! Are you ever going to use that name?" He said, "No, let me tell you about him." I said, "No, I don't want to know anything about him. I just want to use that name." So the name turned up in *True Confessions.* When

I heard the name I had no idea when I was going to use it if, indeed, *ever.* But it was a name that absolutely set a character in cement. We had dinner with Joyce Carol Oates at Princeton once; she was saying that she does the same thing, that she collects those little fillers; she never knows when she's going to use them. She just throws them in a file, and oddly enough, they do stick.

To get back to your question, *Vegas* is the one book for which I can actually pinpoint the moment when it started. I was trying to think of an idea, doodling at my desk while I was talking to my wife, and I drew a heart, then a square around the heart. I found I had written five letters: *V-E-G-A-S.* So, I not only had a subject, but I had a title.

INTERVIEWER

Why is the title of *Vegas* reinforced by the description "a fiction"?

DUNNE

Because I had a contract for a nonfiction book. I always thought of *Vegas* as a novel, but Random House said, "It doesn't read like a novel," and I said, "A novel is anything the writer says the book is, and since I made most of it up, it can't be nonfiction." So we ended up calling it a fiction. A lot of it is true. The prostitute did write poetry, although the poetry I used in *Vegas* is not hers. It was actually written by my wife, who as a child had memorized a lot of Sara Teasdale poems. "I can write you bad poetry," she said. So there are two little poems in there that Joan actually wrote.

INTERVIEWER

What is your state of mind when you are writing?

DUNNE

Essentially, writing is a sort of manual labor of the mind. It is a hard job, but there comes a moment in every book, I suppose, when you know you're going to finish, and then it becomes a kind of bliss, almost a sexual bliss. I once read something Graham Greene said about this feeling. The metaphor he used was a plane going down a runway and then, ultimately, leaving the ground.

Occasionally, he had books that he felt never did leave the runway; one of them was *The Honorary Consul,* though in retrospect he realized that it was one of his better books.

INTERVIEWER

How much do you know about the end of a book?

DUNNE

When I did *Dutch Shea, Jr.,* I knew the last line was going to be, "I believe in God."

INTERVIEWER

Why did you pick that line?

DUNNE

Because that's the line the man would say as he kills himself. I wanted that most despairing of acts to end with the simple declarative sentence, "I believe in God." In *The Red White and Blue* I knew the last line was going to be either "Yes" or "No," in dialogue, and the penultimate line was going to be "Yes" or "No" not in dialogue. The first line of *Vegas* is, "In the summer of my nervous breakdown, I went to live in Las Vegas, Clark County, Nevada." I knew that the last line of that book would be, "And in the fall, I went home." I don't think it's necessary to have a last line; I just like to know where in general I'm going. I have a terrible time plotting. I only plot about thirty pages in front of where I am. I once had dinner with Ross MacDonald, who did the Lew Archer novels about a California private detective. He said he spent eighteen months actually plotting out a book—every single nuance. Then, he sat down and wrote the book in one shot from beginning to end . . . six months to write the book and eighteen to plot it out. If you've ever read one of those books, it's so intricately plotted it's like a watch, a very expensive watch.

INTERVIEWER

You have said that you have a lot of trouble with plotting a book. What makes it move forward?

DUNNE

I have no grand plan of what I'm going to do. I had no idea who killed the girl in *True Confessions* until the day I wrote it. I knew it would be someone who was not relevant to the story. I had always planned that. But who the actual killer was, I simply had no idea. Years before, I had clipped something from the *Los Angeles Times* in the small death notices. It was the death of a barber. I had put that up on my bulletin board. I was figuring out, "Now who . . . ," getting to the moment when I had to reveal who killed this girl, with not the foggiest idea who did it, and my eyes glommed onto this death notice of a barber. I said, "Oops, you're it." One must have enormous confidence to wait to figure these things out until the time comes.

INTERVIEWER

Do you have great affection for your characters?

DUNNE

You have to have affection for them, because you can't live with them for two years or three years without liking them. But I have no trouble killing them off.

INTERVIEWER

Is there a considerable shifting of gears in moving between non-fiction and fiction?

DUNNE

There's a technical difference. I find that the sentences are more ornate and elaborate in nonfiction, because you don't have dialogue to get you on your way. Nonfiction has its ruffles and flourishes, clauses and semicolons. I never use a semicolon in fiction.

INTERVIEWER

Your latest novel is *Playland.* The background is the movie business.

DUNNE

I lived in Los Angeles and worked in the movie business from the mid-1960s until the late 1980s, but except on the fringes, in *The*

Red White and Blue, I had never written about Hollywood and the picture business in fiction. It was like an eight-hundred-pound gorilla. Sooner or later I was going to have to deal with it.

INTERVIEWER

Why did you set the Hollywood part of your novel largely in the 1940s rather than in the period you were working there?

DUNNE

Because I don't think contemporary Hollywood is terribly interesting, and because I don't want any sense of a roman à clef (is your so-and-so really so-and-so?). Mostly I wanted to reconstruct an era from a distance, an era that I kept on getting tantalizing glimpses of from people I knew or worked with who had been there in the 1940s, and had not just been there but had been at the top of the heap.

INTERVIEWER

For example?

DUNNE

Otto Preminger. Joan and I once did a screenplay for him. He was an immensely cultivated man, but he was a tyrant with a volcanic temper. When he lost his temper, the top of his head—he shaved it with an electric razor sometimes during story meetings—would turn beet red. He screamed at most people who worked for him, but never at us; he just got elaborately polite, and he would refer to Joan as "Mrs. Dunne," drawing it out for half a dozen sibilant syllables. He brought us back to New York to work on the script. He said it would only take three weeks tops, but three months later we were still there . . . in this tiny apartment on Fifth Avenue, with our four-year-old daughter and a different babysitter every day. Our daughter called Otto, to his face, "Mr. Preminger with no hair," which he took with good grace. We finally said we were going home for Christmas and we would finish the script there, and Otto said, "I forbid you to go." It was an extraordinary thing to say. We thought he was kidding, but that was the way the studios had always operated and he saw nothing wrong with it. We went back to L.A. anyway, and he threatened to sue us for $2 million. He simply could not understand our lack of deference. It worked out. He paid off our contract at forty cents on the dollar. It was the kind of punishment the old studio system would have exacted. But we always stopped by to see him when we came to New York, because if you were not working for him, he was a charming man.

INTERVIEWER
Who else?

DUNNE
Billy Wilder. In the mid-eighties, he asked me to do a screenplay with him for an idea he had, about a silent movie star playing Christ in a biblical epic. The twist was that the movie star was a dissolute drunk who was screwing everybody on the set, including the actress playing the Virgin Mary, while the actress playing Mary Magdalene spurned him, another twist. Billy wanted him to repent at the end of the picture, and actually walk on water—a gag he would set up throughout the picture, and then pay off at fade-out. Nothing came of the idea, but we had some funny meetings, because Billy has perfect pitch for truly hilarious bad taste. This was a man who won seven Oscars, and he kept them in a closet at his nondescript office on Santa Monica Boulevard. He usually worked with Izzy Diamond, but Izzy was dying or had just died, and Billy always wrote with a collaborator, which is why he had asked me to work with him. Raymond Chandler had worked with him on the script for *Double Indemnity*, and they had detested each other, but they wrote a great screenplay together, which proves you don't always have to like the people you work with. I would ask him about the days of the red scare and the blacklist, and he had this interesting take, which was that no one very good actually joined the Communist party, it only attracted the second-raters. Of course Billy had the most famous line about the Hollywood Ten (or the Unfriendly Ten as they were called) when they had to testify before the House Un-American Activities Committee. Only two of them were talented, he said, the other eight were only unfriendly. We never wrote the script. I had to finish *The Red White and Blue,* and the time did not work out.

INTERVIEWER

Did you work with George Cukor?

DUNNE

I knew George, but never worked with him. We were at a dinner party one night at Peter Feibleman's house. Lillian Hellman was the hostess, and the guests were George, Olivia De Havilland, Willie and Tally Wyler, and then a younger generation——Peter, Mike and Anabel Nichols, Warren Beatty and Julie Christie, Joan and I. We were very much made to feel that we were at the children's table, there to be seen but not heard. George and Willie and Lillian were all to die in the next few years, and it was as if they knew this was the last time they would see each other, and they wanted to settle a lot of old scores. And boy, did they! The interesting thing was that they all liked the old studio system, and the monsters like Harry Cohn and Sam Goldwyn. At one point in the evening, I made the mistake of asking George about Howard Hawks, my own personal favorite of the old time directors, and he rose up and said, "I despise Mr. Hawks, and I loathe his pictures." Betty Bacall once told me Hawks was a famous anti-Semite; he would talk to her about Yids, not knowing that her real name was Perske, and he wasn't supposed to like gays much either, so needless to say George had no use for him. He'd talk about Garbo and Kate Hepburn, both of whom would stay with him at his house in the Hollywood Hills when they came to L.A. I remember once going to a party at his house. He wasn't giving it, I don't think he was even there; he had just lent this perfect little jewel of a house to a studio for a press party for some out-of-town distributors. The studio——it was Fox——had dressed the pool area and put up a tent. At the end of the evening, I went to get my car, and as I was waiting for the parking boy, I picked a lemon off a potted tree by the entrance to the house. When I looked at it, I saw that it had been stamped with the word *Sunkist*. What the studio had done was wire lemons to the trees. That's what studios did. They tried to control everything, even the environment.

INTERVIEWER

Blue Tyler's character in *Playland* seems to have elements of Natalie Wood. Did you know her?

DUNNE

Not when she was a child star. When we first got to California, she was just beginning to cross over from a child actress to a grown-up movie star. She had never really been a child star in the sense that Shirley Temple was a star, able to carry a picture all by herself (the way Macaulay Culkin can today), but the transition from child actress to woman movie star was one that only Elizabeth Taylor had made successfully. Margaret O'Brien hadn't made it, and neither really had Shirley Temple. Only Taylor, and now Natalie. About this time, there was a huge eight- or ten-page photo spread on her in *Life* magazine. I remember one of the pictures especially, of Natalie in the conference room at the William Morris Agency, sitting at this enormous conference table, this tiny slip of a young woman, surrounded by her retainers—her agent, Abe Lastfogel, who was the head of the Morris office, her public-relations people and her accountants, all of these middle-aged men focused on managing the career of this twenty-one-year-old child. We met her a few years later. She was an extraordinarily generous woman. She paid for a shrink for her assistant, a young man named Mart Crowley, who wrote *The Boys in the Band*. Mart was a friend of ours, and through him we became acquainted with Natalie and her husband, Richard Gregson, and then later with R.J. (Robert Wagner, called R.J., who was Natalie's first and third husband), when they remarried. I asked her once what it was like being a child star, and she said, "They take care of you," *they* being the studio. One thing I remember about Natalie was how astute she was about the business of Hollywood, about her own worth and the worth of everyone else. She understood money and investment the way a French bourgeoise does. And like most people in Hollywood, she was a fantastic gossip, knew everything, where all the bodies were buried, and under how much dirt.

INTERVIEWER

How much of this material made its way into *Playland*?

DUNNE

Specifically only two things really—the photo of Natalie Wood in *Life* at the conference table in the William Morris office, and then Natalie saying that the studio took care of her. This is not to suggest that she was the model for Blue Tyler, because Blue was sui generis, and when I got to know Natalie, she was a twice-married young mother. But with all these people, Otto and Billy and George and Natalie, there was the sense of the studio controlling their lives, their destinies in every aspect, and the concomitant sense that however the studio's subjects—the actors, directors, producers and writers under contract—might have bridled under the idea that the studio knew best, they did not ever really rebel. There is a line in *Playland* when Arthur French says, rather sadly about some lie the studio put out, "People believed studios in those days." What he meant of course was that people were so trusting they even believed the untruths, as they were supposed to. That period, the late 1940s, was the last time that the studios exercised total control and had real power. Television was just a dark cloud on the horizon, and the government had not yet forced the studios to divest themselves of their theater chains. A studio's power was so absolute in those days that it simply would not have permitted a contract star of the caliber of Julia Roberts, say, to marry someone like Lyle Lovett, a funny-looking below-the-title singer.

INTERVIEWER

So, you set out wanting to do a novel about Hollywood in this period?

DUNNE

Actually, no. I started out to do a novel about Blue Tyler's daughter. I thought of her as a contemporary Sister Carrie, but I couldn't make the book work. Then Joan and I were asked to write a screenplay about Bugsy Siegel, which we turned down. But there was something about the idea that intrigued me, and I suggested a story about a New York gangster who comes to Hollywood and falls in love with Shirley Temple. Not Shirley Temple herself, God knows, but a major child star, seventeen years old, trying to cross over into grown-up roles, with the vocabulary of a longshoreman and the morals of a mink. We wrote the screenplay, but it fell between the cracks when the studio we wrote it for was acquired by another studio, which in Hollywood is the kiss of death for projects initiated by the acquired studio. The executives at the new place are scared enough of getting burned by their own projects without having to take the fall for failed projects from another studio. They go out of their way to bad-rap the other studio's projects. Much of the interplay between the loathsome director Sydney Allen and my narrator Jack Broderick is a direct result of this experience, although I had no idea at the time that I was going to make use of it. Then I lost a year to medicine. First I had open heart surgery, and just as I was recovering from that, I got blood poisoning.

INTERVIEWER

And it was during that year's hiatus that *Playland* took shape? Or another shape?

DUNNE

Yes. I rethought it. I had this murder book I had acquired while doing another picture, the film of my novel *True Confessions,* which had a crucial scene in a morgue. Now I had never been to a morgue, and so one night at two o'clock in the morning, the director Ulu Grosbard and I were taken inside the morgue, absolutely against regulations, by a homicide detective. We saw the cold room, where the corpses are kept, and we saw autopsies being performed, and the decomp room, where decomposing bodies are stored—the most God-awful smell, I had to smoke a cigar to get past it. It was quite an experience. Afterward, the homicide cop let us look through old murder files. There was an implicit quid pro quo attached: he wanted to be a technical advisor on *True Confessions* and if we saw something else that hit our fancy, money would change hands. It was on this expedition that I read the murder book of an unsolved 1944 murder. The "murder book" is what cops call the history of an investigation, containing police reports, forensic photographs, autopsies, the questioning of witnesses and suspects, correspondence, updates, all the way to the final disposition of the case, in some instances the gas chamber.

The book in this case was still open, as are all unsolved murders. Several things attracted me to it. First was that the victim, who was only seventeen, had gone to the same school my daughter was attending. Second, the apartment building where she lived was one I knew well: it was the home of friends of ours. And third, Shirley Temple was a schoolmate of the victim—her telephone number was in the victim's address book—this was ten years before I even began thinking of writing a novel about a former child star. There was also a riveting forensic photo of the battered and naked girl on a gurney in the morgue. Someone had placed a doily over her pubic area; it was an absurd daintiness considering the circumstances of her death, and the ravages of the assault visible on the rest of her body. The cop said I could have the book for twenty-four hours, so I took it, got it photocopied and the forensic pictures photocopied. It was back in the file the next evening. I suppose one might call the entire endeavor an example of off-the-books free enterprise.

INTERVIEWER

And this is the murder that appears in the book?

DUNNE

Considerably rewritten to accommodate the narrative. I had the file for years, and didn't know what to do with it. I was not interested in it by itself as a discrete literary endeavor, and I did not know how to fit it in anyplace else. What intrigued me mostly were the loops and turns of a criminal investigation, the number of tangential lives it happened to touch, and how in the course of the detective work a mosaic of petty treasons, moral misdemeanors and quiet desperation emerged that had nothing to do with the murder in question, but only with permutations of life itself.

INTERVIEWER

Again, it's interesting how much of the book is based on fact.

DUNNE

Fact is like clay. You shape it to your own ends. For example, I wanted a namer of names before the House Un-American Activities

Committee who was a sympathetic, and unrepentant, character. So I invented Chuckie O'Hara. Gay. A director. An admitted communist before HUAC. But then a wounded war hero in World War II. And finally someone who purged himself by naming names, and then lived out the rest of his days without guilt. It is about Chuckie, at his funeral, that I wrote: "Whatever his transgression, in the end he was one of them. Membership in the closed society of the motion picture industry is almost never revoked for moral failings." That is a coda for Hollywood even unto the present day.

INTERVIEWER

So *Playland* is about this closed society?

DUNNE

I suppose so, yes. Among other things. Like, what is truth? Because no one in the book ever really tells the truth. Half-truth is the coin of the Hollywood realm.

INTERVIEWER

Whatever happened to Blue Tyler's daughter, the one you originally thought the book was about?

DUNNE

She appears for the first time on *Playland*'s last page.

INTERVIEWER

To go back a bit, you started off writing for *Time* magazine. Was that helpful? Why did you leave?

DUNNE

It had to do with *Time*'s coverage of the Vietnam War. The *Time* bureau chief, who was doing the war out of Hong Kong before he moved to Saigon, was a guy called Charlie Mohr. Charlie was one of the first to say this war isn't going to fly. He was by no means a liberal; he just saw it on the basis of his reporting. One week we did a wrap-up on the war, and Charlie sent in a file, the first sentence of which was "The war in Vietnam is being lost." It was a Friday night, and I said to myself, "Uh oh, this is never going into the magazine." I had dinner with Joan, and I said, "I think I'm going to call in sick." She said, "No, you've got to go back and do it." So I went back and did the story based on the file, trying to put in the qualifiers that would get past Otto Fuerbringer, and went home around three in the morning. The next morning the edited copy was on my desk, and on the top it said, "Nice. F." It was the complete opposite of what Charlie's file was and what I had written. Redone from top to bottom. Charlie quit and eventually went to *The New York Times.* I said I no longer wished to do Vietnam. I ended up doing Lichtenstein, the Common Market, realizing that my days there were numbered. Joan and I got married in January. In April I said, "Do you mind if I quit?" And that was it. However, I liked *Time.* It taught me how to meet a deadline, to write fast. It's wonderful training. Writing for *Time* is like writing for the movies: ultimately, what you write is not yours, because you're not in charge of what you're doing.

INTERVIEWER

Joan worked for the Luce people for a while, didn't she?

DUNNE

For *Life.* She had published her first novel *Run River* and then the essays in *Slouching Toward Bethlehem*, and was about to publish *Play It As It Lays*, when she got the offer to do a column for *Life.* I said, "Don't do it. It'll be like being nibbled to death by ducks." She lasted less than a year. It was about that time we got asked to do our first movie, so everything worked out.

INTERVIEWER

Had you thought of writing for the screen?

DUNNE

As a matter of fact I started a novel about Hollywood when working for this industrial design magazine after coming out of the army. I knew nothing about Hollywood and had never been there. It was called *Not the Macedonian*, and the first line was "They called him

Alexander the Great." That's as far as I ever got. I used to write a lot of first lines of novels; the second line was the problem.

INTERVIEWER

How did you come to be asked to do a screenplay?

DUNNE

A wonderful man named Collier Young . . . he was Virginian, I think, and had married four times. Wives two and three were Ida Lupino and Joan Fontaine. He lived up on Mulholland Drive in a place he called the Mouse House. One year his Christmas card said, "Christmas greetings from the Mouse House, former home of Ida Lupino and Joan Fontaine." He was the creator of the television series with the detective, Raymond Burr in the wheelchair. He got fired three segments into it, but he still got paid every week because it was his idea. In 1967, the same year that South African doctor, Christiaan Barnard, did the first heart transplant, Collie came to us and said, "I think there's a movie here." We worked out a story in which a Howard Hughes character, Hollis Todd, needs a heart, and his underlings kill a former Olympic athlete who had become a paraplegic after an automobile accident, and transplant his heart into Todd. All the main characters had last names for first names, I suppose because Collie's name was Collier Young. To our amazement, it sold to some studio, I think it was CBS, which paid us $50,000. I thought I'd died and gone to heaven. The picture was never made, though the screenplay was novelized and called *The Todd Dossier.* The man who wrote the novelization basically took our treatment and just added onto it. That book is still in print. It's sold in seventeen foreign languages.

INTERVIEWER

So you were on your way?

DUNNE

That got us into the Writers Guild and once you are in the Guild you can work. The first screenplay we wrote that was produced was *The Panic in Needle Park.* My brother Dominick Dunne took it to

various and sundry places, and it was finally bought by Joe Levine.
We were told you had to sell to Joe Levine with one line. The one
line that sold it to Joe was: "Romeo and Juliet on junk."

INTERVIEWER

How do you and Joan work when you're doing a screenplay?

DUNNE

With *The Panic in Needle Park* I wrote the first draft in about
eighteen days. Joan was finishing up her novel *Play It As It Lays*.
When I finished she went over the draft and did her version. Then
we sat down and put together the version we handed in. It's generally worked that way with every script we've done. The version
the studio sees is essentially our third draft. A movie is so much
more schematic than a book: you only have 120 pages, because the
rule of thumb is one page equals one minute of screen time, and
movies shouldn't be over two hours long.

INTERVIEWER

Why in writing for the screen is a film rarely done without collaboration?

DUNNE

I'm not sure that's so. Bob Towne works by himself. So does Alvin
Sargent. Bill Goldman. Larry Gelbart. But I cannot imagine doing
a screenplay by myself because so much of it is talking it out first,
so you know where the high points are. With a book you can often
do riffs, which you can't really do in a movie, unless you're a writer-
director. We have never wanted to direct pictures. By the time we
wrote our first screenplay, we had written maybe five books between
us, which was what we wanted to do because we were our own
bosses: with a book you are the writer, director, editor, cameraman.
But I can say without equivocation that the movies have supported
us for the past twenty-six years. We've written twenty-three books
between us, and movies financed nineteen out of the twenty-three.
And we like doing it.

INTERVIEWER

Why is it that it's looked upon with such detestation by people who consider themselves serious novelists and who have gone out there to make the money? Do you think they've actually had quite a good time and just don't want to admit it?

DUNNE

Yes, I do. I've never believed in Hollywood the Destroyer. The naysayers are people who would have been destroyed at Zabar's if they never went west of the Hudson. I simply never believed it. Faulkner wasn't destroyed. Hemingway wasn't. O'Hara wasn't.

INTERVIEWER

Have you worked at doctoring other people's scripts? Is it worth it?

DUNNE

Yes. Six figures a week, if you're any good, hundred grand at the minimum. We've all done it. For a long time, I couldn't understand why they paid so much. If you get a six-figure weekly fee, you think it's more money than there is in the world. The studio, however, is looking at a 40-million-dollar picture, and if it doesn't get done, they are out all that money. So they will throw in writers at a hundred and fifty grand a week to put in jokes, put in scenes just to get the picture on . . . they *always* answer with money. The worst thing that can happen is that the project gets flushed, because then they lose all the money spent for development, which can add up to millions of dollars.

INTERVIEWER

Can you give a few examples of screenwriting at its best?

DUNNE

Chinatown. Robert Towne. It was a wonderfully intricate, well-worked screenplay with an enormous amount of atmosphere. Another one: Graham Greene and Carol Reed in *The Third Man.*

That is the best collaboration between writer and director I can think of. It is the one movie Joan and I always watch before we start a script, because it is so brilliantly worked out. It's very short, an hour and forty-five minutes. What else? I wouldn't say it's one of the best, but Truman Capote's *Beat the Devil*. Oh, and Quentin Tarantino's *Reservoir Dogs*, a terrifying and funny screenplay; I liked it much more than *Pulp Fiction*, which just seemed to rework *Reservoir Dogs*.

INTERVIEWER

I assume a great screenplay can be destroyed by direction and by acting.

DUNNE

There's no such thing as a great screenplay. Because they are not meant to be read. There are just great movies.

INTERVIEWER

So when you talk about a good screenplay you're really talking about what directors and actors did with it. There's no way one could have a recognizable style as a screenwriter?

DUNNE

What the screenwriter is ceding to the director is pace, mood, style, point of view, which in a book are the function of the writer. The director controls the editing room, and it's in the editing room where a picture is made.

INTERVIEWER

Is there a formula to screenwriting?

DUNNE

Not in general. Specifically perhaps. Bill Goldman once said that you start a scene as deep in as you can possibly go. You don't start the scene with somebody walking through the door, sitting down and starting a conversation. Bill said you start a scene in the middle of the conversation, which I think is a very astute observation.

Interviewer

Would you divide the screenplay into acts, as some people do?

Dunne

The studio people talk about first act, second act, third act. We don't do it when we're writing. When we were doing *True Confessions*, Ulu Grosbard came up with a wonderful take. He said the script was a "one-span bridge" and it needed to be a "two-span bridge." I knew exactly what he meant. The screenplay we had went up once and came down, instead of going up twice and then coming down. In other words, we needed a third act.

Interviewer

Is there a connection between a writer who has literary merit and a screenwriter? Is a screenplay such a departure from the novel that one hardly needs to know how to write to become a screenwriter?

Dunne

What troubles me is that screenwriters today seem to have had no life other than film school. They've rarely been reporters, they've rarely gone out and experienced a wider world. I had the army, I was a reporter for ten years, I'd been to Vietnam, not for long, but long enough to know I didn't like to get shot at. I covered labor strikes and murder trials and race riots. The entire frame of reference the younger screenwriters have is other movies. It's secondhand. And if you steal a moment from an old movie, you can probably bet that the moment you stole was probably itself stolen in the first place.

Interviewer

Would you recommend to a young person a career as a screenwriter?

Dunne

I'm not sure I would, because you're really not a writer and you're really not a filmmaker. I once said that the most you could aspire to be as a screenwriter is a copilot. If you are going to write movies full-time, and you don't write books like Joan and I do, then you better aim to be a director, because that's the only way you're going to be in charge, and being in charge is what writing is all about.

INTERVIEWER

You sound downbeat about screenwriting.

DUNNE

Look. It pays a lot, and it's fun. It's better than teaching and better than lecturing, the other compensatory alternatives for writers without jobs. But it is hard fucking work. On our last script, *Up Close & Personal*, it took eight years to get it on. We quit three times. Two other writers came on board and left. In all, we wrote twenty-seven drafts before a frame of film was shot, then we worked for seventy-seven days during the shoot rewriting. The picture was originally supposed to be about Jessica Savitch, a golden girl for NBC News who flamed out and died in an automobile accident. She was a small-town girl with more ambition than brains, an overactive libido, a sexual ambivalence, a tenuous hold on the truth, a taste for controlled substances, a longtime abusive Svengali relationship and a certain mental instability. Disney was the studio, and the first thing Disney wanted to know was if she had to die in the end. And they weren't crazy about an interracial love affair she had, nor her abortions, nor the coke, nor the lesbianism, nor the gay husband who hung himself in her basement, nor the boyfriend who beat her up. Otherwise, they loved the idea. Making that work was work. Eight years worth. Twenty-seven drafts worth. Thank God it was a hit.

—GEORGE PLIMPTON

ACKNOWLEDGMENTS

"Sneak" was first published in *The Studio*, originally published by Farrar, Straus & Giroux in 1969. "Tinsel" and "Memento Delano" were originally published in *The Atlantic*. "Gone Hollywood," "Dealing," "Quintana," "Fractures," "Laying Pipe," "Memories of a Left Fielder," and "Regards" were originally published in *Esquire*. "Quebec Zero," "Induction Day," and "Buck" were originally published in *The Saturday Evening Post*. "To Live and Die in L.A." and "Eureka!" were originally published in *New West*. "Pauline" was originally published in the *Los Angeles Times Book Review*. "Hessians," "Hollywood: Opening Moves," "On the Kennedys," "An American Education," "The Simpsons," "Poet of Resentment," "Birth of a Salesman," "STAR!," "A Star Is Born," "Your Time Is My Time," and "Death of a Yale Man" were originally published in the *New York Review of Books*. "The Paris Review Interview" is copyright © 1996 by *The Paris Review*, reprinted with the permission of the Wylie Agency.